Crawling Horror

Crawling Horror

Edited by Allen Ashley

Shadow Publishing

CRAWLING HORROR

Third Edition 2025
Published as Creeping Crawlers © Shadow Publishing 2015, 2017
Cover by Alexandra Stockmar

(*Notes: The quotations attributed to Donald Medford in Andrew Hook's story* Usl *are from the film: "Them!". The quotations in Gary Budgen's story* Scarab, *from the Egyptian Book of the Dead are taken from the translation by Normandi Ellis.*)

ISBN: 978-0-9572962-2-0
Shadow Publishing, david.sutton986@gmail.com
https://www.shadowpublishing.biz

In memory of Joel Lane:

much missed; the best of us.

Contents

Introduction: Hatched on a Leaf

Allen Ashley

AN INSECT'S LIFESPAN is often brutally short; a book's, thankfully, is generally much longer. Likewise the gestation period. I'd assumed that I first came up with the idea for a "Creeping Crawlers" anthology some two and a half to three years ago but maybe it's not as simple as that. One of the key texts in my development as both a writer and a reader was my first encounter with Franz Kafka's "Metamorphosis". This story opened my mind to the possibility that one could bridge the perceived gap between genre and so-called literary fiction. receptive to a range of interpretations, "Metamorphosis" presents as a horror story—"One morning, when Gregor Samsa woke from troubled dreams, he found himself transformed in his bed into a horrible vermin"; but it's published in the prestigious Penguin Modern Classics line. In the short term, it helped inspire me to finally pen my body horror tale "Dead to the World"—my first major success and my most reprinted story. In the longer term... perhaps it has ultimately led me to collect nineteen brilliantly assorted stories from established and emergent writers on the theme of insects, arachnids, arthropods, crustaceans and their ilk; and, crucially, their relationship with us.

How did I define a creeping crawler? Basically, I went for those creatures that the Natural History Museum in South Kensington would include in its similarly titled gallery. But there may be exceptions...

There are many maxims told about these creatures. King Alfred became so engrossed in observing a spider's web-building that he carelessly burnt the cakes. If two flies mate and have four offspring and then they mate and so on the world will be overrun in forty days. (Thank goodness other animals have a taste for them) Cockroaches are built to survive the nuclear winter. Greater fleas have lesser fleas upon their backs to bite 'em; and lesser fleas have lesser fleas and so ad infinitum.

There are no fleas in "Creeping Crawlers", you'll be pleased to learn.

Much of our relationship with these small creatures is based on fear and dislike: we call in pest control to rid our homes of 'roaches or wasps' nests; we suffer arachnophobia or shiver and scratch when we see crawling things. Some of this hostility may relate to a fear of death—the worms will eat us, the flies will buzz about our corpse, the maggots will hatch beneath our distended skin. Then there are locusts, termites and aphids: their destructive nature perhaps speaks to our own fear that human habits too often mirror their ruthless and no care for tomorrow rampages.

But we can also admire the hard-working leaf-cutter ants or the Sisyphean perseverance of the dung beetle. Nowadays we understand a lot more about bee society. I think it was back in the 1980s that a "Horizon" TV programme first brought to wider public consciousness the complexity and accuracy of the bee's dance, indicating distance and direction of the best available nectar. And this was long before Google Maps.

And yet the fascination may still go hand in hand with the distaste and the phobia. Perhaps it's a matter of macro versus micro: two separate worlds intersecting occasionally and uncomfortably, with lingering mistrust on either side. We may rule our domain but their empire has stood far longer. Their lives remain quite alien to us, mostly hidden away where nobody sees and quite often where nobody wants to look. Up close, magnified, the insectile configuration has a beauty that may be judged as both outlandish and repulsive. The insect class and its associated species and genus—molluscs, arthropods, etc—can appear, in human terms, intensely beautiful but also repellently ugly. Most of us have a liking for brightly-coloured butterflies; the curling motion of a caterpillar's movement might also appeal. But slugs? Larvae? Maggots? How many of them evoke the stroke or cuddle reflex? We default to a family identification with fellow mammals, our red hearts habitually softened by the almost universal cuteness of warm-blooded offspring: kittens, puppies, lambs, fox cubs... and one of my favourites, wild boar piglets.

Meanwhile, wasps ruin our picnics; greenfly eat our plants; mosquitoes, flies and fleas bite us and draw out our blood whilst infecting us with toxins and disease. We may be in the midst of a war or, at the least, subject to uneasy collisions.

Here's a thought: we humans can reliably estimate how many specimens remain of endangered mammalian species such as Amur leopard or black rhino. We can accurately count sheep. But do we really know how many insects, arachnids and arthropods are lurking out there? And what they might be planning...?

Enjoy "Creeping Crawlers".

Allen

•   London, July 2015

Us!

Andrew Hook

When man entered the atomic age he opened a door into a new world. What we eventually find in that world nobody can predict.
                    - Dr Harold Medford

THIS STORY MAY sound fantastic but it needs to be told. Come, stretch those wet wings, ease yourselves out of your egg cases. We don't have much time. Before long, you will follow the males on your nuptial flight. Don't form personal attachments, you will outlive them. The three of you are destined to be queens.

Some of our kind remain as we used to be: tiny, unevolved, perfectly adequate but lacking the advances we have made. Their colonies develop slowly; they have retained the larva and pupae stages of development. I see I'm confusing you, your intelligence is barely forming; but should I delay in imparting this story your instincts will predominate and you will be off, carried by the wind to create new colonies, and without this knowledge our history will be lost. Understanding is crucial to survival. We still have enemies who wish to defeat us.

See how I rub my gaster segment and mandibles to communicate. You also have pheromones. Use them wisely. When you lose the ability to produce one of those pheromones then the workers will raise new queens in the colony.

Are you ready? Over thirty-five thousand sunrises ago our species existed throughout every territory but then we became dominant. Our ancestors of this story led a sparse existence in hot, arid land. In darkness we thrived, but during the day we remained underground, collating, considering, preparing. Occasionally the heat was distilled not just by the night but by rain. For some mornings our scouts had reported activity from a different species, one which seemed to adopt a similar social framework to us. A few of the workers headed outside and observed. After a night of rain and lightning they described a brilliant light, abominable noise. When the scouts ventured into the distance they saw a cloud had formed and found the desert sand melted into light green glass.

We understand now that this was the start. Over the following three thousand two hundred sunrises our mutations evolved. I have already told you we discarded the larvae and pupae stages of development: this created a faster metabolism. The turnaround of males was accentuated. Our size increased: two-fold, four-fold, eight-fold. So it continued. Today we are two hundred times our original form. And let no one tell you different. With size comes power.

Our colonies grew in size but were limited in space. We couldn't remain as we had been. Yet there were barriers to our development. Other species which had to be crushed for us to survive.

Your workers will tell you with pride that we are savage, ruthless, and courageous. We are chronic aggressors who are used to capturing others of our kind for slave labour. In this we had a match. Similar to the species we needed to battle we developed increased communication, fostered creativity within our societies. Unlike the bees with their hive mind, we encouraged individual thought so long as its use was solely for the welfare of the commune. Our history remains oral, obfuscated by time, but the beginning of our foray into new lands begins like this.

We sent scouts into the desert. Our hunger outstripped our resources. They returned reports of two-legged aggressors, the meat from whom encouraged further exploration. We were met with weapons beyond the reach of our stingers. Wherever possible we injected our enemies, but we found our mandibles could also snap them in many places. They had supplies other than their corporeal bodies. Sweet stuff. Some of our originally-sized brethren joined us in reconnaissance. The sweet stuff was the incentive. They followed one of the smaller two-legs whilst she was gathered into their colony. She was mute but they had distilled our poison and woke her. It was then that we discovered they had named us as an enemy: *Them Them Them!*

Those tiny scouts explained the confusion in its colony, as though our size were a stick jiggled in a hole. They too had fliers; these discharged more of their kind through reproductive processes unknown. In their colony the females were less important. Our scouts reported only a handful who took part in the battles, and they remained at the periphery of the action.

Another few sunrises: new queens were ready. Much like yourself; much like ourselves. We needed to be quick. We had just one colony our size. Should it be discovered...

They came at the height of the sun. Shockwaves vibrated our antennae. The heat was intense. A gas different to that essential for survival suffocated many. Our queens were impregnated. Fled. We can only speculate as to the torture of those flamed in the eggs that remained. The line had been drawn. Three queens departed for new territory. The survival of the fittest.

> *We haven't seen the end of them, we've only had a close view of the beginning of what may be the end of us.*
>
> - Dr Harold Medford

We knew we were everywhere, had been for over a trillion sunrises. In some of our colonies they worship ancestors trapped in amber. Yet despite our experience we knew we had disadvantages. Our enemies had superior vision. Their fliers did not lose their wings after the nuptial flight. Their males rarely died after mating. We had strength – the ability for one to lift twenty. Yet our aggressors had non-organic structures which served to augment them. One of our queens entered one of these devices. We know little more than that it sank beneath water with all lost.

Our second queen with her entourage fared better. Flying over further desert, gorging on sweet stuff, they found sanctuary within the heart of the two-legged colony. Dark openings signalled the entrances to ready-made tunnels. Care was advisable. These tunnels held surface water indicating previous flooding, but our heroine navigated an air space and began the process of laying eggs. You will find this possible for over five thousand sunrises after your mating. Those males you hatch will protect, feed, and work for you over procreation. Keep them that way and your colony will thrive.

Our tiny advisors, albeit limited through their intelligence, were able to keep track of our enemies' movements; for whilst our enemies fought with our adapted kind they considered our template no danger. The heat of the day remained a barrier to our activities. At night there were fewer two-legs for feasting. Our scouts had decided the colony should remain hidden even during cooler hours. We became incautious, attacking too close to the nest. After another sunrise, whilst two of their young hid in our colony their disappearance spurred their elders into greater action. Our queen's hiding place was tragically discovered.

They entered with lights and they entered with fire. We attacked and killed. New queens had just been born, their wings flexing as yours are now strengthening. They were almost ready for flight. Our enemies filled the tunnels which began to collapse in the battle. They might have been trapped but so were our queens. Without extending the family the bloodline was extinguished. Fire obliterated their traces.

I see you're stirring. None of us is still for too long. Be patient. Once you are ready for the drones you can select two guides and take flight. Night has fallen. You will be more comfortable under the cover of darkness and have no problem following the pheromones. Find a suitable place for a colony. Break off your wings and care for the eggs. Use the sperm you have stored selectively in fertilisation. Only fertilised eggs bring forth females, unfertilised eggs lead to males. Use this knowledge wisely. But don't be dismissive of the males: they are here to serve us, but we are here to serve the super-organised whole.

The first to hatch will be runts, but good workers. They will assist in finding food, developing the colony, minding your eggs. Those that come later will be stronger, more adept. You will live over five hundred sunrises longer than any of them. Our species will outlive our enemies. You will have many offspring.

We are in hiding. Our enemies ended *their* story with the death of the second queen. They were unaware of our third.

My scouts inform me we outnumber our enemies. We have lived underground too long, our tiny counterparts working overtime to conceal us. Our patience, diligence, and perseverance will come to fruition. We will be the dominant aggressors. Subsuming those in our path.

Take to the wind, my lovelies. My time is near an end. Ten thousand sunrises is a laboured existence. But existence is all there is. Repeat until death.

And remember: *once we were them, then they were them; yet now we are us.*

In the Earth

Storm Constantine

T HE CENTIPEDE WAS cut in two. "Why did you kill it?" Mawde asked.

Jeryl pursed her lips. She was squatting in the dirt of the lower cellar, the frilly skirt of her white Sunday dress pulled up over her knees. "Don't you know what they *do*?" she said.

Mawde shook her head. "Run about?"

"They *burrow*—into *any* hole of your body, and then they start eating."

Mawde grimaced. She couldn't believe that. Why would a humble creature like a centipede do that?

"They *do*," said Jeryl. "I've seen pictures. They ate a woman's eyes from the inside."

Mawde was sentimental about all creatures, whereas her cousin Jeryl seemed fixed with the idea that if anything was small enough to slaughter with a quick stamp of the foot or a blow from a trowel, then it was her treat—or perhaps her duty— to kill it. Mawde's mother said that all animals, however scary and unpleasant they might look, were all part of the Nature's creations and must be respected. Loved.

Jeryl's mother didn't believe in anything. Now Jeryl poked the centipede parts with a stick she'd found.

Outside, the summer was gloomy and thundery, pressing down on the tall wooden house, making its labyrinth of cellars a cauldron of shadows and lifeless air. A smell of old earth surrounded the girls; pungent and musty. Jeryl was staying with Mawde's family for a whole month during the school holidays. She liked to play in the cellars. She said there were tunnels down there, hidden behind the sagging wooden racks and shelves, which snaked right into Pike Mountain, dating back to the start of time. Even when dressed in feminine flounces, within this confection lurked the heart and mind of a grubby little boy. No amount of dressing up would change that.

Jeryl had been looking for tunnels, (hence the digging that had unearthed the doomed centipede), but to Mawde's relief so far none had been found. She liked her cousin's company but wished sometimes her favoured pastimes didn't have to involve danger or fear. It wasn't enough simply to sit in the sunshine on the porch roof, but Jeryl insisted they had to jump down from this height onto the lawn, which hurt Mawde's ankles and feet. They couldn't just play make believe in the cellars but had to look for tunnels—undoubtedly haunted, or so Jeryl said. Neither was it enough to climb the tall old yew trees that clustered like hags at the garden's edge; they had to hang upside-down by their knees from the highest branch they could reach... then right themselves and drop to the ground. Jeryl was always on the lookout for higher places from which they could jump and was unconcerned that yew wood was relatively soft and therefore not the best support for weight, even of a child. She was obsessed with heights, but also liked to push herself physically. "This *could* be too high," she might say solemnly, before holding out her arms and throwing herself into the air. Mawde was afraid of these antics—demands, even—but couldn't bring herself to refuse them. Jeryl's scorn was worse than her challenges. But that aside, she was the most fascinating playmate, unlike any other girl Mawde knew.

Neither set of parents were aware what the girls got up to during their holidays. In all the households Mawde knew, it was common for the children to be shooed out of adult company after breakfast, tolerated briefly at lunch, then sent out again until tea. Unless it was bad weather when they were allowed to play indoors, but out of adult hearing, such as in the attics or cellars. Bizarrely, neither Jeryl nor Mawde had ever hurt themselves, which perhaps—Mawde thought—meant that her mother's stories about guardian angels must be true.

That night another storm came up from the south, crotchety and fevered. When lightning pierced the hot sky it had the look of bruised flesh being punctured by needles. The heat, the anxiety of the sky, infected the old house. It groaned in what sounded to Mawde like dread. Her cousin Jeryl slept in a bed on the other side of the room, but had fallen asleep soon after the curtains had been drawn, and did not wake, even when flickering storm light illuminated the room. The unseen inhabitants of the house—vermin and insects—were skittish, pattering behind the walls and in the cavities above the ceilings, below the floors. Mawde lay awake, thinking of the centipede her cousin had killed, how the halves had curled in on themselves. The creature had felt pain, and it had been so big. What if...?

No, Mawde told herself, *no. It was an insect. Didn't have feelings.*

The rain, when it came, was of the kind that Mawde's grandmother often referred to as the tears of the world—that is, a deluge beyond measure. Even through the curtains, the storm light now seemed watery, running down the walls of the room, threading between the somehow sickeningly large roses of the wallpaper. Despite the rain, the air was hot and Mawde's body felt sticky and uncomfortable beneath her light summer blanket. She drifted in and out of sleep, images flickering across her mind's eye, her head aching. She dreamed of earthy tunnels and myriad feet in the dark. On her hands and knees she crawled through the dirt, then it was as if she slithered along it on her belly, and the scent of loam and rot was like the sweet hearth of home. She was comfortable in this dream, neither scared nor excited, simply... doing her business.

Then, as dreams do, the world shifted, and she was standing barefoot in the middle of her bedroom with the watery light over the walls and the blanket-cocooned hump of her cousin's shape in the bed before her.

Was this a dream?

"Jeryl?" Mawde breathed.

The hump in the bed twitched and a strange little sleeping-noise came out of the blankets, such as a slumbering dog might utter, as it ran across its dream-fields.

Mawde went to the bed and placed a hand on her cousin's

shoulder, shook it. "Jeryl?"

Another noise came out, like dead branches rubbing together, or a bowl of dried peas being thrown down the stairs. Dream-Mawde pulled back the blankets, saw what lay there. A centipede, cut in half, the size of an eleven-year-old girl, the parts curled in on themselves. But the face between the feelers at the head was Jeryl's and now she looked up at her cousin with all the pain of the world, its deluge of tears in her eyes.

Mawde woke with a cry. She felt sick, wanted to vomit, but then the feeling passed. She sat up, glanced fearfully at the bed to her right. "Jeryl?" she murmured. And then louder: "Jeryl!"

"Wassamatter?" came a grumpy reply.

"I had a dream," Mawde said.

Jeryl sat up in her bed too, scraped hair from her eyes. "You're awake now. Open the curtains."

Mawde shuddered. "No!"

Jeryl expressed a disappointed sigh and clambered from her bed, went to the window.

"Why?" Mawde asked.

"There might be angels in the windows," Jeryl said. "I see them a lot at home, especially when I wake up from a dream."

Mawde had not heard Jeryl mention this before. "You *see* them?" she asked timorously.

"Yes, they fill the window, very tall. They tell me things, but I never want them to step out and get into the shadows. It's important to keep them where they are, because then you can see them. They can't hide and whisper things."

An angel is a kind, beautiful creature, Mawde thought, but in that moment the idea of seeing one seemed the most terrifying thing possible.

But all that was in the window was the fluid mosaic of running water and Jeryl's face, half asleep, dripping with the light.

The storm passed away moodily to the north, and summer returned in its wake. The morning was magnificent, inviting, and any echoes of the disturbing dream and its unsettling aftermath faded from Mawde's mind. Now the weather was better, the cousins could ride their bicycles out into the country lanes around Mawde's home, which were empty of traffic during the week, except for the occasional farm vehicle or someone riding a horse. No longer required to wear what Jeryl referred to as 'stupid doll dresses', they were attired in shorts, T-shirts and pumps, riding their bikes from village to village. In nearby Elmslane was a tiny shop that sold ice cream, which they always aimed for before returning home for the day. In every village, Jeryl was drawn to the moss-robed old churches, looking for ghosts or evidence of people being buried alive. She would examine headstones for mysteries. "Look, this woman died two days before her baby, and she wasn't much older than *us*. The father killed the baby because it had killed her. That's obvious."

Ever since Jeryl had started visiting her cousin in the holidays, one of her favourite pastimes was to hide and frighten people, especially those who came to tend graves. As grave-

yards were often thick with yew trees—Jeryl's favourite kind—
she would order Mawde to climb into the branches and stay
very still. A woman might come, or an elderly man, and then
Jeryl would coo something sinister, such as, "Nooo, nooo, tooo
soon." Or simply hoot like an owl or utter a sound like an excla-
mation from a startled dog or cat. They were rarely caught, and
if the victim did spy them, the girls would throw themselves
from the tree and run off like deer. Mostly, the people would
pay no attention, but it was satisfying when a frightened face
looked up, glanced around themselves, hurried away. Then the
cousins would giggle uncontrollably. "Let's go to the next
place," Jeryl would say.

But that day, the graveyards were empty of sport and Jeryl became restless. She suggested a visit to another of their haunts.

At the western end of Dappleheath, Mawde's home village,
was a row of old houses with long gardens. At the bottom of
these summer time jungles was a 'no-man's-land' that didn't
appear to belong to anybody. This was a narrow ribbon of
woodland—holly, birch, thick stands of elderberry, some domesticated fruit trees that had perhaps escaped the gardens—
through which a stream ran. On the other side of the trees was
a school playing-field that seemed inordinately huge and was
rarely used. Not that Mawde ever saw it that often in term time;
her school was somewhere else. After heavy rain, one section of
the stream would swell to fill a shallow sandy pool. Naturally,
as the pool's width varied, and offered on some occasions a

greater challenge, Jeryl liked to take a run and jump it. Mawde was afraid of getting wet, even though the water was hardly treacherous and less than three inches at its deepest point. There was simply something disturbing about the way it was so important to Jeryl that they succeeded in their jumps, as if, should they fail, some calamity would happen.

Today, of course, after the storm, the waters would be engorged and swift—as much as they ever could be—and Jeryl was eager to see how wide the pool would be.

Mawde liked the wood, even if she didn't enjoy the jumping that much. There was such a variety of life within it, as if it were a miniature, and therefore magical, ancient woodland. Rabbits braved the boundary between this small wilderness and the shorn playing-field. A woodpecker lived there; always heard, sometimes seen. The petals of flowers—periwinkle, forget-me-not, campion—seemed more vivid there amid the emerald forest grass that was springy underfoot. Mawde liked to think it was a sanctuary for benign magical creatures, but to Jeryl it was the fortress of capricious fairies, who would steal babies, swap them for a blackened tree stump. They could suck out a beautiful girl's youth, or curse a man to fall in love, then go blind, mad. Jeryl searched for the spoor of these beings relentlessly.

On that day, as Jeryl rooted in the soft, dark earth, like a terrier rummaging for a buried bone, Mawde wondered why—for her—angels were golden and good, and fairies were simply aloof and mysterious, yet for Jeryl these creatures were always cruel and vengeful, full of hate for humanity.

"Look at this," Jeryl said, wonder in her voice. She had uncovered something beneath a stone, perhaps evidence of a fairy atrocity.

But before Mawde could come to look, a harsh male voice rang out. "Hoi! Get out of there! This is private property! Gerrout!"

The cousins stared at each other in alarm, before jumping to their feet. Mawde had a glimpse of an unfriendly male face—elderly—staring over the fence at the bottom of the nearest garden.

"Don't you come back here, you little pests!" he roared as Jeryl and Mawde scampered away. "Private property, you hear?"

Usually, when caught out, and a swift retreat was called for, Jeryl laughed and poked fun at whoever had yelled at them, but this time, when they emerged through a hole in the fence by the lane, where their bicycles lay hidden in the long grass and cow parsley, Jeryl's face was pinched.

"Stupid old git," Mawde offered, hoping Jeryl would then smile and say something even more insulting.

"I'll get 'im," Jeryl said simply, not even with darkness in her tone, just stating a simple fact. She lifted her bicycle from the grass. "No one uses that land. It's wild. No one should stop us."

"*How* will you get him?" Mawde asked.

Jeryl said nothing. She mounted her bike and jerked her head to indicate Mawde should follow.

They went to another woodland place they liked—a copse of oaks and beeches in a hollow in the middle of a hay field. But sometimes other children were there, which neither Mawde nor Jeryl liked particularly. Today, mercifully, they had it to themselves. Jeryl was still not speaking, despite Mawde's efforts to lighten the atmosphere. Jeryl simply rooted, clawing at sodden dead wood and beneath the bracken. She turned over a large log that had to be pulled forcibly from the earth, making a sucking sound. Beneath, the ground teemed with insect life—wood lice, beetles, centipedes. "Oh, look," Mawde murmured. "So many of them."

Jeryl stood up, then, methodically, she began stamping on the tiny creatures, grinding her foot against the soil, all the time making a soft, grunting sound.

"Stop it," Mawde said. "Stop, Jeryl."

Jeryl wouldn't stop, and for the first time, Mawde ran away from her cousin, out of the shade of the wise oaks, across the sun-soaked hay field, and went home alone.

Jeryl did not reappear until tea time. To protect her cousin from any parental chastisement, or indeed herself for leaving Jeryl alone in the copse, Mawde hid in the garden until she heard the whirr of Jeryl's bicycle wheels on the gravel of the drive. Then, Mawde ran from her hiding place, across the lawn. At that moment, Mawde's mother came out the house, no doubt to advise them their tea was ready. She caught sight of Jeryl, muddied and unkempt, then glanced briefly at her tidier daughter. "What have you been doing?" she snapped. "Where have you been?"

Jeryl stared defiantly, shrugged.

Horrified at what this insolent response might evoke in her normally fair-minded mother, Mawde said, "We went fishing and Jeryl fell over in a muddy place."

"Mud?" said Mawde's mother in a voice that might easily have been saying 'entrails?' so disgusted was her tone. Mawde realised then—one of the chiming epiphanies of childhood—that although her mother considered nature beautiful and to be respected from a distance, in her view no girl had any place getting *into* it and letting it dirty her.

"Get changed," she said severely to Jeryl. "And wash yourself as best you can. Bath later." She turned to Mawde, "As for you, young lady..."

"I'll wash and change too," Mawde said, even though she wasn't very dirty. She ran after Jeryl who was stomping into the house.

In the bathroom, Jeryl was still quiet, although she hummed to herself softly. "Are you all right?" Mawde asked.

"Of course," Jeryl answered.

"Jeryl..." Mawde began. She knew she had to speak, say *something*, but the words were reluctant. "You shouldn't kill things like that."

Jeryl flicked a sharp glance at her. "They don't mind dying for me. They expect it."

"*Dying* for you...?"

"How else can I tell them what I want? Beetles don't have brains, but they have eyes. You have to show them." Jeryl threw water over her face, rubbed mud from her arms.

Mawde remembered her dream then, the insect Jeryl in the bed, cut in half. "You're wrong," she said.

Jeryl expressed a contemptuous snort. "*You* don't know anything. Keep your trap shut."

The look in Jeryl's eyes was frightening, so cold and dark, like winter earth; small scuttling things moving behind it. A distinct thought formed in Mawde's mind: *don't make her angry with you.*

"Sorry," she said, and went to the bath where she washed her hands. She didn't want to share the sink Jeryl was using.

That night, Mawde slept deeply and did not wake. To her, it was an ordinary night and the morning that followed it equally ordinary. Jeryl seemed brighter now, for which Mawde was grateful. The sullen, quiet Jeryl frightened her; she'd never been like this on previous visits. While they were washing-up for Mawde's mother after breakfast, a knock came at the back door. Friends and family never used the forbidding front door, which was rarely opened. This visitor came right inside without waiting to be invited—a friend of Mawde's mother called Mrs Cherry. She had a sickly son, who went to the same school as Mawde and was excused sports and swimming.

After the ritual offering of tea, and with Mrs Cherry established at the kitchen table, the woman lit a cigarette, inhaled purposefully and on her exhale, announced with relish, "The Hensons had dreadful trouble last night."

"Who?" asked Mawde's mother.

"Live in End Lane, the one with the green door."

"Oh... yes... I don't know them personally. What trouble?"

Mrs Cherry chewed her words with satisfaction before sharing them. "Vandals got in their garden. Made a terrible mess. Ruined it, you know. Ruined it! Even the greenhouse gone. It's just a mud patch now, I heard. And you know what?"

"What?"

"They didn't hear a *thing*. Got police round now, of course."

"How dreadful..."

Mawde's head had begun to buzz. She felt strangely dizzy and disorientated. End Lane... the wood at the back of the houses where she and Jeryl had been yesterday. She knew her face had gone bright red and that it was important her mother didn't notice this. Jeryl was still washing dishes in a serene manner, as if her mind was far away, as if she hadn't heard.

"Susan Ross just told me that May Henson's kitchen was absolutely crawling with beetles this morning. Unearthed, I expect. They were in *everything*."

Mawde put away carefully the last dish she was drying. "Can we go now, Mum?"

Mawde's mother nodded distractedly. "Yes, sweetheart. Don't be late for lunch."

Outside, as the cousins walked to the shed where the bicycles were stored, Jeryl was again quiet, although she was smiling—a private expression she clearly had no intention of sharing. Mawde wanted to say something, *ask* something, desperately, but was afraid to do so. She sensed endings and change, the summer fading, without understanding why. At the shed, as she wrestled with the padlock—unlocked but as recalcitrant as if it were stuck fast—she said, "Wonder if it was the man who shouted at us... whose garden was wrecked." She glanced up at her cousin.

Jeryl stared back for a moment, then put out her tongue. Mawde jumped backwards. There was a centipede on Jeryl's tongue, still and wet, just lying there. Jeryl uttered a squawk of laughter, then spat. Mawde winced away.

"Told you," Jeryl said.

After that summer, the cousins grew apart. Further details of the holiday became blurred in Mawde's mind, but then perhaps Jeryl had returned home only a couple of days after the garden-wrecking incident—a crime for which no one was ever caught. Later that year, Mawde overheard a couple of whispered, coded conversations that her mother held on the phone with friends. Listening carefully from concealment, Mawde deciphered Jeryl had been in severe trouble at school. Phrases such as, 'difficult child' and 'a bit touched' were breathed down the line. Mawde gleaned that for Jeryl a new and different kind of school had been in order; her mother and father had moved a couple of hundred miles away to be near her. There had been no further holiday visits and the relationship between Mawde's mother and her sister inexplicably cooled. Mawde couldn't divine the reason, and her mother kept her secrets until she died, quite young. Mawde had no idea where her aunt lived, and any questions made to her father resulted only in "let it lie, Mawde. They don't want us contacting them."

Jeryl became a childhood memory; a strange yet intriguing girl. Mawde never spoke about her, and eventually forgot her, except for moments during summer storms, when she lay awake in the dark at night and heard insects in the walls.

Then, by chance, many years later when Mawde was in her late thirties, her work brought her into contact with Meredith Jones, a woman who'd known Jeryl as a child. Mawde had even met her a couple of times at gatherings of Jeryl's family, not that she recognised Meredith's grown up face, and—unlike Mawde—she had married, so her name was different. After an office meeting, as both women were putting away their laptops, Meredith said, "You're not the Mawde Emsley who's a cousin of Jeryl Ashman, are you?"

"Yes, I am," Mawde said, surprised. In an instant, the past came hurtling back and she felt faintly disorientated. She smelled earth.

"You probably don't remember me," Meredith said. "I was a friend of Jeryl's." She laughed. "Well, went to the same school, and was invited to birthdays and so on, but Jeryl didn't really have friends, did she."

"I... well... it was a long time ago," Mawde said, in a colder tone than she intended.

Meredith blinked in a nonplussed manner, clearly unsure what to say.

Mawde made a vague gesture with one hand, looked away, fiddled with her computer bag. "Family thing. There was a rift..."

"Ah." Meredith sighed, then ploughed on bluntly. "Can't say I'm surprised. They had a terrible time with her, terrible. So sad for the parents, having to move away and virtually take on new identities." She offered a pitying expression. "But of course you must know that."

Mawde grimaced, which she trusted would indicate she didn't wish to speak further on the matter, although part of her was itching to interrogate this stranger. The problem was, she didn't know *anything*. This childhood acquaintance of Jeryl's knew more.

"Are you still in touch with the family?" Mawde asked, as lightly as she could muster.

"My mother is," was the reply.

"I wonder..." Mawde now spoke impulsively. "Jeryl and I had no say in... becoming estranged when we were children. I wonder whether I should contact her."

The woman gave Mawde a glance that was full of meaning, bursting with it: a keen arrow of a glance. "That's up to you," she said carefully, "but... she's a very *troubled* person, Mawde."

Polite euphemism, Mawde thought. She nodded. "Yes," she said, "I expect she is. Cut in two." She hadn't meant to say those last few words, but Meredith Jones nodded.

"Yes, you could put it like that," she said. "Tragic."

Mawde muttered a hasty goodbye and fled the room. Outside, it was thundery, the lawn beyond the office building oozing and mulchy. Mawde saw a brief image before her mind's eye of Jeryl crouching in the dirt, glancing up, her smile as secretive and cruel as that of the fairies in which she believed. There were insects on her skin, like a living tattoo. Then she sank into the wet earth until only her eyes remained, peering out.

Running with the Tide

Adrian Cole

A S IF IT WASN'T bad enough to have suffered a continual stream of winter storms and the resultant flooding and interminable, soul-destroying mopping up, the landscape was now being subjected to a drought. It had started imperceptibly in April. Then, day by day, the temperature had climbed untypically into the low 20s. Fine at the time – people loved the early hint of summer: it went a long way to banishing the memory of that miserable winter. When May and then June went by without as much as a rumour of rainfall, the first seeds of unease began to root. Temperatures had reached the nadir of 28 and the humidity took a relentless toll on the land, the wildlife and the population.

By late August it had become hellish. No one could remember the last time a cloud had been seen, and a heat haze shimmered across a parched, gasping land, streams evaporated, river levels subsided to almost nothing, reservoirs fell to record low levels. People devoured the news bulletins, but other distant places, equally as cursed as their own, bore less importance to them than the immediate nightmare. This drought had become a threat – it promised chaos if it went on much longer. The entire infrastructure of the country creaked and groaned, a dysfunctional machine, about to capitulate, beyond repair. Day after day, people turned on their radios, eager for a weather forecast that would bring relief, the promise of rainfall, no matter how small. At night, ironically drenched in perspiration, they lay on their beds and slept feverishly.

Rik Brennan rose at six a.m. Already the air shimmered, thick and uncomfortable. He showered and dressed, white tee-shirt cool on his flesh: he knew it wouldn't be for long. By midday he'd want to peel it off, a discarded second skin. He ate a meagre breakfast and checked his dwindling supplies. He'd have to make his weekly trip down to the village. It would be an opportunity to assess how his neighbours were coping. He'd not made time to get to know them: ironically this god-awful heat wave might give him that opportunity.

Outside, in the glare, he studied the cottage. The small extension remained half-finished. He'd started work on it with the enthusiasm of novelty, coupled with a focus on something other than his break up with Tess. They'd been partners for four years, living and working as teachers in London. He'd accepted the need for change in their lives. Their future had stretched on all too clearly, too predictably. Her promotion and its demands crystallised his own situation, a slower advance towards a landscape that had somehow become too unchallenging. He was thirty, no age, too young to be trapped, he told himself. They'd outgrown each other's drives.

This summer break had enabled him to come to the South West and begin rebuilding, both the cottage and his life. He didn't miss the claustrophobia, even in this oppressive heat.

In the brazen sunlight, the cottage melted into the background of low hills and woodland, its old slates almost leached of colour. The extension leaned against the end cob wall, the beams of its roof frame like clean bones poking up from the emerging body of work. Rik had underestimated the effect of the heat, day after day, and his efforts sagged at times, muscles aching under the increased demands, like working underwater, or in the vacuum of space. More than once he'd regretted starting the project. *Should have farmed it out to a local builder*. It was never going to be finished by the time he had to go back to the college. He twisted his mind from that thought, its anathema.

He got into the car, driving slowly down the winding slope through more of a meadow than a garden. It was thickly overgrown, peppered with wild flowers, although the grasses had become seared, little greenery surviving. Rik wondered if there was a danger of ignition. He'd seen fires on the hillside earlier that week, but they seemed to have been controlled. A fire in this meadow would rage, the cottage under real threat. *Maybe I should take a scythe to it all. More time lost.*

At the bottom of the meadow, a copse spread out across the boundary, a mixture of chestnut, sycamore and alder. The thick canopy was showing signs of losing its struggle with the season as tree roots probed ever deeper for water. Some of these trees would die. Only the strangling ivy seemed to be thriving, as if it would replace the trees altogether. Beyond the copse Rik was immediately presented with a view of the bay, stretched out below him on either side. It curved around to his right in a long beach, eventually turning back towards the Atlantic in the west, its far side ten miles away. Rik had loved this vista when he'd sat on the hillside earlier that year, drinking in the wide expanse of constantly shifting sea with its line after line of creamy white surf. He'd watched the remote black dots of surfers, toing and froing on their boards. He'd promised himself he'd try it, but so far he'd not made the time.

What he saw now made him gape. The tide had receded, not in its usual, twice daily pattern, drawing back several hundred yards from the shore, but well beyond that. Oddly, it was so far out he couldn't distinguish where the sea actually broke on the hitherto unrevealed land. Freakish. A bizarre summer tide, maybe even one that occurred in some occasional pattern of years. He shielded his eyes against the brilliance of the sun and tried to study the exposed sea bed. There were vast tracts of flattish sand, but long lines of rock ran seawards like the bones of gigantic hands and fingers. Some were bare, others were dark with weed: the overall effect was unnerving, unnatural here as the surface of the Moon.

Rik's attention swivelled to the estuary of the river that dissected the bay at its mid-point. He knew that further inland, two miles upstream, was a small port, its quayside still busy. If this tide decided to return, an unheralded *tsunami*, the consequences, especially for that town, would be catastrophic. Could that happen? Or would its return be as gradual as any other tide? What had caused the phenomenon? An effect of the drought?

Maybe they'd know in the village. He drove on, watching the fields where a few sheep and cattle had slumped, hardly any of them on their feet, dumbly accepting the change. The reddish earth looked solid as concrete and the air shimmered, distorting distances like bottle glass.

Before he got to the store, he found the narrow street blocked by a handful of men. Rik knew them as local fishermen. Their leader, Dane Croker, was a big-boned man with a bright, beery face. He gave Rik an uneasy look as he pulled up.

"Morning. Anything wrong?" Rik asked.

"A boat's missing. Some of us are going out to look for it."

"Anyone lost?"

"Two men and a dog. My brother, Mick and his mate, Dan Cloak. Went out on the tide, two days ago. They may be stranded out in the bay. Unlike them not to come back." Rik had never exchanged more than a handful of words with him and the others previously, but their expressions now were anxious, quietly seeking support.

"Need an extra pair of hands?" Rik made the offer almost casually.

"Be glad of it."

Rik noticed some of them were carrying shotguns. "Expecting trouble?"

Croker shrugged. "Can't say. Never seen nothing like what's out there. You got something? Be on the safe side."

"Sure. I'll park up and join you."

35

The staccato conversation was over. Croker nodded. The men went down a long stone jetty. Its weed-smeared base was normally slapped by the tides but now it was perched on top of a shingle ridge: it had an obsolescent look. Rik parked and fetched a long-handled axe from the boot of the car, hefting it uneasily. *What the hell am I expecting to do with this?*

He caught the group of men up as they began the long trudge across the wide open sands. Out here, even with a slight breeze coming in from the sea, it was oven hot; the sand baked hard, the rocks beneath it poking through in twisted hiero-glyphic patterns. Rik was suddenly conscious of the isolation. There were no other people in sight: the emptiness stretched in all directions, unprotected and sun-blasted, the air shimmer-ing. A few thin pools reflected the glare like glass, but even these were no more than stains. The beach had been almost ut-terly drained.

Rik wondered again about *tsunamis*. Everyone was aware of them these days, given the dramatic reporting on television. No one here seemed to pay much thought to the possibility, but even so, if the tide did take a sudden turn and raced in, they'd be pulverised.

They moved across the sands towards the estuary mouth, where the river bisected the long beach. When they got within fifty yards of it, they were all amazed to see how little water flowed out from the land. This river mouth was usually well over half a mile across, but it had been exposed, reduced to no more than a hundred yards, cut deep down into the bedrock, moving sluggishly like a mudflow. Broken branches poked up among the rocks, chunks of weed clogged the banks down to a level never revealed before. They could have taken a small boat out on the waters, but no one suggested it, as though the idea was impractical. Behind them, over the shoulder of the now distant dunes, the land was desiccated and shrivelled, the fields bone dry.

Rik wondered how it would be in London. He'd not contacted anyone there for a few days and its world had receded for him. It would be like a cauldron. A fight for survival. *I can't go back. It's a time for changes. There must be something I can do here. Maybe a transfer, if there are any openings. Even supply work, casual employment, will do for a start.*

They'd finally reached the end of the sands, the land no more than a smudge behind them. There were evaporating rock pools, trapped in deep gouges in the rock, the strata arranged in linear, leaning expanses like miniature folded mountains. The smell of weed was overpowering, the olive green and deep browns of the sea vegetation drying up in the remorseless sun. It became difficult to traverse the minor canyons and scarps, the rocks sharp, almost fanged. The going got slower: from time to time they dipped down into a maritime crevasse, the razor landscape hidden in deepening shadows.

Emerging from one such deep gash, they found themselves on another flat expanse of sand. It stretched away, with still no sign of the retreated sea. The men, who had said very little on the journey, looked at one another, all mentally asking the same thing: do we go on? They were committed, so there was a tacit agreement. Two of their own were missing and they would find them, it was that simple.

Behind them, in the declivities, they heard movement, a soft, sluggish series of sounds, almost as though water might be returning to the pools. Maybe the tide had caught them out and was coming at them from another direction. But the noises were intermittent, whereas a tide on the move would be more consistent. Out on the sand they found a dead jellyfish, the size of a dinner plate, and then others, a whole mess of them like monstrous fried eggs. They stepped through them carefully, the smell of death suddenly hitting them like a foul gust of wind.

It took them a good half an hour to get across the sand flat and its dangerously slippery smears of clay to another outcrop of rock and its tangled mass of weed, which topped it like a stunted forest, initially offering no way past. They had to work their way around it and as they did so, they could hear more sounds above them, as though the weed banks sheltered a flock of gulls, cormorants or guillemots. But no birds took to the air. The skies remained silent as a vacuum. Whatever was in the higher rocks chose not to reveal itself.

At another breach in the rocks, one run of the strata had collapsed, forming a natural path through the weed banks. Again the company wrestled with its own unease and a growing sense of dread. This was an alien place and the stench of weed and decay had become hostile. They had seen almost no marine life other than the pervasive weed, but the smell of countless invisible victims was palpable.

Croker wore his determination like armour. Rik sensed that his companions had had enough. They didn't want to be caught out here in darkness – it was long gone noon. The sunset would be after nine, but they could only go so far out before turning back and being sure of making the village in decent light. Rik sensed it would only take one of them to suggest they return soon, and it would start a unified agreement. Common sense was winning out over sentiment.

"Let's get through this cutting," said Croker, as though he reluctantly shared Rik's thoughts. "If there's no sign of the sea, or the boat, we'll have to go back. Maybe organise a longer search tomorrow. Get supplies."

There was muttered agreement, and relief that enabled them to move a little further. They got through the long cleft to a rocky but flat area that dropped away dramatically, stunning all of them. They were on the lip of an escarpment, the sea bed hundreds of feet below. It would be a difficult climb down, slippery and treacherous, surely too challenging, Rik thought. Looking to the left and right of them, they saw only the remote sea bed. It was as if the sea had removed itself entirely, pulling back out into the Atlantic itself, moved by seismic activity.

How could the Authorities not know this was happening? Rik asked himself. *How could they possibly not have warned us? Maybe they did know. Maybe they wanted to avoid wholesale panic.* Because if people realised what had happened, the sheer scale of it, hysteria would rage worse than any virus.

His thoughts were pushed aside by a sound from far below. Everyone in the group reacted and immediately started talking.

"Quiet!" snarled Croker, glaring down. "Listen. It's Dan's dog. You hear it barking?"

It came clearly on the still air, the definite barking of a dog, as though the creature had scented them and wanted to establish contact.

Rik screened his eyes and studied the far rocks. "There!" he said, pointing. "What is that? Is it a boat? Caught in the rocks."

Croker screwed up his eyes and nodded. "By Christ, you're right. It's their boat. They must be down there, holed up." He turned to the rest of the group, his expression appealing to them. "We have to go down. They may be hurt. We can't leave them out here."

No one relished the thought of the climb, but they were united in their agreement – a rescue had to be affected. Croker braced himself and prepared to shout out into the void. The others watched him, faces grim. Rik could sense their apprehension and was about to say something to Croker, but the big man, who had cupped his hands around his mouth to amplify his voice, slowly dropped them, as if a shout would, after all, be too dangerous, or maybe blasphemous. No one questioned his personal decision not to call out. They were fishermen, but this place was alien.

Uneasily they began the descent, negotiating the intimidating, slippery nooks and crannies of the rock face like hesitant mountaineers. The afternoon sun seemed even more unsympathetic, inexorably blazing down through airless skies. The men could hear scuttling sounds, as if sea creatures that had survived were stirring and slithering deeper into the rocks in search of cool air and pockets of brine. The presence of the humans deterred them, life here retracting the way an anemone draws its feelers back into itself when threatened.

Rik slipped more than once, inwardly cursing the hefty axe he'd brought along. Now that they were out here, it seemed a luxury, unlikely to serve a useful purpose, just as the shotguns were. The men carrying the weapons took some comfort from them, their insurance against anything that might defy their progress. As they neared the foot of the escarpment, the scale of the new rocky landscape ahead of them became clearer – larger, taller outcrops loomed over them as they passed into more twisted folds of rock, mocking, hostile. Rik sensed an unearthly aggression, that and the sense that more and more life moved here.

Eventually they heard the dog barking again. It hadn't left its post, faithful to its masters, if they were there. The men struggled up out of shadows, a smell of decaying fish like a physical blow. Here an entire shoal of mackerel, thousands strong, had perished, snared on the fangs of coral. The dreadful heat had baked them into a rotting paste, spread in a grey-silver sludge across to where the bow of the trawler thrust up at a ridiculous angle at the heavens. Its stern, smashed by impact, was wedged deeply into the rocks, its barnacled keel badly holed: it was as if the dead mackerel had flooded out of the hold.

The dog finally appeared, barking, Rik thought, in a kind of desperation. Its eyes were wild, its mouth soaked in drool from its ceaseless efforts to raise the alarm, but when it caught sight of Croker, it forced its weary body across the rocks to him, its tail wagging almost incongruously. The big man ruffled its matted hide and it looked up at him as though giving him the last of its energy.

"Good dog, Jed. Good dog. Where's your master? Where's Dan, eh?"

The dog whined, its eyes suggesting to Rik that it was afraid of being admonished for something it had done, or failed to do. The other men were looking up warily at the trawler, the jagged edges of damage in the keel.

This time Croker did call out, repeating the names of the missing a number of times, but there was no answer. One of the men went to the nearest hole in the keel and peered in, almost sliding off his feet in the slick weed and dead fish. Other men began clambering around the trawler. Rik found himself with Croker and they managed to haul themselves up one of the rocks beside the prow, hoping to get a better look at the wheel house. Croker was the more adventurous of the two and reaching a point close to the rail, grabbed it and swung himself aboard, albeit at a precarious angle.

Rik balanced himself on top of the rocky spire; it afforded him a better view of the seaward landscape, out to where thick banks of mist obscured any real distance. Those immense white curtains shifted and shimmered, as if veiling some final, unhealthy secret. Huge shapes seemed to be moving behind them, but Rik knew it was an illusion, where the mist thickened and curdled like thunderheads. Maybe, at last, the vanished sea was there, its surface heated up to release the mist, a plausible explanation.

Croker's voice pulled him back to matters in hand and he forced himself to swing across to the upper part of the trawler, almost dropping the axe in the process. Croker was leaning on the wheel house, his face grey with effort and something else, shock perhaps. Suddenly he had become very wasted.

"Are they in there?" said Rik.

Croker looked at him as though he didn't recognise him. Slowly he nodded.

Fear, Rik realised. Like a raw wound. It was a dangerously infectious emotion.

Rik had to steel himself before easing carefully into the wheel house, the twisted tilt of the tiny room distorting everything in filtering rays of sunlight. Those rays, however, did pick out something at the back of the area. Two, thick rubber coats hung side by side: the smell they exuded was far worse than anything Rik had encountered thus far on the trek. It was only when he drew back that the light seemed to shift and he caught sight of the upper part of the coats.

They weren't coats. They were bodies, or the remains of them, as though their entire innards had been removed – sucked out, maybe – to leave them boneless and slack, like fat skins, clothing melded to them, creating the rubbery effect. The

43

heads were shrunken but grotesquely elongated, facial expressions in death pulled down into stretched, eyeless horror. Bloated feet protruded from the sagging lower parts of the corpses, as though the last of their fluids had drained into them, creating an absurdly exaggerated image that in some other place and time might have been laughable.

Repulsed, Rik groped his way back outside. Croker was watching the rocks, as though trying to discern something that might be responsible for the shocking death of the two fishermen.

"What could have done that?" Rik said, as much to himself as Croker. It was only now that he was out here that the implication of the two bodies having been hung up on cloak hooks struck him. It had been almost a *human* action, even if it had been intensely barbaric. He realised now, though he couldn't bring himself to say so, that the bodies – what was left of them – were like trophies.

"We should cut them down, take them home," said Croker, although his expression suggested he had no stomach for it himself, nor for discussing the implications of what they'd found. "Proper burial."

Rik knew the big man was right. His own feelings about religion were indifferent, though there seemed something fundamentally wrong about leaving the dead men in this outrageous tomb. "What are we going to use?"

Croker looked at him askance, as if he had said something heretical. But he managed to grip his slipping emotions and nodded. "Should be some tarpaulin aboard. I'll look."

Rik knew Croker was implying the ghoulish work of taking the two corpses down was going to be left to him. He shuddered, revolted by the thought. Croker was already swinging himself out over the back of the wheel house, hanging dangerously above the wild angle of the trawler. He preferred that to dealing with the dead. Perhaps, thought Rik, he couldn't stomach having to handle his brother, so radically altered by whatever grotesque events had taken place here.

Below Rik the dog had started barking again, though the sound it made was very different to the call that had brought the group here. Now it howled frantically- a mixture of misery and warning. It was facing the seaward side of the trawler and nothing the men could do would silence its incessant, hysterical protest. The message was clear. Something was coming.

"Dane!" one of the men called up to Croker. "That could be the sea, on the turn. If it is, we need to be getting back, fast." The others had gathered and were obviously intent on heading for home without any delay. They all knew how perilously fast the tides moved.

Croker looked up at Rik, silently willing him to make no mention of what they'd found in the wheel house. It would, after all, have to serve as the dead men's final resting place. Rik nodded, sealing their unspoken pact. He began the awkward climb down, risking another look seaward. He could hear something now, a susurration, as if the distant tide was at last sliding back over the shattered rocks. That – or something like it. Something that slithered, or hopped. En masse. A tide, but not the sea. A *living* tide.

It was as though all life here had drawn itself together and was beginning the process of its redistribution. Those mist banks swirled, billowing forward, as if they might be driving whatever vast force was advancing. The dog responded as if it had been dealt a rough kick and leapt forward, yapping madly, trying to race off through the clutching rocks towards whatever was coming, slipping as it went, its abrupt rush forward propelling it beyond the thought of injury. The men stared at it in surprise, no one quick enough to deter it.

It disappeared among the rocks, its bark diminishing until after several protracted minutes, it stopped altogether. After several, ominous moments it became one long shriek, the canine equivalent of a scream. Rik gasped, wondering what sort of horror could have befallen the dog for it to react so violently. The sound broke off, replaced by other, even more sinister sounds.

Croker swore crudely and hefted his shotgun. The dreadful sound seemed to have pushed him across a bridge of decision.

"Get the fuck out of here," he growled to the others. "Fast!"

"What about you?" someone said.

"My brother's out there. I'll find him and bring him back." He looked pointedly at Rik, daring him to spill the truth. "What brought you here?"

"I – I needed a change," said Rik, taken aback by the sudden savagery in the fisherman's voice.

"Yeah, well you got one. The whole fucking world's changing." The big man turned away and went into the rocks, after
the dog, or perhaps, Rik thought, some kind of vengeance. Not
for him the guilt of flight.

The group had no stomach for an argument and moved back
towards the now remote land, loyalty to Croker folding under
the damning pressure of their fear. Rik shared it, his back exposed to whatever was closing in: he felt like a turtle without a
shell. It was impossible to travel quickly, but they covered the
broken terrain as effectively as they dared. On either side of
them, still beyond visibility, the sounds of sea life escalated and
the air was redolent with dissolution, almost nauseatingly
acute.

When they heard another scream, so high-pitched and
distorted it hardly seemed human, they redoubled their efforts
to get away. As they reached the foot of the escarpment, the
rock wall appeared to be twice as steep. A growing panic
hugged them; no one voiced their unified thoughts: something
malevolent and purposeful was crawling in on all sides, using
the rolling banks of mist as cover. The afternoon light was still
strong, but the mist would weaken it considerably once it un-
coiled over them. Reaching the crest of the escarpment became
doubly vital, as though it would magically repulse the mist.

Rik was glad of the axe, but it weighed him down: it took an
effort of will not to discard it. Near the top of the tortuous
climb, one of them men turned to peer down at the grey vague-
ness

below, lapping like a sluggish tide at the rocks there. Over-wrought, the man fired his shotgun – two rounds – out into the void. The sound reverberated around them, repeating itself as if a score of shots had gone off, slowly diminishing. Everyone waited to see the effect.

Below them, silence smothered everything. There was only the mist. Whatever crept and slid through it, that ungodly host, had gone very quiet. Maybe the gunshot had deterred whatever was there. Rik frowned at the thought – how would cephalo-pods understand the sound?

The group moved on, desperation flooding them. One of them, Ruddick, seemed to have taken charge: he was fumbling with a mobile phone, speaking into it while the others glanced at him. Ruddick turned to them with a look of relief.

"They're sending a boat out, down the river. We'll have to bear to the north and make our way along the bank until they can find us. We'll have to go some to beat that mist."

Without any discussion, the group followed him through the cracked strata and weed banks. Overhead the first runners of the mist were sliding across the skies like silk feelers. Rock walls swallowed the men as they headed towards the river bank. They emerged onto a wide expanse of sand, easing their passage. They were tired, but they ran, goaded by fresh fears.

Rik looked back and saw something wriggling out of the rocks, white and bloated. It was far from alone. The air was thick with sound again, those sea-sounds, a seething mass of movement. The sand beneath the men gently vibrated, as if their pounding feet had disturbed something below and it was stirring itself. They saw clumps of dead crabs, some of them as wide across as car tyres. The air grew cooler, the sun's strength weakening. The mist came on again.

By the time the group reached the wide, flat riverbank it was, almost unrecognisable. Each man knew he'd never make it back unless that boat found them. They would be overtaken. The river here was normally underwater, far beyond the lowest tidal point, its features almost indistinguishable from the sea bed. Thankfully it had eroded most of its shores to the point where the going was easier and the men were able to keep up their pace, pausing only when they slipped on the bright green seaweed, treacherous as ice.

Rik's breath was rasping, his throat dry. For once he was glad of the physical effort he had put into the building project; it had toned his muscles. The men were in varying stages of collapse. The fittest of them, fishermen or land workers, were coping with the killing pace, but a couple of them, older men, were losing ground and Rik knew they couldn't go on much longer without a break.

"You get to the boat," one of them said. "Me and Ray'll rest a minute."

To Rik's surprise, no one argued: moments later the two men were left behind. The others exchanged embarrassed glances, but nothing was going to hinder their flight. Rik pushed his own vague feeling of guilt at abandoning the men aside. Images of the two corpses he'd seen in the trawler made that easier. Survival was all that mattered now.

When the mist drew them into its disturbingly cold embrace, the sounds on all sides had increased again. Countless life forms were advancing on both shores, whether in pursuit of the fleeing men, or for more sinister aims. Rik sensed the onset of a kind of madness, grounded in the intensity of his fear: only the sudden appearance out on the river of the boat postponed his mental collapse.

They waded out through the shallows as a small motorised trawler, barely big enough to accommodate them all, drew in cautiously to the bank, barely avoiding getting stranded on the clinging sand banks. One by one they reached the boat and were hauled aboard. As Rik was manhandled into the craft, he heard something out in the wall of mist, more terrible shrieks.

"What the fuck is going on?" one of the crewmen said, trying to see into the mist. "Where's Ray and Archer? Who's out there?"

No one wanted to explain. Shapes in the mist were solidifying, humping across the last of the sand towards the water like elephantine slugs. The men who held the shotguns began firing indiscriminately, shot after shot, reloading and firing again in an uncoordinated, almost insane fusillade. The crewmen on the boat looked on in stupefaction, totally bemused by the mass movement on the shore.

"Just get us the fuck out of here!" snarled Ruddick, reloading his own gun. The trawler swung round easily, its throbbing motor pushing the boat into deeper water before taking it back upriver. Soon it was outrunning the mist. Rik listened, certain that he could hear something else now: the sound of the sea, the tide, racing, close behind the streaming mist. Premature twilight engulfed them.

By the time they had reached the original mouth of the estuary, passing between the tall dunes that reared up on either side, it was late afternoon. They were beyond the mist again; the sunshine brought little comfort: they had become morose and sullen. Rik answered a few of the probing questions of the crewmen, but he knew they thought him evasive. How could he describe what had happened without sounding ridiculous?

The river ran inland for two miles before they reached the small port. The river was a trickle, the harbour no more than a series of gleaming mud banks. All of the men had to wade carefully across them to reach stone steps up to the flat harbour side. Rik was surprised to see a couple of police vehicles, parked like white sharks nearby. There was a pub, chairs and tables scattered outside, but a cordon had been set up: curious onlookers were kept back by several uniformed policemen.

"Get yourselves inside and warmed up," said the officer in charge. Rik and the others needed no second bidding. They were all ushered into the compressed seclusion of the pub and given hot soup. Rik took it mechanically. Afterwards he stripped off his filthy clothes and accepted something more comfortable. He barely noticed the police and other officials around him and his companions.

"Get some rest," said the officer. He seemed to Rik to be

treating this like some kind of natural disaster, a bomb scare perhaps. "When you're all up to it, we've got a few questions we need to ask you all. In your own time, gentlemen."

Rik woke with the dawn. All yesterday's survivors had been housed in the pub's various bedrooms. The police investigation was grindingly thorough. No one was to leave until the police knew what had happened to the five missing men.

Rik switched on the shower, but its spray was stubbornly cold. He could smell the sea, then realised that the water was brackish. He went to wash in the sink, but its tepid water was brown and briny. He dressed and went downstairs into silence. There was no one here.

Outside he drew back in momentary alarm. The police cars had the distinct look of having been abandoned. The light was brightening with the sun, but thick fog closed in, white and clammy. Through its shifting veils, Rik saw the edge of the quayside and heard the soft voice of the tide. He walked towards it and stood on the very edge of the quay. Amazingly the tide had come right in. It didn't appear to have done any damage, just flooded back like any normal tide, fully restored, almost spilling on to the quay.

He could see something gleaming, a number of slimy trails across the stonework, as if impossibly huge sea-slugs had come ashore. Further down the quay, a body sprawled. Was that a policeman?

Breaking through the mist, out in the middle of the river, a shape took substance as it cut through the flat, mirrored surface. Rik studied it with surging alarm, recognising it. How could he forget it? It was the trawler he had last seen with Dane Croker, far out on the exposed seabed. The tide had lifted it and, against all probability, brought it here. As it drew closer to the quay, Rik could discern shapes hunched around its prow, five of them. Men whose faces were, mercifully, obscure.

Dane Croker had brought his brother home. Rik recalled his last words, out in the seabed wilderness.

Sunlight was slowly shredding the fog, revealing that the returning trawler was not alone. There were others coming in on waters that now churned with life. Long lost vessels, seething with marine life as it prepared for a landing.

Survivors

Terry Grimwood

THE WORST THING about interstellar flight, worse than the psychedelic insanities of worm-hole travel, worse than the needle-and-haystack probability of finding life out there, or even a world we could call a second home, worse than the meteor strike and the loss of sixty-eight members of the crew, was time dilation.

Time dilation, the knowledge that when you finally limped home, damaged and grief-stricken, there would be no one left who was there to wave you goodbye twelve years before. Twelve ship-years, that is. Almost two hundred of Earth's.

We took our families. The pain of partings would have been unspeakable, untenable, funereal. The ship was a travelling micro-world on which marriages were made, and broken, and children were born.

And now we were back.

God knew how we did it; half the vessel a holed, uninhabitable crematorium, one drive dead, the other three overworked and nearing catastrophic overload.

Seeing Earth, home, for the first time in twelve subjective years was too intense, too overwhelming, for immediate emotion. One hundred and seventy four survivors and ship-born stood on the cavernous community deck, to stare at the wall-sized view port, and barely a tear shed or word spoken between us.

Earth was not as I remembered it. Earth should be noisy with electronic chatter. This Earth was silent. Earth should be blue, broken by handprints of brown and green, smudged with whorls of white. This Earth was concealed by unbroken, grey cloud, a hidden, worrying place.

But it was home.

A landing party was selected; me among them because I was one of the few left who could pilot the remaining shuttle. No one was certain that the damn thing could still fly. Its pod had been on the periphery of the meteor strike. We would return to the original European launch site; a place that was once Heathrow Airport.

There were four of us: me, Lieutenant John Michaels (pilot and mission commander), along with Engineer (and second pilot) Avni Singh, Doctor (Medical) Alistair Nqbe and Security Officer Marta Hammer.

The descent was a cloud-blind, out-of-control, helter-skelter. Touchdown was not gentle either: a tube blew at the last moment, upsetting our precarious balance and deceleration. The landing gear collapsed, pieces of hull, fin and engine were ripped away. But the restraints held and the womb-seats remained inflated. Everyone answered my shaky roll-call. No one, it seemed, was seriously injured.

We emerged from the wounded shuttle. It was arctic cold. The sky, a brutal, lowering weight of cloud. All structures, buildings and whatever craft had once used the airport, were white-encrusted ruins. A relentless, icy gale whipped snow into gusts of white mist and would have flayed us alive and frozen our lungs if it wasn't for our therma-parkas and masks. We had come prepared.

There were people, headed our way, anonymous figures, obscured by the restless snow-fog. We waited. If they were hostile, well, what would we gain by running? The shuttle was in no fit state to get us out of there. As they came closer we saw that the party was muffled in shabby, patched-up parkas and furs.

"We're humans," I shouted above the wind. "We've come home." My words sounded clumsy in my own ears, almost as if I'd asked them to take us to their leader. Hardly surprising, I hadn't seen or spoken to a stranger for twelve ship years.

One of them, tall, dark-skinned, a woman I realised when she was near enough for me to see her properly, called back to us; "Where are you from?"

"We've... We've been away, out in space. We're explorers. The Fiennes Expedition."

"From Before." It was not a question.

"Before what?" Marta asked, diplomacy not her main strength.

"The war, the end, of civilisation. Before the clouds came and the seas froze."

"Have you heard of us?" I said. "Everyone knew about us... Before."

The woman glanced at the others, then shrugged. "We've

had other things on our minds." She regarded us carefully. "Are there more of you?"

"Yes," I answered then glanced skywards, the action, a reflex. "Up there, in the ship, the Fiennes."

"Are they coming?" The question was matter of fact, not concerned, but not welcoming either.

It was Avni who answered. "Depends if we can repair the shuttle." And that was when the reality of the situation came crashing in. If we couldn't repair the craft, we would never see our friends, families, our people, again. And those, trapped in the Fiennes, could not come home. They wouldn't starve to death or run out of oxygen, the ship's hydroponics and recycling plants would see to that. But the frustration, the emotional devastation at being so close to Earth, yet unable to return to her surface, would be unbearable. There were already tensions, cliques. The ship's social structure was fragile.

"We can help you," the woman said. "There's plenty of spare parts. This is a graveyard full of dead machines. And we're engineers, of a sort."

They lived in the remains of a hotel, one of the big, expensive ones in the airport environs. The place reared out of the snow, its windows blank, empty holes, its paintwork blotched and peeling. It bled wires and pipes, steelwork and panelling. The reception area was a snow crusted, slush-floored cave, its concrete ceiling visible between islands of mouldering ceiling tiles. Naked lights were strung out on cables, which were secured to any protuberance available. The light was yellow and uncertain. On our trek here from the shuttle, we had passed a large copse of industrial-scale wind turbines, blades spinning effortlessly in the endless gale. At least this corner of the post-Before world had electricity.

We were led upstairs, the lifts presumably out-of-order. I lost count of how many floors we ascended, a struggling worm of parkas, our panted breath manifest in rhythmic puffs of vapour. Where there was glass in the windows, the view was obscured by frozen snow. Where there was no glass, the relentless wind reached in to claw at my bones and burn my lungs.

We finally ended our climb. A faded, wall-mounted, plastic number informed us that this was the eighth floor.

We were taken into what was once a function room. Now it looked to be a communal dining hall. Men and women were seated at the long rows of age-battered, wooden tables, intent on their food and drink. These tables were probably the originals, used for countless meetings and team-building sessions. Before. All present wore rough, practical clothes: overalls, combat slacks, frayed sweaters and hooded tops. There was little chatter, and no laughter. They were haggard, intense, undemonstrative. Survivors, that most insular, hard-bitten of species.

It took me a few moments to realise that there were no children.

"Eat," said the woman. She had introduced herself as Lana during one of her rare and brief, bursts of conversation, shouted above the gale as we walked.

We sat, awkwardly, in a gap on a bench, made for us by the shuffling and the redistribution of its occupants. The food was scooped out of a large vat and slopped into metal bowls. Both items of tableware looked homemade, the metal beaten, skilfully, from some scavenged sheet of steel. Apart from the ladle used to serve the portions, there was no cutlery.

The food was a hot, brownish mush. It tasted of meat, interspersed with things that crunched. Its texture and monotonous flavour made it hard work, but these people seemed to live on the stuff, so it wasn't likely to poison us. There was drink as well, a syrupy yellowish liquid that was almost unbearably sweet.

No coffee or tea.

"You mentioned a war." It was the first time Nqbe had spoken. He sounded nervous.

"About a hundred years ago," Lana answered. "The weather turned bad, crops failed. Water ran out in some places, others places were flooded. People fought to survive. It got out of hand; chemicals, germ-warfare, nuclear weapons. The human race punished itself by committing suicide."

"Didn't succeed did it," Marta said.

"No," Lana smiled, faintly, ruefully I think. "It didn't."

"How does this work?" Marta asked. "I mean, you say you're engineers. Where does the food come from? Are you the only ones left?"

"We live in communes and we trade skills. There are farmers

out there, and itinerant construction gangs who keep these ruins from falling down. There are also gangs of scavengers who trade oil and petrol. It's how we heat our living areas at night. And only at night. Fuel is precious, finite. We scavenge a living from the corpses of aeroplanes and space hulks. We make things and repair things."

Space hulks? Did that mean that humankind had continued pushing outwards after we left? Desperately clawing its way into the void, until everything collapsed.

They gave us a room, a few more floors up. It was empty, its window sealed with a sheet of mouldy plywood. Apart from sacking spread over the bare concrete floor, there were no comforts. We would retrieve our thermal sleeping bags, torches etc. from the shuttle and make it our temporary home.

Nqbe sat down in the corner of the room, face in hands. I crouched beside him. "You okay?"

"We shouldn't have come back, John. This isn't our world."

"We always knew it wouldn't be the same one we left."

"We could have stayed on Rigel IX."

He was right. Though riven by apocalyptic storms and erratic, almost hourly temperature changes, the planet had oceans, supported plant life, was enclosed in a breathable atmosphere.

"I couldn't stay, not there," I said. "A lot of us couldn't bear it, you know that."

"I... I'm sorry John, of course."

My wife and two daughters were among the thirty or so, killed on Rigel IX.

The Engineers used a giant hangar as their workshop. They wanted to move the shuttle inside. I was reluctant. Avni disagreed with me. She said that the weather was too brutal for us to carry out repair work outside. I wanted the shuttle in a place from which we could make a fast getaway if the need arose.

"Why will we need to run away?" she demanded. We stood by the hangar doors, away from the Engineers who were, nonetheless, watching us, silent and impassive. Nqbe and Marta were slumped against the hangar wall, further inside, waiting resignedly for us to finish our argument. "These people are helping us."

She was right about that of course. They were under no obligation. But, I didn't trust them. Their quiet acquiescence and acceptance of our sudden presence amongst them unnerved me, as did their lack of protest over the possible influx of an entire community to their starved, ragged world.

I was tired of the dispute. "Okay, Avni, let me put it to you another way. It's an order. The shuttle stays out there. We work on it out there. Now, it's getting dark, we need to fetch our kit."

Later, in our room, in the warm, blackness, I felt Marta unzip my sleeping bag and climb in. She held me tight and I nuzzled her long, fine hair, gently kissed her eyes and for a few moments, the feel of her, eased away the memories that haunted my nights. I clawed at her and she hushed me and touched me and I sank into her and forgot until the dark came and I was –

– digging into the mud with my bare hands as the rains of Rigel

IX tore the clothes from my back. They were under there, suffocated beneath a river of black-grey slime. They were screaming their silent screams, begging me to release them, so that they could breathe, oh Christ all they wanted to do was breathe –

"John!" Hissed into my ear. I felt Marta shove back the flap of the sleeping bag and sit up. "Can you hear it? Listen!"

I did so, bleary and uncomfortable in the stifling heat of the room. A heat at odds with the gale battering at the shattered window's plywood covering.

"What is it?"

"Outside the room. There's a rustling noise."

"There are people in the building."

"I know, but this isn't people. Can't you hear it?"

Marta was making me nervous. I listened, and, yes, there it was, above the steady rhythms of Nqbe's and Avni's breathing. Rustling, scraping. Marta was on her feet, wrestling with her overall, then making for the door.

"No," I said. "Stay here –"

Too late. The door was open. I scrambled to my feet, grabbed my own overall, and woke Avni in the process.

She mumbled blearily. "Woz'appening?"

"Marta thought she heard something. Wait here."

I didn't give her time to protest.

The corridor was as warm as the room. There were no lights but I saw a torch bobbing into the darkness up ahead. It swung round to dazzle me.

"God, Marta."

"Sorry. I can see movement. I think it's... Christ!"

I felt my way to where she stood. Marta grabbed my arm. "Look." She swept the torch beam along the skirting and I saw it too. Insects. Thousands of them, cockroaches, beetles, a mixture of species swarming along the join between floor and wall, racing out of the light. Some were huge, gleaming, things, all were fast. Something clattered past my face, wings brushed my skin. I recoiled. The torch beam shot up, to trap a spiral of flying creatures: moths, flies, wasps, and others too fast to identify.

Survivors, like the engineers and the farmers and fuel scavengers, and possibly the most adaptable of all life forms on Earth, the insect.

"The warmth must have brought them out of hiding," I said.

"They should be eating each other, not swarming together like that."

"Things have changed, survival is survival, Marta."

I heard Avni call my name and a moment later felt her hand on my shoulder. Her disgust was palpable. Something batted at my face and I waved it away. More of them whirred past my ear.

Marta moved off again. We had no choice but to follow. The flying insects were so dense now I had to look downwards to protect my eyes and mouth. Avni's hand was tight about mine as we stumbled, in Marta's wake, out onto the lobby.

"Fuck!"

Marta shone the torch round the space. Every inch of wall, ceiling and floor was hidden beneath a heaving carpet of insects. Avni released my hand and staggered back, beating at her face and hair. "Shit, get them off me. Get them off me!" I heard her move away, towards the room, running, bumping into the wall, swearing and sobbing.

It wasn't weakness. We were tough and travel-hardened, us interstellar adventurers, but we were also fragile; minds, hearts and souls fractured by what we had found out there.

"They're coming from below," Marta said.

She shone the torch onto the stairs and I saw them streaming up from the shadows pooled below us. Many were now mating, coupled on the wing or as lumbering double creatures, struggling over the floor.

Wherever I stepped, I could feel them crunch under my boots. Each time I lifted my foot, it was like dragging it from soft sand.

Or mud.

"We're going back, now."

"This is wrong. We need to find –"

"Back," I snapped. "Marta, that's an order."

We stuffed one of our sleeping bags along the crack under the door. I couldn't sleep; Marta was tense in my arms. I could hear Avni, shivering and murmuring in uneasy slumber. The rustling and scraping noises grew louder. Flying things pattered against the door. Some of them must have found their way in here. I began to feel them on my face, in the sleeping bag. Imagination, reality, either way, there was little I could do about it, but wait for morning.

At some point in the deep, hot dark, the noises gradually died away.

Next day we started work on the shuttle. The cloud broke a little and let in a touch of sunlight. It felt like a good omen, although it brought no warmth. If anything, the momentary brightness made everything seem even colder.

With the engineers' help, we stripped out the damaged parts, and drew up a list of replacements, which the engineers would scavenge for us.

There were decisions to be made if we managed to get this craft back up to the Fiennes. We had found only one non-terrestrial planet fit for human life. I and many others did not want to go back there, even though not that many of us would survive the journey. Damaged as it was, the Fiennes would have to take its time. Rigel IX belonged to our children.

But this was no longer home, either.

The sunlight weakened. Clouds closed over the bright-lit wound. Night was coming.

We had not mentioned the insects to Lana. I hadn't requested our silence. It was an unspoken agreement.

That night we ate in the refectory, and the near silence of the engineers began to unnerve me. Apart from Lana and a big, shaven headed guy, they barely seemed aware of us. The food, the mush, made me gag. My head ached from caffeine starvation. When we returned to the room, I felt besieged.

I was woken from an edgy, dream-laden sleep by the rustling. There were other sounds; buzzing and whirring, the pitter -patter of flying creatures. My skin crawled. Marta sat, torch focussed on the door, until she collapsed from exhaustion. When my own dreams returned, they were full of urgent, scuttling movement.

We worked through the daylight hours. We had little rest. I drove the others on, put up with their protests, their discontent. The cold was enervating. The grey sky bore down on us, the wind burrowed into my skull and danced on my nerves.

And at night, the insects came.

I could no longer find comfort in Marta's arms. She was suspicious, restless, argumentative. Nqbe was becoming withdrawn. Avni was working herself to destruction. Squabbles broke out. The fabric was frayed.

Then, on the fifth night, Marta disappeared.

I woke hot, my head pounding, as grey light seeped in through the gaps around the blocked-up window. The wind moaned, rain or sleet lashed at the plyboard covering. I rolled over and was alone, not unusual anymore. Marta spent too many nights sitting cross-legged, facing the door, listening to the endless noise of the insects.

This morning she wasn't in the room at all.

Okay, it was light. Her agitation could have driven her out early.

But I knew different. I could feel it, in the vacuum of her absence.

"Stay here," I told the others. Then I was out in the corridor.

I met Lana on the stairs. There was no reason for her to be there. It was as if she had been waiting for me.

"What's wrong?" she asked. Her question was a lie. She knew what was wrong.

"One of our people, Marta, she's missing."

Lana shrugged "We'll look for her."

"Don't lie to me. You know where she is."

"Repair your vessel. Go back to your ship."

"Where is Marta?" I was angry now.

"Your people need to come home." She turned from me and walked away. I reached out, grabbed her arm.

I felt.

Movement.

Under her skin.

A brief wrongness. Gone. Never there.

Lana wrenched her arm free, stared at me for a moment. Then walked away. I slumped against the wall, dizzy from exhaustion.

There was no choice but to continue working on the shuttle. I fetched the others. We finished our dry rations. I kept them away from the engineers, hauled them, cold, tired, and hungry out to the shuttle. The engineers had done a lot of work, the major structural problems had been dealt with, the fin replaced, the torn belly patched. They had crawled over the thing like ants. Moved heaven and earth.

By nightfall, we were testing the power plant. She was raw and wounded, but there was a chance the shuttle would make it back to the Fiennes tomorrow, where full repair could be effected.

Before I left the shuttle, I discreetly armed myself with a knife and one of the small flamers concealed under the pilot's seat.

As the light began to fade and we prepared to set off back to the hotel, I took a last look around at the snow blurred horizon beyond the airport perimeter. And wondered what the hell was out there. What world this had become. The desolation, and the mystery of it, was terrifying.

I was always going to search for Marta.

Avni and Nqbe were asleep, exhaustion saw to that. Sleep that was disturbed by mumbled terrors and fraught twisting and turning in their sleeping bags, but sleep nonetheless. Grabbing a torch and pocketing the flamer, I opened the door as carefully as I could and stepped out into the corridor. Before I could shut the door again, I felt some of the insects scuttle over my feet and into the room. I headed for the stairs. Tiny bodies crunched under my boots. Moths and other winged creatures danced in the torch beam. The walls seethed with invertebrate life. Things dropped on my head. I scrabbled at my hair, felt the hard, skittish bodies.

As before, the stairs were alive with the things. Surging upwards, frantic in their mating dances. I took a breath then set off down. The creatures swirled about my feet, over the insteps, so many of them that walking became difficult. I felt them on my legs and quickly gave up trying to brush them away.

I made it to the lobby, which was a scuttling, squirming lake of living things. I felt my gorge rise. I had to keep going. I had to find her. I had left those I loved on Rigel IX. Never again.

The source of the insect flow seemed to be a doorway to the right of the lobby. I drew the flamer from my pocket.

Through the doorway now, deeper into the hotel. There was a smell, a mixture of mustiness, and a bloody, meaty stink. When I passed through the next doorway I found myself in the kitchen. Food bowls were piled up on the worktop, as were the big serving vats. The sweet liquid we drank was stored in huge glass flasks. There was a walk-in freezer.

I opened the door, looked in.

A moment later, I was sick.

There were human bodies in there, hanging upside down on meat hooks; arms limp, hair trailing, mouths open—death open.

My stomach heaved again and again, because now I knew what we had been eating. Marta was not among them, thank Christ.

She was in what had probably been the restaurant, and she was not alone.

The tables were locked together to form a set of long platforms that filled the room, end-to-end. The engineers were prone on the tables. I moved among them and there she was, pale as a corpse in the torch light, and not to be woken. She was breathing, though. There was a pulse; her skin was hot, flushed.

I shone the torch in her face.

A cockroach emerged from her left nostril and scuttled over her cheek then dropped to the floor. Another struggled from her left ear. A third scuttled in from the dark edges of the disc of torch light and disappeared back into her ear. Gagging once more, I shone the torch round wildly. Insects were entering into, and emerging from, the others, glimpsed horrors, caught in the wildly dancing torch light.

Then I remembered that odd movement under Lana's skin.

I carried Marta outside to the shuttle. I hugged her close to me, tried to keep her warm as I stumbled and tripped through the snow, unsure of what I was doing. All I knew was that I had to get her away from that place.

No one followed. There were no insects out here in this frozen version of Hell.

The freezing gale whipped the snow into a blinding fog that raked my face and drove into my lungs. Marta was growing cold in my arms. She stirred, moaned. I told her I loved her. Over and over again. It became a litany. I had never used the word with her before. I thought she was mere comfort in my grief, but now she was going from me, I realised how much I needed her.

And there was the shuttle, almost ready now, patched and bandaged. I clambered inside, slammed the hatch shut and held her tight. The shuttle was dark and cold. I couldn't afford to drain the power cells to heat us, so we burrowed into a womb seat, wrapped in thermal blankets. As Marta's body temperature rose again, I felt the insects stir beneath her skin. I felt them scuttle over my hands as they emerged from her body. Something bit me, a sudden vicious pinch of pain on my hand.

More bites.

Stings.

Exhausted I slipped towards sleep –

– towards the roar of the mudslide, and the screams and shouts of alarm. I was running, back towards the base camp, back towards the great tongue of slime that stretched from the hillside above and covered everything. Everyone. The lightning-riven sky boiled green-grey, and rain slashed down with such force it tore my overall and my skin. I fell to my knees and dug. I howled their names and slithered into the murk like a worm, sobbing and shouting and burying myself until I was dragged back by the others, who were also weeping and shouting and offering their grief to the storm. Almost thirty souls lost, the roll-call of names, soon to be added to the ones we would lose to the meteor strike.

We could have stayed. We would have learned. We had the resources, the expertise. We allowed our grief to drive us back into space, in the vain hope we would find succour back on Earth. We forgot the rules of interstellar travel. We forgot the brutality of time dilation. We forgot why we had brought our families with us...

Dawn broke and, as the light shifted from black to grey, I saw engineers ranged around the shuttle. They were armed, with rifles and flamers, but made no move to storm the vessel. Their patience was terrifying.

Marta stirred, coughed wetly and shuddered. Her eyes opened, showed her confusion, and fear.

"John?" Her voice was hoarse, choked, as if she was speaking around something lodged in her throat. "Help me... Please... kill me..."

I couldn't. I stared, helpless, mumbled that I would take her back to the Fiennes.

She pulled away from me. I saw the movements under her skin, a flurry of activity in her arms, her neck. Then it was still. "No..." she said. "I can't go back, not now."

"What have they done to you? Marta, what's happening?"

"Survival," she said, the fear suddenly gone. "We give them warmth. They give us life... Jesus, it hurts. I'm drowning... suffocating. I want to die..."

"Humanity was a mewling child, poisoned and dying."

I spun round to see Lana in the open hatch. I hadn't heard her approach. There was no threat in her presence.

"There are two species who will always find a way to survive, no matter what; one able to find a hiding place and thrive, even in Hell, the other, able to shape the world around them, even when the world is broken."

"Symbiosis?" The word seemed too scientific, too clinical, to describe what had happened here.

"Yes, I suppose it is."

"Is she still Marta?"

"Marta?" Lana frowned. "She is... she. A part of us."

For a moment I felt an urge to kill them all, even Marta, to destroy this abomination. But I knew I couldn't, and the urge faded. "So, this airport, this community, is a hive?"

Lana shrugged. "We defend it, we sustain it. We trade, and we fight."

I remembered the carcasses, hanging from those hooks. "And steal human flesh."

"We survive."

"You have no feelings? No emotion or... guilt?"

Another frown. "We survive."

"Jesus Christ."

Marta gave a cry and dropped to her knees. She was in pain. Lana made no move to help her. Whatever metamorphosis was taking place, it had to be suffered alone.

"The shuttle is ready to fly," Lana said. "Avni can take it back to your ship and start bringing your people home."

Of course, I would not be allowed to go, or be anywhere near Avni and Nqbe. They were not to know the truth.

And the rest would come, the people trapped on the Fiennes. They wouldn't be able to help themselves. They would be driven here by the need to come home, and when they arrived...

I was taken to the hangar. I sat on a tool chest, Marta beside me. She was quiet, vacant. Someone had given her a sweater and a parka. I helped her to dress. Her flesh rippled. I held her hand and felt them moving inside her. I wondered how long the process took, and how painful it was. She made no sound but I could see the terror in her eyes.

Kill me, she said. Please...

I stared out of the door. It was snowing again, huge clumps of white swirled through the grey and across the bright beams of the arc lights.

I waited. A moment, then I saw them. Lana, a couple more engineers, and two other figures, Nqbe and Avni. They held each other, looked lonely and afraid.

I don't know what Lana had told them, but they must have believed it. Probably that Marta and I had died, exposure perhaps. Avni and Nqbe had to go back voluntarily, they must not know the truth.

There was little time, and even less chance of success –

I grabbed Marta's hand and ran.

I ran and shouted their names.

Marta struggled but was too weak to fight. Lana turned, shouted at me to stop. I yelled back. I saw Avni stop and turn. I shambled to a halt, wrenched Marta to myself and felt the disgusting ripple through her flesh. I saw Avni, take a step towards me. Lana as well. She was armed, a handgun.

"I love you Marta," I whispered.

And, before Lana could shoot, I slashed upwards with the

knife and opened Marta from navel to breast. I heard Avni's wind-snatched scream. I saw Nqbe vomit as the insects poured out onto the red, red snow. Lana fired. Something knocked me backwards, but not off my feet. Nqbe grabbed Avni, hauled her struggling towards the shuttle. I realised I was on my knees now, I felt the warmth of my own blood spread across my stomach. Lana was firing at the fleeing Nqbe and Avni.

I dragged my arm up and flamed her.

Tiny fires tumbled from her burning flesh, frantic and dying.

I felt a second bullet rip through my right side; a third shattered my left shoulder blade. I didn't feel the rest, but lay in the snow, clutching Marta to myself. As I watched the shuttle flee spaceward on a pillar of liquid flame, I felt the first of the insects crawl over my face, seeking warmth, and knew that I was not going to die.

A Taste for Canal Burgers

David Rix

A ND I'M USUALLY such a careful cyclist. I don't go barg-
ing through when I can't see what's ahead. I don't go sailing along trusting the world to get out of my way. I don't even
jump red lights, before any idiots start having a go at me. But
on that cool spring night...

It was around three a.m. Cycling London's canal paths at
this hour is hallucinatory enough at the best of times—they are
narrow unpredictable cracks that plunge through the city,
worlds of uneven pavement, alternating light and deep, deep
dark with low bridges, heavy city always crowding around as
close as it possibly can—and a continuous line of moored narrowboats lurking beside you like half-submerged coffins. But
tonight the slamming of a door still rang in my ears—a voice
sounding stupid and ugly followed me—the memory of words.
Bad words. So I guess I was somewhat distracted. Maybe there
were even tears in my eyes—the world reduced to a half-blind
Gerhard Richter painting of rainy black and orange. At the time
I had no idea what I hit.

I remember balance disrupted. I remember hurtling through
the air. I remember a massive presence to my right—water,
suddenly seeming like an ocean. I remember my mind very
calmly trying to work out what to do to prevent myself impact-
ing that water, working through scenario after scenario in my

head, even until the last moment trying to find one that would work. I remember an almighty bang as my bike and my shoulder hit the hull of one of the narrowboats tied up there. I remember a sudden chaos of black and wet. I remember my bike and everything else vanishing from sight. I remember a lot of cold.

I wanted to scream aloud in sheer rage, but of course I couldn't open my mouth. As if things weren't complicated enough and miserable enough in the world, now this had to happen. Which way was up? Which way was down? Could I align myself to either? To my relief, it seemed I could. My feet touched bottom soon enough with a dull soft-hard feeling, as of muddy stonework, and I could stand again. My face broke the surface. I had gone down in the gap between two narrowboats—a few metres of black open water with the stern of the one I had hit looming over me. I looked round in a panic for a way out of this, but I can tell you, a low wall or the hull of a narrowboat may look insignificant when you are standing up above it, but when you are in the water below, it is another matter. I could see nothing but vaguely sinister fluted metal and the jet black hull of what might as well have been a battleship.

And then—I just about got the shock of my life when a face erupted out of the water about a foot away from me.

I think I might actually have screamed. I mean, okay, of course I bloody screamed. What would you expect? Stuck there in the dark, my nerves already twice jangled. Figures on the towpath I could cope with. Even annoyed and sleepy figures on the boats. But coming up from below, out of nowhere—fuck yeah I was scared.

"Ach—careful," it cried.

But it soon got a lot more surreal than that. There was a flurry as the figure struggled—seemed to struggle—with something in the water. Something that slid past my leg with an indefinable feeling. Something that splashed and swirled. And then there was a sharp pain, as though the something had bitten me...

I screamed again, flailing away from it all until I banged into the massive hull behind me.

"Shhh," the figure begged. "You'll wake the boaters. Hang on..."

I just stared, too shocked for any kind of coherence. But by this time the figure was beginning to reformat itself in my mind from 'monster' or even 'mad human who might possibly be a serial killer' to just plain and simple 'woman'. A pale face with hair streaming over her skin in long wet snakes—a pair of transparent swimming goggles that glimmered at me like the blinded eyes of some cave fish. She grabbed a length of cord that hung down from the side of the boat and did something complicated with it—apparently tying it to something. Apparently to *the* something. To whatever it was she was fighting with in the water. Then she was backing away with a small gasp of relief, as though some minor but troublesome chore was completed.

"Are you alright?" she asked, shoving the goggles up onto

her forehead.

"How can I be alright?" I cried. "I mean, what's ..?"

"Did you fall in?" she asked with an almost petulant frown. "You scared me half to death."

"What do you think you did to me?" I yelled. "What's the heck's going on here?"

She gave me a weird eyebrows-up look. I drew a long, long breath, slapping the drips of water away from my face. It was important not to lose it here—this was not a good place to lose it. Losing it had to be saved up carefully for the right time in the right location...

"I cycled into the canal," I said, trying to calm down. "Hit something on the path."

"Fuck," she muttered. "I hope it wasn't my hose..."

"Your what?"

She shook her head.

"For gawd sake, let's get out of here, okay?"

That sounded a good idea, but—

"Over here," she said, half swimming around to the side of the boat away from the towpath—and away from the tethered thing. She felt her way along the hull a short distance, then grabbed something.

"Wait –" I muttered, turning back. "My bike."

"Uh-uh," she said, restraining me. "Don't. Don't go that way. I'll get it out for you in a moment. This has all got quite insane enough already."

"If you say so..." I mumbled.

"This way," she said, gesturing. I propelled myself after her, half-swimming, half-walking over the uneven canal bed. There was something hanging down into the water from the side of the boat, I realised. A rope ladder.

"Go on—up you go."

I grabbed it and climbed, hauling myself up and landing in a squelching heap on the tiny stern deck, surrounded by unidentifiable boat oddments on all sides. It was illuminated by a small lantern—just a tiny island of light in this canal darkness.

"Mind out," she called, following. "And mind my crayfish." I glanced vaguely at some large white plastic tubs beside me, then slithered out of the way feeling like a sodden half-drowned worm.

I stared up her. For a moment I thought she was stark naked, and you know what? After all this, I wouldn't even have thought it odd. But no. Actually she was just wearing a perfectly normal set of underwear. Wet and clingy and almost precisely not what you expect to encounter at night in London. I sat up and focused on finding reality again. In some kind of search for the normal, I found my wallet in my pocket and opened it, surveying the wet ruin of all my notes and papers. "Sorry about your boat," I managed, my voice quavering. "I think I hit it somewhere on the way down. Is it ok?"

"Oh fuck the boat," she said gruffly. "Are you hurt?"

"Yeah—I—I think I'm okay." I rubbed my shoulder. Nothing seriously wrong there. Then I absently rubbed at my leg—and froze when my hand came away covered with dark fluid. Red.

"Oh gawd," she muttered.

I was trying to remember. That pain had come when—she had—and something—when it almost felt as though...

"What was that?" I demanded. "Something bit me. At least— it felt as though..." I stared at her, a look she returned with a slightly shifty expression. Then I shook my head. "Uh, uh—no, it must have been my bike or... or some metal down there." I peeled my trouser cuff upwards and examined the wound, which she helpfully illuminated with a small torch. It looked rough—shallow and rather torn. Two neat parallel gouges, run- ning a nice river of red down my calf. She leaned in and took a closer look, then shrugged with a hint of unease.

"Get those things off and I'll dry them. And you'd better get inside. Clean that out a bit."

"My bike?" I mumbled.

"Oh gawd yeah," she said, shoving her goggles over her eyes again. "Where did you fall?"

I waved vaguely at the narrow corner between the stern of the boat and the towpath, then glanced at the cord hanging into the water not far away. Something was definitely swirling there beneath the surface, tugging on it.

"Okay, hang on." She hopped onto the towpath and jumped in again with a surprisingly quiet splash. "Gimme that rope," she whispered, gesturing at one lying in a pile on the deck be- side me. I passed one end to her and she vanished underwa- ter—all very routine. Then she was up again and nothing to do but haul the rope in. The bike soon emerged, streaming water, the panniers hanging empty, no doubt leaving their contents behind on the canal bed. I swore under my breath.

"My phone was in there somewhere," I muttered.

And wrapped round one wheel, a length of yellow hosepipe— one end still trailing into the canal.

"Oh gawd," she muttered, looking really unhappy. "I'm... sorry. There's not usually anyone around at this time of night."

"What is it?" I asked with a sigh.

"It's my air supply," she said.

I stared at her feeling stupid.

"For—diving..?"

"Yes."

I glanced down again. The cord was still stretched taut and moving slightly. My leg still bled a nasty little stream.

"Have you been fishing?" I asked dizzily.

"Yes," she muttered, looking a little apprehensive.

"I mean... actually in the water?"

She nodded and shrugged.

"I use the hose sometimes to get under the surface so I can feel around. Just pop it in my mouth—not as if I am going very deep."

I stared at her, wondering vaguely which of us was the more insane. That trailing yellow worm looked the most ridiculous and unsafe thing I had ever seen in my entire life.

"At three A.M.?" I demanded.

She shrugged again. "Well—you know how it is in London. Always someone wanting to interfere—some stupid regulation or other –"

I shook my head. Whatever it was that she had tethered to the end of that rope was not tiny. It was large enough for the cord to hang taut. It must be a big fish. Maybe even a pike? Had she been pike-noodling with her bare hands at three a.m.? In Regents Canal?

This was crazy.

Before I could say anything though, she suddenly got into motion. "Come on," she said with a shiver. "Please get those wet clothes off."

"Yes but –"

"We'd better get you warm and dry at least. I'm standing here in my eddies and I doubt you are any warmer. Get those clothes off and get in that fucking shower."

"You have a shower?"

"Of course," she said, waving at the steps down into the interior of the boat. "All the comforts of home, provided you don't mind water everywhere."

"Ok then," I said with an appreciative smile. "Thanks."

I made for the doorway.

"Out here please," she said with a small thin grin. "That boat gets enough fucking condensation. Get 'em off."

I dithered, feeling a little self-conscious.

"Come on," she said impatiently. "There's nobody about. Have you got a face on your 'arris or something?"

"My what?"

"Arse," she clarified.

I gave a short laugh, aware that there was no real choice about this. It wasn't the cleanest place in the world and if I didn't, I would probably have gangrene by the time I got home—or I would have turned into some highly specific kind of toxic superhero. And besides, the wet was already wicking every mote of warmth out of me. With a shrug I stripped off and, with comforting practicality, she took my sodden clothes and wrung them out into the canal before draping them over the side of the boat in a neat line.

"The shower's on the right, just beyond the kitchen area."

I watched her grab my bike and sling it on the roof in one muscular movement, then I turned away and headed inside, stumbling down the steps and through a haze of cluttered interior—and soon found the shower. It was a tiny cubicle, barely big enough for one person to squeeze into, but I must admit the blast of hot water was utter bliss. Bye-bye chill and canal stink and good bloody riddance. I lingered in there for a few minutes, scrubbing at the wound, then opened the shower door and peered out, feeling awkward and naked but rather more human again. I found her waiting right outside, still looking very wet and shivering.

"You look better already," she said with a tired almost-smile. "My turn." She gave a shaky laugh. "Lemme in there."

She handed me a nice fat robe and pushed past me as I tried to climb into it.

"Thanks," I said, meaning it. "It really is—very good of you,"

"Don't worry about it."

A moment later, her two items of underwear, or eddies as she called them, came tossing out of the doorway—a neat and accurate throw that took them right into the nearby kitchen sink with a plop.

I sighed and tried to relax. It had all been a bit of a flurry, but now at last I had a chance to slow down and look round the interior of the boat properly—and I have to say it was quite striking. It was more spacious than I had expected since the floor was a little way below the surface of the water. It was a long thin cabin, almost like a train carriage, divided up into several spaces. I was sitting in some kind of lounge with a fitted sofa and chairs, with the kitchen taking up one end of it. In one corner, an old woodstove crackled agreeably, radiating heat. Beyond the shower, a doorway let into what I presume was a bedroom at the front. It was a pleasing space, the walls sloping out, then in again making a roughly hexagonal cross-section. It was cluttered—the basic stuff of human life crammed into a long thin box, as well as some more arty touches. Oddments picked up, things collected, things made.

In short, whatever else it was, it was a home. No doubt whatsoever, a permanent live-aboard home. This was nothing unusual. An ever-increasing number of Londoners were moving onto the water into places like this, squeezed out by the impossible housing market.

I couldn't resist getting up and having a look around. The kitchen seemed well appointed—and bloody hell, I've seen smaller ones in the cupboards they call London apartments these days. A cooking range and oven, presumably run off a gas cylinder somewhere, a sink, cupboards, drawers—it was indeed all the comforts of home.

Poking around curiously, I soon found myself noticing the sink, which contained a rather unappetising salad of wet underwear, a few vegetable scraps, and something else that I didn't recognise. Three black things that looked like thorns. At first I thought they were some kind of claw. Then I wondered if they were a squid beak. But they weren't. I picked one up and studied it. It was about a centimetre long, hollow and very sharp.

I had no idea what they were.

Then the shower door opened again and I quickly dropped it. She looked out.

"Um—would you mind..." She frowned. "Oh fuck it." She stepped out, stark naked and hurried into the bedroom—only to emerge a few moments later wearing a robe of her own. It looked hand-made—simple brown material held together with vivid red stitches. Definitely a certain artistry blended with the basic utilitarian. She hesitated, suddenly looking awkward.

"Sorry," she muttered. "I am not used to company. You know, it's about four months since I last had someone visit me here. You'll have to bear with me, I am not—I don't think I am very good at this..."

"So long as I am not in the way," I said, desperate to match politeness with politeness.

She sat down by the stove and handed me some antiseptic and a length of bandage, which I applied to and wrapped round my still slightly oozing leg. As with the boat, I now had a chance to look at her properly as well. Her face was quite thin and there was a continual wary expression on it that bothered me. It was a face that seemed to find it hard to smile or relax without keeping something carefully in reserve. A face that has had suspicion beaten into it over a long period. Her age could have been almost anything from worn-out late teens to 30s—it was hard to tell.

"Your clothes are drying outside," she said. "I'll bring them in and put them in front of the fire in a moment. I, I don't know if you need to go home but –"

I frowned.

"I don't—need to, no," I said. That came out sounding much bitterer than I intended and she glanced at me with a flash of curiosity.

"Are you homeless then?" she asked with a casual tone that gave me a small chill.

"No—not really," I said, tossing my head with a slightly daft defensive gesture. "I just—can't go home for a little while."

The curious look continued. I gave a guilty squirm. I suppose there was no choice now. I had doomed myself to explain. "I had a bit of a row," I whispered with a guilty squirm. "With my, ah—"

"Trouble and strife?"

"Um ..?"

"Other half?"

"Yeah—"

"And stormed out?"

"More like chucked out," I said with a sigh.

She gave a frown. "So that's why you were cycling round the canals at three a.m. Is she crazy?"

"I should be thanking you," I said caustically. "At least you have saved me worrying about phone calls…"

She gave me an embarrassed look and a tiny smile, one that flickered over her face as though unsure if it was allowed to be there.

"And—you're going back?" she asked.

"I—suppose so. Not much else I can do."

"Well, at least that means there's no hurry. Some bloody sanctuary this is, but—welcome aboard. Make yourself at home, as far as possible in this thing. You want to stay the night?"

I stared at her, not used to such offers out of the blue. Not in these paranoid days.

"Would that—be okay?"

"Sure—I don't think my sofa is so bad."

"Then—thanks," I said. "You live alone here?"

"Yeah," she said shortly. "Just me and my boat. You know, the cockney for boat is nanny goat—so I guess this is my nanny. Kind of nice."

I glanced up with interest at the reference to cockney slang— and at last I remembered what the term 'eddies' meant. Eddie grundies = undies. The funny thing, though, was that her voice didn't sound cockney. Instead she had a smooth and almost featureless accent, for all her sometimes colourful language. Maybe she was a lost ex-student, unable to find a toe-hold in the world and thus settling down here in maybe one of the very few lifestyles left that didn't steal your soul.

"Isn't it—lonely?"

She was silent for a while, long enough for me to wish I hadn't asked, then nodded. "Yes. But..." She paused, and then the words came out with unexpected eloquence. "I suppose, sooner or later everyone and everything proves unreliable. Even oneself. Especially oneself. I am better off alone and with what I can hold in my hand."

"Maybe," I said, thinking of my own home without much affection.

"You know, this thing cost about a quarter of just the deposit for one of those swanky flats up there." She waved vaguely at the ceiling and I tried to remember which particular buildings were clustering around. But they all look the same—the same hopeful luxury of any flats near water.

I nodded slowly.

"Sorry," she muttered, sitting up. "I'm not much of a bloody host. Would you—like something to eat? Or—maybe drink? I ought to offer you something hot but I don't really drink tea or coffee, so –"

"That's okay—"

"And... as for food, I haven't much in the fridge, but... Gawd—I'm not... I'm pretty much out of... I've eaten everything I caught and there's only a few bits and bobs left."

She stared at me, an obvious tension in her now—a jittery nervousness that was threatening to become contagious. It was clear she wasn't kidding. She really wasn't used to this.

"Don't worry," I said, trying to be soothing. "It's fine. I'll be..."

"Unless maybe—there's something in the traps outside? Not the crayfish though—they are not ready yet."

"Do you really manage to live off the canal?" I asked, anxious to steer her towards different topic.

"Well—hardly that," she said, "but everything you can find is one less thing you have to buy."

"I always assumed these places were rather dead?"

"You'd be surprised. There's crayfish, and fish. And... and you can find lots of plants. Salad everywhere if you know it. And there's other things around as well, like snails. Earthworms—they make a nice patty, you know."

"Really?" I asked, startled in spite of myself.

"Oh yes. I don't have any though. They need twenty four hours to prepare. You give them wet flour to eat..."

That was not entirely a disappointment, but somewhere at the back of my mind I had heard of this before. Wild food. The foraging lifestyle. Living off the land. But this was the first time I had run into it in the flesh—and the last thing I expected in the heart of the city, where I would half-expect any wild food to put you in the hospital.

"I'm—just going to check my traps," she said. "Otherwise..."

"You really don't have to worry," I tried to say again with some desperation, but she was already stumbling up the steps to the stern deck. I followed her and found her standing precariously half way along the outside of the boat; her bare feet perched on a tiny little ledge. She was hauling in a rope, and something soon came up dripping and gleaming in the dark—some kind of box. Then a second one. She came scrambling back and dumped them on the deck.

"Nothing," she said forlornly.

"Please don't worry," I said with a laugh. "I'll be fine—really."

She gave a sigh. "It's easier to find crayfish—but you can't eat them straight away." She lifted the lid off a bucket, and I leaned over to take a look. Several small lobster-like creatures rested there placidly in a pool of water—all legs and massive claws. I don't think I had ever seen a crayfish before, except maybe on a menu. They looked dramatic things to be wandering round in a London canal.

"Signals," she said. "Not ready to eat yet, unfortunately."

"If I pick one up, will I regret it?"

"Naah—hold it by the body. It won't nip you."

I caught one gingerly, its hard and spiny shell pricking my fingers. Close up, it was hard to imagine anything more alien, with its weird machine-like face and squirming jointed legs.

"They need to spend some time in clean water," she said. "That's the thing. So they can shit out all the crap they've been eating. A sort of detox diet." She gave a shrill giggle. "You need it in London especially."

"Fantastic," I murmured, returning the creature to the bucket. "I'm amazed there's so much here."

"Oh there's more things here than anyone really imagines," she said with a smile, her nervousness beginning to fade now. "You know—there's several types of crayfish all dicking it out for the title of lord and master of the London canals. All of them invaders. My money's on this guy—the Signals. They are tough and cruel and vicious." She waved at the quiet water. "There's a gang war going on here more brutal than anything the city has ever seen."

"What do you mean 'invaders'?" I asked.

"Oh—you know. Species that shouldn't be here. That have come in from elsewhere. London's full them."

"It is?" I said in surprise.

"Fuck yeah. There's exotic spiders, parrots, turtles, snakes, scorpions—all sorts of things. All over the city. There's even a colony of fucking wallabies in Highgate Cemetery. And even stranger things as well."

"What things?"

She was silent. I was sure her eyes had found the rope that still hung over the side. The rope that still moved with a tautness that was nothing to do with the water. Then her face went dark.

"Nobody knows what's down here. Even those entitled clots who live right up there above us have no idea. Because they won't connect with their own fucking world." I looked up at the expensive and anonymous-looking flats. "They love to pretend this is some kind of nice sweet park just for them. I see them swanning down the towpaths, glowering at the cyclists and glowering at us for daring to run a working boat in their precious waterway—but they haven't a fucking clue what is down here. Human, animal, vegetable, mineral—they haven't a fucking clue. This might as well be another world as far as they are concerned."

"I think I prefer your world," I said. She gave me a sharp look, wondering whether I was serious or just patronising her.

"You—umm—really don't mind this kind of thing?" she asked with some caution, waving at the crayfish and various other tubs scattered around.

"Not at all," I said. And it was true. I knew better than to be squeamish about lifestyle choices, lifestyle necessities, eating crayfish or anything else. Even earthworms.

She was silent for a while, then shook her head with a small smile. "Come on," she said. "Let me see if I can scrape together anything at all from what's in my cupboards. I am sure I can manage something."

"Thanks," I said. She was already descending the steps though. I stared after her—and lingered. I was curious. This was a world that I had barely known existed—a lifestyle utterly alien. Crayfish? Earthworms? And what the heck was at the end of that rope? Out of pure curiosity, I reached out for it and pulled.

Whatever it was, it was reluctant to come, though I could feel it moving on the end of the line. I stared at the black water, my mind taking me closer to the Amazon River now than to Regent's

Canal—picturing giant catfish or murky toothy river monsters. Could it really be a pike? If so though, why on earth had she tied it up like this rather than just brought it on board?

Then, as though I had finally defeated its grip, the thing came up with a rush—so fast that it was almost in my hand before I even saw it. And I think I gave a yelp of shock.

Something big —black—long—thin—spiny—formless—that thrashed very unhappily and immediately tried to wrap itself round my arm.

It was... by no stretch was it a fish. I thought at first it was a snake—but no snake is covered in bristles. No snake has spines like that. Then I caught a hint of soft segmentation and it suddenly classified itself in my mind. Worm. Absurd and insane though it seemed, that's what it was. But this was a long, long way from the earthworms she had talked about. This was a grotesque king among worms. A massive predatory bristly monster. I would estimate about four feet long. It moved with a weird sentience, more like the sensitive questing perception of a leech than a fumbling earthworm. This creature, whatever it was, had a certain sophistication about it.

I want to be clear here. I have never had a problem with the small creatures that surround us. I was always fine picking up spiders—even the maybe-or-maybe-not poisonous False Widow spiders that seem to be swarming over London these days. You handle them right, they won't hurt you. I can cope with leeches and slugs and pretty much anything this country can throw at me. But this thing was utterly outside my experience, almost ridiculously so, and anything outside your experience is going to blindside you, at least at first. So no wonder I panicked a little. No wonder I gave a yelping shriek.

There was a clatter of feet on the steps and she stared out—and swore. I looked at her guiltily.

"Be careful," she yelled.

I didn't really need telling. I just let go of the cord, watching it drop into the black water again with a dull splash.

"What the heck is it?" I whispered. She didn't answer, just darted to the side and leaned over.

"Fuck's sake," she growled, "I didn't want you to see that."

"Why?"

"Because—" She hesitated. "Because—well to be honest I am not sure what it is. Not sure anyone knows about it. It's another of those—things that turn up in London. Like the crayfish. But this is my canal and I don't want complications from those fuckers up above."

She tugged on the rope tentatively.

"You going to tell anyone?" she asked with a wooden glance at me over her shoulder. "Any fucking point my asking you not to?"

"I'm not sure anyone would believe me," I said.

She gave a weary sigh and a massive shrug. "Well—now you've seen it, you want it for dinner? I suppose it would be a bit more substantial than anything I have in the fridge."

I blinked at her.

"With a touch of lemon and a bread crust. They make a great worm burger. Better than earthworms any day."

I still just stared.

"Yeah," she continued with a challenging grin. "You gut 'em, boil 'em, mince 'em up. No need to put them on a detox diet—they are so big you can get the gut right out. Then it's butter, lemon peel, salt and pepper. Then bread 'em and fry 'em. Very tasty—very sweet."

She yanked on the rope again and the creature resurfaced. She hauled it right up onto the deck this time and I hastily retreated to a safe distance. But she just grabbed it behind the spiny head, holding it and securing the squirming tail between her legs.

"No need to look like that," she said.

"I'm not looking like that," I said stupidly. "I mean –"

"Hey—you wouldn't care about fancy French escargot or prawns—so why the heck not? Don't give me that British squeamishness crap. You should see what they sell in Chinese markets."

I cautiously stepped forward again, feeling somewhat reassured now because she seemed to know what she was doing. A closer look revealed its structure, which was very complex. The bristles that covered it were arranged in two tufts on each of the segments, with those towards the head end also armed with the large backwards-pointing thorns. It was among these spines that the cord was tied—seemingly the only way to secure it. As far as I could see, its mouth was nothing more than a gummy fold of flesh, around which four feelers or tentacles flopped like flaccid strings.

And those spines looked familiar. Definitely not teeth or claws. Even less squid beaks. Presumably they were defensive—and very sharp.

"I've seen what they sell at the market in bloody Ridley Road," I said gruffly. "I'm not sure anything can surprise any-more." I shook my head. "Are you serious?"

"Of course I'm fucking serious."

"Okay then. I—I—I—I'll give it a go..." Feeling floaty and ethereal, I followed her—and it—down into the boat. Then I grinned. "When my mad girlfriend asks me what the heck I was doing all night, she'll never ever believe me."

It looked normal enough, but then, anything looks normal when it's made into a patty with a bread crust and cooked a pleasant golden brown.

"Want me to go first?" she asked with dry humour.

I picked one up. There was a challenge here and I didn't want to fail it—not some childish game of who went first but whether I could accept this world and respond to it properly. I was trying very hard not to be spooked by the knowledge of what it actually was and the memory of what it looked like—nor by the sight of her stretching the creature out on a chopping board and whacking the spiny head end off with one quick slice, before opening it up lengthways to remove its highly alien anatomy. She'd handled it with great proficiency and pragmatism, even though it had squirmed for a long time, even when she had finished prepping it. Even when it was little more than a strip of meat. I have a strong stomach and only so much patience with squeamishness, but I wouldn't have blamed anyone for freaking out at that bizarre spectacle.

But understand this: I wasn't forcing myself here. I wasn't trying to prove anything to myself or anyone else. I wanted to try this—it was that simple. Because—hey, it's interesting, right? There's a lot of experiences out there that you've never had, so why fight them when they turn up?

In the end we pretty much chomped on the things simultaneously. And inside the crust was a subtly flavoured filling that my taste buds couldn't quite place. Definitely something unfamiliar about it though. I can attempt to describe it—I can say it was mild and smooth with the faintest hint of scallop and a touch of pork fat, but it is so hard to describe flavours in any meaningful way. I guess you will just have to try it sometime.

"Do you like it?"

"It's... yeah, it's rather good actually." I tried hard to keep a note of surprise out of my voice but I probably failed.

I went for another mouthful. Tasty. And the patty had vanished.

She gave a smile—I think the first real broad comfortable

smile that I had seen from her. Picking up a second patty, I looked dreamily out of the window, maybe thinking some crap about how you never know where life is going to take you next. Or other barely acknowledged thoughts like *how long would it take to save up for a narrowboat?* Or maybe just registering the hint of dawn light that was beginning to flood the old canal.

On the towpath, the first commuter cyclist raced past with a brief rattle, eyes on nothing but the slabbed path and mind no doubt on anything but what might be residing in the dark water beside her.

Mariposas del Noche

Pauline E. Dungate

FROM THE MOMENT he arrived on the island, Toby was enchanted by the large, dark-winged witch moths. A pair fluttered into the wooden hut that served as the arrivals hall and spread their wings on the rafters. If he hadn't been queuing to pass the table that was the customs desk, he would have un-shipped his camera and started taking pictures.

"There will be plenty more of those," his companion said. "This is the time of year that they emerge. Now, if you would collect our suitcases while I complete the formalities, we can find our transport."

Dominic Carter was effectively, for this trip anyway, his boss. The seventy-year-old entomologist was here to record the six-legged inhabitants of the archipelago. He'd been coming annu-ally for more than forty years and only in the last five had he bothered with a photographer. Toby Lansdowne had been his choice. Up until then, Dominic had captured and drawn his specimens. Two things caused him to change his routine—the new conservation laws that discouraged collection and the ar-thritis that was beginning to prevent him grasping his paint-brushes firmly.

As the car travelled down the straight road that ran from end to end of the island, red-backed crabs scuttled out of the way and other black moths fluttered across their path, neither taking notice of the human travellers. Once they had arrived at the resort centre, the only decent place to stay, Dominic declared that he would rest until lunch when they would discuss the schedule for the next week. In the meantime, would Toby check that the hire car had arrived and was suitable. By that he meant that it had air conditioning, spare wheel and off-road option.

Toby had time when that was sorted to wander. He had been to the Caribbean before but was always looking for better pictures, better angles and the perfect specimen. The moths intrigued him. He didn't expect to see them out during daylight, at least not ones as conspicuous as these. They didn't settle where he could photograph them, though. They always landed out of sight, tucked behind vegetation or angled into a crevice.

They shared the open dining room with anoles, bananaquits and cats, the last being totally ignored by the former two. Dominic spread a map of the island out on the table.

"I want to explore all of it," he said, "but most of all, I want to get out to here." He stabbed the map with a swollen-jointed finger. It was a small island off the northern tip.

Toby squinted. "Isle de Mariposas," he read. "That's a bit of a weird name. It's neither French or Spanish. Or English."

"Don't forget that all three countries squabbled over the islands around here. The name is probably an historical relic."

"Isn't mariposa Spanish for butterfly?"

"Or moth. There may be nothing to see. It may have been named after a rock formation or the shape of a bay but it may have an isolated population of some kind of insect." The excitement in his voice was palpable. "There must be at least sub-species there."

"Wouldn't they be able to fly from the main island?" Toby asked.

"Prevailing winds. They would carry them out to sea. See the alignment of the islands. The wind cuts across them both."

"Don't some butterflies travel long distances?"

"It does happen but it's rare. How are you about camping?"

Toby shrugged. "Okay, I guess." Though he preferred a comfortable bed, he'd endured nights in the wild to get the required pictures. And if the old man was prepared to, it would seem mean to object.

"That's settled then. I'll organise a boat for later in the week."

Work started seriously in the afternoon with Toby driving to one of the quadrants Dominic had specified, then collecting, cataloguing and photographing anything with six legs. Both of them would spend the evening hours assessing the day's data.

Next morning, Toby had already breakfasted and was trying to get a flying shot of a troupial darting in and snatching sugar packets from the table, when Dominic arrived. He slumped in a chair looking despondent.

Toby waited for him to be served tea before asking, "Problem?"

"I'm having difficulty hiring a boat. No-one I've spoken to wants to take us out to Mariposas. I've been brushed off with a variety of excuses ranging from nowhere to land, the currents are too strong, to the place is cursed."

Toby laughed. "Really? They think it's cursed? That's nonsense. Did you try the dive centre?"

"I did ask if they could drop us off there on the way to a dive site and pick us up on the way back. They told me the boatmen won't go near it. It's haunted."

"There's only one solution. We hire a motorised canoe from one of the villages at the other end of the island. We don't have to say where we're going."

"And if they ask?"

"I bet there are some bays it's difficult to get to by road. We can go in by boat."

"Good idea. Can you sort that, in case they've had word of the crazy old Englishman who wants to go to the haunted island?"

"No problem."

The boat Toby finally managed to hire was a fibre-glass hull with an outboard motor attached. They pottered in a couple of bays so that he could get used to handling it. Dominic was happy catching a variety of flies that skimmed the water beneath mangrove roots. Toby couldn't get excited about the small black things that might or might not bite. It was disappointing that the dragonflies that feasted on them perched on twigs too high to focus on properly. The witch moths, though, flitted amongst the aerial roots, too elusive for Dominic to net.

As they made their way up the coast, Dominic said, "If we leave early tomorrow, we need only spend one night over there. Make sure we have plenty of fuel. We don't want to get stuck."

Toby nodded, deciding it was better not to say anything. He'd already purchased an extra can. He wondered whether Dominic just liked giving orders to reinforce his authority as the one paying for the expedition, or whether he genuinely considered Toby too inexperienced to think of these things for himself. The age gap was sufficient to make Toby the same age as Dominic's grandchildren.

There was an obvious current sweeping between the two islands but nothing the outboard motor couldn't handle. Toby was pleased that he hadn't had to try paddling across. The best beach was a spit of land covered with lumps of bleached coral rolled ashore by the waves. Toby had to wade knee-deep in order to haul the boat ashore against the tug of the water. He looped the mooring rope round the bole of a tree to drag the canoe up above the high water line, tying it firmly to prevent any chance of it stranding them.

Once they stood beyond the front line of trees, the sounds of wind and wave were cut dramatically.

"I don't hear any insects," Toby said.

"They will be here," Dominic told him. "The inter-island distance isn't that far. I noticed sea-grape flowering on the beach. Where that is, there will be insects."

"Can't hear any birds, either."

"All out fishing perhaps? An uninhabited island ought to be

a desirable nesting place."

"Maybe." Toby pushed his way into the shrubbery. The inevitable witch moths took flight. There were taller trees towards the centre of the atoll. He looked up. In the sea he had been concentrating on finding a suitable landing spot and hadn't really been looking at the vegetation. Now he noticed clumps of webs shrouding the branches.

"What are those?" he asked. "Surely there aren't that many spiders around here."

Dominic crossed to where there was a web on a lower branch. He pulled his magnifier from his pocket and peered through it. "Not spiders," he said. "Lepidoptera."

"You mean caterpillars made them?"

"Almost certainly. Don't touch them. The species that show this kind of behaviour weave hairs into the web. They are frequently irritating."

"You mean they'll make me itch?"

"Or worse. Breathe them in and your symptoms will be similar to asthma."

"I don't think I'll be sniffing them, thanks. Should the tents go in the centre of the island or nearer the shore?"

"Centre is safer in case of high wind. A storm can lash the waves right into the trees."

"Right." Toby was anxious to get the camp pitched so he could hunt for good pictures. Islands like these often had a plethora of hermit crabs and some of their shells were spectacular. Around resorts locals swept them into the sea to prevent visitors' toes being nipped. A waste of time, Toby reckoned, as they were always back the next day. He did a tour of the atoll and came back, puzzled.

"Dominic, why would a place like this have a complete absence of hermit crabs? I didn't spot any ghost crabs either."

Dominic frowned. "Are you sure?"

"I circled the place twice. There are shells—mostly damaged—but no crabs. No sign of birds either. I'd expect to startle at least one heron."

"Hmm. We can dig a pit-trap on the edge of the tide-line and see what we can catch overnight. I also want to set moth sheets between the trees."

"Have you found any wildlife of significance?"

"I've been concentrating on the webs. They seem to be of all stages, which is unusual. Mostly life cycles are synchronous. It allows for plant regrowth."

Toby brightened. "I should be able to photograph an instar progression. There are so many webs, breaking a few won't matter."

"They will repair them. We will need to handle them with gloves and I would prefer you to wear a mask."

"Yeah, okay." It was irritating but if what Dominic had said was true, Tony didn't want to be breathing in itchy hairs.

They spent the afternoon dissecting webs. Dominic was right in that the caterpillars were at different stages. Some he preserved for detailed lab examination when they got back home, a handful he put in a collecting box intending to rear them and see how fast they went through the cycle. What surprised Dominic was the type of debris found in old abandoned web masses. It wasn't just the fragments of insect carapaces but the number of small bones as if small birds or lizards had become trapped and decayed where they died. He packed away an empty web with its grizzly contents for analysis later. Toby was delighted with the colours. They changed as the caterpillars did, from tufts of turquoise on the smallest to iridescent purples and blues in older ones. The biggest they found were scarlet.

As the light faded, they ate and waited to see what, if anything, would be attracted to the illuminated sheet hung between the trees. They got witch moths. Photographed with flash they showed patterns and colours not visible in daylight.

Toby woke in the middle of the night. He lay still, listening. Through the canvas, he thought he could make out the sound of waves but not wind in the trees. Most tropical islands had insects calling throughout the night. Not here. And they hadn't seen any except the moths. There was something beneath the range of his hearing that made his skin itch. Toby reached for his torch before unzipping the tent and stepping outside. The camp site was limned with shadows cast by the near-full moon. He caught a movement in his peripheral vision and cast the light around.

The beam illuminated the trunk of a tree. Moving down it was an undulating procession of caterpillars, four abreast. He followed them down with the torch. They moved purposefully onto the ground and across the sand. Toby dived into his tent groping for his camera. This was too good to miss.

As he took the first shots he banged on the roof of Dominic's tent. "Wake up. You'll want to see this."

He heard movement from inside the tent and a muttering. Then Dominic stuck his head through the entrance flap. "What the hell's going on?"

"Look!" The flash showed up the rippling lines of caterpillars as they trekked across the sand.

"It's a processionary," Dominic declared. "Get movie footage."

"I don't care what it's called," Toby said. "I've never seen anything like it."

"Some moths do it. Follow them. See where they're going." He ducked back into the tent, re-emerging with his sandals, collecting box and a torch.

The larvae headed in a straight line for the beach. The stream diverged, splitting into two trails that followed the edge of the water. Occasionally, a larger wave would sweep some away, the bodies being pushed up onto the sand with the next wave. The gap in the line immediately closed. The tide was on the turn and as pools appeared at the edge of the sea, the corpses sank to the bottom. In the torch light, Toby saw tiny crabs and fish dart out of the crevices to nip at the meal that had unexpectedly fallen their way.

"Are they going anywhere in particular?" Toby asked.

"They often do this when they are looking for somewhere to

pupate," Dominic said. "Or looking for a fresh food plant."

"They seem to be all sizes."

"Food, then."

They walked beside the line, careful not to step on any, expecting to find the head of the line, to see it turn landward again. Instead, they found other runs of caterpillars heading seaward and circling the island.

As the tide receded, the pools drained. They left behind the corpses not just of the drowned caterpillars but shrimps, small fish and crabs. As the water went, the living larvae ventured onto the wet sand.

"Dominic," Toby said, "the caterpillars. They're eating the dead fish."

Dominic crouched down to examine them more closely. "I do believe you are right." Excitement coloured his voice. "This is just what I was hoping for."

"But caterpillars are vegetarian."

"The word is herbivorous. But you are right. Most of them are. The caterpillars of the African Apefly do supplement their diet with insects when food is scarce. This is marvellous. I hope you are getting lots of video footage."

"Why is this so special?"

"Don't you see? There isn't enough vegetation here to support the population. The hairs are irritant because they are toxic. The ones that drown are poisonous. They kill the creatures that think they have a free meal, then get eaten in turn. It's an evolved behaviour. And we are the first to see it."

"Would they eat us?" Toby felt slightly nauseous at the prospect of being gnawed while he slept.

"Oh, I doubt it. There's not enough poison to kill us and we
would feel them before they got more than a mouthful."

"That, Dominic, is very comforting," Toby said sarcastically.
"I intend to thoroughly search my tent before I go back to
sleep."

Toby had decided that he had enough images and retired to
his tent, leaving Dominic pottering around outside, excited by
the phenomenon. He didn't know what time he finally retired.
When Toby awoke in the morning, he realised there was a
problem. The zip on his tent flap was difficult to undo, the result, he discovered, of the tent being covered by a layer of web.
His hands instantly began to itch. Whether that was because he
had brushed them against hairs caught in the web or because
he expected it didn't matter. He headed for the beach, checking
that the boat was still secure before stripping off and immers-
ing himself in the sea. The brine took away the itching though
he noticed red weals in the backs of his hands.

There was no sign of the caterpillars. Toby presumed that
they had retreated to the vegetation. Even the corpses had disappeared, washed out by the retreating tide. He did a circuit of
the island, peering into the rock pools.

He dressed and made his way back to the camp site. Anything they had left outside was now covered with web. He broke
a web-free branch from one of the shrubs and washed it thor-

oughly before using it to poke the webs. Nothing appeared to be alive in them. Then he set about clearing the front of Dominic's tent.

"What the hell are you doing?" came the older man's grumbling voice from inside.

"Don't come out yet," Toby told him.

"Why the hell not? You're not shy, are you?"

"No, the tent is covered..." Before Toby could finish his sentence, Dominic unzipped and stuck his head through the flap.

"Oh shit," Dominic said as strands of sticky silk clung to his head and face.

"Wash it off in the sea," Toby told him.

Dominic wriggled out of the tent and disappeared rapidly towards the water. When he came back, he surveyed the camp site. "I presume you have pictures?"

"Not yet, my camera's inside."

"Pictures are a priority, Toby. We have to record this phenomenon. We have investigations to carry out. Do you realise how important this is to science?"

Toby gave an exaggerated sigh. "Dominic. We can't stay here."

"Why not? We brought plenty of supplies."

"Which are now thoroughly webbed. Even if we cleaned it all off, there's no guarantee it'd be safe."

Dominic stared around as if taking in the state of the camp properly for the first time. His shoulders sagged. "I suppose you are right." He brightened. "We'll leave as late as possible. A little hunger won't hurt us and we owe it to science to find out as much as possible."

Toby really would have preferred to leave as soon as possible, but supposed this was the best compromise. "What do you want me to do?"

In the end, they salvaged as much as they could, carefully wrapping the tents inside out, after dunking the canvas in the sea. They abandoned most of the items they'd originally left outside the tents during the night. Dusk was beginning to gather as they headed back to the main island. At intervals, Toby noticed flares of light as if fires were being momentarily lit in the bushes and extinguished moments later. He wondered if it was one of these traditions that they would probably never know the reason for.

Back at the resort Toby carried his gear to his room, dumping it on the floor. He wanted a proper shower and clean clothes before he even thought about dealing with the tent. He shooed out a dozen witch moths that fluttered in when he opened the door. At least Dominic had been right about him seeing a lot more of them before the trip was out.

Next morning they drove to the top of the island opposite Isle de Mariposas to quarter the section Dominic had designated their next area of investigation. The most noticeable thing was the black patches in the trees and bushes. They pulled off the road to examine them. Black ash crumbled at Toby's touch.

"That's what those lights were last night," he said. "They were burning something."

"The webs," Dominic said. "Look, you can see the charred corpses of the caterpillars on this one. Why would they do that?"

"Perhaps they only meant to get the empty ones. They do look unsightly decorating the trees."

"No excuse. It's desecration."

"Perhaps they don't want the caterpillars near their crops."

"What crops?"

Toby gestured at the landscape. "Bananas, coconuts, mangoes."

"There's enough for everyone, including the wildlife."

Toby kept quiet. He wondered what would happen if a plague of meat-eating caterpillars started marching into the villages.

All the way back to England, on the long flight across the Atlantic, Toby had to listen to Dominic's mutterings about the destruction of habitats and the missed chances to observe evolution. Toby refused to get drawn into the argument, wondering why the locals hadn't taken torches to the Isle de Mariposas long ago.

He was relieved to be able to escape Dominic's company once he had seen him safely into a cab at Heathrow.

"You will let me have copies of all your pictures?" Dominic said as the door closed.

"As soon as I've processed them. I'll drop a disc with them on round to you." After all, that is what Dominic was paying him for. Not that he'd get everything. There was no point passing on out of focus images. He got jobs like this by word of mouth and didn't want any poor examples of his work on the loose to be ridiculed.

"How long?"

"I might be able to get it done in a week." He'd have to work long hours but he'd prefer to get it done before relaxing.

"Good. Call me first."

"I will."

It took Toby a longer than he anticipated to go through all his images and weed out the worst and with the other commissions that had piled up while he had been away, it was nearer three weeks before he was able to call on Dominic. With some clients, emailing the images would have been sufficient but Dominic wanted them delivered personally. When he arrived, the old man was almost bouncing in his enthusiasm.

"Come in, come in. You must come and see this." He led the way through the house to a bright, sunny conservatory on the back of the building. A large part of it was filled with a framework covered in fine mesh. Plants grew within it.

"Look, look!" Dominic drew him over to the structure. Some of the plants, Toby noticed, were covered in webs. A sudden sense of dread poked at his memory.

"Please don't tell me you brought some caterpillars back," he said.

"No, no. Just some eggs. And they hatched. They've developed very fast. In three weeks, they've almost reached their final instar. They'll pupate soon."

Toby looked more closely at the webs. They were small compared with those that had infested the trees on Isle de Mariposas. He imagined he could see some movement within the nearest. He almost didn't want to ask the next question. "Are they carnivores as well?

Dominic shook his head. "Not so far. Though I have offered them meat."

"Perhaps you need the pressure of numbers."

"I have considered that. So I've reduced the food supply."

"Would it be true evolution if they only eat meat out of necessity?" Toby asked. Another thought occurred to him. "If they are carnivorous, what would happen if they escaped?"

"Don't let that worry you," Dominic said. "These are tropical insects. Our winters would kill any that escaped. Not that they could. This cage is very secure."

Toby hoped that he was right.

That had been a year ago. He hadn't seen Dominic since; though the older man had sent him copies of the magazines with the pictures he had taken of the processionary caterpillars on the way to the beach. He had done a little research himself— moth larvae building webs wasn't new. There were several species in Europe that did it. They weren't that rare but it was only occasionally that numbers were so great that they were noticed.

Then the broadsheets announced plagues.

When the webs started appearing on the plane trees in London, Toby decided to investigate. A set of pictures as contrast to the witch moths would be fascinating. He walked along the avenue of affected trees, his mind sizing up angles and alignments, seeking the best images. Bunches of leaves were cocooned in swathes of sticky silk. In some places the trunks of the trees were coated in it as well.

Ahead of him, two men in white hazard suits had set a ladder against the bole of one tree. One of them, tank on his back, hose in one hand, had climbed up to spray insecticide over one of the webs. Toby took a few shots of him silhouetted against the sky, then the skyline.

"It won't do any good," he said as the man descended. Both took off their head-pieces.

"Why not?" one asked.

"The webs are waterproof. They have to be or the masses would be washed away in the rain. Your spray will just run off." Toby knew he was going to lecturing mode. It was a bad habit when he came across ignorance.

"We're only doing as we're told. Council thinks tourists will get worried if they think spiders will drop on their heads."

"It's not spiders. There are caterpillars in there munching away at the leaves. If there wasn't any traffic, you'd be able to hear them."

The man shrugged. "Makes no difference. Spray 'em, we're told, spray 'em we do."

"Burning would be more effective."

The man snorted. "Bad enough using insecticide. Imagine the complaints if bits of flaming webs started drifting over the road."

"Can I go up the ladder for a closer look?"

"Shouldn't let you. Safety, you know. Just don't blame us if you fall off."

"I won't." Toby changed the lens on his camera and set it up for a macro shot before climbing up. He was very careful not to touch any of the webs.

That evening, Toby settled down to sort through his new images. As usual he had the BBC rolling news on in the background. The phrase 'legions of caterpillars' caught his ear. He turned up the volume. A pretty, female reporter was standing at the entrance to a small park talking earnestly into the camera. Then she turned to a witness.

"Tell me what you saw," she said.

The interviewee was the kind of average Joe they always seemed to find for this sort of thing, an attempt to engage the masses, Toby thought.

The man said, "They was squirming everywhere. Come down from the trees they did. Like a river. There was this dog, see. Went to sniff them. Like dogs do."

"What happened then?" the reporter said.

"Well, this dog, see, it howled. Like it were stung."

"And then?"

"Don't rightly know. It rolled over, squashing them buggers.

The owner picked it up and went away with it."

The reporter turned to the camera again. "A spokesman from Butterfly Conservation says that this phenomenon is called a processionary. The hairs on the creatures are irritants and apparently a few people are highly allergic to them so the advice is, if you encounter any marching caterpillars, don't touch them."

By this time, Toby was only half listening. He shrugged into his jacket and grabbed his camera, equipment bag and tripod. This was the opportunity he wanted. He had seen the name of the park on a plate behind the reporter and recognised it as being the one near Dominic's house. It wouldn't surprise him to see the old man out there, sketching the larvae.

It took him almost an hour to get there and find somewhere to park. By that time, the park gates had been closed and most spectators had vanished. Maybe the caterpillars had gone, too. Toby looked for a likely place to climb over the fence. He had a torch in his pocket but he didn't need it. A combination of street lights and the full moon gave him enough visibility. He looked first for the webs in the trees. The silk tying together the branches gave them a distinct knobbly pattern against the orange tinted sky. The procession was easy to find. The caterpillars flooded across the path, undulating nose to tail. Careful so as not to crush any, Toby knelt beside the line and took a couple of shots before checking the images. He was struck by the colours. In the flash, they scintillated with turquoise, purple and scarlet—like those on the Isle de Mariposas.

An ice crystal formed in the depths of his abdomen and spread upwards as he scrolled back through the memory card to find those earlier pictures. His fingers felt numb as he compared the images. Then, mouth dry, he ran.

He didn't remember scrambling back over the fence before pounding up the street to Dominic's house. He wanted to be wrong. He needed to be wrong. He leapt the three steps to the front door and jammed his finger on the bell. He didn't care if he woke the old man up. He just wanted to be wrong. With his other fist he pounded on the wood. He could hear the echo of bell and thump from inside, but no movement.

Toby stepped back to stare up at the windows, looking for a curtain twitch. It wasn't always wise to open a door past midnight. Nothing. He stooped down to peer through the letterbox, hoping to see something in the hallway. It was covered. He could see nothing.

Toby knew he was working himself into a panic. The sensible thing was to go away and come back in the morning. To apologise to Dominic for making a nuisance of himself in the night. He deliberately took a deep breath and pulled out his phone. He should have thought of it earlier. Selecting Dominic's number he called, pressing it to his ear to be sure it was ringing. It was ringing inside, too. He could hear it. No-one was answering.

He had to know. He had to be sure one way or the other. Toby took a step back, then gripped his tripod firmly by the legs and swung it at the window of the downstairs room. The sturdy metal platform at the top bounced off the glass. The second swing produced cracks and the third shattered the pane. He glanced around. For once he would have liked to have seen a policeman running to apprehend him. He took off his jacket and wrapped it around his arm before pushing out the shards of broken window before hauling himself over the sill.

His feet crunched on the glass. Toby retrieved his torch from his pocket and shone it around. The room was innocent. Largely as he had seen it last; the only difference a newspaper lying on the arm of a chair and an empty tumbler on the floor beside it. He crossed to the door to the hall and opened it. He was about to blunder through when he saw the silk threads glistening in the torchlight. A glance up and down the passage showed him more.

He had noticed a poker by the Victorian style fire-place. Fetching it, Toby used it to break his way through the webs that clustered more thickly towards the back of the house and the conservatory where Dominic had set up his insectarium. The space was lined by the webs but Toby could see no sign of movement. They looked recently vacated. He wondered where the spinners had gone walkabout. Carefully he backed out, making sure he didn't brush against them.

Toby stopped at the bottom of the stairs and called out. He was an intruder here, an invader into Dominic's privacy. He'd never been invited to the upper floors. Getting no response, he began to climb. The webs festooned the banisters but the treads were largely clear. In the upper passage, Toby became aware of small sounds. It was like the rustling of leaves, and something else. At first he couldn't identify it. It was like a scratching, a rasping.

The door to one room stood open. As he shone the torch inside, he noticed the absence of webs. The beam passed over a shape in the floor. He made to take a step towards it, then stopped. It moved. It wasn't the movement of life, it was a rippling underneath the pyjamas Dominic was wearing. As he touched him with the end of the poker, the cloth disintegrated. His skin was writhing with larvae in the same way as a rabbit's corpse squirmed with blowfly maggots. Toby felt sick. He turned and fled down the stairs and into the untouched sitting room.

He stood in the centre of the room, swallowing convulsively, feeling his pulse race and sweat cooling on his skin. The sensible part of his mind urged him to run, to get away as fast and as far as possible. The rational part said, deal with it.

Toby scooped up the newspaper and started twisting the pages into wands. He needed matches, a lighter, anything to make fire. That was the problem with modern living—few smoked, candles were only for decoration, central heating needed no lighting. The kitchen! It didn't matter if Dominic cooked with gas or electricity, there would be heat enough to ignite the paper.

The door was one less enshrouded by webs. Toby used the poker to clear it enough to open it, winding the silk around the metal the way he had seen gardeners removing strings of blanket weed from ponds. The gas hob sparked to flame instantly. Toby hesitated briefly, knowing he could be putting others in danger. But the caterpillars had to be destroyed. He thrust the taper into the flame. Carrying it swiftly up the stairs he threw it onto Dominic's corpse. It flared immediately along with the stench of burning hair. He lit another twist of paper, dropping it in the passageway as he retreated downstairs. The remaining ones he threw into the conservatory. Smoke was already curling down the stairs as retreated to the sitting room.

Toby stood across the road from the burning building, watching the fire-engines soaking the place, steam mingling with black smoke. He hoped the fire had done enough and contained the contamination.

A shadow passed in front of the street light. The large moth circled it before fluttering down. Something made Toby hold out his hand.

The witch moth perched on his finger, its proboscis gently probing at the minerals coating his skin. The dark wings opened and closed, trembling with pleasure. It was absorbed in its task, unaware of its surroundings. All it took, Toby thought, was one of these delightful creatures to spread the plague. To-morrow, he would begin his crusade—to burn all the webs he could find.

Slowly, cautiously, he raised his other hand to cup the creature from above. Then with one swift movement, he crushed it between his fingers.

Wet Season

Dennis Etchison

MADDEN WATCHED THE black crowd on the other side of the moving gelatin wall, as rainwater poured down in translucent sheets over the windshield. He did not listen to the patternless tattoo. Instead he followed with his eyes the group of black shadows floating past the car.

"I... I shouldn't have made you come, Lorie," he said at last to the black figure next to him.

She turned from the window, her lidded eyes not disapproving. "That's enough, Jim. I wouldn't have felt right, otherwise."

Madden pressed his chin to his chest, squeezing his eyelids shut. He cleared his throat and rubbed his eyes, and his fingers came away moist.

Again his wife spoke, very quietly. "You... were very close to her, I suppose. James, I only wish there were something... Forgive me if I'm crude. But I only wish I could have gotten to know her better. That she might have become, in time, my little girl as well."

He pressed her cool hand.

"It was—just—all the mud around her—" He bit his lips and started the engine and roared up the cemetery road, spinning out and spattering mud as he went.

The Ford geared to a slippery halt under the wet sycamores.

Bart stood at the end of the cracked driveway, behind the main house, propping open the sagging screen door to his apartment.

Through mist Madden saw the controlled, mildly pleas-ant line shaping his mouth, leaving the face somber in a new and ill -fitting mask.

"Forget about the rug," said Bart. "It's filthy anyway."

"We're so sorry to do this to you, Bart." Madden's wife brushed water from her clothing. "But we thought the twins were really too young to, well, exactly have their faces rubbed in it."

Bart smoothed a hand over his protruding, black-T--shirted belly. "The kids are in the bedroom. Rain must have got 'em drowsy. Left them staring out the window, counting drops or something," he added gently to Mad-den, testing a smile.

"Let me see to them." Madden's wife started across the room.

The men waited until she was gone.

Bart faced him. "Come over here and have a drink."

"No.

"Really, boy, really now. You know how I mean it. Come on."

At once Madden felt his joints chilled and tired. "No, Bart. I... I don't need it." He lowered himself to the sofa that was bulging and splitting like a fat man's incisions.

Bart watched the misty screen door and compared it to the pale Scotch and water in his hand. Twice he shaped his lips to stillborn beginnings. He shook his head and said nothing.

"You look at the hole, and the mud," Madden began finally in a low voice, "and you think of... that human being there in a box, being lowered into the ground, and you wonder how it can be that—that a part of your body, a piece that has come from you like an arm or leg, can be cut off, killed and buried away, and you never being able to feel with it again.

"But you know, I worked with a man once who had lost an arm in the war; and he said he could close his eyes anytime and suddenly it was there again, the nerves were restored and he could feel down into his fingertips. But when he opened his eyes to see why he hadn't touched what he was reaching for, his eyes told him there was nothing there anymore."

Rain began to tap erratically on a metal vent somewhere in the roof.

"And you know, I can still see the world through my little girl's eyes, feel it as she felt it, even... even though she's been cut off me, like one of my sense organs. I still *feel* her, feel *through* her, and my nerves, my ganglia just won't listen to the goddam facts."

Outside, water continued to fall and fall illogically, relentlessly, in what seemed to be the result of a vast macrocosmic defrosting.

Giggling, the twins came out of the bedroom.

Madden saw them and smiled wanly from the sofa. The two little boys acknowledged him peripherally and grinned, grasping their mother's hands more securely.

"How did it go, boys?" inquired Madden, generating concern, and immediately hated his own detachment. *You are my sons, now*, he thought, *my only sons, and I should hold you tight against me—*

"We had fun, Da-da. We had samiches."

"An' we tooka nap an' went out an' played an'—"

Why, noted Madden wearily, *they're actually speaking directly to me... She almost never lets them do that. What is this, some kind of show for Bart?*

"Out? But it didn't let up today, did it, Bart?" he said.

"Well, uh," the dark man gestured firmly to Madden, "they—" and he dropped his voice, ready to spell out words before the children, "they begged to go out. You brought them in their raincoats and, you know, it was one of those things. For a few minutes is all. Made 'em real happy. God knows I have no practice in child-rearing. Jesus, Jim, I hope they didn't catch anything."

"Tad and Ray never catch colds," stated Madden's wife, smiling her wide, smooth, peculiar kind of smile. "You did fine, Bart."

Madden watched his wife. Svelte in the grey light, she snaked an arm around each of her children's shoulders.

"We'd better go," she said. "It's Sunday and I have Women's Guild meeting tonight."

"Thanks, Bart. I mean it more than I can say."

They walked together, heads down, to the door. Sunday comics section for her hair and Lorelei and the giggly children clamored down the shiny, fragmented driveway.

Bart gripped his arm, looking deep into his eyes and nodding.

"You know I know. I can't say it. But I remember the Sunday we buried Mama." Hearing it said now, Madden felt no longer a memory of pain but a bond with manhood. "Just so's you know I know." And a slap caught Madden between the shoulder blades and sent him into the rain.

To a car where a somehow strange woman and children waited.

He switched off the ignition and sat very still, staring into the liquid pattern on the windshield.

"Ready, children?" asked Mrs. Madden, not looking to the back seat, taking her purse into her lap.

From the back seat came giggling.

Madden lay his head back to let his eyes trace the headliner of the car. Half a minute earlier, shutting off the wipers, he had caught himself hypnotized as the twin arcs of the wiper blades melted away. Now, the motor silenced, he listened to the sound of endless beads beating their pattern into the top of the automobile.

In the back seat, there was whispering like the swishing of cars down an empty street.

"Let's go, children," prompted their mother. "There'll be plenty of time for secrets when we get in the house."

Abruptly Madden snapped to. He focused his eyes from the windshield to the woman next to him, attuned his ears from the drumming overhead to the whisper of cloth on plastic as the children slid across the back seat. He touched the handle of his wife's door; it was cold. Almost as cold as his hand.

Behind him, someone giggled.

Outside the picture window, premature dusk settled along the block like silent black wings.

"Won't... won't you eat something?" asked Mrs. Madden tenuously. She leaned into the living room, spoon in hand and spoke in silhouette from the yellow kitchen doorway.

He cleared his throat. "What?" Madden's five finger-tips moved involuntarily to the pane. The glass was cold.

"Well," she intoned maternally, "you should have something. It's almost dark. Let me turn on the—"

"It's all right, Lorelei." *For God's sake,* he thought, *don't patronize me. Not now.*

Chilled and fatigued to the marrow, he sat in the newly rearranged and alien living room and tried to release his senses from the pain of here-and-now. He shut his eyes and tried to let his thoughts blow with the storm on down the blurred panorama of empty street.

She puttered for a time in the kitchen and Madden, curiously detached in the dark and the overstuffed chair, noticed again her effortless, liquid movements. The way she had of gliding over a floor as though it were polished glass, her legs flowing out and back with each step in a charming suggestion of no gristle or bone. No deliberate, angular bend to Lorie's arm, no; in her, stirring and pour-ing out and rinsing away became a Siamese rubber-arm ballet.

"Your soup is in the oven, keeping warm. And the twins are tucked in, so don't—I mean, they shouldn't give you any trouble."

Mrs. Madden paused in silhouette, then glided behind the enormous sagging hand that enclosed her husband.

"Lorie," he swallowed. Away in the bright kitchen, an electric clock hummed.

She sat on the armrest.

"Lorelei, do you ever... think about the decision you made ten months ago?" He tried to stop his teeth from chattering. "I mean—"

Her arms reached a pale circle around his shoulders. "You are the finest father my boys could possibly have. And I..." And she smoothed his hair with her oddly flat hands and did not finish. "Do you need to talk, Jim? The Guild meeting—"

Yes, he thought, pressing his eyes tightly shut until shards of grey light fired inside his eyelids, *yes, I need something. I hear your words but they're only words, I need more than talk, 1 need you warm against me, I need to live—*

He drew her into his lap. And at once it struck him.

She was *not* warm. Her skin was cold, cold almost as—

He pushed her away.

"Jim, I'm sorry. Is there something I can do for you?"

"No." He stared ahead into the night-filled room. "They're waiting for you already. There isn't anything you can do for me."

Picking up coat, purse and overshoes, Mrs. Madden pulled back the front door to a sheet of rain. A reminder about the soup, and she entered the falling sea.

The telephone refused to warm in his hands.

A sputter and crackle of rain and whispers on the wires between and across town, a mile away, a phone purred to life.

And purred. And purred.

"Yeah?"

"Hello, Bart. What am I interrupting?"

"Jimmy? That you, boy?"

"I hope I'm not interrupting anything."

"No, no. Listen. Lorie gone to her meeting?"

"That's right."

"Then you're alone." Pause. "Everything all right over there?"

"Yes. Aw, look, I shouldn't have called."

"You wanna talk, Jim?"

"I guess. No... Bart, is someone coming over to-night? You going out?"

"In this weather? Look, is everything all right?"

Pause. "Uh, Bart, I wonder... I just wondered if... aw, never mind, I shouldn't have bothered you."

"Look. You wanna come over here? We could talk, if you want."

"Can't leave the kids."

"They're asleep, then, and you're alone over there. You want me to come over? Talk or something until Lorie gets back?"

Pause. "I have no business bothering you."

"Crap. Look, I'll come over, okay? We can talk, you know, like we used to."

"I'm pretty bad company tonight, I'm afraid. And the weather. Sure you want to?"

"My idea, isn't it? And look, how can you turn down a lonely ol' bachelor like me? See you in ten minutes."

"Thanks very much, Bart," but he had hung up.

Madden waited on the back porch, listening.

Far down in the darkness, the throaty thrumming of the frogs met with the rushing of running water.

All about his thin figure, dirty streams dripped from the roof to mingle with puddles at his cold feet, to slip on down over the slanting yard, to join larger tributaries that splashed their way through the thorny shrubbery of the ravine to feed at last with violent churning into the shrouded riverbed far below.

From in front, Madden heard wet brakes grip to a splashing stop. Shivering, he turned inside.

The two men sat across from one another in the living room, two men who knew each other best of all in the world. There was only a pale-moth glow from the kitchen. They spoke, and they did not speak, and from time to time Bart laughed and sipped from the brandy snifter in his lap.

"... But then they threw the next game to the motherin' Angels," Bart was saying.

"Yes," said Madden.

Bart rose and ambled to the black picture window.

Abruptly Madden was aware that his brother had stopped talking.

Madden stared with him. He saw his brother frown. *Do you feel it too?* he thought. Vaguely illumined beneath the street lamp was Bart's car, leaning against the curb, weath-ering the storm. Idly, Madden had a vision of the rain pouring off the metal top, streaming over the rolled-up windows and down into the innards of the door, where the handle and lock mechanism were.

"Jimbo. God damn it."

Madden watched him. "What's wrong?"

Bart drained his glass. "I don't wanna say it. I don't even know I'm right. Or if I oughta say it."

"It's all right—I can talk about Darla. Probably it would do me good." He massaged his face, trying to relax. "I know I have to face—"

"No. That's not what I'm talking about." Bart pivoted from the window and the rain. "Listen to me, kid. *Do you feel it?*"

"Feel what?"

"Something, about this house, this town. I don't know how to say it. But can't you feel it?" Bart glared into the empty brandy glass.

"Something like what?" Madden lounged back into the cushion, ready to listen. *Now,* thought Madden, *this is the way. It won't prove a thing unless he says it first.*

"Damn," breathed Bart. He turned back to the night and lit a cigarette. "Maybe I'm going off the deep end. Look. Can I ask you a question?"

"Shoot."

"Something about this house. I don't know. The way it smells now, the way the chairs creak when I sit down, the color of the *light,* for God's sake, like the room is under-water or something. And all since she moved in." The cigarette reflection burned in the window. "Naw. Man, you're the one needs to talk at a time like this. I'm supposed to cheer *you.*"

"So you're cheerin'. Shoot."

"Look, it's just that—haven't you noticed anything, well, different about the place since Lorie and her kids moved in? That it isn't really yours anymore? I mean, it's like every person has a rhythm, a pattern to his everyday life. You go into a man's bedroom, it *smells* like him, the bed bends a certain way when you sit on it, because it's been shaped to fit every angle and bulge just right over the years. And you go into the kitchen, the way the dishes are piled up in the sink tells you more about the guy than a look at his diary, if you know what I mean. It's like the house soaks up what you are, the way you feel about life, and everything in the house gets to feeling the same way, too. And not only the place, but the woman he marries: she seems to fit right in, fit him, and the house... and that's part of it, too, Jimbo. She's—and I know I'm steppin' way over the bounds on this, but dammit, man, she's *not you*, you know? Let me ask: don't you notice anything unusual about Lorie?"

Madden shut his eyes impatiently. "She's an unusually attractive woman, if that's what you mean."

"No. But then I promised myself not to bring up any of this with you, at least not for a long time...

"But it isn't just this house. Hell, we both grew up in Greenworth, I knew every turn in the river like the lines on my hand years before the government moved in. And it's changed now, somehow. First, it was just the way the trees started growing crooked along the banks, but lately the whole town seems, I don't know, *funny*. The way the air smells, the paint on the houses... I don't know. I just don't know. But I'll tell you this: if I were blindfolded and left here, I'd never in a year guess this was the same town we grew up in."

Outside, the moon slipped for a moment through a pocket of clouds, washing Bart's face fishlike-pale by the window.

"Bart. What is it?"

"I wish I could be sure, kid. Maybe you should forget it. I pray to God I could. Jim, do you know how many storms like this we've had in Greenworth in the last twenty-five years?"

Madden stirred.

"I'll tell you: three, before two years ago. And not one raised the river more than a few inches. But in two years, five big ones. Here." Bart spilled his coat pocket onto the coffee table. "What the hell—I spent yesterday in the library looking things up, I don't know what for. Some-thing made me do it. But God, I've gotta show you."

Madden reached to the lamp.

Little white slips of paper fluttered in Bart's hands. For the first time in his life Madden saw his brother trembling.

"God!" he laughed nervously. "Help me, will you, Jim? Here are the pieces to a crazy jigsaw, it doesn't make any sense, but something in the back of my head keeps me from getting any sleep lately. Here, look, read it all and then tell me I'm nuts and send me home, but *do something!*"

"'Deaths by drowning, County Beach: this year and last, total 31. Previous two years' total, 9.' What's this for?"

"Don't stop now." Bart fumbled at the liquor cabinet.

"'Total rainfall in inches, adjacent counties last year, up 300%.'"

"See! It's spreading."

Another slip of paper. "'New residents in Greenworth, past 24 months: Broadbent, Mr. and Mrs. C. L.; Marber, G.; Nottingham, Mr. and Mrs. Frank R...'" Madden leaned forward intently.

"There's two dozen more."

He scrutinized his brother's now twisted face. "So?"

"So? So you're right, they're nothing separately, but put them all together—Let me ask you: Lorie never told you where she moved from when she came here, did she?"

"Now that you bring it up, no. But what—?'

"Listen to this. Last night I got out the phone book and dialed these new listings. Twenty-one are married couples. And every woman—" Bart emptied his glass. "Every woman is in the Women's Guild."

Ice water poured into Madden's stomach. "So?"

Bart jerked forth a folded clipping. "This was in the Gazette when one finally moved in twenty months ago."

Madden fingered the newspaper photo of 'Mr. and Mrs. Peter Hallendorf, newly-established real estate broker and his lovely bride.'

"Use this." A pocket magnifier hit the coffee table.

She *was* lovely. There in the enlarged dots was a face that was— "I don't see—"

Bart's shaking finger jabbed at the indistinct eyes, the mouth.

At first he didn't see it. Just that her eyes were softly, lethargically lidded.

Bart snatched a framed photograph from the bookcase and tossed it to his lap.

And there.

There were two sets of lidded eyes, two wide, smooth, peculiar smiles, side by side. They might have been sisters.

Madden groped. At the bottom of his consciousness, the pressure was rising now and he felt his finger giving way in the dike.

"Jim," grunted Bart. "I called the Community Center this evening. They never heard of it. *There is no Women's Guild!*

"And now. Just one more question. I hate to remind you, boy, but you've got to have all the pieces in front of you." Bart leaned over him, breath coming fast and pun-gent. "Tell me again how it was your little girl died."

Madden bit his knuckle. "Man, I don't know what you're driving at. Please—"

"Just say it!"

"She... she, you know. She drowned—in the—bottom of the tub." He fought up out of the chair.

Both men faced each other, white-faced.

"Goddam," breathed Bart, turning back to the darkness. "Goddam me for saying it."

Walking in the wet, Madden knew at last that he could leave the house behind and give himself up to the storm. Slimy, tangled brush grabbed at his sopping clothes, but he did not think of it and slid down the ravine to the churning riverbed. In the glistening night he saw the swell-ing rush muddying over collapsing banks, and he remem-bered the first and worst storm, two seasons ago: how the ravine filled steadily to the brim, spilling up over the back yard; and then, weeks later, how the yard blossomed alive with all manner of new, unnamed wild plants and shoots and bloomed-faced flowers. And how he suddenly awoke one night to discover the moldering ravine an amphitheater of swollen hordes of singing insect life, a thundering of bullfrogs, a sweltering din of mosquitoes, a screeching chorus of crickets. Latent with life, pollen and cyst and egg had been carried by the water and given birth at long last.

Madden stretched through the wet growth to the river's edge. Facts and meanings swirled and eddied within him.

He saw the fresh water flowing on past, headed for the sea.

A paper boat or a leaf could float the five miles to the turbines, and beyond to the sea. But only something living could do the opposite.

Suddenly, as if by a signal, frog and insect ceased their noise.

In the new silence, above the rain, Madden heard a car door slam.

He began tearing savagely at the shrubbery. His hair and chin dripped and his clothes were torn and caked with mud below the waist, but he did not think of these things as he climbed his way to the porch.

He smeared a wet trail across the kitchen.

Lorelei came through the unlighted living room.

"Why James, I thought you'd be in bed. And your clothes, why—"

"Wh-where have you been?" He shivered.

She reached to touch his clothes. He jumped back.

He saw that her clothing, too, was dripping. Much more than from a run from the car.

"Why, James—"

"Get away! Who are you?"

The sound of giggling.

He ran to the bathroom door. He kicked it in.

Grinning in the stark white porcelain bathtub were the twins, Tad and Ray. They splashed and curled eel-like appendages up over the edge.

"What is this?" muttered Madden, blinded by the light.

"What are you boys bathing for at..?" Then he saw their smooth, shining skins glistening in the water in a strange new way.

So this is the way Darla came upon them that day, he thought. *So that was why, that was why. So now I have no choice...*

He fell upon them, pushing their small heads under the water until bubbles floated up.

They came up grinning.

"So you know," she said.

He turned.

The bright, white tiles around him.

Lorelei, dripping, came toward him, holding out her arms as if to embrace him. An alien scaliness glittered anew along her neck, her boneless arms.

Behind him, the little ones giggled.

Madden stepped back before she could touch him. His legs met the tub and he tumbled backwards, seeing in a flash the bright walls and ceiling.

There was a resounding splash and then violent churning. And giggling.

And the sound of the rain outside.

Scarab

Gary Budgen

A T SOME POINT the shelves had collapsed spilling books across the bedroom floor. There was David Attenborough's *Life in the Undergrowth,* popular, beautifully shot, fruit of the first days of microphotography. There was Gullan and Cranstonthe's standard reference and, of course, E. O. Wilson's books on the social insects. Then there was my own little contribution, *Back Garden Mini-Beasts*, dedicated to my wife, already dead by the time it came out. There were lots of others, a lifetime's worth.

I didn't look at them much. When I tried to read the punctuation marks crawled off on their merry own way like mites. And then there were the pictures: dragonflies with crystalline wings; a beetle's elytra gleaming like a sports car's; the fleshy engines of earthworms. The pictures just made me want to weep. At first I took to drink, bingeing on vodka. I drank so much that when I finally stopped I spent a night with the vanished bugs of the world crawling all over my skin, drenched in a nostalgia for all that had been lost.

My daughter, Aliza, was worried about me. She kept calling till I agreed to go to the parties. I supposed I'd always been the groovy dad. These parties were good, at first. You'd walk into a room in some flat. It would be up a few storeys but still with joss sticks burning to cover the stench from the streets. They'd be dancing so frenzied that it could only have been performed by people who had no future. The thump of the beats drowned out the orgies that everyone knew were happening in back rooms.

But this time the party was quieter. People sprawled in armchairs, on the sofa, curled up in corners zonked out. The end of the world wasn't as good as it used to be.

Aliza came over and twined her arm through mine, she looked rough, older than she should at twenty-three but I could still see the child I'd known, a being just beneath the surface of her worn skin.

"Here," she said, holding something out.

"What is it?" I asked. But I knew what it was.

"It's a gift, Dad. Right up your street." She handed me a cardboard tube, like a thumb-sized firework. On the side of this was a symbol, a brand mark, a stylised *scarabaeidae*, of the sort the Egyptians had used as amulets to protect their mummies. This was the beetle who rolled a dry ball of dung imitating Ra pushing the sun across the sky of the ancient world.

"Well..." I said. But already she'd gone over to sit on an armchair and was downing the contents of the tube.

Of course I'd heard of the Scarab.

Some people saw a worm, others a spider, some an insect. Maybe these visions were all different or—since most people were not experts—these were just different words for the same thing. It was obvious wish-fulfilment given what had happened.

I opened the tube and swallowed. In my mouth was the taste

of dust. Then I was gone.

It felt like I knew everything... No, not just that. I didn't know everything I *was* everything. I was a landscape, a world and there were no other people but me. Yet I was not alone.

There was a plain, and it was twilight or else this place was further away from its sun. Something was crawling across the endless dust, its multiple legs treading softly, slowly. It was still a distance away at first but all I wanted was for it to be closer.... Did I reach out my hand towards it? I think I did.

When I came to I was slumped on a sofa, my fingers stuffed into a tear in the upholstery rubbing the foam stuffing. I felt dehydrated and it was an effort to get up. Other people were stirring. The little coffee table in front of me was covered in fag ash, beer cans and the empty little tubes of Scarab. I didn't want to be here anymore.

Somehow I got up and managed to get to the kitchen. Aliza was at the sink, stooped over, gulping water straight from the tap. She looked back at me for a moment then went on drinking.

"I need water," I said.

Eventually she moved away, leaving the tap running for me. I looked around for a glass but there weren't any so I stooped down too.

"What do you think?" she said, standing behind me.

I finished drinking and faced her. She looked terrible, the skin of her face stretched over her cheeks as brittle as dry leaves.

"I'm never doing that again," I said, forcing a laugh.

We both knew I was lying.

There'd been a picnic once. I'd taken Aliza up to Epping Forest, to High Beach with its pub and little green, woodland centre and refreshment vans. I'd bought her an ice cream and then we'd walked off, away from the dog walkers and bikers admiring each other's Harleys. There was a little pond, surrounded by beech trees and hornbeam. Here we'd spread the tartan blanket on the ground. Out on the pond, Hawker dragonflies were circling, zooming after midges and mosquitoes; and down by the edges of the water were damselflies holding their metallic wings aloft, showing their brilliant cyan heraldry.

I did Scarab again at another party that Aliza got me to. She handed me one of the small cardboard tubes. I'd been watching TV all day; the world was getting worse and I wanted out of it.

"I knew you would," she said, "It's the best. It'..."

But she didn't finish, just caught my gaze for a moment and looked away. Beneath her cracked smile I tried to find the child again but this time she wasn't there.

I tipped the powder in, letting it linger, savouring for a moment the dust taste in my mouth. Then I swallowed.

On the plain the creature stood against the horizon. In the twilight I couldn't quite make out its shape. For a moment it was like the silhouette of a fallen pylon, then it shifted to become a dark unfathomable bulk.

It spoke a silent communication of feeling, of immensity. I was everywhere, as though—if this were the internet—I was visiting every website at once; and I was also the internet itself. But I knew that this was so much more than the interconnected wires and servers, ether and screen that humanity had kidded itself was ubiquity.

Then the creature moved forward and the distant sun touched the sleek surface of its carapace so that it shone with black light.

When I jerked awake my mouth felt as though I'd been chewing ash. I stared at others around me, most groggy, some still lost in the beauties of the Scarab. The kitchen was full of people so I drank from the bathroom tap.

Aliza was curled under people's coats in the bedroom.

"Where do you get it from?" I asked her when she woke. I tried not to look at her directly; it was though she had aged years.

"Some guy," she said, "It's no problem. It's cool."

And she told me.

We lay on the tartan blanket just back from the edge of the pond and Aliza began to unpack the picnic basket, carefully bringing out the sandwiches she'd helped me make standing on a chair so she could reach the kitchen counter. Then she took out a large pack of salt and vinegar crisps and some mini cartons of orange juice.

We sat and ate a cheese sandwich each, Aliza taking a bite of her sandwich then a handful of crisps. Then she went to climb a tree at the pond's edge leaving her half-eaten sandwich on the blanket.

*

I used the last of my rations in the government shop. Dried mycoprotein again; now even the stocks of tinned goods were running out. Then I worked for two days with a shovel and mask to earn some ration coupons. I scraped up stinking piles of refuse from streets, forecourts and front yards. Then I tipped this into a lorry that would take it out onto farmland where it would be dumped since nothing could grow there now that the earthworms and beetles were gone. Even with the mask on the stench soaked into me, washing around my nose and mouth.

Taking my ration coupons I walked out along the dual carriageway, following the white lines, only going over to the side when the occasional car passed. I counted six in the hour it took me to reach the retail park. It had been abandoned months before: who needed pet supplies or model aeroplane glue anymore? The car park had become a makeshift dump and was covered with matted food scraps and packaging sodden with rain but stubbornly refusing the final release of decomposition.

In the pet store I saw my contact, sat at a desk surrounded by tanks floating with dead fish, glass cases with reptiles that had starved to death without insects to eat.

"I'm...a friend of Aliza's," I said, for some reason not wanting to say she was my daughter.

He looked like something out of one of the dead vivariums. Skin flakes fell from his cheeks when he grinned.

"I can sort you out," he said, speaking slowly, almost croaking.

I held out my coupons; they represented hours of shovelling shit. He took them and stared at them for a moment before handing them back.

Then he held up his hand and recited:

"*A beetle wanders in the night tasting dust, smelling worms, feeling the ground. He pushes and pushes the seed of himself, a dried ball of dung. Insanity!*"

"You don't want these?" I said looking at the coupons in my hand.

"It's a gift," he said smiling. And he reached under the desk and pulled out a little bag, the sort of paper bag you used to do pick-and-mix with in Woolworths, a bag that you would fill with sweets. It was full of the little cardboard tubes of Scarab.

"Where does it come from?" I asked. I wasn't a conspiracy theorist but I assumed it might be some government thing, something to ease us all into oblivion.

He winked, one eye closing slowly with all the elegance of an arthritic lizard.

"It's a gift," he said, "from God, from Khepri, the sun at dawn. Does it matter?"

As I walked out he was reciting once again.

"*Through the belly of darkness, he creeps, struggles with his burden, at first small and soft, now a large, hard, heavy stone.*"

I thought about that as I trudged back along the dual carriageway. Khepri the sun represented as a beetle. Ancient Egyptians had seen the young scarab emerge from a ball of dung and thought the creature created itself from waste, from shit. A symbol of life and renewal.

At the flat I made sure I did things properly, cleaning as much of the accumulated house dust off the duvet as I could, giving it a good shake. I filled a litre water bottle and put it on the bedside table. Then I emptied the powder into my mouth.

On the plain the creature was where it had been before, just poised beyond full perception reaching out with its invisible influence that connected me to everything, everything that was also me. And yet, now I realised that it wasn't just me. I was the centre, the Omphalos of the universe but so were all the others who were the same as me, or were with me.

The creature took a few steps forward, a slow ballet of stick legs and the graceful sway of its great armoured body. At its front delicate antennae waved slowly; beneath these were thicker, hair-covered palps and the sharp edges of mandibles. I wanted to reach out but couldn't, or dared not. I felt the paradox of being everything and yet being unable to act. Along the infinite lengths of an invisible network my desire was echoed and amplified by all those I was connected with.

I woke and reached for the water. My arm was stiff and I saw the skin on my hand had cracked. After a while I managed to get up and picked up some of my old books. I wiped the dust off

and looked through them, studying photographs and line draw-
ings of insects and arthropods. But I wouldn't find the creature
here. I let the books slip off the bed back to the bedroom floor.
I'd reached for the sweetie bag, looked at it for a moment and
then put it down. In the living room, I slumped on the sofa
sending up the inevitable cloud of dust.

The TV news was all about food shortages, waste disposal
initiatives and outbreaks of cholera. Then there was a feature
about Scarab, about the spread of the problem; increasing levels of addiction. The newsreader spoke in a measured tone, her
heavy make-up unable to mask her grey, desiccated skin, the
patterns where layers had peeled away.

I watched the news all morning, the revolving stories pulling
me through to the evening as one newscaster replaced another,
once pretty young women, middle aged men with gravitas,
young PR types. All of them had the same dry look, partial
mummification—all of them were heads into the Scarab.

At dusk I got out my little sweetie bag.

The creature was closer now and I tried to work out what it
was again, applying all the knowledge I'd accumulated over the
years. Although it looked something like a huge beetle it had
more than six legs; I was sure of that as I sighted along its flank
to the pole-like structures there, row on row stretching away.
Perhaps it was some species of myriapod, centipede or milli-
pede, with a long succession of segments stretching back further than I could see. For a moment, its head bent down towards me and I was caught in the intricacies of its eyes, the

countless hemisphere lenses. I might have even seen myself there, on the plain, a dry husk crawling across dust and rubble, humbling myself in devotion. But I was not the only presence in the screens of that great compound eye.

Then a rush of reassurance enveloped me, a certainty that I was everything because the creature existed, that it existed for me, that it was the world that was me. Its influence reached out again and I felt that sense of connection with all the others who were here I was no longer me.

Later I drank water and watched TV again. The breakfast news reader's face looked like burnt paper. She tried to read from an autocue but was finding it difficult, syllables like air through a reed. There had been more crop failures, more land declared barren. There were alcohol riots in Birmingham and food riots in a list of places. Then, at the end of her report she began to tell a story that was hard to follow, her words rasping, slowing. Unconfirmed reports of deaths of Scarab users, possibly overdoses. She looked as though she might weep tears of dead skin.

I called Aliza but there was no answer so I left a message. I knew I should go and see her but the thought of going anywhere made me want to crumble.

I lay back on the blanket feeling the sun on my face, listening to the buzz of the dragonfly on the pond.

"Daddy," Aliza said.

"Hmm?"

"Daddy!"

I sat up. Aliza was shaking her finger at the blanket.

"You've let the ants onto the picnic."

A crowd of black garden ants, *Lasius niger*, were swarming over the remains of Aliza's sandwich. Others were crowded on the blanket foraging, hard to make out in the tartan pattern.

Aliza stamped her foot.

"Don't," I said.

"But they're ruining the picnic."

"It's OK."

I got up and threw the sandwich with its ants out onto the grass, picked up the bag of crisps and then lifted the blanket to shake it off.

"I'm sorry," Aliza said, her lip pushed out. She was about to cry.

"Why?" I said.

"I killed one."

And I explained that all the ants in a colony were really like one animal, so all she had done was hurt it a little. I told her about the army ants who march through Africa, about Leaf Cutters and Honey Dew ants some of whom are so full of honey they look like amber grapes and how the other ants in a nest feed on them.

"But," she said at last, "They do ruin picnics."

I left another message with Aliza. Back in bed I opened a tube of Scarab and poured it into my mouth, letting it linger there, feeling it cover my tongue, cake against my palate. It was as though I were deep in the earth, stuffed with dust.

The creature was on me, caressing with two long forelegs, its mandibles opening and closing slowly. It felt good to be so close. I knew that everywhere others were experiencing the same sensation. I knew at once that trying to classify the creature, to even name it would be futile, almost sacrilegious. I shed at last that constant, gnawing need to know that had been with me all my life and I felt an almost sexual release. I was discarding the hubris I'd been part of, the centuries of sorting and naming that stretched back through Carl Linnaeus and beyond. All those worthy Enlightenment gentlemen, collecting, classifying in their attempt to diminish creation, crush it beneath the boot of reason.

The edges of the mandible pressed against my cheeks, increasing in pressure. When they began to cut into my flesh there was an instant of pain but then I just drifted into the embrace of a soft darkness.

When I woke up I could hardly move. I reached for my water bottle but I'd left it somewhere else. I wanted to take some more Scarab; I knew that I'd reached the point of revelation, when everything would become clear.

But I made myself get up and went to the kitchen and drank a measuring jug of water. There was a message from Aliza.

"Yeah, I got your call... Your messages. I'm all right." Her voice hissed until she cleared her throat. "Just... well...You know how it is. Funny I was thinking the other day about the time I came home from school crying because Martina Smith had told me Mum was being eaten by worms. And you remember what you said? 'Don't be silly, Mummy was cremated.' And then you started to say that anyway it wasn't about worms there were blow-flies and flesh-flies, ants and rove beetles... You went on the way you did. How you must miss them all, all your little creatures. It must be worse for someone like you..."

There was a pause and then she said something I didn't catch, it was like a hollow breeze down the telephone line.

"It'll be OK, Dad", she said at last. "It'll all be OK."

I knew I should go and see her. I would go and see her.

On the TV were more riots, more crop failures. Scarab was dangerous. There had been deaths. The make-up mask over the cracked skin of the newsreader crumpled as she said this and as the camera zoomed I thought I saw pieces of skin fall away, dull with stage make-up and fakery. I wasn't sure if I was imagining things.

I rang Aliza again.

"Pick up," I said to the messaging service, "I need to know you're all right. I..." My own voice was a feeble series of rasps and breaths.

Soon I would get up off the sofa and go. But I felt so tired. I couldn't remember the last time I went to collect my rations or when I had eaten. If I just had a little more energy I would go.

I went back to the bedroom and lay down, ripped open a paper tube and poured the powder into my mouth.

The creature drew back and I longed for its bite again. It

took a further step back and I reached out, yearned. Then the light changed, the distant glow flared and the sun grew brighter. What I had taken for twilight had really been the dawn. Before me the creature reared up and I saw it for the first time in all its magnificence.

It had multiple segments of limbs wriggling and it rested on a thick tail like a scorpion. I watched its dark carapace come apart to reveal its forewings which stretched away in a great arc. The light of the sun shone through them and like the wings of a butterfly there were panes of ruby, steamed blue, emerald. It was as though I was gazing up at the stained glass of a medieval cathedral.

This was a true communion and I knew now that the creature was social, like a bee, like an ant and that I was linked to all the others of its kind, in all the inner landscapes of Scarab users everywhere. Soon we would merge into a single vast existence.

There was a voicemail from Aliza.

It was whispered, broken, hardly coherent. I think she was saying goodbye. When I called back there was no answer. My own voice, as I tried to leave a message, was just like the air passing through the circulatory system of an insect.

I went through the motions of leaving, standing under the shower for twenty minutes, getting clean clothes from the drawers and shaking the accumulated dust from them. I drank glass after glass of water. On the threshold of the flat I stopped. I went back in again and picked up my little sweetie bag. There was one tube of Scarab inside. I could just take it and be back where everything was perfect. I stood for a long while thinking about this before I managed to stuff the bag in my pocket and leave.

Years after the picnic and Aliza all grown up, off to university. I'd persuaded her to come with me that day as we'd got the campaign mini-bus up the M11, then the A11 and then some side road off into the depths of Thetford Forest, the land of air bases and a private research station for an agrichemical company.

When we got there other protestors were already there, staring at the perimeter fence with its lines of private security and police. We stood in the rain. Some young activists tried to storm the gate, pushing at the police until they were sent back under a barrage of truncheons.

Inside, beyond the fence and the foreground, beyond the trees and in some hidden laboratory, they were creating miracles. There would be a spray soon that would switch off the reproductive genes of cockroaches. Soon there would be no cockroaches. Then no mosquitoes. Then no parasitic flies that ate into people's eyes. It was all perfectly safe, we were told, no danger of any chain reaction. The world would be a much better place. A golden summer for a picnic.

"What's the point?" Aliza asked, laying her placard on the ground as it began to grow dark. We were cold and wet through.

I wanted to tell her that we had to keep protesting, that we couldn't let them get away with this. That is was all so dangerous. But I couldn't find the right words.

The streets were quiet. I realised I didn't know what time it was and the overcast sky gave no hint. In the High Street there were a few cars in the middle of the street, looking as though they'd been abandoned. As I crossed, I saw the driver in one; he was stiff, skin tawny and knotted like a cocoon. One of the dead.

I tried to jog, to hurry but I was exhausted after just a few strides.

I went back to one of the other cars. The keys were in the ignition but the car was empty. I brushed some odd multicoloured grit off the seat and drove.

Aliza's apartment block had been nice once but now the ground around it was the usual mat of organic waste, the smell of it something you never got used to.

The foyer was covered with a sheet of dust and the lift was broken. I climbed the stairs, each one difficult, hurting my legs. My stomach felt odd, pains churning inside. When I got to the door of Aliza's flat I banged with my fist as hard as I could but by now I was feeble. When there was no answer, I rang her phone and could hear it ringing inside. Finally the door opened.

"Aliza," I said.

But it was someone else who answered the door, the man from the ruined pet store, who'd given me the Scarab. He had become little more than a walking corpse with skin of bark wafer. He looked at me, taking me in.

I found my little girl on the bed. Like the driver of the car she was lifeless, shrivelled. No longer lost in Scarab dreams. I held her in my arms and it was like cradling a hollow piece of driftwood dried in the sun. I could hear a scratching, a rattle. I thought it might be my stomach. I didn't want to think about Aliza's organs disintegrating.

Scarab man opened the bedroom door and came in.

"Khepri," he said, his dry tongue running across his lips.

"What? What you on about, can't you see that she's..."

He spoke clearly now, intoning something long prepared.

"It is one hour before dawn. Breezes blow. The ball of dung turns to gold. In the light of day, the ball breaks; beetles fly into the sun. That is Khepri."

In my arms, Aliza fell into fragments; dry clods of what had been her body flopped onto the bed, disintegrating into powder. The ochre dust of her flesh was full of tiny oval gemstones: of aquamarine, coral, and opal. I watched as they shuddered on the bed, cracking open. The tiny creatures that hatched were of many species but none that I knew: there were creatures like insects, like spiders, like lice, there were twisting worm-things. All of them unfurled delicately veined wings. They fed on Aliza's remains, clearing it quickly until all that was left were the tiny pieces of coloured eggshells like those I had seen in the abandoned car. Then the hum of beating wings filled the room and as one great host the creatures took flight.

The Scarab man stood beside the open window and we watched together as the swarm flew out into the morning, a gift that would replenish the world.

For the Love of Insects

Mark Howard Jones

THE SMALL STATION was deserted. It had a run-down look as if it had always been deserted: abandoned before a single train had either arrived or departed. Each discoloured tile told a tale of neglect. Filth clung to every corner. No timetables or posters had ever been hung on its walls, it seemed.

Had he got off at the right place? There were no signs anywhere. The train sounded its horn once, a mournful farewell, as it rounded the corner and disappeared behind a hill. Alex clutched his shoulder bag to him; it contained the few essentials he'd brought along.

He noticed a dust cloud moving towards him from between a line of houses. Suddenly a large black car appeared, slowing slightly as it negotiated a crossing over the railway tracks. Grinding gravel under its big tyres, it crunched to a halt just a few yards away.

The car was a huge black Soviet-era limousine that glistened even in the milky sunlight. The artist obviously took great care of it; he'd probably had it restored at some expense. Inside, it looked roomy but not particularly comfortable.

The man seated behind the wheel glared at him for a moment before opening the door and climbing out. He was tall and wore a baggy black shirt and grey trousers. The gravel crunched dryly under his huge work boots as he strode forward.

He extended his hand, closing it again tightly. The hand-shake was surprisingly soft. "Modril," he croaked before cough-ing loudly and repeating his name in a more audible tone. Alt-hough taken aback by the extraordinary volume of the man's cough, the new arrival managed to squeeze out "Hello. I'm Alex McCarthy."

Modril let go of Alex's hand and nodded. "Yes." It was said in a tone of satisfaction, as if he was pleased he'd found the right person.

The big man walked around the front of the car and opened the passenger door. Alex noticed that he walked with a distinct limp, as if the leg was malformed or injured in some way. "Get in," barked Modril, his voice now obviously fully recovered.

Modril settled himself into the driver's seat and bullied the car into life. A small, sad-faced cat watched the car speed by. As the driver put his foot down, Alex was shocked to see that the end wall of the station was pock-marked with bullet holes.

He'd been warned by a gallery owner in Bucharest that Mo-dril disliked empty flattery or idle chatter, so Alex decided ahead of time to hold his tongue for the duration of the journey to the painter's home. Now that he was face to face with his in-tended interviewee, Alex knew he wouldn't find it difficult to keep his promise to himself; the man was huge and his eyes held a stern expression beneath large, dark eyebrows.

Alex felt relieved that at least Modril's English was likely to be good. The few words he'd already spoken were in a distinct but slight accent and he could clearly be understood. Alex's own language skills were poor and he'd struggled to understand the few dialects he'd heard on the exhausting train journey from Brussels.

He didn't know where the artist had learned English, but he was grateful that his tutors had done such a good job. Of course he'd known Modril could speak English already—otherwise, how could an interview even take place?—but it was one of the few certain things that was known about the enigmatic painter.

No-one was even sure if Modril was a first or last name. Just Modril. Always.

In the few monographs and catalogue notes on him, there were very sparse biographical details. 'Originally from Eastern Europe' was the most detailed that Alex could find. But the man's face seemed somehow more exotic than that. There was something about his eyes.

The car ascended a narrow road with unfamiliar road signs dotted here and there. At one point, Modril nearly ran three workmen off the road, sending them scurrying into the trees for safety. But he seemed not to notice.

They'd been driving for less than 10 minutes when the landscape levelled off. Another few minutes and Alex could see another hill ahead, with a large house built near the top. Modril grunted softly and nodded as if to indicate that this was their destination.

The hill was covered in trees. Probably the remains of ancient woodland, thought Alex. The mist still clinging between the trees, even this late in the morning, looked like deftly-spun spider gossamer.

He looked at the big man sitting next to him. According to some, he was the heir of the great Surrealists like Max Ernst and Dali. And there had also been comparisons with Giger.

But he was greater than any of them, in Alex's opinion. Modril's exquisite and terrifying images of humans and enormous insects, locked together in curious embraces or puzzling dances, were quite unlike any other work ever created. The look of rapture on the faces of the people he painted was inexplicable, haunting.

The trees made the approach to the house dark and Alex kept craning his neck for a glimpse of the building around the next bend. And the next. When the house finally loomed up before them it came as a great relief to him.

Modril parked the huge car in the courtyard before the house with less than diligent care. The machine rocked for several seconds on its tortured suspension before the big man leaped out with a grunt.

The house was large. In fact, Alex wasn't sure 'house' was the right word, as it seemed to be more a complex of buildings joined together by low corridors. Maybe it had been used as something else once, mused Alex.

Modril almost bounced up the few steps to the front door and threw it open with a flourish. Alex followed him obediently.

Just inside the door, he stopped in his tracks. On the wall was a John Curtis illustration of a crane fly, its perfectly delineated long limbs reaching up into the air. The slight yellowing of the paper told him that it was an original and must have cost Modril a small fortune to obtain.

"This way. This way." The artist's voice sounded impatient, so he followed him quickly into the inner darkness of the house.

Modril stood holding a large oak door open for him. "Down here, Mr. McCartney," he said.

"Uhhmm... McCarthy. My name is McCarthy," corrected Alex.

The big man nodded. "Yes, sorry... I must have been thinking of The Beatles."

No doubt, thought Alex as he caught sight of the numerous examples of coleoptera displayed on the wall. Beetles had always made his skin crawl. For the next few days, he'd be running the gauntlet.

The corridor was lined with deep, glass-fronted picture frames, each containing delicately mounted butterflies, moths, various other insects or spiders. He stopped before one frame. It held a single specimen of a large, remarkable-looking creature. It seemed as if the thing within the frame couldn't decide whether it was an insect or a spider. Certainly it was an arthropod, but he'd never seen anything like it before. It was horrifying but fascinating.

His host had lingered, waiting for him to catch up, so Alex took the opportunity to ask what the creature was. Modril merely chuckled and gestured to him. "Come on, there'll be plenty of time for all this later. You need some rest and refreshment after your long journey."

The two men sat facing each other in a large lounge at the centre of the house. There were no windows but a large, decorated skylight revealed that the room was stuffed with art and artefacts. Some were by Modril himself but others were of more obscure origin, Alex noted.

A large coffee table stood between the two sofas on which they sat. The table looked as if it had been carved from one solid piece of wood. Alex guessed that it must be immensely heavy.

"Thank you for your hospitality, Mr. Modril," ventured Alex. The artist frowned slightly. "I am not Mister. I am just Modril. Please just call me that." Alex nodded, feeling suitably chastised after his clumsy attempt to divine the artist's full name had fallen to pieces.

An emaciated looking maid delivered a tray to the table. She wore a neat black uniform and looked to be in her late 50s. She looked briefly at Alex with dark, sad eyes before Modril said something to her in an unidentifiable language, after which she left quickly.

"Please," said Modril, indicating the coffee pot and cups on the table. As Alex reached forward to pour himself some coffee he almost snatched his hand back in panic. There were various books and objects scattered about the table but Alex hadn't noticed the evil-looking piece of sculpture at first. He took his eyes off it only to ensure he wasn't spilling the coffee while pouring it.

Although of poor craftsmanship, the statuette was obviously

of the odd creature he'd seen on display in the corridor. Whoever had created it had made it a hideous mixture of antennae and multi-jointed legs. They'd very obviously got the details wrong, giving it an impossible number of limbs and appendages. It was a nightmare. One roughly cast in some dull grey metal that had barely been polished.

When Modril caught him looking at it and said "You may pick it up if you want," Alex did his best to conceal a shudder at the thought. He didn't want to touch the repellent thing.

Yet, the more he looked at it, the more he had to admit it had an odd allure. He disliked it, most certainly, but something in him wouldn't let him look away. When he found himself reaching for the foul-looking object, something inside his mind snapped in desperation and he let his hand fall to his side.

"It's from Indonesia, in case you were wondering," said Modril. "It's quite rare. I don't think they are made any longer."

Alex took the opportunity to press the matter further. "The insect itself is also from Indonesia, then?" Modril simply dropped his gaze and nodded, pouring himself some coffee.

"I've never seen anything like it. What's it called?"

Once again the painter simply ignored the question. He clattered his cup down onto the saucer, placing them on the table before springing from his chair with astonishing grace and speed. "We will talk tomorrow. Tonight we will eat and we will keep the art until the morning. I should show you to your room now. If you've finished...?"

Alex nodded, not wishing to antagonise his host, even

though he still had half a cup of coffee left.

As he ushered Alex out of the room, the artist added: "My wife will join us later... before dinner."

Despite all the interiors being painted in light colours, the rooms of the house were cool and dimly lit. There was an odd chemical aroma everywhere that Alex didn't recognise. It wasn't paint or anything to do with painting, he was sure. He eventually dismissed it as being due to some cleaning product that he was unfamiliar with.

Alex opened the small window that looked out upon a line of dark trees. He unpacked the few things he'd brought and lay back on the bed in a feeble attempt to recharge his batteries. What he needed was sleep but he was too keyed up to drop off.

Who knows, maybe this will be the only interview Modril will ever give—it will certainly be the first—and I'll be the one to get it, thought Alex. He'd be 'the man who talked to Modril'. By definition he'd become the world expert on the artist. At the very least he'd get his PhD and a book out of it.

He remembered Professor Aitchison's remarks on the day he'd received the summons from Modril. "Be careful. Some called him Madman Modril, you know." Alex had assured him he would be. "You can forget the rest of your work towards your PhD if this comes off. This interview will be enough to secure you your doctorate... and make your reputation on top of that!" his tutor had added.

As he'd closed the door, he'd added one final caveat: "And

you'll have to do something about this idiotic fear of insects that you have, Alex. That'll hold you back."

Easier said than done, thought Alex. He resented the Professor dismissing his fear so lightly. His fear of the multi-limbed creatures had been with him since his early childhood when a picnic had been ruined by a veritable swarm of ants. The miniature monsters had been everywhere; they'd coated the food with their awful black bodies, and they were in his mother's hair when she'd bent to pick him up. As she'd held him close to her, they'd begun to crawl over him, too. Some had even got up his nose. He was only five and it'd taken his mother nearly half-an-hour to stop his crying and shaking.

Alex had paid a hypnotherapist for three sessions before leaving London. He hoped to God that would be enough to hold off his phobia long enough to get this interview over with.

Alex got up, went into the small bathroom and splashed some cold water on his face. He felt exhausted. In a way he was glad Modril didn't want to give the interview until tomorrow.

He had dozens of questions that, even if the artist was evasive, should shed more light on the mystery of Modril.

There were only nine of his works in public collections. But they'd been enough to excite several laudatory articles and monographs on his work. Those, and some learned catalogue entries, had been sufficient to provide him with an enviable reputation.

But there wasn't a single interview with him. Much of what had been written about him was simply guesswork.

About four years ago, there had been rumours that Theo de Caestecker was writing a book with the artist's co-operation. But the book never appeared and then de Caestecker died suddenly, so that was the end of that.

Then the note had arrived. It had said simply 'Come for an interview' and given a time, a date and a place. Brief and to the point but equally unsettling, Alex had thought.

He could only assume that it was the reputation of his tutor, Professor Aitchison, which had secured this rare opportunity. The Professor had contacted the artist through a friend of a friend of a friend who owned a gallery that had shown Modril's work. After six months had passed with no reply, they'd assumed that the message had sunk without a trace.

But now he was standing in the artist's home with his heart in his mouth. He sat on the bed and surveyed the small but comfortable room.

On one wall hung an enormous painting, dominating the room. It was nearly eight feet wide and depicted a bizarre landscape filled with entwined figures. In the foreground lay a pair of figures locked together. The insectoid creature was as large as a man and lay atop a woman, its proboscis extended around her neck. The woman's expression was difficult to read but he found the impression of erotic asphyxiation impossible to escape.

Behind the two figures the picture plane tipped up sharply towards the viewer. It showed a flat area with a building of some sort a little distance back. The building was painted in such a way that it might have been ancient or very modern. The terraces of the structure were all but obscured by similar insect and human figures; whether they were embracing or struggling was impossible to determine from this frozen snapshot. In the background of the painting there was the suggestion of trees.

To one side a dense patch of foliage, sensuously painted with long brush strokes, gave Alex the impression that the scene depicted a humid place.

In the bottom left-hand corner, just below the artist's familiar signature, were some words. He presumed they were the title but there was some slight damage to the canvas and the paint had been scratched away. All he could read was ' ... tual'.

It made him feel uneasy. The more he stared at it, the more uncertain he became as to whether he was spectating on an orgy or a slaughter. Every other one of the artist's paintings that he'd seen had an indefinable air of eroticism clinging to them, but not this one. Perhaps he'd been unable to sell it, and that was why it was here.

He didn't know if the painting normally hung here or if Modril had deliberately placed it here for him to see. But Alex knew it was unlike any other of his paintings hanging in museums or public galleries.

Quickly he took a photograph of it. He felt like a criminal but didn't want to lose such a rare opportunity. He didn't yet know if he'd dare mention it in his thesis, at the risk of angering the artist, but at least he would be able to gaze on it in private.

Alex had managed to doze off on the soft bed. He didn't know how long he'd been asleep when he was woken by a knocking sound. Dazed at first, he thought it might be part of a dream. But when it came again, he realised it was the door.

When he opened it, he found the maid standing there. She looked concerned and then opened her mouth to speak haltingly. "He zay to coomb now and tork. Now." She laid a hand on Alex's arm to underline the point. "Now."

Alex was surprised, delighted. Maybe Modril had changed his mind and this would be the 'big interview'. He grabbed a notebook and pen and followed the maid. "Where are we going?" he asked.

The maid did not answer but simply kept on walking, glancing just once over her shoulder at him. She'd obviously learned what she'd been told to say parrot-fashion and had no grasp of English.

Alex followed her into a part of the house not visible from the front. Partway down a long corridor, the maid stopped and turned to him. She looked flustered and began to hiss to him in her own language. Staring back down the corridor the way they'd come, she jabbed and pointed. She repeated what she'd said then fished a piece of paper from her pocket.

Unfolding it, she showed it to Alex. On it was a crude ink drawing of what looked like two people dancing. Or perhaps engaged in something more intimate. It looked like it had been scrawled by a child. If it was the maid's own work then Modril clearly hadn't employed her for her artistic ability. She insisted on repeating her words for a third time, still in a low whisper.

He had no way of understanding her so he just said "Umm... yes. Yes," and nodded emphatically. She stared at him as if he'd just made a very bad and cruel joke at her expense. Then she walked past him and went back down the corridor.

Alex watched her go then turned to look towards where Modril must be waiting. He presumed that he was expected, so he continued on his way.

The corridor was relatively dimly lit but there was a skylight at the far end. Alex headed for the two doors lit by the pool of illumination.

Near the end of the corridor was a largish photograph, elaborately framed and hung just at eye level. It showed an obviously younger Modril, very smartly dressed and standing next to a seven foot tall version of the hideous statuette he'd seen in the living room. The craftsmanship of this version was far superior to the object he'd seen earlier. The sunlight glinted off its smooth surface, each segmented section of its underbelly sculpted precisely enough to make Alex shudder. Although partly obscured by a spray of leaves, there was a disturbing suggestion that some of the limbs were disappearing behind Modril's back. Impossible, of course, he thought.

Alex was speculating as to whether the giant thing was an idol, worshipped by the Indonesian natives, when one of the doors a few yards away opened and Modril's figure filled the frame.

"Alicks. Here you are. Didn't that stupid maid show you the

way?" The big man took Alex by the arm and almost threw him into the room before slamming the door emphatically.

Alex found himself in a large studio with the last of the daylight streaming in through two elaborate skylights.

The artist insisted on showing him his brushes, manufactured nearby from the finest horse hair. "Very soft, very good," he kept repeating.

Again Alex noticed Modril's difficulty in walking, just as he had at the station. Alex tried not to stare or draw attention to his interest. But it appeared as if the man's knee worked the wrong way round—bending backwards instead of forwards— and that he was struggling to conceal it.

Unsure of whether this was to be an interview or not, Alex asked polite questions about the brushes and the house. If he could put Modril at his ease, then maybe Alex would get what he wanted.

After several minutes, Alex asked the question that was burning a hole through the very centre of his mind. "Why do you paint insects, Modril? And such large ones?" The query was almost child-like but it had the desired effect. The artist turned to him with a new light in his eyes.

"Without the insects there'd be nothing. They are the most successful and numerous creatures on the planet. And they render us so many useful services... they are the base that we all stand upon. You... I.... everybody..."

"They were here so long before us—I have no doubt they will

endure once we are gone. After all, they were building cities while our ancestors still slept each night in the trees.

"They have far greater nobility then a mere race of contemptuous simian upstarts... Compared to them we are pathetic creatures, don't you think?"

Alex disliked Modril's attempt to get him to agree. It was obviously some sort of test but, at the risk of appearing ungracious, he remained silent.

"Mankind." Modril pronounced the word with a chuckle. "So many battles fought, so few victories won, hhhmm?"

Alex felt uncomfortable with having to listen to Modril's ramblings. In his opinion a little madness was desirable in an artist, possibly even essential, but this was taking things too far. And there was no way he could agree with his host's musings about the many-legged monstrosities, though he knew better than to say so.

Alex's belly was beginning to complain, as well, which didn't put him in the most receptive mood for such extreme views. He was looking forward to dinner, which he hoped would be quite soon. He hadn't eaten properly since breakfast. If only Modril's wife would hurry up and make an appearance.

"Errr... will your wife be joining us soon, do you think?" asked Alex, attempting to move the topic on to more pressing and mundane matters.

Modril looked at him as if showing pity for some terribly slow pupil, finding his lessons too hard. This was clearly not the interview Alex had hoped for.

By now Modril was standing in front of a huge canvas, largely obscured by a cloth. It was obviously a work in progress.

"They are gods. They deserve to be worshipped." Seemingly intent on not being deflected from his favoured topic of conversation, he pulled at one edge and the cloth fell away from the huge canvas.

Alex's mouth dropped open involuntarily. The painted scene was vast and horrifying.

The figure of the insectoid creature was familiar; it was a variation on the horrifying form seen in his other paintings. But the human figure was unlike any other he'd seen in any of Modril's other works. It looked like something splitting apart or flying back together after being torn to pieces, all frozen in a moment. The absurd phrase 'Francis Bacon with a hangover' came into Alex's mind.

The figure appeared to be in a kind of delirium, its mouth gaping open in a sigh of surrender.

The artist ran his hand slowly across the surface of the canvas, smudging the paint into one corner after nearly erasing half of the human figure. "I like to think there are worlds beyond our own where the order of things is very different."

Alex didn't know how to respond. Best try to sound professional, he thought. "Perhaps we can talk about that in the interview tomorrow, too."

"My paint stands in for my words," spat Modril. "I don't need to give interviews."

"Then why am I...?" Something deep inside Alex turned

black and withered in the light of new knowledge. "No-no..." he breathed.

Modril smiled and pointed to a spot behind Alex's left shoulder. "Ah, here is my wife now..." Then the man made a bizarre series of clicks and scraping sounds with his mouth. Alex's scalp crawled with fear as an answer to Modril's greeting came from somewhere behind him.

Frozen with fear, he was unable to turn his head more than a fraction. Yet, out of the corner of his eye, he saw a dark shape lowering itself from the ceiling a mere yard or two behind him.

Slowly the shape moved around so it was almost directly in front of him. Alex gasped in terror as he recognised a gigantic living example of the bizarre insect displayed in the hall. It dawned on him that the photograph he'd seen minutes before had showed Modril not with a carved idol but with the nightmarish thing that stood before him.

The creature was enormous, stretching upon its rear legs to tower over him. It hissed softly but didn't make any threatening moves. Alex heard Modril cooing to the huge monstrosity in his own language and wondered if they were instructions.

The thing moved closer to him. The strange chemical tang that Alex had noticed on arrival was nearly overpowering now. He gagged and coughed at its intensity.

His head began to swim and he saw images of a vast green plain. Where and when it was, he didn't know, but he'd seen it before in the large painting in his room.

Then the huge creature came into focus once more. Lost in

the great hollow of dreams, as if adrift amidst the humming, insect-heavy summer air, he watched as a bead of light journeyed across the compound lenses of each eye. He was fixed to the spot, unable to think, let alone move.

The sunset sent rosy light through the skylight as the sun prepared to depart. The creature clicked with what might have been pleasure. The light caught the sensuous sheen of her carapace, highlighting its lustrous blue-green hue. Her mandibles moved with a softly clattering nervousness.

He could see now how beautiful she was, how elegant and sleek. At last he understood Modril's intoxication with her and her kind. All Alex wanted was to belong to her, to be with her.

In the gloom behind her the wall was now crawling, alive with invertebrate witnesses to their outlandish union.

He almost lost consciousness, overwhelmed, as her impossibly long limbs enfolded him. The blend of terror and ecstasy was close to unbearable, forcing him to gulp down each breath painfully.

Now he was almost immobilised. Suddenly there came an agonising pain in the middle of his back as the huge creature stung him. He bucked hard against the thing's segmented body as the pain bit into him, his arms too tightly pinned to escape. Alex couldn't feel exactly where the wound was, but a hot numbness began to spread through him. He tried to cry out, but his voice failed to reach beyond a whisper as the creature clicked excitedly.

"Don't worry. She will be most gentle," whispered Modril.

"Isn't she exquisite?" he added in a tone filled with almost idiotic reverence.

As Alex's eyelids swelled, closing one eye altogether, he caught a final glimpse of Modril sketching furiously. The last sound he heard was of charcoal scratching roughly across canvas, faster with each stroke. He couldn't help wondering if he'd be on public display or part of a private collection.

Mere seconds before the numbness spread down his body, he felt his abdomen being pierced by something large, his previously empty belly filling to near bursting point.

Alongside the bitter tang of the venom on his quickly-swelling tongue, Alex felt a deeper bitterness when he realised that he wasn't to be her lover after all but merely a larder for her young.

Woodworm

Marion Pitman

H E WAS VERY small when his father burned the horse. It was old and tatty, with neither rockers nor wheels, and only a threadbare tail and mane of wool, but he was attached to it, would gallop around the house astride it, until the evening when his father looked at the horse, abandoned while tea was eaten, frowned, and picked it up. He turned the horse upside down and stared at it in alarm, then said, *"Woodworm!"* in tones of horror and disgust. Before the boy fully knew what was happening, his father had carried the horse out of the back door into the garden, where he strode across to the heap of brushwood and weeds waiting to be a bonfire, tossed the horse on to the heap, took out his matches and set fire to it.

The boy screamed then and tried to run out, but his mother pulled him back, and in a moment his father had returned, demanding to know what all the noise was about.

"Full of worm!" his father said. "If we kept it in here, next thing we know they'd get into the house, whole thing could come down round our ears. Now stop that row. You've got other toys. Don't be such a baby."

His mother comforted him and said she would buy him another horse—she never did—but he was stunned by the idea that somehow his wooden horse could make the house fall down. His mother explained, in a vague sort of way, about woodworm, and the power and horror of it took possession of his mind. A few days later his mother found him stamping on a worm, and that led to the discovery that woodworm was actually a kind of beetle, and not a worm at all. After that he was more circumspect, knowing that there was more than one kind of beetle.

He began to have nightmares. The woodworm swarmed towards him, tiny, menacing, champing their minuscule jaws, and he couldn't get away, couldn't move, and the house began to collapse around him, and as he was buried alive he woke, screaming, and his mother came in, half asleep, trying to be sympathetic and not angry, and couldn't make out what he was trying to say, and after a bit she went away again, and he lay in terror for what felt like hours, till sleep finally got the better of him.

His mother sympathised with his fear and horror of beetles—she was not too keen on creepy crawlies herself. She was disturbed, however, when he developed a terror of wood. One holiday they went on a tour of a stately home, and in one room, entirely panelled in wood, the boy noticed some small holes near the floor, and he began to shake, and tugged his mother's arm, saying, "Please can we go? Can we leave this room, please?"

She frowned, hoping his father hadn't heard. "In a minute," she said, "we'll be leaving in a minute."

"I'm afraid," he said, "it's all wooden, and it might fall down."

"Don't be silly, it's not going to fall down. It's been here for hundreds of years."

He bit his lip and carried on, but there was more panelling, and great wooden tester beds, and huge chests and presses, all potential hiding places for the deadly beetle. By the time they left the building the boy was almost in a state of collapse, sobbing quietly, unable to speak. His father threw him a glance as they got in the car.

"What's up with him?"

"He's not well, dear. I—I think he's got a stomach upset."

"Too much cake. I said you were spoiling him."

The nightmares came regularly, the black, swarming hordes flooding towards him, crawling over him, and eating, eating, at floors and ceilings, till he was buried again and again in splintered wood and beetles. He woke, sweating, panting for breath, his skin crawling, his body tingling all over with terror; but he managed not to cry out, not to disturb his parents.

His mother secretly indulged what she saw as a childish fancy that would pass, and made sure that at least all the wooden furniture in his bedroom was painted. He told himself that the woodworm would not eat through the paint, surely it would poison them. He got sort of used to the nightmares.

He got through school without disgrace or distinction, which irritated his father: "You'd think he could be good at *something.*" He was teased and bullied, being nervous and odd, but he put up with it all silently, neither hiding nor explaining the bruises, which again enraged his father, who told him to stand up for himself.

He managed good enough results to scrape into an obscure university, where he studied physics for a year before having a nervous breakdown. The dreams were almost continual, meaning he slept very little. He saw a therapist for a while, and told him about the dreams, and the woodworm obsession, but not about the horse. That was both too personal and too horrible; he could not put it into words.

It was the therapist who suggested he study beetles; confront his fear in the hope of doing away with it. It was while reading doggedly about *Anobium punctatum* that he discovered there were whole companies dedicated to the eradication of woodworm. It was clear, this was his call. The way to defeat his horror was to defeat the cause. He started to apply for jobs.

His father's reaction was predictable: "Did I pay for a good education so he could be a bloody pest controller! Might as well be a rat catcher! Useless and always will be."

But the job enabled him to leave home—his mother was glad, coping with his father was easier if she didn't have to worry about the boy. He found a flat in a block that was built entirely of concrete and steel, and furnished it with metal and plastic. All his clothes and linens were synthetic; the thought of moth made him sick.

The dreams continued, the shiny black carapaces marching towards him, wing cases flexing, jaws snapping; they got bigger as time went on, they were the size of stag beetles now, crunching their way through furniture and walls, doors and ceilings, and the house grew taller, and fell further to bury him deeper; and he woke sweating and swearing revenge.

The people at work were nervous of him, his fury and bitterness were so great. "It's only a job," they said sometimes; but so plainly for him it was a mission, a crusade, a personal vendetta. The chemicals he used were purifying unctions; the protective clothing was a suit of shining armour. He was making the world a better place, roof space by roof space.

He had little social life; too often it involved going out to pubs or other buildings that were full of wood. An atmospheric old world inn with huge worm-eaten beams in its ceiling made him so uncomfortable he could barely make conversation; he sat silently with a pint, trying to breathe normally, thinking he could hear the jaws of the woodworm larvae—he knew it was the larvae that did the eating, now, but could not stop picturing them as tiny black beetles—champing and chawing at the building around him, could feel the beams softening, powdering, about to crumble about his head... He finished one pint and left, pleading a guts ache.

The dreams were an uncomfortable background to his purposed and dedicated life. Now, more often than not, instead of the swarm, there was one huge beetle, towering over him, and sneering, withering him with its contempt. He was paralysed with terror even before the walls fell in. But he soldiered on, knowing that he was fighting the enemy, spurred on to greater and greater effort.

185

It was a blow when he started to notice the breathlessness, and the shaking in his limbs, and the doctors told him he had been poisoned by the chemicals he had used when he began the fight. At first he was devastated, he felt that the woodworm had won, that they had at last defeated him despite all his effort and perseverance; but gradually, after he was given early retirement, and a generous settlement on condition that he didn't sue the company, he began to see his condition as honourable wounds, and felt he had done his best. The dreams diminished in frequency, though the size and disdain of the giant beetle grew no less.

He took to spending a lot of time on the internet, and it was there, one morning, that he found the article. He read it three times, then sat with his head in his hands, the world reeling and crumbling around him. He went back to the computer, searched for confirmation. There were other articles. He stared in horror; his chest tightened, his hands shook, his vision darkened; he thought he would die, sitting there. In panic he forced himself to his feet, walked round and round the room, gasping for breath, sensing a great, contemptuous beetle seizing him and clamping its mandibles about his throat. He flung out of the flat, walked randomly down the road, instinctively avoiding the pavements with trees. He walked and walked, despite the shaking and the shortness of breath, till he had to sit down on a garden wall. When he was able to stand again he found a bus stop and went to see his mother.

His father had been murdered in a road rage incident a few years before, and his mother asked him now and then to move back in with her, but he resisted: too much woodwork in the house, he could not bear it. But he managed to visit from time to time—she had metal chairs and table in the kitchen, and as long as they sat in there he could cope.

He had a key, still, and let himself in. His mother was in the kitchen, drinking tea and reading the paper; although it was nearly lunchtime, she was still in the overall she wore for housework. Since his father died she had let a lot of things go, he thought. She looked up with a smile, which faded when she saw his expression.

"What's wrong? Are you ill?"

He shook his head, and took out his i-pad.

"I'll make some more tea," she said, and went to fill the kettle.

By the time she put a mug of tea in front of him, and took the lid off the biscuits, he had found the article.

"Read that!" he said, "Read it! Wasted, all wasted!"

Bewildered, she began to read, the article that said that woodworm larvae needed a certain degree of moisture, that they were unlikely to be found in old, dry wood; that unless a house had serious damp problems, woodworm holes were likely to be very old, the larvae no longer active; that old wormholes were not dangerous, and could not infect anything else.

She read it; she looked up at him still puzzled, concerned; "I'm sorry ... you mean, you feel what you've been doing is unnecessary? You needn't have used those chemicals -? I'm so sorry."

He leapt up, paced the floor—"It's not just that! The whole thing—my whole life—wasted—needn't have done *any* of it—the horse—the horse—wouldn't have brought the house down—all nonsense..."

"Horse—?"

"The horse! The horse Father burned! It couldn't have done any harm..." He looked at her. She looked blank, clearly wondering what he was talking about. He sat down again.

"Mother. The horse—the wooden horse, that Father burned because he said it had woodworm. When I was small. About three, four?"

She frowned; "I remember you had a toy horse... I don't remember what happened to it..."

"What?"

She shook her head; "I'm sorry, I really don't remember. Are you sure?"

He began to feel dizzy again. She didn't remember. The thing that had ruled his whole life, and she didn't remember. His father probably hadn't remembered either. It was nothing. Nothing to them, and a complete mistake. Everything, everything wasted. No houses were ever going to fall on him. His whole life... He stood up again, and took a step towards his mother; the great dark beetle towered over him, its feelers brushing the ceiling, its shadow drowning him in darkness, overwhelming the anxious, helpless figure of his mother. Loomed, loomed as it always had, casting them both into the shade, into blackness and madness and oblivion, preparing to fall and crush them. He made a convulsive gesture with one arm, as if to fend off the huge, hideously carapaced figure, to fight his way past it.

His heart was hammering; all the years, the wasted years, pressed on him intolerably, ached in his throat; and suddenly the horror of it turned to anger, anger at the great, dark, sneering figure above him, and as he fended it off with his left arm, his right swung round, without any premeditation, his hand closing into a fist, and smacked into the creature's body. It seemed to connect, to connect horribly with the hard casing of the creature's thorax, but instead of the bruising pain his fist was expecting, the casing gave way; it crumbled, collapsed, fell to nothing like a dead moth. Free. He was free of it. All the wasted years, the wasting of his body, all for nothing, but at least for the rest of his life, whatever it was, he would be free, free to be himself... Something inside him seemed to split, to break open, in a flood of light, and a flood of feeling, of all the emotions he had not allowed himself to feel as long as he could remember—anger, resentment, desire, grief, hatred, love—

Through the darkness and the dazzle of light he strained to see his mother, sitting there, gazing at him, uncomprehending but distressed, with so much in her eyes that she, too, had never been allowed to feel; then he fell to the floor, knelt at her feet, and for the first time in his life, laid his head on her lap and sobbed.

Foreign Bodies

Edmund Glasby

"HELL, I NEVER thought I'd ever hear myself say this but I'm with the Chinese on this one." Colonel Frank 'Gunner' Kennington of the US Marine Corp. stared at the large screen, watching the live subtitled updates that were being broadcast direct from the U.N. Headquarters.

Yet another emergency meeting of the Security Council had been arranged and the Chinese ambassador had once again vociferously called for an immediate air-strike on the off-sea Douglas-McKray exploratory drilling platform which lay some thirty miles off the Ecuadorian coast. Both the Russians and the French were coming around to his proposal.

"You know as well as I do that our government would never authorise such action while we're still receiving transmissions. Admittedly they're becoming weaker and God knows how any-one can still be—" First Lieutenant Bill Henderson stopped ab-ruptly as the images of the diplomatic arena changed and imag-es of the drilling platform—or rather what it had now become—appeared on the screen.

The footage, taken from the relative safety of a circling news helicopter, showed the huge rig encased within a weird, blue-green, frogspawn-like jelly. The camera zoomed in on the sur-face and it was possible to make out various structures under-neath the thick, semi-transparent, membranous coating.

"You know, when I was a kid the world held its breath worrying whether Kennedy and Khrushchev were going to blast us all back to the Stone Age," commented Kennington. "In 2001, millions watched the attack on the Twin Towers. Now this... whatever the hell it is, is on every TV in every country."

"To be honest with you, I'm surprised that our government decided to go public with it," Henderson replied.

"News would've leaked out sooner or later. This wasn't something that could've been covered up like all the other stuff we can't talk about." Kennington sat back in his chair as the delegates at the U.N. Headquarters reappeared on the screen. "The thing now is how to deal with it. I think we can expect to get the call very soon."

"So you really think that we'll be asked to investigate?"

Kennington grinned. "It's what we do, isn't it?"

Fourteen hours later, Kennington, Henderson and a dozen hand-picked, heavily-armed marines stepped from the U.S. Air-Force military plane on to the landing strip at Manta. The flight from Fort Bragg, North Carolina, had gone without incident although everyone aboard the aircraft knew that this was far from a routine mission. It had now been three days since the first emergency call from the drilling platform had alerted the Ecuadorian coastguard to something strange happening and over ten hours since all contact had been lost.

An Ecuadorian military official, who introduced himself as Colonel Edgardo Paz, greeted them on the runway, ushering them towards a nearby hangar. Once they had all assembled inside, he led Kennington and Henderson to a side office whilst the marines set about checking their equipment.

There were two other men in the office—a short, plump, bespectacled man with a balding head and a young Japanese man.

"May I introduce Professor Gleeson of the marine biological institute based in Quito and Doctor Yang-Si of the seismological team here in Manta," said Paz. "Both will be accompanying you."

Kennington gave a brusque nod, the limit of his greeting. He was the one in charge and it was important that the others knew this as well. "So, have there been any other developments since we lost contact with the Douglas-McKray?"

"None whatsoever," answered Gleeson. "However, the latest film images taken from one of the survey helicopters seem to suggest a change in the *constituency* of the substance which has formed over the rig."

"A change? What sort of change?" inquired Kennington.

Gleeson removed his glasses and gave them a clean. "Well, from a purely visual perspective, it would appear that the coating has hardened, altering from a semi-liquid to one which appears more solid. Indeed, portions of it have now coalesced into denser segments. It's hard to say whether such solidification is a result of time or a reaction to air or sunlight."

Kennington's steely gaze hardened. As a man of action, he had little patience for academics. As far as he was concerned the likelihood of there being any survivors out there on that rig was now negligible and thus the sooner it was sent to the bottom of the sea, with whatever weird contagion had spread over it, the better. It seemed to him unnecessarily dangerous to lead a detachment of his men and these two 'eggheads' out there to discover just what was going on and yet those were his orders. "You're the experts. What's your explanation for this?" he asked.

"As representatives of the scientific community we're as baffled as you are," replied Gleeson. "This is completely unprecedented. Not until we obtain a sample of whatever that substance is for analysis can we begin to formulate a hypothesis. However, Doctor Yang-Si believes that it may in some way be linked to recent tectonic movements on the seabed." He gestured to his colleague.

"That is correct," Yang-Si affirmed. "At this stage it is but a theory. There have been slight, yet observable, seismological movements along the seabed in the vicinity of the drilling platform. The fault line between the Nazca and the South American Plates lies less than a thousand kilometres from where some of the investigatory boring was performed. It's possible that in the drilling process a substratum reservoir of an as yet unidentified mineral has been tapped, resulting in an immense chemical reaction the oxidisation effects of which are plainly visible."

"I was of the understanding that this was a living organism," countered Kennington. "If I get you right you're suggesting that it's some kind of chemical. Something like tar thickening on a road?"

"That is my belief." Yang-Si nodded. "However, as Professor Gleeson has said, not until we can analyse it can we reach an accurate decision."

"What about survival chances? Do you think anyone could still be alive out there?" As far as Kennington was concerned this was the fundamental question.

Gleeson rubbed his chin thoughtfully. "I'd think it unlikely. Given that this substance seems to have completely smothered the exterior of the rig, I think we have to go on the assumption that it has leaked into the interior as well. There may well be pockets free from its contamination but, of course, we have no idea as to whether or not there are any other biological hazards to be on the lookout for: gaseous emissions, toxicity levels and, of course, radiation."

"You think it may be radioactive in origin?" asked Henderson from where he stood near the door.

"It's possible, although readings thus far obtained have indicated only ambient levels," answered Gleeson. "However, we've no way of knowing what it's like inside. Which is all the more reason to go out there and find out."

Despite having seen and experienced many things over the course of his highly-decorated military career, Kennington found it hard to fully take in the enormity and the sheer alienness of the sight visible through the porthole windows of the military helicopter. Even from this distance, he could see that the entire structure was cocooned in a weird, crystalline crust which extended all the way from the uppermost buildings down to the very sea level—and perhaps deeper. The fact that none of the rig's personnel had managed to escape via the emergency helicopter suggested to him that whatever had occurred here had been both swift and merciless—the initial encasement within the more gelatinous matter perhaps occurring in one monumental, disastrous, geyser-like upsurge. Such a view strengthened the opinion that in the course of the investigatory boring some subterranean reservoir had been punctured resulting in a high pressure release. The thought made him think of the pictures of gushing Texan oil wells he had seen.

"It's like something out of *The Blob!* It's... bloody unreal," commented Henderson. Like Kennington, he too had his eyes fixed on the befouled edifice.

"It's real all right." Kennington turned to face the gathered marines, all of them dressed in their chemical and biological protective suits. "Once we get aboard we stick to the plan. For now this is a search and rescue mission. I don't want any heroics."

The helicopter banked slightly, righted itself and began to hover, the almost deafening sound of the rotor blades drowning out all other noise.

A door was opened and a gust of foul-smelling air blasted inside.

Kennington looked down. Thirty feet below him, he could

see the dark green and glistening surface. It looked like a kind of strange algae. Some parts were mottled a disgusting, dark, watery red, giving it the obscene appearance of blood streaked catarrh which had somehow coagulated into a dense crust.

The first of the marines—a veteran of the war in Afghanistan named Max Wilbur—clipped himself onto the line and, with a final nod to his commanding officer, abseiled down, his bulky protective suit impeding his progress.

Kennington watched him go, half-expecting to see his man sink into the hellish depths of the unearthly surface but, to his relief, the other did nothing of the sort.

With a thumbs-up, Wilbur unbuckled himself from the line and stomped down hard with a boot, signalling to Kennington that the surface was solid.

Over the course of the next ten minutes, the rest of the team lowered themselves from the helicopter. Like astronauts on a foreign planet, some began taking readings and samples from the surrounding biosphere; the air was sampled and, with the use of geologist's hammers, chippings and portions of the bizarre crust were collected and bagged.

Having come to the realisation that his surroundings posed no immediate biohazard, Kennington lowered his face mask and went over to where Gleeson was eagerly conducting a few mineralogical tests. "Well, what have we got here?" he asked.

The chubby marine biologist removed his face-piece. "I'm not sure. It's definitely organic. High levels of iron with numerous terrestrial trace elements, so I think we can safely rule out anything from another planet."

Kennington nodded. "Any idea how thick it is?"

"It varies. Initial probing suggests between six and ten feet."

"Right. Let's see about drilling through this stuff."

Equipment and boring apparatus were lowered from the helicopter and soon a team of marines set to excavating through the strange coating. It proved to be a lengthy and difficult process; the solidity varying between rock-hard and gelatinous with each foot they delved.

After twenty minutes a slime-covered aperture, wide enough for a man, had been tunnelled, at the bottom of which could be seen a metallic surface.

"Going by the layout, I'd say that's the top of the main canteen," said Kennington, peering down the hole. "If we drill through we should be able to create an access point."

Dutifully, two of his team set to the task. The space was widened and a remote surveillance camera was lowered. A technician hooked it up to a portable monitor and Kennington and the scientists looked on apprehensively as images of the deserted canteen appeared on the screen. There were no signs of life... nor were there any bodies. Everything was still.

"There could be anything down there," muttered Gleeson.

Kennington snorted. "I'm going down. I want Henderson, Wilbur and three others. The rest of you stay up here and remain in contact at all times."

"I plan on accompanying you," said Gleeson a little reluctantly. "No disrespect, colonel, but it might do to have a little brains in the expedition. Besides, I may be able to get some better samples—discover just what this stuff is and find out what caused it."

"Okay, Professor, but let's get one thing straight. This isn't *Star Trek*. I'm not Captain Kirk, my men aren't expendable red -shirts and you're not Spock. We take this nice and easy."

A chill dankness hung over everything yet the air was breathable although some men chose to wear their masks as a precautionary measure.

It came as no surprise to find that the electrics were out. Consequently, three of the seven carried high-powered flashlights. The shadows danced strangely as they panned their light sources around the walls and countless surfaces. Darkened, obscured windows reflected the light back enabling them to discern that they were now effectively cocooned.

Noting the multiple exits leading from the room, Kennington assessed the situation. "Okay. Two groups. Gleeson and Wilbur you're with me. Henderson, you take control of the others. Check out the main mess hall on the level below this one and the sleeping dorms." He checked his watch. "We meet back here in thirty minutes. Then, if we find no survivors, we get the hell out of here and send this rig to the bottom of the sea. Check -in every five minutes on the radio."

Henderson nodded, gathered his marines together and set off for a darkened opening on the far side.

Once they had disappeared from view, Kennington led the

two who were accompanying him in the opposite direction. Shadows seemed to flow and shift as they progressed through the labyrinth of dark rooms and corridors, their footsteps echoing disturbingly. A network of massive flanged and riveted pipes twisted their way throughout the structure.

They soon came to a metal stairway that descended into the inky depths.

"Strange that we've yet to find a body," commented Gleeson.

"Could be that they're all holed up in one room, perhaps waiting to be rescued," replied Wilbur optimistically.

"Let's hope so." Kennington started down the stairs. Suddenly his radio crackled and Henderson reported that all was well and that so far there was no sign of anyone and that he was going to continue the search on a lower level.

Gleeson stared around nervously having now regretted venturing inside. A strong sense of claustrophobia bore down on him and it took a great mental effort not to scream out loud. Bile rose to his throat as a troubling thought developed in his brain—a thought, that, for the time being he forced himself to keep private as it was so extreme and irrational that the very concept bordered on the insane.

Noting the professor's discomfort, Kennington turned to him. "Maybe it would be best if you got out now. There's no telling what we mind find in the lower levels and the last thing I need is for you to start playing up."

"Don't worry about me. I'll be all right."

"Suit yourself but don't say I didn't warn you." Kennington

started down the stairs, the temperature dropping with each tread.

The level below was, like the one above, empty and predominately devoted to recreational spaces; a games room, a library, another mess room and a small gymnasium. However, everywhere they went they now found web-like patches of green slime adhering to the walls. Some of the furniture was likewise covered. In one room, a small cinema, a huge swathe of web-slime stretched from the ceiling to the seats below.

The call came in from Henderson, reporting that he was now deep in the rig and that his party too had found great pools of slime. Some of the lower passages and rooms were impassable.

Kennington was about to call off when there was a dramatic change in Henderson's voice.

"*Jesus Christ! What's that!?*"

"Henderson?" Kennington shouted.

"Holy shit, you're not going to—"

The loud report of automatic gunfire blasted from the radio. Then came the screams. More gunfire was followed by a chittering, slurping noise; and then silence.

An unsettling minute or so passed as the three men stared at each other in shock and horror. That something terrible had happened to the other team now seemed obvious for there was no more radio contact.

"What do we do?" asked Gleeson, his face sickly-looking in the shadowy light.

"Time to go," answered Kennington. "We should never have come here in the first place." He walked briskly for the exit and the passage leading back to the stairs.

They were crossing one of the rooms they had previously explored when something long, segmented and multi-legged detached itself from the ceiling and landed on Wilbur's head and shoulders. Like some snake-lobster hybrid, the thing's body coiled around the unfortunate marine's neck as, with a barbed stinger which dripped green venom, it stung him full in the chest easily puncturing his protective suit.

"No!" Kennington yelled, his pistol raised, knowing that if he were to shoot he would, in all probability, hit Wilbur. Although, given the network of blue-violet veins that were breaking to the surface of his face and the manner in which his eyes bulged and reddened maybe it would be for the best. With that thought, he pulled the trigger several times and turned to flee only vaguely aware that Gleeson was already bounding up the stairs in front of him.

"*Come on!*" the professor shouted. "Quick, get up here with the torch. I can't see a thing!"

Kennington leapt up the stairs. He shone his torch directly ahead. A short stretch of corridor was all that now separated them from escape.

Suddenly a door further along on the left burst open and a dark wave of nauseating black liquid within which were con-tained shapes—human-like shapes, ghastly and screaming – poured forth. Squelching obscenely, the revolting, oleaginous effluent crashed against the opposite wall, splashing halfway up to the ceiling before rushing forward towards the two men.

Gleeson was terror-stricken, paralysed with fear.

"*Run!*" Kennington gripped the professor and hauled him away, dragging him back the way they had come. With a powerful kick, he booted a door open, threw the other inside and slammed it shut behind him. His heart was thumping inside his chest, threatening to explode. Something was happening here that he could not even begin to understand. It seemed as though the thoughts that were moving and pulsing inside his brain were not his own and he felt his sanity begin to slide away from him. Beyond the door, he could hear the slopping and squelching noises as that amorphous, corpse-saturated horror oozed outside. Then, to his horror, the metal door began to bulge inwards. Around the jambs and from underneath seeped pools of viscous blackness within which small, luminous, tadpole-like creatures swam and wriggled.

The two men backed away.

With a loud crash a door behind them was thrown open.

"*Colonel!*"

Kennington turned to see one of his marines—a young man named Steve Williams—stood in the doorway. His face was pale and bloodied, his protective suit covered in unsightly splatters of grey-green slime. Still, at least he was alive.

"Come on! There's another way back to the exit!" Williams shouted. "Follow me!"

Tar-like, midnight-black pseudopods bubbled into the room

as Kennington and Gleeson dashed to join Williams. They had just reached the far door when the foul outpouring engulfed the metal portal and, like some hideous afterbirth, flooded into the room.

Chaos raged inside Kennington's normally highly disciplined mind as he ran, only dimly aware that Gleeson and Williams were ahead of him, their shadowy forms visible in the madly swinging torchlight. Then there came a burst of automatic gunfire as the young marine blasted something or other in his path. There was a high-pitched mewling sound, followed by the mass scuttling of dark shapes.

The passage they were charging along seemed to be filled with small half-crab, half-trilobite-like creatures which scattered like a cascade of dropped marbles as they ran on, heading for the stairs at the far end.

Gleeson screamed as one of the monstrosities fell from the ceiling, landed on his head and nipped at his face, seeking to gain purchase. It sheared off half of his right ear with one of its pincers. Yelling in agony, blood streaming down his face, he grabbed it and dashed it to the floor.

"*Quick! Up the stairs!*" Williams stood at an open door. Pushing the professor inside, he then gave a burst of covering fire which illuminated the dark passage, targeting whatever was on Kennington's heels. Slime sprayed.

Crunching some of the hideous creatures underfoot, Kennington sprinted for the door. Brushing past Williams, he started up the stairs.

The young marine stood his ground, putting down a deadly barrage of gunfire which rent the dark asunder, the deafening report mercifully drowning out much of the dreadful wails and cries that came from the darkness. After a few seconds of sustained shooting, he slammed the door shut and rushed up the stairs, joining the other two on a small landing from which two more doors gave access to other parts of the rig.

"You're the expert. What the hell's going on?" Kennington demanded, his eyes boring into Gleeson. "And what are these *things*?"

The professor was wiping his glasses, his face streaked with sweat. "I... I don't know. I honestly don't know. They're unlike anything I've ever seen before."

"Thankfully, I don't think that blob-thing can get up the stairs," said Williams.

Now that there was no imminent danger, Kennington asked: "Henderson...?"

By way of answer, Williams shook his head.

Kennington cursed volubly. There was an open door directly ahead of them which led to a long stretch of passageway.

"The canteen we first entered is at the end of this passage-way," revealed Kennington. "It looks clear." Tentatively, he stepped out into the space beyond, his gun held out before him, ready and more than willing to blast anything that got in his way.

They were within ten yards of the canteen when a side door burst open and a grasping mass of black, semi-solid tentacles shot forth.

Through terror-stricken eyes, Kennington saw Williams engulfed as the multiple appendages lost much of their solidity and became more like an oleaginous flow which drenched the unfortunate marine from head to foot. Rapacious vine-like tendrils squirmed from the ceiling, grasping him around an upraised arm. The soldier screamed and tried to free himself even as the colonel and the professor backed away.

Somehow, Williams managed to pull himself upright but in that next instant two more grasping pseudopods latched on to him—one coiling around his left leg, the other entwining itself about his right arm. Kicking and screaming, he was raised off the ground and held firm, like a fly trapped in a spider's web.

Thunder roared from within the canteen as two grenades, dropped by those above, exploded, peppering the room with deadly shrapnel and bringing down the ceiling directly ahead. A splatter of purplish goo gushed forward, burying Williams and blocking the way ahead.

Things other than flesh crawled down here. Things that scampered, scurried, slinked, skittered and slithered. Things that lacked name or identification. Things that no biologist, no matter how desperate for knowledge or fame, would care to study... at least not too closely.

For the time being, these horrors were absent, hanging back from Kennington's torchlight, their unnerving movements heard as opposed to seen, their very invisibility enough to instil terror into the two men. A demoralising, fear-induced sickness had befallen them so that now, as they took refuge in a small storage area, little larger than a closet, they dared not leave and yet they knew that their survival necessitated them doing so. Unable to establish radio contact with the outside and well aware that there was only so much battery life remaining in the flashlight, they knew they could not hide here indefinitely.

Thoughtfully, Kennington looked at his pistol, knowing full well that it would be of little use against the multitude of alien creatures that were out there but—

"You might think me crazy but I've had an idea going around my head regarding what's happening here."

Kennington looked at Gleeson, the professor's words shaking him from his morbid thoughts. "Go on."

"These creatures—they're unlike any aquatic or terrestrial life-forms known to man... and as for that disgusting jellied mass, well..." Gleeson paused, unsure how to continue.

"Well what? Come on, spit it out!"

"Well...I think they're all acting as part of a whole. It's as though we're the intruder and they're the 'cleansing agent' for lack of a better description. The best explanation I can give is that these things are seeking to purge us from this rig. Like antibodies combating a disease within the human bloodstream. We're the infection—don't you see?" There was a mad, staring look to Gleeson's face. He was shaking slightly, though whether due to the cold, fear or something else it was hard to tell. "Yes, that's it!"

"You've lost me," said Kennington.

"Imagine the rig's a mosquito. Its drill is the insect's proboscis, piercing deep into the Earth, penetrating God alone knows what in an effort to extract a precious fluid. The casing which has formed around the drilling platform is the scab. These creatures are doing their best to eliminate us. *It's as though we're the foreign bodies!*"

"Nonsense!" Kennington shook his head in disbelief, certain that the other had completely lost it. Christ, if that was the case then just what the hell lay two miles or so beneath them? Some truly gargantuan, continent-sized, chthonic leviathan with an immune system comprised of nightmarish creatures? This theory was insane.

"We're never going to get out of here and you know as well as I that they'll never send another rescue party," Gleeson muttered.

"So, what do you suggest? Stay here until whatever's eradicated the others eradicates us?" replied Kennington. "I say we wait for a while and then see about finding an alternative way to the canteen. There must be more than one route."

"We'll die if we go out there."

"We'll I'd rather go down fighting than rot my life away hiding in here. Besides, think how it's going to be when the light gives up."

Gleeson shivered at that very thought. It would be the most horrifying of experiences—sitting, huddled in the corner of this room, straining every sense in order to pick out the slow, insidious advancement of things eager for his blood.

Gun in one hand, flashlight in the other, Kennington edged his way forward, the professor close behind him. Each step was slow and silent. Navigating through this warren of corridors, stairways and rooms was tortuous and laden with terror, each new shadow or darkened opening a potential nightmare-in-waiting.

Both knew that death could come at any moment and from any direction. It was all around them; waiting, biding its time, readying itself for the strike. They were the flies blundering ever closer to the spider's web.

Kennington stopped. There was a sound, muffled and yet somehow familiar.

Gleeson heard it too. "The helicopter! We must be near the canteen!" Emboldened by a new strength of purpose, he rushed for the nearest door and pushed it wide, finding with some relief that they had arrived at their access point. "Help!" he shouted, hoping to alert those above.

Scanning the area and noting the damage wrought by the two hand grenades that had exploded earlier, Kennington stepped into the room. All was quiet. He paced over to the hole through which they had descended little over an hour ago—although it seemed a lot longer—and peered up, seeing nothing but the dark tube of strange jelly with a welcoming circle of blue sky beyond. His heart sank however as he heard the sounds of the helicopter diminishing.

"Help! For God's sake get us out of here!" Gleeson hollered up the pipe.

Gently chewing his bottom lip, Kennington tried to quickly think things through. It was clear that the remaining men had given up any hope of finding survivors, including the exploratory team, and had decided to head back. Perhaps they had been attacked by the same creature or creatures that had plagued him, hence the dropped grenades. In the end it came down to the same thing. To use a military term, they were now well and truly in the shit.

"They've..." The professor stared at Kennington in utter bewilderment. "They've...the bastards have left us here!"

"It would appear so." With the use of one of the canteen tables, Kennington hoisted himself up to the ceiling. It was going to be hard work clambering back up the opening but he did not think it would prove impossible. Drawing his combat knife from its belt-sheaf, he began to cut handholds into the walls of the spongy pipe. In this manner, he created a ladder of sorts and began to ascend.

"Go on! You can make it!"

His resolve strengthened by Gleeson's words of encouragement, Kennington climbed higher forever fearful that he would lose his precarious grip and slip back down, crashing on the canteen table beneath him. This was far worse than the countless obstacle courses he had subjected his subordinates to—a vertical mud crawl. And then, just as he thought he was never going to make it, he reached the top. Digging his blade in deep, he pulled himself free and rolled over on to his back feeling the warm, sane, welcoming sun on his face, physically and mentally exhausted. A sudden scream jolted him back into action.

"For God's sake, help me!"

Looking down, Kennington caught a fleeting glimpse of Gleeson before a tide of black liquid surged over him.

Vomiting a mouthful of bloated, maggot-like creatures, the unfortunate marine biologist broke to the surface, his face now covered in bleeding lesions. And then he was gone.

The sun was setting in a spectacular cauldron of crimson and yellow as it sank on the far horizon. A chill wind picked up as the temperature plummeted.

Kennington sat alone atop the vast, corrupted drilling platform gazing out across the expanse of sea, wondering about his chances of survival. It would be suicidal to jump into the sea— thirty miles or so from land but he would consider it if anything were to emerge from the opening nearby. He could only cling to the possibility that morning would bring with it a surveillance craft of some kind. However, even these residual hopes were instantly shattered, as in the far distance, he saw lights in the heavens, mere sparks that grew in intensity as they neared.

His mouth twisted into a wry smile as the first of the missiles zoomed unerringly towards him.

Dissolute Evolution

Alan Knott

REPORT ONE

THE ORGANISM, ROUND at one end, about 15 centimetres in diameter, was attached to a shiny, tentacled body approximately 30 centimetres long; atop was the head; snake-like, incongruous in its appearance. The eyes of the creature were as buttons, black as pitch. The nose (if it could be called such): slender, Romanesque; the mouth: cruel, and deadly.

Those who saw the thing could not help but be repulsed by it. Like a mechanical machine, it tunnelled the earth—disgorging mucus-enriched soil at the rear—100 times its size.

A demonstration subsequently staged as a prelude bestowed its attributes.

The phenomenon, it was keenly stated, would eliminate famine and all other related parallelisms: disease, pestilence, barren soil, leaving the earth enriched and cleansed ready for organic horticulture; no longer would there be a need for insecticides.

The invertebrate behaved as it should; the vast tank of earth placed at its disposal crawled with harmful pests, yet, within a matter of moments (10 to 20 at the most)—consumed. The loam passed by the creature, enriched with nutrients from the residue ready for planting.

The animal itself would die after 48 hours from lack of digestion and no longer be a potential pest in itself. Its regenerative processes thereby kept strictly under control.

Nothing like this had succeeded before. Questions abounded: How many of these genetically engineered grubs would it require to clear an acre? What of the cost to farmers? How much fertiliser would it save..? Will it breed?

The company's spokeswoman informed the assembly that a cast-off worm, kept alive after performing its duties, could, if nurtured properly, produce a more resilient strain capable of faster irrigation underground. The intent therefore was to supply both male and female components to some agriculturists in order that they may produce (under appropriate license) another strain. She looked around the vast hall:

"A good strain will return a more successful quota with selective breeding and thereby reduce costs, particularly in underdeveloped countries." When asked to expound upon this she looked down at her papers. "Well –" she hesitated. "At the present day only two in thirty thousand survive—but those that do produce a stronger element. It is therefore in the interests of agriculture to improve and develop a stronger breed."

She clarified, "The advantages far exceed any possible disadvantages. Now is the time to take the next step in human development—a revolution of sorts; all peoples of the world freed; with no hunger, no starvation; total conformity... This is within our grasp. In short—we stand on the threshold of a new paradise on Earth."

DISSOLUTE EVOLUTION

A few years pass...

—following clearance of the pests (it was programmed to feed upon) a rogue constituent did not expire within the prescribed 48-hour period as intended. Instead, it changed its feeding pattern—absorbing *normal* earthworms—and something more: it increased in size. Crossed with a female by the unscrupulous, it produced similar strains. Illegal farms bred the new entity for their own purposes and sold them cheaply to developing nations for a quick profit.

In hotter climes, an abundance of worms / insects / beetles and similar arthropods extended the life cycle of the voracious consumer and accelerated its progressive proportions.

—From tip to tail, they now measured 2.5 metres. The width—0.5 metres.

Subsidence now became a countrywide problem; in Brazil, a block of flats toppled over. To all intents and purposes, the common earthworm was defunct. The new strain had taken over completely. Outlawed, it became a pariah, and plans were drawn to have it destroyed.

Geneticists fought hard to safeguard the creation pointing out that in the developed countries it performed as it should—remained comparatively small and lived alongside the indigenous earthworm without interference. The current cycle—then in existence—gradually died out in the Western democracies due to prohibition. In less fortunate climes, however, the mutated species proliferated and had to be tracked down one by one; then exterminated with flame-throwers, in order to avoid the excessive use of biological sprays.

...Then, an episode occurred in the U.K.

REPORT TWO

A farmer ploughs 4 acres of arable land—the last thing he envisages is to uncover is a tentacle measuring four metres long by two metres round. The genotype wraps its intestinal body around his right arm, dragging him off the vehicle. The weight is so great that it presses him into the soil; his cries for help muzzled by the tunnelling vermiform. It is a long duration before his half-buried body is discovered unconsciousness and rushed to the nearest hospital.

The doctors—unsure of the cause—decide a period of rest and natural recuperation to be the best choice. The withered arm puzzles them—it is almost as though rigor mortis had already set in.

Uncontrolled, the condition gradually spreads around the shoulders onto the chest and finally reaches the heart. Remedial action fails. Pronounced dead, the body is passed to his estranged wife. She takes the corpse and arranges burial alongside their only son in the extensive rear garden of the house she occupies.

*

In the summer months this stone-built dwelling proved very cold. Although a large cherry tree sheltered the accommodation, it blocked direct sunlight. The front had exposure, but when the sun moved to the west, the heat was gone by mid-morning.

During this time the householder slept fitfully in the rear bedroom, her mind clouded with dreams of her late husband—of the times they had, including the bad ones. She still loved him and somehow felt she was responsible for their divided marriage and blamed her own selfishness.

While she slept, something dug down in the garden—down and down—until it reached the coffin, prising open the lid and pushing it back; exposing something sticky, a tentacle of mucus succeeded by a snake-like face—the eyelids missing, revealing coal-black pupils and dripping lips that moved awkwardly as though trying to speak.

The nocturnal switchback writhed upward as if blindly searching for the light. A dull yellow with greyish rings, a metre apart along the trunk; the skin, although quite hard, cracked open, spitting like red-hot fat under the glow of the full moon.

The veneered coffin broke as the thing pushed upward—a long body wriggling from the bowels of the earth—seemingly never-ending; unwinding like some foul smelling intestinal discharge; crushing the newly buried loved-one against the walls of the burrow. The ground quivered as it tore past him; spiralling around the base of the cherry tree; using this as a prop; sliding its moist body along until it reached the top of the branches; swaying in mid-air. Until, eventually, it touched the roof of the house.

The immense weight dislodged the guttering—bringing down the fall pipe, wrenching several slates in its wake, the tip of the chimney pot sent flying.

In an effort to find the earth, it penetrated the roof, dragging the tail behind still endlessly unwinding from the despoiled grave—boring through the loft, bedroom, lounge, and below into the cellar.

Once the head had buried itself sufficiently in the grit of the cellar floor the tail followed swiftly with frightening speed. All that remained was a dilapidated building: choking dust, dislodged plaster, regurgitated earth smothered in slime that had safeguarded the denuded burial site. A witness called the fire brigade but combat units brandishing flame-throwers came on to the scene.

Mechanical diggers dug into the soil—unearthing what appeared to be a mining tunnel.

As the team of specialists scrambled in, taking with them high-powered lanterns and burning torches, a guard removed the body of the deceased.

No matter what dangers the hunters faced, they pressed on, determined to find their target, for this thing threatened the lives of many. The excavation left behind by the beast was so large that it allowed the men to proceed along its passageway without the need to lower their heads. The front one established that they had already walked a mile and would soon approach the city boundary.

He brushed aside dripping slivers of phlegm that the worm had spewed in its train. "This sticky stuff won't hold the roof aloft for very long... Let's hope we can find the aberrant bastard before it drops... There's no telling how far this thing may have travelled."

Another of the disparate four spoke up: "It's the biggest one we've encountered so far, exceptional. We are quite clearly dealing with something truly abnormal; we should go back and consult with the professor."

The words sank in his throat: the worm had doubled back; now it challenged them burrowing in from the side.

The sound of burning heat rushes past their ears as they turn the flame-throwers fully on. The ground beneath them trembles. The mucilage-covered walls collapse—systematically targeted, the earth gives way and they tumbled into the deep cavity of a sinkhole.

Plunged screaming into the unknown they are gripped by a sea of organisations that seize them with teeth sharper than scalpels of steel...

"Four men dead. This thing must be quelled as soon as possible—eliminated with quick despatch before it has time to strike again," General Hard commanded.

The professor informed the group that the growth cannot be stopped metabolically, "It will continue to grow with each month that passes..."

The enormity of the crises is such that no announcements are authorised and a blackout is placed on the press for 48 hours.

Fully briefed of the dangers, equipped with the latest tools that technology has to offer, the disposal squad made ready with desperate urgency; they were the elite of the elite...

During the early hours on a Monday morning, it struck; ascending through the flooring of an apartment block. The massive body, now measuring no less than ten metres in length and thicker than three houses abreast, pushed aside the walls as though they were constructed of Lego bricks. The very cells of the creature were visible due to the enormity of the increased magnitude; the abnormal head wavering in the hazy sun as it careered out of control struggling to free itself from the confines of the structure. As the beast rose to unprecedented height, the high tower broke apart; debris showered the pavement; the few people who were around fled in panic.

Motivated by superior force, it dragged its huge, naked body from the wreckage, smashing and shattering everything in its path—parked cars, supermarkets, department stores, office buildings, churches; including the gothic cathedral, which had survived many a tempest over the centuries. Nothing sacred spared.

Along the municipal bypass, a steady rivulet streamed. When the creature shook its mighty head, dust adhered to the mucus coagulating it to adhesive mud. Civilians; commerce, public transport and traffic; the very heart of the city brought to a standstill...

Wearing breathing protectors, 'Operation Crack-Force' is put into action: they presumed to subdue the mutation with a special gas that evaporated quickly. Flame-throwers bore upon the tail in an effort to turn its head

"We must force the head this way to fire the gas."

"Maybe we can burn it in half instead?"

"No—No!" the professor pushes forward. "That will create two monsters instead of one. It must be subdued with tranquilliser darts or the gaseous ether."

Ten canisters were unloaded from the truck. It proved impossible to reach the head with so much rubble blocking the highway; the only other option was to scorch the tail.

The pungent smell from burning tissue proved intense; so much so that had they not worn the masks, they would have choked from the sulphurous smoke.

"—It's turning! Coming this way! —"

The animal had breathed in the toxin. Several more canisters followed in quick succession. The head rose vigorously; and the nostrils flared. Then it struck: downwards; twisting; the teeth slicing through concrete, snapping the thick pavement blocks.

"I believe it's slowing—The gas must have done the trick! Call the professor over."

"It's incredible." He surveyed the prostrate form in the underlying clay. "By all the laws that govern nature this creature is an impossibility." Then he indicated that he was going to paralyse it with a genetic innovation—a little invention of his own that would immobilise it. "It will then stay helpless for quite a while and can be dissected."

Taking care, he sliced crosswise cutting open the vast body of the invertebrate coiled in a spiral to fit the available space in the sanitised laboratory. A thin sliver was taken and placed under the microscope:

"The cells seem very excited—cancerous, even."

"Do you think it wise to cut it up into so many small pieces before we know for sure it truly is dead?"

"*Not dead*," the professor emphasised to his chosen associate. "Only paralysed. I appreciate it might be dangerous—all the pieces could evolve into individual worms should it revive before we have time to complete the examination. However, we can discover more while it still lives."

He brought forward a glass box. Fleshy mutations writhed within the enclosure; freak maggots with long, pointed snouts tracking the air. "These will devour the pieces when we are done."

While the professor and his handpicked team worked on the dissection, the city cleared away the mess left by the renegade and the populace returned to a careless life of repetitive routine.

When something is at odds with reality such as this, then the tenuous thread that connects the mind to outside influences may have slipped. In this respect, Professor Demurer became uneasy.

"Are you OK, Professor?"

"Yes, I—I think so, I'm just a little confused, I have something to think over."

His own precepts now came back to haunt him: that it is possible to detect whether a basis for authenticity is real or not by the rendition of some out-of-place element.

Work continued long into the night; by the time they were finished, it was nearing dawn.

"We'll call it a day—*or night*. Freeze these few pieces for later inspection and revive the mutations tomorrow."

The inner security door slid open and was automatically sealed when the professor and his associate stepped over into the intervening space; then the outer lead door opened, slipping shut behind them as they entered the corridor...

With the imposition of the blackout now lifted, the evening news carried a full report of the incident. Maintaining the confidence of the public was now all-important—the pressure on Professor Demurer and his colleagues to find a solution quickly became intense. The premature release of the mutated grubs into the worm's burrow bore fruit: all the siblings in the cavern were impregnated by the parasites and the Professor was able to announce the termination of the species.

After a while larvae were approved for distribution, and officialdom authorised delivery to all danger areas with instructions for them to be released whenever a rogue element appeared.

With the gradual destruction of the genotype, it seemed the problem might have been resolved until an insidious side effect developed... insects—the size of rats—suddenly surfaced within the confines of previous encounters. Genetic information of the genitor had entered their DNA and the Professor and his team were at a loss to explain the phenomenon.

Some time later they realised the remains of the vermiform had trapped oxygen within its inner linings enabling the larvae to pupate.

Demurer's tone became distracted: "The larvae are growing disproportionately. They may have already entered the food chain; flying insects that feed upon the grubs will process the contagion and undoubtedly spread it through pollination; creating a dark cloak upon our atmosphere. A poisonous force we take for granted has brought this about—*oxygen*—"

With the advent of spring, birds fed upon the newly born insects: caterpillars grew larger than they should; brown woodlice big as fists gorged upon rotting rose buds sucked dry by aphids. Ladybirds broad as a thumbnail feasted upon them. Every crawling thing doubled in size.

The gatherings of wasps and bees droned noisily in accordance with their mass. Gardens, woods, forests, meadows formed a formidable hazard. The transformation of the small had travelled far. There was no turning back.

With the worms now eliminated, the remaining grubs were defunct, having no means of reproduction. Conversely, the rise in oxygen levels raised the humidity. The human species had to adapt to the new situation their elected overlords had created. Forest and bush fires became commonplace, leading to yet another rise in temperature levels.

Invasive houseflies multiplied. Other pests grew alongside them: cockroaches and those associated with hotter climes— equatorial dragonflies; mosquitoes, millipedes; locusts; a plague of outsized invertebrates—

Current insecticides were useless in coping with the swamp-like conditions. In the aftermath, Humankind tried to correct the mutations but the arthropod population continued to multiply resilient to any new pathogen. In order to combat the problem the production of natural predators—such as birds—were *re-sized*, spreading disproportionate excreta—in a world overrun by parasitic monsters. Every window remained tight shut; doing little to protect them or their children from the inexorable rise of the genetic mutations.

A leap in dissolute evolution had begun...

Little Helpers

John Grant

EVEN THEIR MOTHERS, if the two knights hadn't long ago murdered their mothers, would have balked at calling Sir Gawm and Sir Madder the finest, most upstanding bastions of chivalry. But they *were* knights, and proud of the fact. It distinguished them from the peasantry, whose allotted purpose in life was to be *used* by knights like Sir Gawm and Sir Madder.

They were also knights on the lam. It was a state to which they were fairly accustomed, the peasantry, annoyingly, having different ideas about that allotted purpose in life. A few days ago the two knights had been comfortably ensconced in a tavern, their bellies full of coarse food and the astringent liquid the folk in these parts called ale, pleasantly tired after an evening's ravishing, when the subject of payment had come up.

"The ravishing's on the 'ouse," explained the landlord with measured courtesy, "but you'll have to pay for the victuals."

Pay? They were *knights!*

Sir Gawm, his sword in his hand in a flash, struck the impertinent cur down where he stood. Sir Madder neatly caught the full tankard that fell from the man's lifeless hand, and drained it, at the same time using his free hand to tug his own sword—the mighty golden blade he called Gutwallower—from its scabbard. All around the smoky room, men paused in the act of rising from their seats.

"And so shall be served all those who dare besmirch the honored name of Gawm!" cried the knight, the landlord's blood dripping from his blade.

"There are," said a small boy somewhere in the back, "only two of you. And we are five and twenty."

The man nearest to them cackled toothlessly. There was only menace in the sound.

"He has a point," said Madder. "Perhaps we should leave."

They'd escaped the village with only a few scars and assumed that would be the end of it, but a few hours later they heard a din from far behind them and realised they were being pursued.

"They just don't know their place in the world, do they?" said Sir Madder. He and Sir Gawm, astride their underfed battle steeds, were at the crest of a low hill. They could see their pursuers like a tangle of ants in the distance.

That had been four days and many leagues ago, and the two knights were now fairly sure the villagers had abandoned the chase. The fugitives were also very hungry. They'd paused at an isolated farmhouse the day before yesterday, but the foodstocks they'd found had been meager and they'd been too nervous for any but the most perfunctory ravishing. Now their empty stomachs were growling again.

Sir Madder pulled from its sheath by his saddle the scroll map he'd been consulting from time to time in hopes of keeping track of where they were.

"The next hamlet we come to," he said, peering at the inked

parchment, "is called Karmlawth."

He tended to keep the fact that he could read from all but Gawm, for fear of being laughed at as French.

"Karmlawth?" said Gawm.

"Big place, by local standards." Madder scrutinised the annotations running alongside the illustrated strip. "A dozen houses, maybe even more. And a manor. I'd say it's the home of a kinglet."

The companions weren't much impressed by kings, who were two-a-penny in this area of the country. The population was quite sparsely spread, so it was open to anyone to annex a tract of land and set himself up as a king. Not like knights. You had to be born into the right family, one in whose veins the blood ran rich and blue, if you were to qualify as a knight.

"There'll be grub a-plenty," said Sir Gawm with a grin.

"And ale and mead to be quaffed until our stomachs burst," agreed Sir Madder, carefully returning the map to its storage place.

"And wenches."

"All the good things of life," said Sir Madder, "and only two or three hours away if we make good speed. We should be there by nightfall."

The horses were even wearier than the men, but they allowed themselves to be persuaded into a reluctant trot.

Karmlawth lay between hills that sheltered it on three sides, as if the hamlet were being held in a gloved hand. There was a small, clear-watered river, barely more than a stream, running alongside the cluster of houses Sir Madder had seen on his map. Two rickety-looking bridges linked the houses to a large, ill defined field where sheep, chickens and a couple of cattle mingled amiably. A little distance away from the town, on the far side of the field, there was another hill which the two knights guessed, from the regularity of its shape, must be one of the burial mounds the dignitaries of the Old Folk had built themselves.

They wondered if it had been looted.

They wondered if they could loot it.

The knights were accustomed to being challenged by sentries as they approached settlements even as modest as this one. Here, however, the only welcome they got was from a couple of filthy-faced urchins in torn clothing who scampered up to them, showing no fear and very little curiosity.

"Where you from?" said the little girl, somewhat older than the other child, who they guessed must be her brother.

"From a land beyond the seas," said Sir Madder airily, waving an arm to indicate vast and exotic distance.

The girl looked him up and down. "Well, you're here now."

They conceded this was true.

"We have traveled many leagues, and are tired to our bones," explained Sir Gawm.

"Then you'll be staying at the big house," the boy piped up. "Dad always offers lodgings to strangers."

The knights allowed themselves a sly grin. They had few

greater allies than the laws of hospitality, in those parts of the country that observed them. Clearly this was one such part. There'd assuredly be feasting galore tonight, and without the cumbrance of a tavern bill to pay—or, as was the knights' habit, not pay.

"Tell your da... the king that we are two worthy knights questing for the source of all virtue," said Sir Madder.

The girl looked at him incredulously.

"Just lead us to him," said Gawm.

She and her little brother trotted ahead of the horses along a beaten track that led between the drystone cottages. A few of the villagers stared at them from glassless windows, but most seemed completely devoid of concern about their presence. Within minutes the knights were in front of the great oaken doorways of the king's manor. The girl and her brother melted away around the side of the building. The manor seemed built of stone, like the cottages in the hamlet, but the walls had been covered in brown clay and the windows of both lower and upper stories had glass. A standard the knights had never seen before flew from a pole on the roof.

The horses moved restlessly.

Sir Madder dismounted. "I've never known a place with so little interest in visitors," he said, raising his fist to beat against the door.

Which opened just before he struck.

"Greetings," said the figure standing there in the cool gloom. He was tall and lightly built, dressed like the knights in military garb of leather and serge. But his jerkin was polished until it shone like a horsechestnut and the rest of his garments were clean, marked only by the occasional neatly stitched repair. The two strangers were all too uncomfortably aware that, beside him, their own nobility was scarcely apparent.

"Greetings," responded Sir Gawm, who was still on horse-back. "We are two weary and dusty wayfarers who... "

"Yes, I know that. The children told me. Come on in. I'll have someone fetch your horses to the stable. Shut the door behind you."

Clanking, they followed him down a long passageway lit only by narrow windows high overhead. Threadbare tapestries orna-mented the otherwise austere walls to either side; the hangings moved sluggishly like woken ghosts when the knights' shoul-ders brushed against them.

At the far end of the passage the man opened a door onto a brightly lit kitchen. The day outside had become cool as even-ing fell, but in this room the warmth was almost painful. At one end of it a great fireplace framed a roaring blaze. An improba-bly fat woman clad in black was doing something to a pot that perched precariously in the flames. Along each of the longer walls was a row of five sconces holding eagerly burning torches. The two children who'd led the knights through the village were sitting on one of two benches pulled up to a long, roughly hewn table in the middle of the floor. With them was a sweetly slen-der woman whom the knights guessed must be their mother, her finely combed ash-pale hair drawn together behind her head and then cascading down her back.

"Gwen," said their host—the kinglet, he must be—"here are our guests for the night."

She looked up at them with a smile the two knights could have drowned in. "Welcome to our home."

Sir Gawm found himself bowing deeply. Out of the corner of his eye he saw Sir Madder doing the same. He couldn't recall the last time either had paid their respects to a mere woman in such a way.

"It'll be just us"—she gestured at the two children and her husband—"and Doreen, of course." The large woman by the fire turned a round and shining face toward them, then continued tending to her task. "And Merle, Arctos's battlemaster. We'll have stew, as usual, and our own homemade mead to wash it down. No," said Gwen over a rising chorus from the children, "there'll be no mead for you two. The last time you tried some, Harry, you were puking for a week. I thought I'd never get the stink out of the house. Now, you and Daisy go and get your faces and your hands washed and tidy yourselves up to look your best for our visitors."

The children departed, chattering.

Sir Gawm cleared his throat. "Strong stuff, this mead, is it?"

"As strong as need be," said Arctos. His face, which had been near expressionless 'til now, broke into a smile.

He excused himself and left to fetch a tun of it and to tell some unseen servant about the horses. Doreen decreed her pot of stew could be left to bubble on its own for long enough that she could show the two fine gentlemen where their room was, and the bath. She waddled briskly along a trio of passages and up a flight of stairs despite its looking far too narrow to accommodate her breadth. Soon, with a promise to bring them bath water as soon as it could be heated, she was gone.

"My friend," said Sir Madder, as soon as he was sure Doreen was out of earshot, "we seem to have fallen on our feet. This place is ripe for the plucking."

Gawm sniggered. "There's not a scratch on Arctos's battle jerkin, did you notice? He's fought nothing fiercer in that than a bad cold, I'd say. He won't last two seconds against our fine steel."

"That wife of his," said Madder.

Neither of them said anything for a few moments, words proving inadequate.

Gawm broke the silence once sufficient moisture had returned to his mouth. "Plenty of mead," he said. "Milk and mutton, eggs and poultry. And did you smell the baking bread as we came into the house?"

Madder dumped his weapons and his jerkin in the corner and threw himself down on one of the room's two trestle beds, which hardly creaked at all. "Heaven on earth," he pronounced.

"Of course," said Gawm, "there's that battlemaster of his. What did Gwen say his name was?"

"Can't remember." Madder yawned. "Wake me when it's my turn to use the bath."

*

It was certainly *cozy* in the kitchen, the two knights had to concede that. The children prattled, as children do. Doreen dolloped out great steaming helpings of green-grey stew, and there was copious coarse-grained bread to go with it. Gwen smiled serenely at all around her. Arctos's battlemaster had yet to arrive; a space had been left for him at the end of the table opposite to where Arctos sat. Gwen and the children were on one of the benches that ran down the table's length, Sir Madder and Sir Gawm on the other, Doreen between the two men. The only grumble was the size of the goblets the mead came in. Even though their host replenished them frequently from the big bronze jug in the center of the table, it somehow didn't seem the *same* as full-blooded quaffing from a tankard the size of a bull's head, which was surely how quaffing ought to be done.

Things would be different once the knights had eliminated Arctos and taken Karmlawth over.

Which wasn't the way Arctos himself saw the future, not at all. In his slow, gentle tones he enervated the conversation by telling of his plans.

"The people of this island have been tormented too long by bandits and brigands," he was saying. "Rogues have dragged knighthood into the swamps of disgrace. They've sown fear and misery far and wide, so that people hardly dare to leave their homes at night, most especially the womenfolk."

"Ah, yes, the womenfolk," said Sir Madder, leaning forward as if eager to hear more of the madman's pratings.

"And yet," said Arctos, holding upright his dagger with a juicy lump of dripping mutton impaled upon it, "and yet there *are* fine and honorable knights among all the scum. Yourselves, I am sure"—he looked as if he almost meant it—"and others like you. Gentlemen who are as sick as I am of all the suffering and evil."

"But how do you plan to change things?" said Sir Gawm. "Surely it's only human nature that this should be so?"

"I've sent emissaries throughout the land, finding virtuous and valorous knights and directing them here to Karmlawth. Together, once they are all gathered here, we shall regrow chivalry, make courage and honesty once more the marks of a true knight, render—"

There was a noise at the door.

"That must be Merle," said Gwen. It was clear she'd heard her husband's tales too many times before.

Sir Madder and Sir Gawm had expected the battlemaster to be as big and as burly and as scarred as they were themselves, but instead the figure who slipped into the kitchen was as slight as a boy. His hands were delicate and white, with long tapering fingers. His hair was rust-red and cut to the shoulders. His face was as smooth as a virgin bride's.

With difficulty Sir Gawm repressed a derisive chuckle. He and Sir Madder had agreed to wait until they'd assessed the battlemaster before finalising too many plans about making Karmlawth their own. They needn't have been so cautious. This man could hardly be out of his teens. He looked more like a cleric than a warrior.

As Arctos performed brief introductions, Merle bowed to the two knights, one after the other. He had grey eyes, oddly pale beneath his red brows. He had thin lips.

When Doreen put his dish of stew in front of him, he acknowledged her with a nod.

Taciturn, thought Sir Gawm.

The mead was beginning to go to Sir Gawm's head, even though he seemed not to have drunk nearly enough of it to affect him. Arctos mustn't have been joking when he talked about the stuff carrying a kick. It was sweet, too, warm and delicious and rounded as if you could feed it to a baby. Gawm looked forward to the time when Karmlawth's mead cellars would be entirely at the disposal of himself and Sir Madder. Presumably it was Gwen who did the mead-making—her or Doreen. Once that weakling Arctos was out of the way...

"And so you're King Arctos's fine battlemaster, are you?" Sir Madder was saying. His voice was a little louder than usual, his face ruddy. He was speaking his words with controlled clarity, a sign, as Sir Gawm knew only too well, that his old drinking companion was likewise becoming smitten by the booze.

Merle looked up from his meal and nodded, then returned to eating.

"And you've fought a good many battles, then?"

"He's fought enough," said Arctos with that mildness of his.

"But where"—Sir Madder swept a magnanimous arm, almost brushing Gwen's face on the far side of the table—"but where are all your scars?"

Merle shrugged and paused from his eating to pull a piece of vegetable fiber from between his preternaturally white, even-spaced teeth.

"I've always believed," said Arctos in the kind of quiet voice people less drunk than the two knights might have had the sense to fear, "that boasting of your scars is like boasting about the battles you've lost."

Madder ignored him. "And where are the armies you lead into battle?" He opened his eyes wide and stared around him in mock perplexity. "All we saw as we came through the village were women and children and old men who've reached the babbling age. If there are fifty souls in all of Karmlawth, I'll bite my own nose off. Who have these battles been against?"

The battlemaster looked up again. The grey eyes seemed bored. Still he said nothing.

"Does he *speak*?" said Sir Madder to Arctos with heavy irony.

"When he needs to," the man said, a hard edge starting to become audible in his voice.

As he reached for his annoyingly small goblet of mead, Sir Gawm recognised that Arctos was filling with resentment against the local laws of hospitality. These bound hosts to offer travelers lodging and friendship and civility; somehow they were always less binding on the guests.

"Have you ever had a woman?" said Madder directly to the battlemaster.

Merle didn't even deign to react to the question.

"Gwen here," Madder continued. "She's as beautiful a woman as you'll gaze upon if you journey to the farthest corners of the world. Don't you ever dream of finding yourself in her bed?"

"Children," said Gwen quietly, "it's time for you to retire for the night."

Harry and Daisy slipped off their bench without argument and crept from the room.

Gawm looked at Arctos and could see the fury mounting within the man. Good. His anger would make him all the more vulnerable when the time came for Gawm and Madder to strike. Gwen, too, was clearly holding in her wrath with an effort; there was a flush beneath that porcelain-clear skin that drove Gawm's desire for her to an even higher pitch. By contrast, Merle remained absolutely calm, as if he'd heard nothing of the insults Madder was pitching his way—no, as if he'd heard them, all right, but only as one might hear the buzzing of a fly.

Madder seemed unaware of anything happening around him. His hands outstretched on the wooden table in front of him, he was still staring at Merle.

"Or are you frightened by the very idea?"

A moment later he was gazing at Arctos's dagger, quivering in the table in front of him, neatly between one of his fingers and the next. It had appeared there so swiftly that neither Gawm nor Madder had seen their host's hand move. Gawm could see it dawning on Madder that the blade could have just as easily punched right through his hand on the way to embedding itself in the wood.

"You are our guests, and so I may not kill you," hissed Arctos. "But at the same time I cannot permit you to continue insulting my dearest friend and loyalest lieutenant. You question his courage, and yet he alone in all the world has been able to face down the Grindle, the crawler of the mound, to turn aside its breath of flame, to make it dim its lights until they're merely candles illuminating the night so he can see his way. This is the man you think is craven? Cease your vile outpourings. If you've had more mead than your head can accommodate, go to bed and sleep the fumes off. Otherwise, just hold your peace."

"I think my comrade is weary from the journey," said Gawm. "Long travels with too little food can do this to a man. Let me see him to his bed. Tomorrow, I'm sure he'll seek to apologise to you all, and especially"—a nod to the fair Gwen—"to you, my good lady."

"Will you be needing hot-water bottles?" said Doreen, seemingly oblivious to all the tensions in the room.

Sir Gawm found himself being prodded awake. Through the window he could see a three-quarter moon in a crystal-clear, star-studded sky.

"Go away," he said. "What do you want? I thought you'd be dead by now."

Sir Madder chuckled in the darkness. "I slept an hour, but since then I've been too drunk to sleep any more. It's time for us to engage in a little mischief, my friend."

"Can't it wait 'til morning?"

"I've been watching from the window. Not many minutes ago, that young fool Merle bade his goodnights to Arctos and the lady and headed for home. He lives over by that mound we saw on the far side of where the animals graze."

"So?"

"So Karmlawth's only two warriors"—Madder snorted—"are separated now. We can pick 'em off one after the other."

"There may be men in the village," Gawm observed. "Stronger men than these two. Men toughened up by long days' labour with the plow."

"I think not. You saw them. Besides, you know how villagers are. They'll do whatever anyone in the manor tells them to. They won't care if it's us or Arctos dishing out the orders."

"Doing the ravishing."

"That too. Though I can't see either Arctos or Merle being of the ravishing persuasion—more the kind to warble poetry at a wench until she lifts her skirt to get them to shut up. But enough of these idle words! The night is wearing on. Get up, man. Get up!"

So Sir Gawm clambered off his bed and pissed in a pot and buckled his belt around his belly. His sword slid smoothly in and out of its scabbard. His ax hefted just right as he tested it a couple of times against the room's dusty moonlit air before putting it into its own small holster, right next to where his sword hung.

He'd assumed they'd deal with Arctos first, although it occurred to him he had no notion where the house's occupants slept. Sir Madder had other ideas anyway, leading the way outside the house to where there was absolute stillness in the moonlight. No lamps burned in the village, the cottages seeming as lifeless as scattered knucklebones. There was no sound except the quiet music of the stream. It wasn't cold—their breath didn't steam in front of them—but Gawm shivered nonetheless.

Trying not to let their weapons clank, the two knights picked their way quietly between the cottages toward one of the small bridges they'd seen as they arrived. Gawm paused halfway across the span to stare down into the dark water beneath. His head was still achy from the mead and, if it hadn't been for Sir Madder's urging, he'd have gone down to the streamside to bathe his face in the coldness and drink deep.

"Hurry *up!*" said Madder. Even though he'd whispered, the words sounded very loud in the silver moonlight.

They made slow progress across the field, avoiding animal droppings as best they could. The moon behind them was bright enough that it was as if they were following their shadows. Here and there around them somnolent beasts snickered or squawked, disturbed by their passage. Once a cow suddenly arose directly in front of them and moved away a few yards, mooing softly, leaving only its sharny odor behind. Gawm wondered if the villagers stationed dogs out here and, if not, why the domesticated animals weren't plagued by foxes and wolves.

He wished he hadn't thought about wolves. The packs rarely ventured so far south as this, but a rogue solo wolf might. All of a sudden the moonlight seemed to be less an illumination than a cloak.

Ahead of them the burial mound, if that was what it was, was blocking out more and more of the stars. Now that they were coming closer to it, Gawm could distinguish a brighter patch on its flank, as if there were a doorway there leading to a dimly lit chamber.

"He doesn't just live *by* it," he said in a low voice to Sir Madder. "He lives right *in* it."

"Who cares?" his companion replied. "By morning he won't be living *anywhere*, so what difference does it make?"

They grew more cautious in their movements as they neared the mound. It was all very well, back in the safety of the manor, to joke about the callowness of Arctos's so-called battlemaster, about how wet behind the ears he was with his smooth and girlish cheeks, but out here in the moonlight the two knights were conscious that Merle was an unknown quantity. There are limits to how far looks can deceive, and they hardly expected Merle to transform into a berserker, like the Norsemen sometimes did. But he might put up a far tougher fight than they anticipated.

They were right beside the mound now, creeping along toward that brighter smudge Gawm had seen from afar. Madder led the way, with Gawm close behind him. Some light spilled out from the aperture onto the stubbly grass, but barely enough to show against the moonlight. The animals had ceased their noises and the stream was too far away to be heard. It was as if the two knights were alone in the world.

Silently they drew their swords.

"Are we sure he's alone in there?" breathed Gawm.

"We'll never know 'til we discover."

Gawm was still trying to work that one out when Sir Madder gave his famous battle cry and leaped forward, turning to face the opening into the mound.

The battle cry changed into a scream and then died.

In a moment Sir Gawm was at his friend's side, his breath coming with difficulty.

He found himself staring into not a doorway but a vast pair of jaws, wide open, perhaps twice the height of a man from top to bottom and the same distance wide. All around the circumference were hundreds or thousands of fearsomely sharp-looking teeth, coated with a greenish liquid from which, here and there, came little puffs of smoke. At each of the tooth-tips guttered a fierce-looking white flame. In the instant that Sir Gawm glimpsed the interior of that dreadful maw, he saw one thing that scared him almost more than everything else.

The small flames erupting from the wicked points along the upper arch of teeth were burning *downward*.

Then a forked grey tongue flickered, just the once, and Sir Gawm felt rather than saw his old companion-at-arms being plucked from where he slumped.

The jaws slammed shut with a terrifying finality.

Sir Madder was gone. Only his sword was left, the mighty blade Gutwallower, lying there on the rough grass.

Sir Gawm was not entirely a coward. Put a sword in his hand and he'd face up to a rabble. He'd fought his battles and he bore the scars to prove it. But this was something entirely beyond his ken. He'd heard of wyrms, but always thought the tales were merely dreams of drunkards. Yet what other kind of monster could lie beneath the hill like this? Could the child-faced battle-master have adopted a wyrm, if wyrm it was, as his familiar? Was this why Arctos valued him so highly? Because he was a wizard who could make even great monsters bend to his will?

And where *was* Merle?

So lost in his panicked thoughts was he that Sir Gawm hardly had time for fear. He knew he was as dead as if he'd already joined Sir Madder in the monster's guts.

He was jolted back to alertness by the slow opening of the enormous jaws, and the gale of hot, noisome breath that poured forth.

Sir Gawm prepared to be seized by that lethal tongue, chewed by those countless teeth.

Instead, Arctos's battlemaster Merle picked his way gingerly over the daggered fence of the creature's lower jaw and took a couple of paces toward where Gawm shakily stood.

Gawm dropped his sword, his ax after it. He spread his hands to show his surrender.

"Your friend was a bad man," said Merle.

Gawm realised this was the first time he'd heard the

battlemaster talk. Quite light, not deep, the voice could have been mistaken for a woman's, but really it seemed neither male nor female. Gawm was reminded of how Arctos's voice, too, held this mildness.

"And so," Merle continued, "are you."

"I'm a knight!"

"A knight who brings shame to knighthood."

Sir Gawm couldn't refute it.

"The difference between your companion and yourself," Merle said, "is that you're aware of your own corruption. There are times you've woken in the dark and heard the screams of all the innocents you've murdered, the women you've defiled, and you've known guilt."

"I—Yes."

"So, where your friend was of no use to the world except as fodder, you, Sir Gawm, may be worth sparing."

"I'm not going to beg."

"I wouldn't want you to. If you were so craven as to abase yourself in hopes of saving your sorry life, you'd be no better than Madder was."

"What is it you want?"

Perhaps, just perhaps, Sir Gawm was going to live through this.

"I want you to tell the world what happened here."

"You do? But then kings will send their armies here to destroy your monster. There'll be thousands of men like Sir Madder and myself—like us and worse. Things won't go well for the folk of Karmlawth. They'll be put to the sword, trampled underfoot, burned alive for warriors' merriment. There won't be one stone left atop another of Arctos's manor. As for Gwen and the children..."

Merle laughed. "I'm not afraid of that. It won't happen."

"Believe me. I've seen the way that armies act."

The battlemaster made a small gesture with his hand. The subject was closed. Gawm knew better than to argue further. One of them would be proved right, in the due course of time. It was a cruel world full of crueler people. If Gawm spread the tale abroad of what had happened here, it was as sure as God's own goodness that Karmlawth would be razed to the ground before the year was out. There'd be only death here. They'd build fires around the mound until the wyrm either baked alive or came out to face a deadly hail of spears and arrows...

Perhaps I should do these fools a kindness and tell no one.

"You must tell the tale wherever you go," said Merle, as if Gawm had spoken his thought aloud. "And you must tell the people you tell it to to tell it in their turn, until the whole land knows of Karmlawth, and the dreams of a fine man called Arctos, and the goodness of his wife called Gwen. The tale will get all muddled, of course, and more muddled with every fresh telling, but perhaps the heart of it will live. That's the task I lay upon you, Sir Gawm. That's the price of your life."

Yesterday Gawm would have promised with his hand held to his heart to do the battlemaster's bidding, then blithely forgotten his oath as soon as he was out of sight beyond the next hill.

But now he knew, knew so deep within his bones that it was as if he'd been born with the knowledge, that he'd keep any promise he made. Merle was truly a wizard—for only a wizard could thrall a wyrm into being his helper. Wizards could sense the deeds of men no matter how great a distance intervened. Wizards could take the forms of venomous night creatures to exact their revenge, or raise the dead from their graves to do the same. No one broke a pledge he'd made to a wizard—no one did that and lived.

Perhaps a wizard could even beat off the armies that would assuredly come to exterminate the monster.

Sir Gawm went down on one knee. "My lord," he said.

"Go," said the battlemaster, turning away from him.

When Gawm looked up, the side of the hill was closed.

As the knight made his slow way back across the field, it seemed completely empty. The cattle and sheep and chickens were gone, even their droppings. When he reached the stream, he had to wade through it; there was no sign of the two unsteady bridges he'd seen before. As he climbed out of the water, leggings dripping, feet freezing, and approached the little village, he found there was no village there to be approached. Arctos's manor was gone, too. Where it had stood there were only the knights' horses, too bone weary to run away. The cupped hand of the hills held nothing, nothing but himself and the two steeds.

He looked back across the empty field. On its far side,

bathed in silver, the beast's mound still loomed. It was perhaps the only real thing he and Sir Madder had known since their arrival.

Gawm shuddered.

Everything else had been illusion and magic, the people as much as the stone cottages and the lowing cows and the giggling children. As he hauled himself up into the saddle, he thought about wizardry, and the ways of wizards, and who wizards were.

Merle was no wizard. Merle was just another illusion given the semblance of a man by the true wizard, the one who dwelled within the mound.

The wyrm who wanted the land to be saved.

What had Arctos called it? The Grindle.

Sir Gawm turned his horse toward where the roadway ran, and coaxed the beast into a slow walk. There were places to go and a tale to tell.

And who knew how long the tale might live?

The Tarantata

Richard Mosses

THE DOORS OF the plane opened and heat rippled through it. I had to stop and catch a breath before continuing up the aisle, my rucksack, packed with a few days' clothes and essential toiletries, hugged high to my chest. As I approached the door, the light was already blinding. I squinted through the haze of fumes and crossed the runway to the shade of the terminal. The airport was a world apart from so many serviced by small airlines. Air-con cool, polished marble chic and bright neon travesty, the terminal looked as if it had been opened yesterday. I could smell fresh plastic and new carpeting above the ozone of the air conditioners.

I got into the small Fiat I'd hired. My sunglasses blotted out a bit of the light. Using my phone, I navigated through a bustling town, and then headed south along the coast on a pristine highway. How many more of my preconceptions would be blown away? I might as well have stayed in Glasgow and visited an Italian restaurant.

The arid limestone landscape of Puglia seemed as alien as Mars. The Adriatic Sea stretched out dark blue beneath an azure sky. San Laurentius was an old fishing village of narrow streets, an ancient harbour, and stray dogs—the picture postcard Italy I'd been looking for. I endured a long, warm greeting from my landlady before I retired to the cool gloom of the two rooms that would be my home for the next week or two.

Once late afternoon arrived I decided to take a closer look at the village. It was like visiting Portmeirion, a Welsh village modelled on places like this. A Mini Moke could tear round the corner and a former spy, dressed in a white-trimmed black blazer, would interrogate me brusquely on the identity of Number 1.

San Laurentius had fewer pastel shades and palatial buildings, being whitewashed and more humble. There didn't seem to be a point where one building ended and another began, each side of each street was one long intermingled terrace of apartments reached by staircases. Tall narrow windows opened onto small balconies enclosed with wrought iron.

A group of kids played football in one street, scrambling in a free for all over a scuffed leather football while older boys looked on, smoking cigarettes. Now and again a noisy moped disrupted the game. The arrival of its occupants led to either outcry or a hail of welcomes.

I stood out a mile: tall, pale and clearly not dressed like a local—my lightest summer clothes were still too heavy for this climate. While the kids hassled me I hadn't a clue what their taunts meant and ambled along amused and embarrassed.

In the harbour a few boats were tied up next to a high wall. The wall was part of what looked like a castle jutting out into the sea. Lobster pots sat on the shore and a few fishing nets were hung over frames. Smaller boats were dragged up onto the beach. The sharp smell of the sea I was used to was somewhat sweeter and less chemical here. A couple of small restaurants were starting to prepare for meals later that evening.

I walked parallel to the sea until the village ended. Scrambling over rough rocks, to wander down by the water, I cut through sharp grasses and thistles. I took off my shoes and socks and stood on the hot sand. Rolling up my trousers, I walked into the warm water. I smiled as I paddled.

The sun began to go down, much earlier than I had expected, as I walked back into San Laurentius. The lights were coming on in the harbour area—street lamps and pretty garlands of plain yellow bulbs attracted flickering moths and fireflies.

A young woman smoked a cigarette and stared out to sea. In the gloaming the red coal of her cigarette resembled one of the fireflies. Her eyes met mine and held them until she smiled playfully and her eyes darted away. She was the only woman of her age that I had seen in the village—early twenties, only a few years younger than me. I passed her by and went into a restaurant.

Dinner was excellent, many dishes, all pleasing to the senses—fragrant breads I teased apart with my hands; bitter olives, green and black; grilled fish, cooked in garlic, that crumbled under my fork; crispy salad with large slices of tomato; cheeses that combined delicate flavour and the odour of wet boots; all of them slathered in bright, tangy olive oil. I drank a whole bottle of wine and rolled back to the apartment to the amusement of the locals.

The sun was barely up before me and I was grateful I had no hangover. I hadn't bought any food, so I went to find some. The air was fresh and a cool breeze came from the sea. The streets were empty save a few kittens mewling for their mother. I couldn't find a shop, never mind an open one, when I smelled fresh bread.

It was a real bakery, a rarity back home, barely ready to serve anyone, never mind an awkward foreigner. The old baker understood me well enough. With bread wrapped in brown paper and a carton of fresh milk I returned to my rooms to plan the day ahead.

Checking in with the office nagged at me like a sore tooth. No one would be in yet. Almost as maddening was the need to check my email. I took a few quick photos but saved them rather than sharing them. I even resisted a quick web search for local sights.

With my leftover bread, I got into the car as the village started to come to life. Winding through the streets, waiting patiently for kids and dogs to get out of my way, I headed up towards the hills that lay beyond the village. There on the last road out of town I saw her, one hand on hip, the other thumb jutting upward.

"Hi," I said. "Where are you going?"

"Where are you going?" she said, her accent erotic. She bent over and looked into the car through the window. I had a perfect view down her dark dress. And I knew she knew. And this added to my excitement.

"I don't really know," I said, my voice thick.

"How lucky. That's where I'm going." She opened the passenger door and slid into the seat.

"Iain," I said. She looked at my hand like I was offering her a wet fish.

"Angelina," she said.

I tried to concentrate on my driving while Angelina smoked a cigarette, exhaling out of the window.

"Where did you learn English?" I said.

"School and tourists," Angelina said. "You're not the first foreigner to visit here."

I felt a pang of jealousy. "Have you been to Britain or America?"

"No," Angelina said. "I haven't left Puglia. I will one day, soon." She looked out the window.

We drove on in relative silence. Conversation was frustrating and difficult. What did I need to do to get her to open up to me? I had driven up into the hills and was heading north. We must have been close to the centre of the peninsula that formed the heel of Italy. It was arid and hot even by mid-morning in September. I should have brought water with me.

I saw a gleaming city in the distance, white, sitting over the summit of a hill. The houses looked like each sat on the row below, circling round the hill, climbing ever higher to heaven, a bright Babel. At the very top sat a church. I imagined this was a perfect city, a city of light—a city of God.

Speeding along towards it I began to notice fairy homes set back from the road. "What are those?" I said.

"What are what?" Angelina said.

"Those buildings, with the cone-shaped roofs."

"Trulli," she said. It sounded like truly.

"Stop the car," Angelina said.

I slammed on the brakes and we slid to a halt in the dust. "What's wrong?" I said.

"I didn't want to go any further," she said. "We can look at a trullo."

We had stopped next to one of these Trulli. It didn't appear to be occupied. The house had walls of stone to about shoulder height, parts of which had been plastered and whitewashed. There was an elaborate arched doorway that I would have to duck to get through. On top of the house were three cones made of flat, rectangular stones, arranged like a dry stone wall, with a small stone cross sitting in the very top. It looked as if the house was wearing a number of wizard's hats, or dunce's caps.

"If you take the plug out of the top, the roof will fall in," said Angelina. She stood so close behind me I could feel her breath on my back and sense the heat of her body.

"Why would you want to do that?" I said.

"In days gone by," Angelina said, her dress rasping on the cloth of my shirt as she brushed past, "when lords came to get taxes on houses, people could demolish their homes quickly."

I walked round the back of the building, following Angelina, as intent on the rhythm of her hips as the odd oval shape of the building. "That really doesn't make much sense," I said. "These walls look a metre thick, how would you not notice the remains of the building?"

Angelina just shrugged.

"There's no windows," I said.

"Can't possibly be a house then, can it?" Angelina said.

On the way back to the car I saw a statue in a small niche in the stone wall next to the road. It appeared to be the Virgin Mary, but white paint covered the traditional blue cloak. Red paint ran from her eyes and had been splattered on her outstretched hands and the hem of her white dress. A small red rose, dried in the sun, lay at her feet.

"Someone has defaced this shrine," I said.

"It's not a shrine, it's a border marker. That's normal," Angelina said.

"Normal? People here normally paint over statues?"

"That's what The Lady looks like to us."

I had always found impaled icons disturbing, but this Lady chilled me even in the afternoon heat.

"I want to go home," Angelina said, climbing into the driver's seat.

"I could do with some shade and some nice cool water," I said. I was disappointed we hadn't visited the white city. There was always tomorrow. It was actually cooler in the car, even without the air conditioning on.

"It's only forty degrees, what are you complaining about?"

"I'm not complaining," I said. "I'm just not used to it."

"What do you want to do now?" I said, as Angelina stopped the car outside my apartment.

"What do you think?" she said.

"Oh." I hadn't come here for a holiday romance, and certainly hadn't expected things to progress so quickly. I got out of the car and made my way towards the steps leading up to the flat.

"Not here," Angelina said in a whisper. She headed down the street towards the harbour. I saw the curtain twitching out of the corner of my eye.

I'd not been out this way to the beach before. The blue sea lapped on the sand. Angelina slipped her hand into mine, bumping into my shoulder as we walked. We clambered over slippery rocks and there was a secluded cove with a small shack set back from the beach. Once it had been painted blue, but now the paint was crinkled by the sun. The roof of the hut extended out the front, over a veranda with a low rail, providing a shaded area.

Angelina opened the door, wood creaked and dry hinges protested. She entered the dark hut and closed the door behind her. I sat on the deck, cross-legged and squinted out at the water, wondering if I could see Greece in the distance. After a few moments she returned with two wooden bowls brimming with fresh water.

"Where did you get this from?" I said.

"There is a well," Angelina said.

I hadn't heard any noise. It seemed unusual to have a well so close to the sea. The cool water washed away one thirst. I put down my empty bowl. Mites, some red and others blue, crawled over knots in the wood.

Angelina sat close beside me. She put her arm across my tense back and lay her head on my shoulder. I couldn't remember the last time that I had last been this close to someone. She sighed, long and remorseful.

"What's wrong?" I said.

"Nothing," Angelina said, avoiding my eye. She kissed me. I kissed her back. Warm lips, her light tongue darting into my mouth. I don't know how long we stayed that way. My hand rested on her thigh.

A sound disturbed me and I broke off. I saw a woman close to the hut, but then she was gone. Angelina cried out.

"Are you okay?" I was worried I'd done something wrong, something too soon—that I had misinterpreted the signals.

"I've been bitten," she said, her voice tight. "Find the spider."

On the floor of the veranda I saw a large spider with a black, bulbous body with a red tear shape on its back scurrying towards a crack between the boards. I stamped on it.

"What did you do that for?" Angelina said. "I'll never be cured."

"What are you talking about?" I said.

"Get me home."

I picked Angelina up in my arms, struggling with the dead

weight of a petite woman.

In the village a small crowd formed around us. A couple of boys ran ahead as I went to the waterfront. I was greeted by a number of dignified villagers—I recognised the baker and my landlady. All, mostly women, were pleased to see me. The youngest was in her forties. Some wore black lace shawls over heavy black silk dresses. I saw pendants round their necks, like single teardrops of blood or emerald, nestling next to crucifixes.

The baker indicated to me to lie Angelina down. The street seemed a poor place for her to recuperate.

"Is there a doctor?" I said.

Smiling faces, cracked and worn, nodded at me. I was reassured and patted on the back. I had no idea what I had done to deserve this thanks. No doctor came.

A small boy with a cheeky grin pushed through the crowd. Carried in his arms, as I had carried Angelina, were a fiddle and a bow. The baker took them from him. A small cheer erupted from the crowd as he played a quick melody and Angelina twitched.

The baker said something to me. I looked at him. He repeated what he had said and I caught the word 'tarantula'. I guessed he meant the spider, even though it bore no resemblance to any tarantula I'd ever seen. I motioned that I'd crushed it with my foot. A murmur ran through the crowd. The baker said something else to me. I shrugged my shoulders. The elders talked amongst themselves. An order was barked out and a wiry young girl emerged from the crowd. "Signore," she said. "The spider. It colour?"

If I'd caught the spider the locals would have known whatever anti-toxin would revive Angelina. Feeling even more foolish, I demonstrated its size with my fingers and showed myself weeping. "Tears. Red, rouge, russet. On its back," I said, desperate for the girl to understand.

"Rosso?" the girl said.

"Yes."

She explained to the elders. There was a lot of nodding and this seemed to meet with the approval of the baker.

"What's going to happen?" I said.

"The dance of the tarantula. The Tarantella," the girl said.

"A dance? Now?" I said. "She needs medical help."

"Dance away the poison. You dance too."

"I'm not poisoned and I can't dance."

"The stranger dances."

Someone shouted and the girl slipped away. The baker plucked at his strings, tuned them and took up the bow once more. The crowd hushed. I heard the distant cry of a gull. The baker milked the moment before playing a lilting melody. His fiddle wept, so sorrowful was the music he played.

Angelina moved—her limbs twitched and spasmed. I thought she was having a fit and rushed forward to help only to be held back by a hundred arms. Angelina arched her back, her feet and neck still on the street, then sprung upright and began to sway with the rhythm of the fiddle.

The crowd clapped and quickened the tempo. Angelina danced, a shuddering dance, angular and jilted, like someone was pulling her strings. Her eyelids flickered open—her eyes were rolled back showing only the whites. I was transfixed.

Angelina's shaking began to become more fluid as she moved her arms and feet, dancing to keep up with the tune. Parts of her movement reminded me of Indian dancers—the way her head moved from side to side or a swift, stabbing motion with flattened hands. Meanwhile the baker played on, lost in a trance himself.

My stomach rumbling told me that lunchtime had come and gone. The sun was starting to turn my skin red. I desperately needed a drink.

Then there was a brief pause, perhaps for the baker to rest.

If what the girl said was true, it seemed that they intended to sweat the poison out of Angelina. She remained motionless, a discarded doll, strands of her hair stuck to her face. The baker, placing the bow in his back pocket and holding the fiddle like a guitar, resumed with a halting pizzicato, plucking at the strings. >zing zing< >zing zing< Angelina stamped, one foot hitting the floor in time with each pluck. Then she moved as though throwing out long threads in directions all around her. >zing zing< >zing zing< The baker brought out his bow once more and repeated the rhythm playing a similar note, but now adding an insect resonance to the sound, like a grasshopper.

Angelina scuttled out from the centre of her stage. Round and round and round in ever widening circles, a spiral was marked out by her feet, before she scuttled back to the centre again, and waited. The notes changed to a pulsing, flowing cadence that produced in me floating, darting, halting sensations. Then there was a rising struggle, a frustration—a bluebottle battering itself against a window. Angelina's head had followed the movement, her feet felt the tremors and then in a sudden sprint she danced towards me, pouncing.

Angelina kissed me on the lips—her tongue darted into my mouth. I thought I tasted bitter metal. Then she fell to the floor.

The crowd went wild, cheering, clapping. I was lost and bewildered.

A murder of old crows flocked past me and descended upon Angelina. I couldn't see what they were doing.

Another elderly man emerged from the crowd carrying an earthenware cup and handed it to me. The cold water shocked me and I began to find it hard to breathe. The crowd, the street, the town all began to recede down a dark tunnel.

In the darkness my joints ached and I imagined the venom racing its way to my heart to be pumped out into the rest of my body.

Then I heard it calling, a siren song, drawing me forward. That violin. Weeping for the loss of innocence, yearning for forgotten youth.

I opened my eyes and Angelina stood before me. I was surprised to see her eyes open, standing on her own. It was clear she wasn't present. She didn't move and barely seemed to breathe. She was in a thin white shift—the sunlight silhouetted her body beneath it. Surrounding us was the coven of crows, forming a black circle, and beyond them the crowd of towns-people. The baker continued to play. New notes were woven into the tune—a movement from a mournful pavane to some-thing full of fire.

Angelina jigged along with the music. Starting slowly she gyrated and stretched, lithe and supple. Twisting and rotating, she became a hurricane of hair and hands. Her movements be-came more lurid as she thrust and gestured, groaned and moaned, shaking her ass and clawing at the air.

I was the subject of her attention. While her movement aroused me, especially as her sweat soaked shift clung to her breasts and thighs, I was also aware that I was surrounded by people who were probably her grandparents and great aunts.

A swirl of music got under my skin. I felt the music infect me, inducing the urge to move my limbs and my detachment was destroyed. Drawn to my feet by Angelina, we whirled and twirled, arm in arm, hand in hand.

We danced close, her body up against mine. I could feel her heat, smell her sweat. We were joined together. I let out a whoop of delight and lost myself. I danced until I felt my limbs were ready to fall off. The ache in my joints subsided and I smelled the same coppery bitterness on my skin that I had tast-ed on Angelina's lips. I could go on no more and fell to the ground, exhausted.

The baker's tune shifted up a final desperate gear and Angelina danced on alone, her movement becoming more frenzied.

Was this dance some kind of voodoo rite? What Loa might be riding the horse? Superimposed over Angelina I saw a woman. Hazy at first, a phantom taking form. This was the woman I had glimpsed just before Angelina was bitten. I had seen this apparition before, out in the shrine at the trullo.

This thing was weeping blood beneath its long black hair—blood like the dark stains on its hands and the wine soaking the hem of its white dress.

I managed to stand on weak legs—the creature spotted me and came over. Stumbling back, I disrupted the circle of old women celebrating.

I had to leave, to get away. The crowd couldn't see what I saw and pushed me back into the circle.

Trapped, panic was rising within me.

I turned and saw The Lady, claws outstretched, gore dripping on the floor from its fingertips.

I fell down and put up my arms to protect myself. As it came closer I shut my eyes and waited for the end.

It passed into me. An icy feeling chilled my insides, like breathing in deeply on a frosty morning.

Angelina collapsed, conscious but exhausted.

Lifted from the ground, I began to dance again, cold and rigid, driven by my possessor to close the ceremony. The baker's tune returned to its melancholic melody and my dance slowed.

The fiddle stopped.

Heat returned to my body as I lay there on the stones of the street, shattered. I was in turmoil. What was that thing? I felt sick at the thought of it inside me.

The baker stepped forward and presented Angelina with a blood-red teardrop on a thin gold chain. She had joined her sisters—the Tarantata—the women who had all danced the Tarantella.

I awoke in my apartment still wearing my clothes, unsure of how I got there. My arms and legs were sore and stiff. My head felt heavy, my stomach grumbled and I fought down a boke as I recalled the revenant being inside me.

In the main room, the baker sat waiting, changed from his flour-dusted trousers into his Sunday best. He smiled, shook my hand and then embraced me. I freed myself and went into the bathroom. It was morning again.

The baker had gone when I returned. A bowl of olives in oil, a large fresh loaf and a jug of cold red wine had been set on the table. I tore into the loaf, drained the jug and felt the heat in my forearms and across the back of my neck.

I couldn't handle staying here, a stranger in a land of lost rites. I threw my clothes back in my pack and booked an early flight home.

Before I climbed into my car, Angelina approached me. She carried herself differently. There was a look in her eye. She had a gravitas I associated with women rather than girls. She drew me toward her, in a full embrace, and kissed me deeply.

Without fear, without thought, I kissed her back. I wasn't

lost at all. She broke away, eventually, and she laughed.

"Thank you," she said. "You helped me and the village. We would like you to stay. I would like you to stay."

I was tempted. "Thank you. I want to go home."

"I'll come and see you in Glasgow," Angelina said. Part of me hoped she would. "I have something for you—a good luck charm. The Lady will always know where you are. She never loses one of her own. You and I are alike now." She passed me a tissue paper packet, kissed me again and left me longing.

I opened the packet on the plane. Inside was a blood-red teardrop on a gold chain. I hesitated for a moment then put it on.

There was an article in the in-flight magazine on global-warming. Spiders from the south of Italy could now be found in northern France.

You Dry Your Tears If They Don't Work

Ralph Robert Moore

O VER THE LONG, long years of our lives we live in so many different places. Some we can't wait to leave. Some that make us sad when we have to zip the suitcase, look around at the walls one last time. Walk out the door, forever. Alone again.

Of all the places he had lived, across so many state lines, this room was his favourite.

A modest room. Window, desk, chair, bed, closet. Some books. Mice in the white plaster walls. Sometimes he woke up with spider bites.

I could grow old here. Die in that comfortable bed.

Sitting at the desk by the open window, and the desk wasn't his, any more than the window, he watched the snow drift down, taking its time. There is no hurry. The snow is doing what it does. And until you wake up the next morning, you don't realise what it's done.

Irish face. Black hair, dots and dashes of grey. Those blue eyes that must have looked like an adult's even when he was a child standing next to a refrigerator in the kitchen. So direct in their gaze it must be hard to come off as polite. He'd have to hide his stare while he talked, direct it elsewhere, at his hands, a room's furnishings. Make up for it with smiles and shrugs, to seem less intense.

Not an idyllic childhood, of course. But still, a nice childhood. Walking down a side street, small with hands in pockets. Finding on the black tar of the road the pale symmetric seed pods spun down from Maple trees, like wings.

Biscuit slinked through the open doorway. Wiggled his hind end on the floor below the desk. Orange eyes gauging effort. Leaped up onto the desk. Lay his long body across the opened book Mike had been reading. Typical chess move. Lifting his head sideways, eyes squeezed shut, whiskers reflecting light. As Mike stroked under his chin. Biscuit never lets out an audible purr. Which is rare. But as Mike continues scratching under his small, uplifted jaw, his fingertips can feel vibrations in the cartilage of the throat. A sneaky purr. Someone who pretends they're indifferent to what you're doing to them, but it's clear they like it. And don't want you to stop.

From below, the doorbell.

Mike went down the rich wood of the front staircase, smelling cinnamon. Angels and devils have spread their wings across these walls. Fingertips checking the straightness of his collar.

The front door had no peephole. All about faith.

A priest younger than him on the stone porch, luggage by his black shoes. Dark hair, bright eyes.

"Father James?"

James extended his hand. "Father Mike?"

After the handshake Mike stepped back, maybe a little too formally, inviting him inside. The two of them carried in James' luggage, from the cold of the porch to the warmth of the hall.

The sort of make busy that let both men hide their shyness.

Mike shut the front door, but didn't twist the lock.

From where James stood, rubbing his upper arms, his eyes bounced around at the hall's open doorways, the curving stair rails of the second floor. A rectory's quiet mysteries. Trying to learn more about his new home.

He became aware of Mike's gaze. "Your directions really helped."

"I avoided the temptation to type them in Latin."

The smile of a dog being petted on his head. "Much appreciated."

Awkward silence.

Which Mike broke. It helped that James seemed more nervous than he was. "I'm sure we're going to be sniffing under each other's tail, but in the meantime, do you want the grand tour?"

"I'd like to see the church first, if that's okay." His face, although handsome, was thin. As if he didn't like eating, or worried a lot.

Mike led him down a side hallway, towards the rear of the rectory.

They came out on a large kitchen, long table in the center.

All chairs empty but for an elderly priest, white collar loosened, halfway down one side, sipping soup.

James smiled. "In my previous parish, they didn't allow a TV in the kitchen. In fact, we only had one TV in the entire rectory. That one was kept in a closet and only rolled out for papal elections and presidential debates."

"We're very twentieth century here. Of course, it's the twenty -first century, but... The TV was a donation."

On the TV, live coverage of the downtown riots, which seemed to have escalated.

"Father Ferraro? This is Father James. He's been assigned to our parish."

Ferraro laid his spoon in his soup bowl. Didn't shave his neck this morning. "Animals."

"It looks like it's gotten more violent."

"They drag people out into the street and beat them. Like animals."

"We'll have to pray for them."

"I pray for the people getting beaten by these animals."

"We can go out this side door here, into the grounds."

Outside, bare black trees, a few benches along the path. Empty. Faint suggestion of the moon in the dark blue sky. Not yet a full circle. The wind was picking up, swirling drifts that had already fallen. James watched the upward spirals of snow. "When I was a child growing up in Buffalo, my grandfather told me these were the spirits of the dead, trying to rise to Heaven."

It relaxed Mike even more that James was trying to impress him with his cleverness. "Nothing morbid about that."

"Is it unusual to get snow here this early in the season?"

"Actually, it is."

"Are those pumpkins?"

"Yes! Each Fall we have a pumpkin patch, for the kids." Snow sparkling atop the wide orange shapes, like sugar. "Part of our environmental consciousness program. In the Spring, we have the children plant radish seeds. We start harvesting the radishes a month after we put the seeds in the ground. Great lesson for the kids, since they tend to have short attention spans."

They crossed the courtyard to the side door of the church.

Hedges, still green.

Mike let James go first.

Side by side, walking through the quiet front lobby, past the cheerful posters and public restrooms. Towards the nearest doorway leading into the church proper.

Mike reached his hand through the doorway, armpit touching James' shoulder, flicking on lights. Leaning this close to the other priest, Mike could smell him. Peppermint and cumin.

And the interior of the church was in fact magnificent. Built in the late eighteen hundreds, dozens of arches rising up to the blue and peach frescoes painted across the concave ceiling. Heaven in a bottle.

Walking backwards, face tilted up, like a tourist in Times Square. "Guess I'm not in Nebraska anymore."

Mike watched, hands held in front of his vestments. Those mature blue eyes. "It means a lot to me that I live here. That I get to work here."

James's eyes, under his black eyebrows. "I know." Lips curling up. The female parishioners are going to love him. His charm, their awkwardness. He's going to get knitted scarves and casseroles. "This is where I'll be living, and this is somehow

273

a vow of poverty?"

"That's why I love going to national monuments. Mount Rushmore, the Statue of Liberty, Yellowstone Park. I don't own them, but they are mine. Ours. Who needs possessions?"

James gestured towards the rear of the church. "Mind if I get up on the altar?"

"Please!"

They walked down one of the aisles, passing wooden pews.

The giant plaster cross at the rear of the altar, bolted to the back wall. Christ with his head lifted sideways, staring up.

"That was installed about a decade ago, by Monsignor Geller. He didn't want to show Christ in death. Christ triumphant, obedient to the Father."

James walked in his slim black vestments over towards the lectern. Looked back at Mike. "May I?"

"Absolutely. I'll still be performing the high masses, but the rest will be yours."

He stood behind the lectern, hand grasping either side of the wood. Looked out over the empty rows of pews. "This is much larger than my old parish. How many parishioners do you get?"

"The church is usually full for the eleven o'clock masses. Some people standing along the walls, and in back. Probably some of it because of our choir. We have a men and boys choir. I'll introduce you to the choirmaster this Sunday. He's lay, but very dedicated to the church. Mr. Donleavy. Small, slight. His forehead gleams with sweat while he's conducting. For your masses, at eight-thirty each Sunday, we usually get a three-quarters attendance."

"That's impressive, these days."

"We have a mostly Latino congregation."

James nodded. Glanced over his shoulder at Mike. "So, are we bonding?" Such confidence shown in the way he stood. Like a beloved. His charm must have never failed him.

The tall door at the front of the church swung open.

A small boy.

Door closing behind him, the boy shuffled over to the holy water stoup. Clearly unaware of the priests. Dipped his right hand in the basin, using that fingertip wetness to make the sign of the cross point to point from forehead, heart, left shoulder, right shoulder.

"That's Carlos. One of our altar boys. Very devout. Carlos?"

Carlos jerked his face towards the distant altar.

"Let me introduce you. He comes from one of the more stable homes."

Mike stepped down off the marble of the altar. Strode briskly down the center aisle. James following behind.

"Carlos, I'd like to introduce you to our newest addition, Father James."

Carlos shrank back, rubbing his wet fingers against the side of his trousers.

"Carlos? Are you okay?"

Dark eyes looking up at the priest. "I did something wrong, Father. Really bad."

Mike went to brush snow off the boy's shoulders. But

stopped his hand's advance when Carlos flinched.

In a quiet sideways voice only James could hear he said, "They're like wild animals at this age. They want the food in your hand, but they're ready to flee. You have to constantly reestablish trust. What did you othat was so bad, Carlos?"Carlos wobbled his head. "I can't talk about it, Father."

"Would you like me to hear your confession?"

"No."

Of course, Mike had been placed in the spotlight now, and how he handled this matter would surely influence James' impression of him.

"Why don't we go over to the rectory? On a cold night like this, I'm sure we could all benefit from some hot chocolate."

The three of them walked back through the courtyard. The snowfall had gotten heavier. The stemmed tops of the pumpkins were buried in whiteness.

The two priests walked behind the little boy. Mike glanced at James. "I see this as one of our primary missions, to comfort the young."

"As the twig is bent..."

The kitchen was deserted. Father Ferraro's empty bowl still on the long table, spoon handle slanted up over the rim.

And the TV was still on. The riots had gotten even more violent. A police helicopter set down in the middle of a boulevard, overhead blades rippling trash away from its landing. Immediately overrun, blue-uniformed officers pulled out of the side doors of the copter, beaten. Pops from guns being fired.

Both priests stood in front of the screen, bowing their heads, hands held in prayer.

Mike put some milk on to boil in an old aluminum pot with a blackened interior.

Took a box of Hershey's Cocoa down from a shelf. Measured into the pot.

The three of them sitting at the end of the table nearest the stove. Each took a tentative sip of the hot cocoa in their mug.

Mike watched Carlos' troubled face as he swallowed, both small hands holding the mug. Looked over at James. In a priest's quiet voice: "Would you like to try?"

James put his mug down. Waited until Carlos had done the same.

"Whatever it is that's upsetting you must be something major." Looked to Mike. Who nodded approvingly. A good overture.

Carlos said nothing. Picked up his mug, drank some more. The stall of a child. And some adults.

"We've all done things we're ashamed of. Things we wish we hadn't."

The priests could tell by his dark eyes that Carlos, although not responding, was listening.

"When we were weak. When we forgot our body is a temple. But God forgives. God forgives everything."

"Yeah?"

"Yeah. And whatever it is you did, you can rest assured plenty of others have done the same thing as well. You may even have enjoyed it at the time. That's okay. God forgives. What does matter is that it made you feel bad about yourself."

Tiny little teardrop in Carlos's left eye.

James looked at Mike for guidance.

Mike nodded.

"This thing that happened—" James interrupted himself. "Was it an action, or a thought?"

"An action."

"Were you alone when this action occurred?"

"No, Father."

"You were with someone else?"

He's doing a good job.

Carlos stared down at the tabletop, swinging his legs. "Yes."

"Was this other person young, like you, or old?"

"It was two other people, Father."

"I see. Were they—were these two other people older than you?"

"Yes. One was."

James' sad eyes met Mike's sad eyes. "How much older than you would you say, Carlos?"

"Couple of years."

"Oh. Okay. Were they male?"

Carlos shook his head.

"Both were female?"

Carlos nodded.

"Did you know them?"

"Sure didn't."

"Where did this happen?"

"My momma's house."

"Did they talk to you?"

"Yes! One of them. The older one."

"How did it happen that they talked to you? Were they already in your house when you got home?"

"No. They rang the front doorbell and I was the only person home so I opened the front door and they were standing there."

"Did you invite them in?"

"Not really. But the girl that was older was very pushy. I don't like pushy people."

"I don't like pushy people either. What happened when they came inside? What did they say?"

"She said to me, Where's your mother? And I said, She's at my aunt's. And she said, Do you want to see what I have in my purse? And I said, I don't know."

"How were they dressed?"

He twisted his head around on his shoulders. "Kind of fancy. Like they were going to church. They had really clean dresses on. They wore eyeglasses. They had plastic purses."

"So what happened?"

Carlos stared down at the brown-rimmed bottom of his mug. "She said, Wanna see a picture of me and my dad? I said, Not really. She opened the top of her purse and pulled out a picture anyway, then shut the purse real quick. Here's the picture. I looked at it, because she was putting a lot of pressure on me. She was real pushy. "

"That's not right, when people are pushy. What did the picture show?"

"It was this old guy in a suit, with a vest. He was sitting down. The girl who showed me the picture was sitting in his lap, on one of his knees. She was looking away. Her father was looking right in the camera."

"Is that what upset you?"

"She said, Wanna see my trick? I didn't say nothing. I was wishing they would leave. But she said, I'm going to show you my trick now, okay? I may have started crying a little. I don't remember. She was acting like she was an adult, and I was just a kid, and I had to do what she told me to do. So she puts the picture back in her purse, and she reaches into her purse with her hand, and she takes out this big, black spider. It was the biggest spider I ever saw." He started tearing up. "And I was thinking, this can't be a real spider, because it's too big. It was as big as her hand. And it started flexing its legs and I thought, it has to be some kind of toy, where she's pulling strings I can't see, and that's making it move, but then she held it up in her fingers and I saw it was a real, live spider. It didn't have a face but it had eyes. And she said, Wanna see my trick? And I said, No! I don't want to see your stupid trick. And she said, Watch!"

Carlos' two hands, grasped together on the kitchen table, struggled against each other, knuckles whitening, like angels.

"And she rolled her head back and opened her mouth, she opened it really wide, she had whiter teeth than me, she must have a rich family, and she lifted the tarantula above her mouth and started lowering it into her mouth, but she had to keep lifting it up a little and lowering it again because the legs wouldn't agree to go in her mouth. They were waving around like really long licorice strips, over her eyeglasses and around her chin, and up her nostrils, but finally she got the whole spider lowered into her mouth and she closed her mouth, her cheeks were bulging and her eyes were bugging out behind her eyeglasses. She was probably feeling that big, black tarantula moving its legs around in her mouth, trying to find a way to crawl out. And she just stared at me. And then she lifted her hands up to her shoulders and gave me a look like, See?

"And I said, Stop that! Stop it! I was crying but I was frozen. And she looked at me like, I'm a girl, but you could never do this. You're a sissy. And your dad probably knows you're a sissy. He probably knows you like to play with dolls and take their clothes off, even though I never, ever play with dolls, Father. My mom has some dolls, in a box at the bottom of her closet, but she turned all their heads around, so they're flat below their faces, they don't have two bumps on their chests."

Carlos had white spittle on his lower lip. Those angels were wrestling.

"Finally she opened her lips and the spider started crawling out. It looked like it was really happy to get out of there. It was reaching its front legs down and feeling around for something to climb down to. She lowered her face and put her palm under her mouth so the spider would have something to stand on. Its legs were really wet with her spit, it was drooping off the spider's legs like raw egg whites. She looked at me and grinned, with wet tarantula footprints across the lenses of her eyeglasses.

"Then she went, Ow! Ow!

"And I sat up in my chair. Did the spider bite you?

"No, she says. I got a cut on my knee." Carlos pushed his black eyebrows together. Still confused by what had happened. Evident by his eyes.

"So I say, I'm sorry you got your knee cut. And she says, Could you kiss it for me? Make it better? And I'm like, What? But she wants me to kiss her knee. I look down at it. I don't want to kiss her knee. But she says, My Dad would kiss it, but he's not here. And she, like, blushes. So I want to get her out of my house, so I can go back to watching TV, I'm missing my programs, all these comedies, so I get down on my knees, and I kiss the tip of my finger and then touch it to the cut on her knee while I make a kissing sound. And so she gets all huffy and everything and she says, That's not kissing my knee! Not really! So I say, Oh for God's sake—Sorry, Father—and I kiss her knee. Then she says, Would you lick the blood off? I'm like, I don't want to lick your dirty blood off your knee—I'm thinking this, I don't say it to her—"

Carlos's face, jerking up, flinching. Coffee cups falling out of the overhead kitchen cabinets. Spinning on the floor, handles and rims. James stepping sideways, trying to grab the edge of the table, to steady himself. The pain in Mike's ears as the explosion runs up in decibels, drifts back down.

Silence in the kitchen. Three males.

"What was that?"

Mike looked at the stove. To make sure no gas was escaping from the little black jets.

James had his fingers to his forehead.

Carlos got quietly out of his chair, crawled under the long kitchen table, still holding his spoon.

Mike was senior, so he looked around, slapped James' upper arm. "Okay. I thought the explosion came from outside."

James nodded, still in a daze.

"Carlos, get out from under the table, please. Christ walks with you, no matter where you go. Our Lord will protect us."

The boy reluctantly shuffled on his hands and knees until he had cleared the underside of the table's edge, and could stand up. "So how many Hail Marys do I have to say, Father?"

"We'll discuss that later. I think the explosion came from the courtyard. James, I want you to treat Carlos as your charge. You can hold his hand if you need to. I'll go first."

Back in the courtyard. Cold, now. Snow piling. Branches bending down. Where they had walked earlier, a large pit, black and grey smoke rising.

Both priests felt the heat rippling from the pit.

Mike reeled up the black beads of the long rosary hanging from the belt of his vestments, until he had the tiny silver crucifix in his fingers. Advanced towards the pit.

Splashed deep down inside the pit, helter-skelter across the caved-in sides, lines and triangles of what looked like metal.

Emerging from the pit, slithering in all directions, markings in the snow.

Bloody feathers scattered at the bases of the nearest black trees.

"We need to go inside."

Side door shut, Mike strode over to the refrigerator. Picked up the handset of the landline phone on the counter. Pressed 911.

The front doorbell ding-donged.

He hesitated. Hearing the rhythm of rings in his ear. Put the headset back on the receiver. "Let's see who that is. It may be a parishioner in need of help."

Men on the rectory's front porch. Arms at their sides.

The man in front, grey hair, square jaw, looked at Mike. Smiled. "May I ask who I'm addressing?"

"I'm Father Mike Corrigan. This is Father James Foley. May I ask who you are?"

Mike looked at the photo ID held up by thumb and index finger. George Bennett. Homeland Security. Of course, Mike wouldn't know if the ID was fake or not.

Bennett looked over Mike's shoulder, into the interior. "May we come in?"

"For what purpose?"

Three men behind Bennett. One with eyeglasses. The other two younger. The two younger men stepped forward.

Bennett held out his hand, sideways, not needing to look at them. "Absolutely you can ask. You had an explosion in your courtyard. Right?"

"Yes."

"We're here about that."

Mike went into thought.

"Kind of cold out on this porch, Father."

Mike let out a breath. "Come in."

"How do we get to the courtyard, Father?"

Mike led them through the quiet rectory hallways, framed religious images on the walls, into the kitchen. The man with the eyeglasses stared at Carlos.

"Steve, Oscar. Check it out."

The two younger men went out through the kitchen's side door.

Bennett looked Mike in the eye. "What a handsome boy. May I ask why he's here?"

"He's an altar boy. He's paying us a visit."

"This is Dr. Majewski. He'd like to examine the boy."

"Why?"

Bennett let out a sigh. Put his hands on his hips, flaps of his coat pushing back.

Mike looked down. Black automatic strapped to his side.

"I'll need to contact Carlos' mother first, to get her permission."

"That is not going to happen, Father. We just don't have the time. We appreciate your cooperation."

One of the younger men came back through the side door. Snow blowing around his high, broad shoulders. He looked at

Bennett. Drew his right index finger horizontally across his Adam's apple.

Bennett turned away. Raising his eyebrows. Caught himself. Toughened. "Steve, get the boy ready. We'll do it on the kitchen table. Doctor?"

James hung back. Mike stepped forward. "Nothing happens to Carlos until we contact his mother."

"Steve, I want you to place this priest in custody."

Steve advanced towards Mike, chuckling. "You ever box, Father?" Looking directly into Mike's eyes. Pulled out, from behind his hips, a set of handcuffs. Hard steel. "You ever been handcuffed before? It really hurts the wrists. Pinches nerves."

I should never have let them in. Of course, if I had refused them entry, wouldn't they have just forced their way in? Escalating my loss of control of the situation? Heavenly Father, guide us in these times. So that we may see things clearly and act according to your wishes. "I want to be present while Carlos is examined. We don't know any of you."

Steve flicked a look at Bennett.

Bennett's head stayed still. And then, after the longest time, the slightest inclination.

Steve backed off.

Dr. Majewski walked over to Carlos. Touching his eyeglasses, to make sure they were straight. Blond hair that looks like it's dyed, but probably isn't. "Up on the table, boy." Patted his palm on the wood. Getting ready to examine a dog.

Carlos' frightened brown eyes. Swiveling to the one face he

trusted in the room. "Father?"

What do I do?

James stared down at the floor.

Bennett and Steve focused on Mike. Waiting for his answer.

"I think we should cooperate with these men, Carlos. I'm going to stay right here, by your side." He switched his eyes to Bennett. "If anything goes beyond where it should, these gentlemen know I'll contact the local papers, and TV stations, and reach out to some of my Catholic friends in state government. So I don't think they'll be so foolish as to overextend themselves. Because a priest always looks good on TV. People listen. Politicians listen."

Bennett smiled. "Most of the priests I see on TV these days are being hauled off, cowardly hands covering their faces. Father."

"Not this one."

"Not yet."

Carlos sat himself backwards up on the kitchen table.

Dr. Majewski pulled out a stethoscope. Probably the least intimidating thing he could have removed from his side pocket. "Take your clothes off, boy."

"Father?"

These men weren't leaving. That was clear. "Remove your shirt, shoes, socks and trousers, Carlos. This won't take long."

It sickened Mike to say that. But not the first time he had said or done something that had sickened him. Still sickened him.

All the grown up men standing in the rectory's kitchen. Watching Carlos, seated on the edge of the long table, awkwardly remove his clothing, eyes never leaving Mike's face.

Dr. Majewski reached into his side pocket again. Pulled out a syringe. Carlos sat up straighter in his white briefs.

Steve reached into a green duffel bag. Lifted out a heavy microscope. Plunked it on the table near Carlos's hips.

"What's going on?"

Dr. Majewski, irritated at all the questions. "We believe this boy has an infection. One he received an hour or so ago. I'm going to try to locate the infection inside him, and draw it out with my syringe."

"Shouldn't this be done at a hospital?"

Dr. Majewski, eyes exasperated, gestured with both hands at the ends of the stethoscope he had placed in his ears. I can't hear you. Laid his hand on Carlos's bare chest. Pushed against the chest, to get Carlos to lie down on the table, on his back.

While everyone watched, he traveled the circular end of his stethoscope up Carlos' left arm, listening. Got all the way to the shoulder. Pushed Carlos's arm up, over his head. Elbow bending. Left hand dangling by his ear, like a contortionist. Slid the listening end of the stethoscope up into the left, hairless armpit. Straightened up, alert.

Stuck the pointed tip of his syringe into Carlos's armpit.

Carlos jerked the upper half of his body. Off the table's surface. Until Steve, leaning forward, pushed it back down. Hard.

Carlos twisting his face. Letting out a yelp.

Dr. Majewski, irritated.

Mike reaching his hands forward.

Bennett making a big fist. Showing it to Mike. Steve's eyes.

And slipped out, the syringe's hard steel tip.

Bead of bright red blood in the dark armpit.

Dr. Majewski brought the tip of the syringe over a Petri dish. Helicopter over a town square. Gently squeezed out the blood.

Slid the Petri dish under the microscope.

Lowered his right eye to the microscope's eyepiece.

Tapped his fingers, at the bottom of the scope, around the rim of the Petri dish, sliding the dish this way, that.

Pulled his eye off the eyepiece. "Nope!"

"I didn't know you'd be sticking needles in him."

"Well, now you know!"

"You can't keep doing that to him."

The spectacles angling towards the priest. "I can do anything I want to do. You don't like it? Go off in the corner. Say the rosary."

James? Looking down at his black shoes. Not so charming anymore. Little white lies like, I wasn't the one in charge.

As Mike watched, flinching, flinching. Dr. Majewski sticking the syringe point into Carlos's flesh. Poking the steel point, hovering elsewhere, poking the steel point, let's try down here, poking. Dimpling the dark skin. Pop! Through the skin's surface tension. Sliding that stainless steel down into red meat. Back to the microscope each time. "Fuck!"

Carlos gave up protesting. Because he knew protesting

wouldn't stop what the men were doing to him. You dry your tears if they don't work.

A break. Everyone needed one.

Carlos was allowed to get off the table. Stretch his legs. He immediately slid over to Mike. Standing next to him, silently asking for protection. Like Biscuit would quietly stand in the middle of the kitchen floor, where his bowl would be placed, asking for food.

And that did it.

"It ends here."

The visitors didn't even bother replying to Mike. Ignored him.

"It ends here. Get out."

"What?" Dr. Majewski. Incredulous as a frat boy. Wet lips twice as large. "We're just getting started. I'll poke this boy, and poke him, and keep on poking him, until I decide when it's over."

And God spoke? Or didn't.

The long kitchen table slid sideways. Titanic. Crashing into the wall.

Clumsiness. All the men, like their strings had been cut, falling on their elbows.

Outside the windows. Orange flames billowing up. Floor of the kitchen thundering.

Father Mike, black vestments twisted around his body. Swimming to Carlos across the floor. Pulling on the back of his hair. Dragging him to the hallway.

Staggering back into the kitchen, getting Carlos's clothes.

"Dress! Quickly!"

Big brown eyes. "Okay, Father."

Down the rectory hallways, palms pushing off the walls, propelling. Find the closet, pull off the hanger an overcoat.

"Put this on!"

Oversized for Carlos, but not so long he would trip in it.

Behind Father Mike, the sound of the others getting to their feet. Cursing. When something terrible happens and yet you survive, that's what the evil do. Curse, instead of laugh with joy at being spared.

The dark wood of the front door to the rectory gets pulled open. Framing the cold whiteness of street beyond. No birds.

"Carlos, I want you to run. Don't run to your home, because they'll find you there. Run to a relative, then when she answers your knocks, ask her to take you right away to a friend of hers. Ask that friend to take you to one of her friends, and on and on, until you're somewhere safe."

Cursing in the hallway.

Carlos going down the steps, out into the world of snow.

Hand on Mike's shoulder, jerking him around.

Bennett. Angry. Angry like a dog. Foam at the fangs. "What the fuck do you think you're doing?"

Father Mike, as we'll remember him, blocking the front doorway with his outstretched arms.

Bennett lifting his side arm to Father Mike's face. "Move the fuck away!"

Father Mike not moving. Arms outstretched. Fear in his blue eyes.

Carlos running down the snowy, lamp-lit street. At the end of the block, skidding around a corner.

"Move or I'll blow your fucking head off!"

Carlos, fleeing in the cold. Looking for a new place to live.

A place where he can be safe.

Father Mike, not moving, staring at the gun barrel. Seeing into its dark, cylindrical depth. In those deep shadows, the copper grin of a bullet. Frightened face wishing he were in his bed, even though it wasn't his bed. The mice in the walls, the waking up with spider bites.

Bennett pulling the trigger.

To wake up feeling sickened, what a horrible way to start the day, but that was always the way he woke, sickened, yet still, even more horrible, waking up, like most men, loud noise, with an—

Guano Dong Baby

Robin Lupton

THE GUANGDONG Shēng Yù Néng lì House of Holistic Chinese Medicine was sandwiched between an American Fried Chicken place and an Oxfam. I stood outside rubbing my foot on the greasy pavement and eyeing a solar-powered, waving cat in the window. Next to it was a blue-tacked laminated, anatomical drawing featuring a naked woman speckled with acupuncture spots. None of these things filled me confidence in the establishment's fertility services.

I have always been dubious about alternative medicine. There is something about it that reeks of new age hoodoo-voodoo that reminds more of medieval bloodletting than solid science. I understand the placebo effect. I know that herbs have medicinal properties. Meredith has shown me countless journal articles illustrating how Chinese holistic medicine has been shown, if not proven, to boost fertility. I know all these things, but I still have my doubts that holistic medicine will do anything more for us than take our money and give Meredith a warm fuzzy feeling inside. This may have something to do with the fact that every time Meredith has mentioned Guangdong Sheng Yu, something happens inside my brain mutating the words to Guano Dong She-goo , which I immediately translate to English as 'bat shit dick she goo'. It's hard to trust a service whose name reminds you of a climactic moment with a knob made of bat turds. The truth is that after our first failed attempt with IVF Meredith and I are getting desperate.

If Guano Dong, (it's hard for me to think of the place as anything else now) makes her feel more relaxed and gives her hope that can only be a good thing. It definitely can't hurt.

"You ready," I asked squeezing her hand. Meredith was looking closely at the anatomical figure covered in red needle points. Meredith doesn't like needles, but one of her friends from work, I think her name might be Sarah, was treated here and swears her recent pregnancy is the result of a well-placed needle in her foot.

She nodded and we went inside.

The interior was deserted and looked exactly how I expected. The south wall was dedicated to flat pack square IKEA shelving units. Each square proudly displayed a large glass jar containing different roots and herbs in various shades of brown and stages of decay. The back wall featured a hallway which I assume led to the treatment rooms. Next to the hallway was some sort of box or cage covered in a white sheet. To the right of that was a reception desk. A stick of jasmine incense smouldered at its base next to a few tired looking pieces of fruit and a brass Buddha. In front of the shelves was a small waiting area which contained red plastic chairs and a coffee table stacked with out-dated *Cosmo*'s and a book on the history of Chinese medicine. Based on the magazine selection I was willing to bet Guano Dong got a lot of middle class 30 and 40 somethings using their services. Meredith and I did not sit. Instead, we stood in nervous silence giving each other what do we do now looks until a Chinese woman emerged from one of the treatment rooms and walked up the hall toward us.

She looked to be in her late thirties. Her hair was pulled back with ornate mahogany chopsticks, their delicate grooves catching the light. She was hugely pregnant and I knew if I turned to Meredith now she'd be watching the woman's bulging belly with covetous eyes.

The kimono the woman wore was overly fancy and I wasn't sure if she was a client or staff member. The dress was golden brown and made of a strange crispy diaphanous fabric with an opalescent sheen that twittered as she moved. I was about to ask her if she knew where the receptionist was, when she extended her hand and asked how she could be of service.

"My friend Sarah Tate and Dr. Shukla recommended you. We are here about your fertility services."

"Fertility is our specialty."

The Chinese woman's name was Dr. Zhāngláng. She sat us down in the hard-backed plastic chairs and began asking us questions about our failed attempts to get pregnant. When she had all the information she needed she began recommending a treatment plan for Meredith which would consist of a mixture of acupuncture and herbal supplements in the form of tea.

"We call it fertile-i-tea," Dr. Zhāngláng said with a smirk. Meredith and I smiled and nodded appropriately at the weak pun, but I wasn't really listening.

Somewhere in the room I could hear rustling, like grass shifting under tiny legs followed by the countryside sounds of birds or crickets. I struggled to track the chirps and trills and listen to Dr. Zhāngláng and Meredith's conversation at the same time. Over the thrum of invisible insects I heard Meredith asking if acupuncture had any links to birth defects.

Meredith had read in a few places that after 35 the risk of Downs Syndrome increased to something like 1 in 250. Ever since then she had been silently terrified if we ever did get pregnant she would conceive some sort of horrifying flippered creature that would consume our lives. We'd want to love it, but couldn't help resenting it. She wouldn't talk about it, but on her 35th birthday, after she blew out her candles, she went into the bathroom and cried. I told her there was nothing to worry about, that things would be fine, but I was silently scared too. Over the whisper of tiny feet, Dr. Zhāngláng assured us, that there were no birth defects associated with holistic medicine and that we were in good hands.

When our consultation was finished, Dr. Zhāngláng and Meredith walked down the little hallway to one of the treatment rooms. Over Zhāngláng's reassuring murmurs that the needles wouldn't hurt a bit and the click of the closing treatment door, I could still hear the shuffling clicks and trills of something alive. I wandered around the room listening until I realised the sound was coming from the covered box next to the hallway. I was suddenly sure it was some sort of bird cage and it would contain canaries or maybe a rare Chinese rodent you can't feed after midnight. I carefully lifted up a corner of the sheet and was hit by the earthy aroma of basements and waterlogged garden sheds.

It took me a moment to understand what I was seeing. The cage was split into several layers, each with its own little door. The layers were covered in hamster hay upon which was a wriggling black mass. It took a moment for my brain to realise what my eyes were seeing. It wasn't just one moving mass; but instead, hundreds of shiny brown backs attached to thousands of little legs scurrying deeper into the hamster hay. Cockroaches. The cage was swarming with hundreds of cockroaches. My stomach tightened and bile lapped at the base of my oesophagus, making my mouth taste hot and sour.

I wanted to put the sheet back down, grab Meredith and leave, but a disgusted compulsion made me lean forward. I was a rubbernecker watching a terrible accident unfold. Something about watching the creatures move independently and en masse was awe inspiring. Each one was nearly two inches long, not including their antenna. Their exoskeletons glistened an opalescent golden brown and sparkled sickly in the fluorescent lights.

I wondered why Guano Dong kept a cage full of roaches, when most their cliental were aspiring yummy mummies who would find the creatures disgusting. It was unhygienic for one. Cockroaches carried diseases. I wanted to move away. To sit down in one of the hard plastic chairs so I could stare down Dr. Zhāngláng when she finally emerged from the treatment room with Meredith. Then I could tell her how disgusting and out-dated holistic medicine is. Instead, I leaned closer to the cage and watched the roaches scuttle and trill across the mulch.

"I see you discovered our cockroaches," said Dr. Zhāngláng from behind me. I hadn't heard her approach. "Beautiful, aren't they?"

I let the corner of the sheet slip from fingers and spun to face her. "Where's Meredith?"

"She's relaxing. I'll go get her as soon as I've made her fertile -i-tea"

"What are the roaches for? Are they pets?"

"No, they have several medicinal purposes. They are particularly good for enhancing fertility."

"Don't roaches carry diseases?"

"That's a common misconception," she said as she approached the cage. She moved passed me and hooked the corner of the sheet over the top of the cage to keep it out of her way. Then she opened one of the doors about half way down. As she slipped her hand inside, she cooed something softly in Chinese. She was like a woman whispering affections to a beloved house cat. In response to the coos was a flurry of clicks and trills and a rustling from the cage and I wondered if the roaches had been trained to recognise a summons for food or were smart enough to know their master.

When she pulled her hand free from the door she held a fat long cockroach in her palm. It didn't struggle or try to get away, its wings glinting golden in the light. "Roaches" she began, "live in the most disgusting places in the world. They've had to evolve good defences and special enzymes to protect themselves. They never get sick. They could theoretically live forever. This is what makes the cockroach such a good aid for fertility. They destroy everything that stops life from flourishing."

She flipped the roach over and pulled something from its abdomen. It gave a weak trill. Then she flipped it back over and ran a finger along its wings affectionately. When she was finished she put the insect back inside the cage and shut the door behind it. She whispered something else to the creatures then lowered the sheet again. When she turned back to me she held the thing she had removed from the cockroach's stomach. It was hard, yet smooth, flesh coloured, oblong that looked like it had been forged from layer on layer of secretions.

"It's an oothcea, an egg case. It is essentially the cockroach's embryonic stem cells. Like man's stem cells, they are able to change into most things: eggs, placenta, and oestrogen. This will help give your wife whatever she lacks to help ensure her pregnancy."

Next Zhāngláng pulled down a pestle and mortar from one of the shelves then set about putting different herbs in the mortar. Last of all went in the egg case.

My stomach lurched as I listened to the oothcea crunch and break under the weight of pestle as it was ground into the other herbs. When she was finished, she poured it into a large white envelope then sealed it shut with a sticker featuring a Chinese symbol. She handed it to me.

"Now every night after dinner, you need to brew her cup of tea with two teaspoons of this. You shouldn't drink the tea."

"I don't think that will be a problem," I said putting the envelope into my jacket pocket.

"You don't believe this will work," said Dr. Zhāngláng.

"I have my doubts. Honestly, I don't want to offend you but it seems pretty disgusting."

"This is not some backwater cure like using powdered tiger genitals to cure erectile dysfunction, Mr. Matthews. Chinese medicine has been practiced for thousands of years. This will work."

In honour of our trip to Guano Dong we ordered a Chinese takeaway for dinner. I probably should have waited until after dinner to tell Meredith about the special ingredient in her fer-tile-i-tea, but I couldn't help myself. It was too disgusting, so between mouthfuls of duck pancake and Singapore noodles I told her about the cage of roaches and the oothcea. Meredith almost spat her food out in a fit of disgusted giggles when I told her how Dr. Zhāngláng talked to the insects like they were pets and the sound the egg case made when she crunched it with the pestle.

After dinner Meredith started flipping through Netflix for something to watch while I pulled out my tablet and ran a Google search on the medicinal value of the cockroaches. "I just don't see how it can be sanitary," I said, swiping through the search results.

Several journal articles came up, but I ignored those. I was looking for something more sensational. Then I found the article about the cockroach taco.

"Ew, Mer, listen to this. Some lady in New Mexico ate a taco that had a pregnant roach in it. Apparently, before she could swallow, the roach laid its eggs in her mouth. Well her mouth was all nice and warm and wet. The perfect incubator for cockroach eggs. The eggs started developing in her mouth. She got big sores all over her tongue and on the inside of her cheeks. To get the eggs out and stop the roaches from hatching in her mouth she had to have huge chunks of her tongue and the inside of her cheeks removed."

Meredith's eyes went wide and she laid her hand protectively on her stomach.

I knew it was cruel but I couldn't help myself. I kept pushing. I laid the tablet in my lap so I could better taunt her.

"Can you imagine? Hundreds of little baby roaches running around your tongue and burrowing between your teeth." I made my fingers into little legs and made them shuffle up her thigh. She shivered.

"You are making that up."

"No, I'm not, it says it happened right here. You probably shouldn't drink that roach tea."

"Let me see the article," she snapped, and then plucked the tablet from my lap.

"This is from a website called *Surreal Stories from the*

Southwest. What a load of rubbish. The next article is about Bigfoot," she said handing the tablet back to me. "Do you not want a baby?" she asked with the corners of her mouth pulled down so far they tugged at her eyes. She looked so sad, I could hardly breathe. "If you really didn't want to try Guangdong's you could have just said."

"Of course I do. I didn't mean... it's just that, I don't really buy that roach eggs will make a difference."

"But it's not going to hurt," she said. "We agreed we'd try it. There is good research out there that says Chinese medicine used in conjunction with IVF increases your chances of pregnancy. I felt really good after my treatment today, I feel like you are trying to ruin that."

"That's acupuncture, not cockroach tea."

"Whatever," she said, getting to her feet. She collected the remaining takeaway boxes and walked to the kitchen. Her walk was angry and annoyance radiated off her. I'd only meant to tease her, but I'd gone too far.

"Mer, I'm sorry. You know I want a baby."

She didn't answer. I could hear her huffing around the kitchen. I should go to her, but before I did I wanted to find some sort of evidence to prove the tea would help. Anything that would put her mind at ease. I heard her put the kettle on and the whirl of boiling water was muting the sounds of her loading the dishwasher. I spoke louder as I swiped through the internet for a more positive article.

"Mer, baby, I just found an article that says roaches are both delicious and nutritious. It backs up all the stuff I was telling you that Dr. Zhāngláng told me about roaches never getting sick and their super bacteria killing enzymes. "

The only sound from the kitchen was the whistle of the kettle and the clink of crockery.

"Mer, did you hear me? Roach farming is a big industry in China. It's completely legit. I'm sorry for teasing you."

Meredith appeared in the living room doorway holding two cups of tea.

"And this one says some of the big US drug companies are going to start using roaches in their medicines, so Guano Dong is definitely on to something."

"Guangdong," she scowled. "Good, here is your fertile-i-tea." She handed me a cup. The liquid was so dark it was almost black. It smelled of dirt and rain.

"Dr. Zhāngláng said this tea was just for you. I'm not supposed to drink it."

"Hey, you're the one who started this by trying to freak me out by saying baby roaches were going to start growing in my mouth. You're drinking it."

"But Mer..."

"Come on, it's both delicious and nutritious."

Six weeks later Meredith was lying in bed, her autumn coloured hair cascading over her pillow and a book in her hands. She had been to the doctor's that day to have three fertilised eggs implanted in her womb. Right now she lay there full of hope and contentment, taking sips of cockroach tea and looking beautiful.

I slipped off my shirt and started to get into bed.

"What's that on your stomach?" Meredith asked me, peering over the brim of her glasses.

"What's what?" I looked down my chest, pooching out my gut, to see my belly more clearly, but I couldn't see anything out of the ordinary.

"I don't know. It looks like some kind of rash. Come here."

I knee-walked across the bed too her. She sat up to examine my stomach. She poked a spot and a strange but pleasant ache radiated from the blemish.

"What is it?" I asked.

"I can't tell if they're bug bites or spots."

"Pop one and see." I love popping pimples. I always have. I also love asking Mer to pop the hard to reach ones for me. She hates it. She thinks it's gross, which is what makes it even more fun for me. I know popping spots isn't good for you and that it scars, but there is just something so satisfying about squeezing out a white bead of puss from angry inflamed flesh. It must be similar to the feeling a farmer gets when he pulls a maggot out of the earth and crushes it between his callused fingers.

"You know I hate doing that. Plus if they're bug bites you don't want to mess with them"

"But what if it's not a bug bite? What if it's a spot?"

"Either way it will go away on its own and if you mess with them, they'll scar. And I happen to like your stomach, just the way it is." She leaned forward and kissed the trail of hair that descended down beneath my pants to prove it.

I leaned over and kissed her belly too. "I love that sexy stomach of yours as well. And if we are lucky, pretty soon, it might have even more things about it to love."

"What if all three eggs take? We could end up with triplets. Can you imagine?"

"We'll have to get one of those fancy three-seater pram things," I said, lying down next her. She shifted over until her head was resting on the crook of my arm.

"Yeah but how will we feed three babies at one time? I only have two of these." She squeezed her breasts teasingly.

"I'm sure we can work it out."

Once she was asleep I softly probed the spots on my belly. I counted five in all. I gave one an experimental squeeze, then felt the familiar satisfying crunch of a spot getting squished.

"I can feel and hear you playing with your pimples," Meredith said in the darkness. "Leave them alone."

"I thought you were asleep."

She slid her hand over my stomach and rested her palm protectively over my belly button. "If I hadn't pointed them out, you never would have noticed."

"Okay. I'll leave them alone," I lied, knowing I would slowly and satisfyingly pop each and every one over the next few days.

I popped the second spot in the shower. I like to see how much white I can get out before the puss breaks in half or starts bleeding. This one had been particularly good and I had pressed out a four millimetre bead of white before smearing it with my thumb and rinsing it down the drain.

I popped the third spot on Saturday morning after breakfast. Just in case the pregnancy had taken, she made an elaborate pregnancy approved brunch of overly hard scrambled eggs and bucks fizz sans the fizz. After I scraped the last bit of egg and toast in my mouth I disappeared up to the loo with a cup of coffee and my smart phone, but instead of playing angry birds I played with the spots.

I was surprised by how much bigger they had gotten in just a few days. They were nearly the same size as a pencil eraser. The skin around them felt tight and inflamed, but unlike normal whiteheads these spots were hard, almost as if they were covered in fleshy armour.

They were becoming more difficult to pop, too. Every time I tried to press on one, the fat on my belly shifted and they slipped from my grasp. The hair blocked my view, but I persevered. I chose a smallish one just below my belly button and squeezed. It hurt and a stinging sensation I could hardly tolerate spread through my stomach. When the white squished out, it was followed by a wake of red and its juice smeared pinkly over my skin.

For half a second I swear I felt the white thing on the tip of my finger move and saw it raise its maggoty head. I held it up to my face to examine it more closely but it lay still, like a dead worm, like the little, lifeless, lump of puss it was. The movement must have been a trick of the light.

Meredith had been in the bathroom for ages. It had been two weeks since the fertilised eggs had been transferred to her uterus and she was taking her first pregnancy test. I was getting antsy waiting so I was distracting myself by playing with the two remaining spots on my abdomen in the downstairs loo.

The spots had gotten even bigger and they were starting to worry me. They should have healed naturally by now, but instead had grown to the size of a 10p coin. When I showed them to Meredith that morning she told me what I already knew. That they weren't normal and I should go to the doctor. I would, but I wanted one more chance to pop them on my own.

I chose the largest spot that rested just above my hip bone and squeezed. I squeezed until tears pricked my eyes and I thought I was being stabbed. All at once there was a satisfying crunch that vibrated through my abdomen and a trillish wail. As I squished the blemish together its contents emerged slowly and grudgingly. The thick white mass reminded me of larvae. It came out in one piece. First came a decidedly human looking head, then a pair of white thin arms, then a second. Each arm was fitted with a five human looking fingers. Then finally two little legs, six limbs in all. I pinched the thing in my hand, its head falling slack to the side. Its chest was caved in from where I had squished it. Fragile milky white wings clung to its back. It could have been the foetus of a fairy. It wasn't a spot, it was a baby.

I was so terrified I nearly threw the thing into the wall, but the same combination of disgust and attraction that caused me to lean forward to look at the roaches, that same sick need that makes me pop my spots, made me hold that fragile baby thing in my hand and hold it close to my chest. I swallowed a scream.

I didn't know what to do. The thing in my hand looked more like a baby than an insect and it had been growing inside me. My free hand went to the remaining spot on the left side of my abdomen. It was smooth and looked to be made up of layers of secreted armour.

Too many thoughts ran through my head at once. The article about the New Mexican woman and the roach taco. Dr. Zhāngláng saying, "It's an oothcea, an egg case. It is essentially the cockroach's embryonic stem cells. Like man's stem cells, they are able to change into most things: eggs, placenta, and oestrogen. This will help give your wife whatever she lacks to help ensure her pregnancy."

Could it have ensured a pregnancy in me as well? Is that why she said not to drink the tea? I felt dizzy. I sat on the toilet cradling the baby thing in my hand. It had cried when I'd squashed it. I had killed it. I'd killed all of them but one. Tears pricked my eyes and waves of guilt and terror washed over me.

I didn't hear Meredith's tread on the stairs or realise she was calling me until she tapped on the bathroom door.

"Is everything okay in there?"

Then I remembered she had been upstairs taking the pregnancy test. As soon as I opened the door I would find out if we were having a baby or not. I wasn't in any state to comfort her if we'd failed. What would she think and say when she found out I'd been slowly killing the closest things we might ever have to children, even if that child was twisted and different?

Mer turned the knob and the movement shook the door in its frame. "Baby, can I come in?" she said breathlessly. "It's... it's, good news." I could hear the joy bubbling out of her voice. The test was positive and she wanted to kiss and cuddle and celebrate, and I had just killed something that could have been a baby.

I leaned forward and unlocked the door, then sat back on the toilet while Meredith came in. Her eyes bright and full of happy tears, her smile radiant and relieved.

"It's positive," she said, holding out the pregnancy test. Two little purple lines were displayed in the window.

"That's great, baby," I said and a few tears escaped from the corners of my eyes.

Then I held out my hand revealing the child thing curled on my palm. Her smile cracked. The joy in her eyes dimmed. I felt wretched for diminishing this moment for her.

"You were right, I shouldn't have popped them."

Meredith placed the open shoe box on the desk before Dr. Zhāngláng then stood silently at my side. She hadn't taken her eyes off the box since we left the house. During the taxi over she had repeatedly raise the lid to peek inside, then whispered in my ear so the driver couldn't hear, "It looks a bit like you." Another peek, another whisper, and: "It looks like a fairy child." Peek, whisper, "Do you think it suffered?" Peek, whisper, "Do you think there is one in me?"

Dr. Zhāngláng's eyes widened at the sight of the curved white creature with its crumpled wings in the shoe box. Without saying a word, she stood up revealing her still heavily pregnant belly and the same gold and brown dress she had been wearing nearly eight weeks ago when we first met her. She moved silently to the shop door and locked it.

When she turned back to us her eyes were glassy. "I told you not to drink the tea."

"What kind of warning was that? You didn't say why. You didn't say, 'Don't drink the tea because you might conceive a roach-human hybrid.'" I waved my hand wildly over my stomach and the shoe box.

"I didn't know it would. This is an exceedingly rare occurrence. You should need additional support. As people who want children, you could consider it a blessing."

"Are you saying this has happened before?" Meredith asked.

Dr. Zhāngláng didn't move her arms, but her golden brown kimono parted down the middle and began to open as if she were opening a robe. The kimono spread up and back behind her, folding into glorious golden wings of a cockroach. They looked like stained glass. With her wings behind her, I could see Dr. Zhāngláng wasn't pregnant at all. Folded across her thorax was a second pair of arms. She was beautiful and terrible and reminded me of one of the Hindu goddesses with additional limbs.

"My father's wife died in childbirth," she began. "He was devastated and lonely. My father was an entomologist. He specialised in cockroach reproduction. He wasn't the first to drink the tea. They'd been drinking it in India for centuries. That is what inspired the drawing of Lakshmi, the Goddess of fertility and abundance. You may recognise the arms." She spread her additional limps out in front of her delicately. "Even with the tea, the chance of conceiving is exceedingly rare, as I said. This shouldn't have happened."

"I don't understand. Is Meredith pregnant with a baby like you, too?" I asked. I hoped not. Meredith had been dreaming of a normal human baby for years.

"No, the baby growing inside Meredith's womb is human. The baby in the box and the one still growing inside you is a hybrid. In many ways it's more advanced than a human will ever be. For example, once they mature it's almost impossible for us to get sick and we are very hard to kill. Roaches seek survival at all costs.

"When you drank the tea the eggs travelled through your system and you fertilised them internally. You don't have a womb so they secreted themselves in your abdominal flesh. As it grows it will fall out naturally. When it grows up, it will look like me, and you," she said, relaxing her wings back around her body and hiding her second set of arms.

I stood stunned looking at Meredith and Dr. Zhāngláng and the child I had killed and stuffed unceremoniously in a shoe box. The shock of everything that had happened in the last two hours was more than I could handle. This felt beyond science and medicine and even magic. I wanted to ask what we should do now. Clearly if the baby was like Dr. Zhāngláng it was so close to being human, killing it would be wrong, but what did Meredith think? Would she want to take care of a baby that was this different? Raising a child with special needs had been one of her biggest fears. Would we even know how to take care of a creature like Dr. Zhāngláng? There were so many things I wanted to ask and say competing to come out of my mouth they jammed in my synapses and left me silent.

Meredith came to my rescue. I felt her hand wrap around mine.

"Looks like we had more than one egg take after all. We better go get one of those fancy multi-seater pram things."

Spinnentier

David Birch

THE FIRST TIME they caught me with fly spray, mother squirted it in my mouth until I choked and threw up. That was also the last time they caught me.

I learned that stealing meant punishment. Lots of things meant punishment after we moved to the new house. Trying to go outside by myself got me put in the cage. They bought it for a dog but I'm small for my age, and we never got the dog.

It's always messy in the new house, which is really an old house, with dirty windows that make it dark all day. And we're not allowed to tidy up. Gran squeezed bruisers into my arm with her bony fingers just for moving a pile of old slippers from under the staircase.

"Wiiicked boy," she said in her long dry voice. She talks slowly but moves fast for an old person. She watches while I eat my breakfast and as soon as the last spoonful of cereal is in my mouth she's clearing the table but the dishes never get washed, not by her, she puts them in the basin then leaves me alone.

"You have to be your best around your Gran," mother tells me if I start to complain, "she won't put up with any of your nonsense." I stay out of the way when I can. My room is my safe place and it's the only clean place in the house. They don't come in so I tided it. But the sheets still make me itch because mother washes them, which means she doesn't. Father goes out to work, he has clean clothes for that, he puts them on like a spacesuit and goes through the front door like something might grab him.

I don't go to school so I read books. There's a TV in the corner, you can hardly see the screen through the dust. I turned it on once. They acted like I'd set the house on fire, running around and shouting,

"Turn it off, turn it off,"

I sat there laughing. Gran crawled across the floor and caught hold of my ankle, and shook me.

"Make it stop," she hissed.

I turned it off and waited for my punishment. But none came, no cage, no being put in the cellar in the dark, listening to the scratching sound from the hole. The one that looks like a well but isn't because the edge looks too dry. Instead they left me. I heard them argue in the kitchen but I don't know what they said.

The next day the plug had been taken off.

We have curtains hanging everywhere in the house. Thick grey white curtains we're not allowed to touch, I called them webs once and didn't get fed for two days. Father has started bringing home boxes full of flies. He lets them out in the house; they don't last long. They buzz around and get caught in the curtains. Then the spiders come. Mother and Father and Gran all sit and watch the struggling insects being bitten and wrapped in silk coffins. This is their TV.

I said, "I feel a bit sorry for the flies," they laughed at me and Gran said I should think myself lucky I wasn't a fly. I kept away from her even more after that.

They took me to the park as a birthday treat, eight is a special number. I explored the trees and the bushes and ran on the grass. The wind was warm and I let it blow in my face, so different from Gran's stuffy house. I paddled my feet in the pond while ducks swam around quacking at me for intruding.

"Can I have an ice cream?" I asked Father.

"It can't hurt, this once," he gave me a rare smile and a five pound note.

"Do you and Mother want anything?"

"We've got what we need right here," he said and I saw mother sat by a hawthorn bush, spiders crawling over her face and along her arms. I ran to the ice cream van at the top of the hill, taking one look back I decided I'd seen it wrong, because I was running and a bit far away, it looked like my parents were picking flies out of the webs and eating them.

At the van were some other children. They were dressed in bright colours that made my blacks and greys look old. I tried to talk with them but it was difficult. They must not have been to school much either, most of them couldn't even make proper sentences. Half of them didn't even use proper words.

I stood eating my ice cream and looked down the hill. Mother and Father were having a great time; a dark blanket moved around them and crawled over them in waves. The edge of the park was very close. There was a street, with shops, I went.

They've started buying more and more food. Mother spends hours cooking in the kitchen and we eat until we're almost sick. Except Gran, she just watches. Last week we had visitors. Five people, one I think used to come around our old house, the rest I don't know about. We sat at the big table and everybody stuffed themselves, except Gran. Then they all took out little boxes full of big fat flies and watched the spiders come. Not just on the web-curtains, some of the flies had their wings pulled off and the spiders ran out from all their hiding places in the old slippers and under the dusty furniture and bit the flies. The flies tried to run away but it's not really their thing. The noise was horrible but our visitors looked like they were listening to a symphony.

The next morning I saw a dead mouse hanging by the pantry door, wrapped like a giant fly. I don't know what kind of spider does that.

The visitors didn't leave which makes them guests. They don't say much, just watch the spiders. The spiders don't hide as much; they scurry around over the furniture and the people. I let them even though they make me cringe. I know better than to kill one.

Gran has been ill, everybody fusses over her but they won't allow a doctor.

"It'll be over soon," they keep saying, standing around the

bed and rubbing ointment on her skin. I think she might die. She says stuff but the words are too dry, and I'm not sure her eyes are working because she turns her head whenever anybody moves. I stay in my room and nobody bothers me. But then I feel guilty because she is my Gran and she let us live here. So then I go and see if I can help. The house is full of curtains now. The windows are covered but we're not allowed to turn on the lights.

I woke up during the night. I heard a kind of a scream. It mixed in with my dream, where I was running through the house with a huge can of fly spray blasting the curtains and filling the rooms, and it's raining dead spiders and then I see my Gran, she screams and I wake up.

Except I knew it wasn't just in my dreams and it wasn't her voice. I crept out onto the landing avoiding the criss-cross of silk threads, sure breaking one would give me away. I crept halfway down the stairs: I know where the creaking starts. I saw Gran hunched over dragging or carrying something back into her room. I opened my mouth to shout, scared she would hurt herself but I saw a spider as big as a fist drop on a thread and land on her shoulder. And I think I saw a paw before the door was closed. Looks like we got a dog after all, just not one I could stroke.

I went back to my room but couldn't sleep. I heard voices. People were moving. It must have been hours; outside the birds are waking up and starting to sing. Inside I'm watching as the guests carry Gran out of her room on a stretcher, she's covered in silk. Spiders are dropping off her after adding their bit. She must have died.

They took her into the cellar. Mother caught me spying and I was ready to be beaten but she hugged me instead and took me with her. I couldn't see the cellar walls or the ceiling, everything was covered in thick silk. Spiders hung like Christmas decorations in a horror film. I felt as if they were watching me with their round black eyes.

The guests carried Gran to the well. They were going to throw her in, I looked at Mother.

"It's the way of things," she whispered to me, smiled and gave my hand a little squeeze. I looked between two guests, a man and a woman, and watched as Gran was lowered into the well. I pushed past them and saw. It was full of webs. She sank through a little but they were spun so thick and she was so thin, the silk took her weight and held her.

Then the spiders came. All sizes and colours, they spun themselves in one after the other until the white was black. It looked like a cocoon made out of dying arachnids. That's what they call spiders. It's written above Gran's front door in German, so it's not spelt the same but Mother told me. She said we should know this, that it's important for people like us.

After we left the cellar with Gran wrapped in the well Mother gave me a book to read. Then she and Father and the guests started boarding up the windows. The doors were next. I put down my book and Mother sat beside me.

"It's better this way," she said, "unbelievers aren't welcome now."

A few lamps were lit. I noticed the spiders were gone.

"They've gone to help your Gran," Father told me.

"It'll all be over soon," Mother said. I went up to my room. I put a chair in front of the door and checked to see if the fly spray I'd bought on my birthday was still there. I took off the top and sniffed it. I touched my finger on it but stopped myself from spraying it. I wanted to save what I had.

I brought food and drink up to my room and a torch I found under the sink. It's weird in the house now, all those webs hanging empty. I don't know why but it feels a little sad. It's quiet as well, I mean it was never a noisy place but now nobody talks, nobody does much. The guests spend most of their time in the cellar. I try not to be noticed.

I've put the chair back against my door but I don't think it will help. And I wish I'd bought more fly spray, tons more.

Mother took me into the cellar, said, "I had to go, to be good for Gran, like the others." It was dark in the cellar. I thought the guests would be sitting or kneeling near the well. I was wrong.

They were hanging. Wrapped in their own silk blankets on threads as thick as rope, they swayed as Mother walked past them to where Father stood looking down into the well. I waited just inside the doorway.

319

"Come on, you mustn't be afraid, this is how it should be, what we've been preparing for," Mother held out her hand for me to go and take hold of. I stepped forward. Then one of the guests twirled and her face looked down on mine. Even through the strands I could see it wasn't the right shape. The forehead bulged out because the rest of her head had been sucked in. Something had been eating her, from the inside.

I looked over at the well.

"It's alright," Mother said as a huge claw as big as my head reached up over the edge of the well. I screamed and I ran. And I know I couldn't have but I'm sure I heard Gran's long dry voice saying, "Wiiicked boy."

Now I just hear a scratchy, tack, tack, on the wooden floors, sometimes downstairs and sometimes outside my door. Mother and Father never came out of the cellar, and I'm staying in my room. I listen and watch the chair pushed under my door handle. And clutch my can of fly spray.

The Sweet Meat and the Beet

David Turnbull

The Beet Chamber

S OLDIERS CAME SCURRYING to the nursery and roused them from the nest.

Danding blinked sleep out of his eyes. Somewhere in the gloom, Koren started to wail and bawl. "Not yet. It can't be time." His beseeching set off some the infants. Their crying echoed against the mud walls of the chamber.

Weevill nannies rushed to soothe them, gently nudging them with their snouts, suckling them back to sleep with syrupy drops of aphid honeydew. Danding found Pashina's hand. They rose as one and stumbled to the muddy floor of the chamber.

"Stay close," he told her as they were herded with two dozen of the older children into the murky mouth of a tunnel. Pincers clacking, the soldiers drove them forward, heads bumping against the gouged ceiling, shoulders scraping the curve of the walls, Koren's sobs echoing all around.

The floor of the tunnel seemed to spiral upward in steep gradients. Danding kept hold of Pashina's hand, her fingers entwined with his. Within minutes they arrived at the hollow of a new chamber. Danding gasped for breath, his heart pounding in his chest.

An overseer was waiting. His nymph scuttled and shifted as the soldiers jostled the children into an assembly. The staccato movement of the nymph caused the overseer's withered limbs to flop flaccidly about. With his mistress's pincers firmly embedded in the crusty scars on his side he looked like one of the grass

dollies they used to play with in the nursery.

"From today onward it's all about the sweet meat and the beet," said the overseer.

Pashina edged closer to Danding. Their grass skirts rustled. Her green eyes were full of apprehension. She toyed nervously with a lock of her matted hair.

The nymph moved again and the overseer's arms swayed pendulously. Danding could see the veins that marbled his arms and the black rot that was eating away at his redundant hands.

"You have been brought to the Beet Chamber to do your duty," he said

"I want to go back to my nanny," sobbed Koren.

The nymph darted forward, antennae snaking wildly above the overseer's shoulders. The overseer's harsh voice echoed around the chamber.

"It's time to put childish things behind you."

His nymph rose on its rear legs, thorax bending as it lifted him high above their heads. "What is our purpose?" demanded the overseer, looming over them.

"To serve the Queen and the Little Master," they recited.

The nymph lowered the overseer down. His useless feet dragged along the ground, twisting his legs to unusual contortions. "For the foreseeable future," he told them, "the way that you will serve will be to mash the beet."

He looked up to a wide hole in the ceiling.

"The beet will come tumbling down," he said. "It will fall into the pit. The foreman will show you what you must do."

The foreman entered the chamber. He was naked. His body gleamed with sweat and sticky splatters of beet juice. He strode over to the wall and picked up the largest of the white shinbones that lay stacked there.

"Work hard," said the overseer. His nymph turned and scuttled into the tunnel, back legs kicking up dirt.

"Choose a bone," barked the foreman.

Still holding onto Pashina's hand, Danding followed the other youngsters to the wall. Once everyone had selected a bone the foreman ordered that they form a circle around the pit. They waited. From above them there came a dreadful rumbling. Koren started to cry again.

The beets came down in a thunderous avalanche that soon filled the pit to the brim with pale, ugly tubers. Danding blinked and coughed out dust. The foreman dropped to his knees and raised his shinbone above his head. His gleaming muscles tensed as he brought the bone down full force onto the pile of beets, splitting their fibrous skins and breaking off jagged chunks.

One by one he looked each of them in the eye.

"Get on your knees."

They did as he commanded.

On his signal, they raised their bones above their heads.

And down they all came.

A dull thump echoed in the muddy chamber.

"Learn the song," said the foreman. "It will help you to keep time."

"Beat the beet!"

Thump!

"Smash the beet!"

Thump!

"Crush the beet!"

Thump!

They already knew the words. They had been hearing them all their lives, hammering away in the mud ceiling above the nursery and reverberating through the hollows of the tunnels.

"Beat the beet! Smash the beet! Crush the beet!"

Endlessly it went on, till Danding's arms ached, and his shoulders burned, and he was drenched in the juices of the beet. When, at last, the foreman felt the mash was good, a procession of worker drones came scampering into the chamber, skin baskets held in their pincers. With industrious precision, they scooped up the mash to transport it away to the Cauldron Chamber.

There were only a few minutes respite before the next load of beet came roaring down. Danding raised his bone. Pashina did too. And all the others. Koren's face was streaked in dirt and tears. But he joined the chant and did his duty.

"Beat the beet!"

Thump!

"Smash the beet!"

Thump!

"Crush the beet!"

The Meat Chamber

The Meat Chamber also had a wide hole in its muddy ceiling. The meat would come tumbling down to accumulate in a twisted pile that filled up the pit to its ragged brim. In the Meat Chamber there was a clear division of labour.

The overseer was an ill-tempered old woman, with greasy grey hair that hung down over her sagging breasts. Her limbs were as flaccid as those of the Beet Chamber overseer, but her nymph was slow and bumbling, so they weren't often caused to dance around that much.

Many, many sleeps had passed before the soldiers came to herd them through the narrow tunnel that joined Beet Chamber to Meat Chamber. They were older and bigger, biceps and shoulders taut and sinuous from all the constant mashing.

When they had assembled, the nymph had passed ponderously along the line, while the overseer carefully examined their outstretched hands. Some were assigned to the boning and skinning crew, some to the gutting crew, and the remainder to the grinding crew.

Danding and Pashina ended up being assigned to different crews. The separation was unsettling. In the nursery they had shared the same nest and had fallen asleep each night, drowsy

325

on honeydew, staring into each other's eyes as their cheeks rested against the cooling camber of their nanny's ochre shell.

Now they were parted by duty.

When the meat came down into the pit Danding's crew would scramble first for the legs and arms. Hurriedly they would set to work with sharpened slithers of slate, peeling away the skin, then slicing the meat from the bone and cutting it into fist-sized hunks that were tossed into skin baskets.

Meanwhile Pashina and the other gutters would have hauled out the torsos and sliced open their bellies so the organs and intestines slopped out into the skin baskets they held wedged between their legs. That done they'd reach in and pull out anything that stubbornly remained in the hollow—a heart, or a lung, or a kidney. Then the clean torsos would be passed back to the skinners.

Last to do their bit were the grinders, to which Koren had been assigned. Once the shinbones had been set to one side for future use the grinders would shatter the remainder with rocks and then scrape out the marrow with little sticks. Finally, the splintered bones would be forcefully ground into a fine meal between two huge boulders.

There were revelations to be had in the Meat Chamber.

Unlike his sullen Beet Chamber counterpart the foreman on the boning crew was affable and talkative. "The bone meal goes into the porridge you were weaned on in the nursery," he told them. "Another type of porridge is made from the marrow. It feeds the grubs in the hatching cells."

He picked up a flayed torso that had been passed to him by one of the skinners.

"The cured skin is pulled over baskets woven from sticks to make them watertight." He reached for his cutting implement. "The meat is bound for the cauldrons to be boiled with the sugar beet mash that gets served to the Queen and the Little Master. The dregs from the cauldrons go to the winged alates. The rest, all the shit—the guts and the gristle—goes into the stews that feed us and the drones."

"Outside," he replied when they asked him where the meat and the beet came from.

"What's outside?" asked Danding, hacking wet, flaccid meat from a forearm.

"It's the place beyond the great mound," replied the foreman. "The ceiling outside is called the sky and there is a yellow circle called the sun."

He worked his piece of slate dexterously in and out of the ribs of the torso. Beside him, Danding set the bone of the cleaned forearm to one side and dropped the chunks of meat into his skin basket.

"There's nothing beyond the great mound," he said.

"There is," insisted the foreman. "There was once a man on my crew who had worked in the fields where the beet is grown..."

"What's a field?" asked someone.

The foreman shrugged.

"Anyway, this man injured his leg and the soldiers brought

him back down here to work in the Meat Chamber. He told me all about the sky and the sun and the fresh air."

"What's fresh air?"

The foreman shrugged again.

"The man said it smells nice and tastes nice. It's cool inside your lungs."

"I wish I could taste the fresh air," sighed the blood-splattered girl sitting crossed legged next to Danding.

The foreman traced the edge of his flint down the spine of the torso.

"If you're lucky that's where you'll all end up. Outside in the fields."

Danding narrowed his eyes.

"This meat?" he asked, reaching for another forearm. "Is it us? Do we become the meat?"

All of the crew looked down in horror at the ragged limbs they were working on.

"The man told me there are other humans on the outside," the foreman assured them. "They're bred as meat, not workers, fattened up on a sticky soup made from bone meal and the sweet meat slops chewed up and regurgitated by worker drones. He said they can't talk and they're as stupid as aphids."

The Cauldron Chamber

Danding watched the smoke as it was sucked up into the dark maw of the chimney. He wondered where it went. Might there truly be such a place as outside? He closed his eyes and found himself daydreaming about blue sky and fresh air.

Pain shot up his arm. A gob of hot syrup had splashed onto the back of his hand. He winced at the sharp sting of it and turned his attention back to stirring the contents of the stone cauldron with his big wooden paddle. The flames from the fire that licked the belly of the cauldron sparked red cinders at his legs and made him jump some more.

Through the vaporous haze he saw Pashina, carefully dropping red chunks of meat into the swirling churn of the sugar beet syrup. She gave him a coy smile, then turned her head away. Many more sleeps had passed. They had been moved on again. Now they were back on the same crew. But an uncomfortable awkwardness had developed between them.

Both of them were undergoing physical changes. Pashina's breasts had started to protrude and become rounder. Her bony hips stood out more noticeably beneath her grass skirt. He, in turn, was growing sharp little whiskers on his chin and wiry black hairs in all sorts of places. His voice seemed to alternate between high-pitched squeak and low, sonorous baritone.

At night when they lay side by side in the grass nest, exhausted and reeking of the sickly scent of the syrup, they'd be tense and apart, not hugging for warmth as they'd done so often in the nursery. He'd listen to her breathing and it seemed to set off strange, harmonious rhythms within him. He'd feel his heart pounding so forcefully he'd think he was about to die. And a pleasant, but somewhat unsettling fluttering would start in his belly.

He wove her a grass dolly out of straw from the nest, arms and legs hung loosely from loops through the tightly twisted torso. Pressing his thumb and finger tightly against its side, like the pincers of a nymph, he shook it about to make the limbs dance.

"I'm the overseer," he said in a gruff voice. "And you will do exactly as I say."

Pashina smiled and took the dolly from him.

"Into the cauldron you go," she said, plucking the limbs one by one.

They laughed. It was like they were little once more.

The Breeding Chamber

The woman that Danding had been forced to lie with had huge breasts. Her fat arm was wrapped around him. He could smell the stench of the sour sweat that emanated from the matted hair beneath her armpits. She told him her name was Meret. He shuddered when she planted a wet kiss on his cheek.

"You didn't think they would let you stay with your little girlfriend once she fell pregnant, did you?" she asked.

She tried to straddle him, but he managed to push her off.

The chamber was full of the sounds of urgent copulation, punctuated by the occasional ejaculate moan. Somewhere in the dark recesses of one of the chamber cells sat Pashina, belly growing fatter by the day. Danding missed her. Missed her kisses and caresses. Missed the way they had learned to delve and buck in ecstatic unison.

"What happens when the babies are born?" asked Danding.

"They let us keep them on the tit till they can walk," explained Meret, tweaking his nipple crudely between her fat finger and thumb. "Then they send them down to the nursery to suckle on the aphids and get mollycoddled by the weevil nannies."

"And then we move on?" asked Danding, brushing her hand away from his chest.

"You'll stay a while," she replied. "You've got good seed in your balls. They'll expect you to plant a few more before you go."

Another sickly shudder ran through him.

"And what about Pashina?" he asked. "Will she come with me?"

Meret snorted.

"Only boys and barren girls move on. Your little girlfriend can take a seed. She'll be kept here now. When the next lot of boys come up from the Cauldron Chamber she'll have to spread her legs and let them fuck her till another seed takes."

"No!" he yelled. "I won't let that happen."

Meret clamped a sweaty palm across his mouth.

"Hush," she whispered. "Or you'll have the overseer and her nymph down on us."

Danding started to weep.

"It's not that bad," she breathed into his ear. "They treat us good. Sometimes we even get a bit of sweet meat and beet, as well as the usual stew."

Her stinky hand remained firmly clamped over his mouth. Her wet tongue poked grotesquely into his ear. "If I take my hand away are you going to promise to keep quiet?"

Danding nodded his head. His mind was racing, thinking about the dreadful prospect of never seeing Pashina again. Meret removed her hand. She traced it slowly down the wiry hairs on his belly to his navel.

"How many babies have you had?" he asked, starting to feel feverish.

"If you get me seeded it'll be ten," she said. "I reckon I'll still be good for a few more after that."

Danding wanted to be sick.

He jumped when she reached down and grabbed his limp penis.

"Now, let's see if we can wake up this little soldier," she said, squeezing him hard and digging her dirty fingernails into his flesh. Danding felt bile rise up in his throat. He tried to struggle free, but she sat on him, knees jabbing into his ribs, pubis grinding against him.

The Feeding Chamber

There were ventilation bores within the honeycomb of the Feeding Chamber. The chant and thump rising up from the Beet Chamber could be heard constantly. "Beat the beet!" Thump! "Smash the beet!" Thump! It was like the great pulsing heart of the mound. Danding's heart seemed to pulse obediently in time with it. As if it was as much a part of him as his own heart.

He found that if you listened closely near some of the vents you could hear the infants crying down in the Breeding Chamber. He knew that three of them were his. Another was on the way. But his only thought was of the pink little boy he'd fathered with Pashina. That was his son. The others didn't matter. *They* were made from obligation.

"I'll find my way back to you," he'd yelled to Pashina when the soldiers came scuttling into the Breeding Chamber to drive him and the others through the tunnel to the Feeding Chamber.

"You won't," she'd insisted, nursing their son against her breast. "But I'll always remember you in my dreams."

Danding blamed the Queen for his woes. It was because of her that he found himself endlessly pushed from chamber to chamber. She was the cause of his separation from Pashina. Soon she would cause their child to be separated from Pashina. And the whole sorry cycle would start again.

The Queen demanded obedience and subjugation. Her huge, bloated form wriggling grotesquely in the royal chamber, endlessly oozing eggs, as the Little Master fussed around her, and the entire mound toiled to serve her needs.

Danding hated the Queen.

In his wildest fantasies he would go to the chamber to serve the Queen her sweet meat and beet. He would bow subserviently as he set the huge clay tureen before her. Out of the gloom she would ripple monstrously forward, mighty, slavering maw at the ready. And just as she was about to take her fill he would

plunge his hand into the syrupy stew to retrieve the slate boning knife that was submerged amongst the bobbing chunks of
meat. Before she could screech out an alert to the Little Master
he would plunge the knife straight into the soulless black of her
eye.

He knew though that this could never become a reality.

The throne chamber was protected by an entire battalion of
the Queen's fiercest soldiers. Besides, he was not even on the
crew that served there. It was the handful of girls who had not
been able to conceive a child that the Feeding Chamber overseer selected as serving maids for the Little Master and the
Queen's winged alates. The honour of serving the Queen herself
had fallen to Koren, tall and broad, and no longer such a cry
baby.

Danding was instead selected for the crew that fed the blind,
squirming grubs in the hatching cells. His task was to dip his
paddle into a clay tureen and shovel great, slopping heaps of
meal and marrow porridge into the gluey orifices of their impatient mouths.

It often occurred to him that one of these grubs might transform into a winged alate that would fly away to become Queen
of her own mound. If he couldn't kill the Queen then maybe he
could kill one of her heirs. He considered using his paddle to
beat one of the grubs to a pulp. Smashing and mashing it into a
gelatinous soup the way he'd been taught to do with the beet all
those long sleeps ago. As he fed them the porridge he'd find
himself absently chanting under his breath.

"Beat the grub! Smash the grub! Crush the grub!"

And he'd thump his paddle in time against the side of the tureen.

There were days when his hands held the paddle so tightly he felt sure he was about to go through with it. But then he'd remember his promise to Pashina. She didn't believe he'd be able to find his way back to her, but he clung with a passion to the notion that it might be possible. If he killed a grub he'd be torn to shreds by soldiers within moments of the deed.

His anger went unrequited, bubbling away inside him like syrup in a cauldron.

Some days he felt like a shinbone that was ready to snap.

In the end in was Koren who became the subject of his ire. They were all settling down in the grass nest for the night, bellies sloshing with the gut and gore of their daily stew, when he came strutting cockily into the sleep chamber.

"Great news," he announced, chest puffing out, grass skirt swaying to his swagger. "I won't be coming with you when you move on. I've been selected to become a foreman. Who knows, one day I might even become an overseer."

Everyone went to congratulate him. When it was Danding's turn he balled his fist as tightly as he could. Koren gave him a huge, toothy smile. Danding smiled back, then slammed his fist as hard as he could into the cry baby's side.

Koren squealed and fell to the floor, writhing in the dirt and straw.

"You bastard, Danding," he howled. "Why did you do that?"

335

Danding hovered over him, fist still clenched.

"I thought you might like to feel what it's going to be like with a pincer stabbing into your side," he growled.

Koren kicked out at him.

"I'll report you to the fucking overseer."

Danding just sneered and spat in his face.

The Beet Field

Sweating profusely Danding climbed the slope of the mound, lugging his fourth overloaded basket of sugar beet tubers. The sun was high in the morning sky, casting long shadows from the mound's towering pinnacles. He liked the blue sky but he wasn't sure yet if he liked the sun. It blistered his skin and made his eyes water.

He emptied the contents of his basket onto the beet pile. A procession of busy worker drones was gathering up the tubers in their pincers and dropping them down into a wide hole a little way up the side of the mound. Danding imagined them tumbling down into the Beet Room.

Further up, he could see grey smoke belching from the wide mouth of the mound's chimney. The fires beneath the cauldrons were being stoked up. His gaze followed the trail of smoke across the verdant miles of the beet fields, green leaves shimmering in the gentle flow of the warm breeze. He could see the soldiers shepherding the pickers out into the furrows to dig out the rows of ripened beets with their hands. He was glad the overseer had selected him as a lugger, even though the work was back breaking.

One of the other luggers emptied his basket and stood beside him. His hair was long and straggly, his beard matted around his chin. Danding stroked his own wiry whiskers. The lugger handed him his water satchel. Danding swallowed down two mouthfuls.

"You don't remember me, do you?" said the lugger.

Danding wiped some sweat from his brow and held his hand over his eyes as he squinted at his companion. There was nothing familiar about the weather-browned face that looked back at him.

"Hercas," said the lugger. "We were in the nursery together. I tried to steal your porridge once. But you wouldn't give it up."

Danding placed him now. Hercas had been one of the older kids when he was little. A bit of a bully, he seemed to recall. Danding felt his forearms tensing. Since the incident with Koren, he'd become very handy with his fists.

"You'd better not try anything," he warned.

Hercas grinned through his beard.

"I wasn't planning to. Actually, I wanted to show you something."

Danding handed him back the water satchel.

"We need to go a little higher on the mound."

Danding cast a worried glance at the worker drones, still diligently picking away at the pile of beet tubers.

"They won't trouble us," Hercas assured him. "Once they're set a task that's all they focus on. They won't deviate."

Danding followed Hercas. The higher they climbed the more he could hear the sombre calls of the meat herds in the fields on the other side of the mound. "Maaa!" "Gaaa!" He hated the unintelligible noises they made. It always put him in mind of the Meat Room, ragged limbs and torsos endlessly tumbling down into the pit.

Hercas came to a halt. Danding stood slightly down from him on the steep gradient of the mound. "You see those shapes just beyond that line of trees?" he asked.

At first Danding wasn't sure. But then he saw them, odd looking shapes, silhouetted by the glow from the sun, like dozens of fingers pointing up to the sky.

"What are they?" he asked.

"Human mounds," said Hercas. "Built thousands of sleeps ago, by our ancestors."

Danding spat onto the dirt.

"Humans don't build mounds," he said. "That's for Queens and Little Masters."

"They were built by humans," insisted Hercas. "And humans lived inside them."

Danding looked back at the objects.

"How do you know?"

"Someone went there once."

"Someone lied," laughed Danding.

Hercas looked down the slope at him

"I heard you once worked on the boning crew."

Danding nodded.

"Did the foreman tell you about the yellow sun and the blue sky and the taste of fresh air?"

Danding nodded again.

"And did you believe him?"

Hercas stared to lay emphasis on his point.

Danding climbed a little way up the slope to get a better view.

"Some of us plan to go there," said Hercas.

Danding felt his sticky brow creasing.

"How?" he asked.

"There's an area just beyond the far fields where there's only ever one soldier on patrol. We've sharpened some shinbones and hidden them behind the nest huts."

Sharpened shinbones?

The old anger awoke within Danding like a raging hunger.

He felt his fists clench.

"If you reach the human mounds, what then?" he asked.

"If it's good there we'll come back and help more to escape."

Danding's thoughts turned to Pashina and his poor, lost son.

"Including those still inside the mound?" he asked.

Hercas thought for a moment.

"If we could find a way, we'd surely try to get some people out of the mound."

Danding looked to the line of trees once more. The objects were like huge sticks planted upright in the ground. He didn't think humans could ever have had the intelligence or the wherewithal to construct such things. Yet he found himself seized by curiosity.

"Could I come with you?" he asked.

Hercas grinned back at him.

"I was hoping you'd say that."

Dusk was falling when they crawled on their bellies through the dirt of the sugar beet furrows. In addition to Danding and Hercas there were four others—two men, one a lugger, the other a picker, and two women, both pickers. The weapons they had wrought from sharpened shinbones were strapped to their back by twines of grass.

They reached the end of the beet field and crouched in a low semicircle behind Hercas. They could see the six-legged soldier scuttling back and forth as it patrolled its designated territory. Just behind it were the long acres of the grass, where the pickers were sent to gather straw for the nests between beet harvests. Once the deed was done they were going to sprint to the forest beyond.

Hercas withdrew his weapon and rose slowly to his feet. Danding and the others followed his lead. The soldier stopped. Its bulbous head snapped in their direction, antennae twitching, pincers clacking. Its segmented rear rose slightly from the ground as it excreted glistening beads of dew. A dreadful, putrid scent came wafting towards them, making them hack and sneeze.

"Go for the underbelly," said Hercas.

Danding blinked and held out his weapon, eyes streaming

from the pungent odour.

The soldier launched itself forward, pincers raised high.

Hercas ran to meet it.

Danding made to follow, hatred a fire in his belly.

Somehow he couldn't move a muscle. He didn't know if it was the strange scent that the soldier had let off or whether his courage had simply failed him. But he was frozen to the spot, his anger consumed by a melancholy lethargy. Around him the others stood still and unmoving, weapons lowered, eyes wide with fear.

Hercas must have felt it too, because at the last moment he seemed to stumble and skid to a halt. The soldier danced eerily before him and hacked up a paste-like regurgitation. A sticky puddle of resin oozed around Hercas' feet, firmly trapping him where he stood.

The soldier was on him in the blink of an eye. Its pincers closed around his waist. He dropped his shinbone as he was raised high into the air, strands of translucent resin stretching out behind him. His legs juddered. He cried out in pain. The soldier closed its pincers and snapped him in two. The pieces of him fell to the ground, spurting blood and gore.

One of the women screamed.

Danding saw soldiers, dozens of them, rapidly skirting the beet field. Behind them came the wizened Beet Field overseer, leathery limbs flipping and flapping to the galloping motion of his nymph.

His voice echoed over the shimmering green leaves of the

beet.

"What have you done, you fools?"

The Culling Fields

Danding dipped his head to the clay trough and sucked up a mouthful of the oily regurgitated swill. It was sickly sweet and gritty with fibre. He fought back his gag reflex and swallowed. In the fields this was all there was to eat, so he had no choice but to endure.

A sharp pain on his left shoulder caused him to jump, spluttering out a second mouth of slop. His head snapped round. A female child had bitten him on the shoulder. "Gaaa!" she said, trying forcefully to squeeze into his spot. "Gaaa!"

Danding slapped her away and dipped his head for another mouthful. All around him the meat jostled and barged for a place at the trough. They were broad shouldered, hirsute and shaggy headed, laden with layers of fat. Danding wiped his mouth with the back of his hand and stepped back from the trough. The child immediately tried to slip into the space he'd left behind, but one of the males caught her by the hair and tossed her several feet across the field.

Danding staggered away. This had been their punishment for trying to escape. With the overseer's curses ringing in their ears the soldiers had chased them to the Culling Fields and abandoned them there. The meat herds were millions strong. In the chaotic melee of their brutal existence he'd quickly lost the others. He had no idea where they were, or even if they were still alive.

The fields were trodden into a swampy quagmire. The meat defecated and urinated where they stood, trudging their waste into the mud with their big, lumbering feet. As Danding splashed and slipped his way across the field one of the obese females fell prostate in the filth before him, hairy buttocks raised in a grotesque dance of erotic enticement.

He heard the familiar skitter of insect feet skimming over the mud as one of the herder drones rushed to cajole him into copulation. He felt its pincers prodding at his shoulder blades. He hung back. He'd learned that if he hesitated the situation would soon resolve itself. Sure enough a brawny male barged past him. It dropped to its knees, sending up foul splashes of effluence. Within moments it was rutting and grunting.

Job done, the herder drone skittered away.

Danding pushed on across the field. To his left he could see the stone dykes that formed the birthing pens where the impregnated females were driven. Some worker drones were chasing a clutch of infants into the fields. They were bawling and howling as they slithered and skidded around in the mud.

Ahead of him was his destination. The shallow lake over which the meat was driven to the area where the butcher drones waited. They'd splash and panic through the water, making their guttural noises, to emerge clean for the slaughter.

Danding watched as a group of herder drones corralled a hundred or so of the meat by the edge of the lake. He'd been observing this for several wakes now. Soon the first of them would be sent across. The butcher drones would move swiftly.

The decapitated heads would be tossed, spinning through the air, to the regimented rows of soldiers, waiting patiently to be fed. The limbs would be removed by the deft snipping of pincers. A procession of workers would then transport the arms and legs and torsos to a pile beside the hole in the side of the mound that led down to the Meat Room.

It was cold and efficient.

But Danding had observed that there would always be a few from the herd that would not be taken. Perhaps they were too scrawny, or maybe diseased. Possibly some other factor was at play. All that Danding knew for sure was that four or five of these rejects would quickly be shepherded away by waiting soldiers.

It had set him thinking. Could there be other chambers in the mound? From its enormous size this seemed entirely plausible. There had to be chambers where the baskets were woven and the skin pulled taut over them. There had to be chambers where the kindling for the cauldron fires was chopped and then stirring paddles fashioned. There had to be chambers where the hollows were hewn into rocks for the cauldrons themselves.

He had convinced himself that these chambers were where the rejected meat was taken. There to be taught to perform simple tasks. And he saw in this his chance to get back inside the mound, to somehow find his way back to Pashina and then to find their son.

It was a dream that he clung to.

Didn't they all have dreams? Dreams were the stuff of the human heart. They were the difference between humans and their oppressors. Unlike a soldier or a worker, a human who held true to his dreams could easily deviate from the task expected of him.

Danding looked at his reflection in the lake. He'd gained weight from wakes of feeding on the slop, but he was nowhere near as corpulent as a male should be in its prime. Surely he'd be rejected and hopefully conscripted to work once more within the dank labyrinth of the mound.

As the herders cajoled the first of the meat into the water, Danding skirted the edge of the lake. Stealthily, without drawing too much attention, he managed to insert himself between two of the filthy, bellowing brutes. The slaughter had already commenced. He watched a shaggy haired head sailing through the air, leaving crimson spray in its wake as it fell to the waiting pincers of a soldier.

When he waded into the water it felt cool around his mud caked thighs.

Chemical Glide

Andrew Darlington

'NOT WITH A BANG'

THE FOLLOWING MORNING the sun comes up over the ramshackle rooftops. Its bloated light ignites rainwater pools in the street, turning them into reflected blood. It sets fire to stagnant areas of brackish water beyond the town's perimeter of fields, and riddles listless shrouds of shore-mist with multi-legged columns of light. Within the adobe houses brown-skinned people with thousand-year-old eyes are already stirring. Inca-ancient women move to prepare meals. Barbarian children slink from disinterested parental eyes to infest the alleyways. Later, as the sun climbs, men who look as though they've been carved from mahogany slouch on mud-rutted street corners glancing out towards the misting bay, to where the gently decaying wooden boats have been beached, hauled there to sleep upturned like basking crocodiles, and neglected fishing nets hang like ill-repaired spiders-web from drying frames. The men smoke huge ragged cigarettes, spit long brown comets of dirty saliva, and exchange desultory whispered phrases in Aztec-Spanish. A line of eight drying octopus hang like descending aliens.

Another stupid day... only this time, Kaukonon is dead.

"Kaukonon?" He registers blood spattered in odd patterns on the wall. At first they resemble cryptic messages from psychiatric inkblot tests splashed across crumbling plaster. Then Paul Quinn's eyes grow accustomed to the gloomy half-light of the room's interior, and he can see the body sprawled across the rumpled bed, lying curled into a foetus-shape. Casually. As though he's asleep. But there's no movement, no sound to betray the rhythm of breath. The corpse-skin is pale, the wrists open and already fly-crawled. His hand is a claw, drawing ridges of soiled sheet into it. And the blood lies in circling accretion discs, one within the other. The outer rim has already dried to a powdering of fine flakes. Inside, through contour lines of denser reds, it becomes a congealing liver-black jelly directly beneath the opened wrist.

Is he lying there relaxed and peaceful? The kind of peaceful relaxation he'd never found in life? Standing here, it's tempting to make such an argument. But that just comes down to failure of empathy. His features are still as only the features of the dead are still. And in those eyes, the stare that only the dead can have. No. No relaxation. No peace. Just nothingness. Nothing.

Another stupid day. Confused, Quinn stands in indecision. There's blood. A blood-drip. Drip drip-dripping. And something he must do about it. But more urgently, a squirming in his gut prompts him forward towards the lavatory located at the far side of Kaukonon's room. He catches faint traces of its stench as he stands with his thoughts slowly separating out into a series of layers. The discovery of the suicide means there are actions he must undertake. But the thought of passing so close to the body is seriously repellent. The bile at the back of his throat is already choking. So instead he carefully retraces his earlier footsteps, a measured tread shuffling backwards out of the room. Pacing silently, as though the slightest noise will disturb Kaukonon's sleep. As though he's going to turn and open his eyes. That's illogical. But even now he's checking that the door handle is free of blood. Less so as not to leave evidence undisturbed, more that he's loath to touch spilled bodily fluid. It's only as the result of a conscious effort that he's able to reach out and turn the handle. It rattles, loose and ill-fitting.

One, two, three steps, through the door, and out onto the landing. He breathes hard. Down the stairs, then right into the communal room where a wall-mounted TV is still flickering silver soundless symbols. Morse patterns of snow-storm static washing at the black walls. In the room there are sleeping figures. His eyes trace the configuration of limbs, recognising Huxley and Vendon, then the shape of Ahriman—lost somewhere on the third day of his Chemical Glide trance. It's only then that he registers a girl's eyes watching him. Naomi.

"It's Kaukonon. I think he's dead. In fact, I know he's dead."

"What do you mean, dead?" Her cold eyes resting on him.

"How many ways are there of being dead?" He can think of nothing else to say at her.

'DESERTS OF VAST ETERNITY'

The horizon is sudden. Light hangs on the world's edge, a dawn frozen in the act of breaking. The plain is bleak. Perhaps the air is thin? But as no actual breathing is involved, it doesn't really matter. Anyway, unstructured wisps of spindle-limbed plants are hung on what little air there is. And they're strung in bizarre constellations like models of complex molecules in a science exhibition. Or incomprehensible messages in psychiatric inkblot tests. A mystic code, if only he's able to decipher it. Below them, in the shadows cast by the scrawny plants, tangles of long-legged spiders move purposefully. Except they're not spiders. Not quite what you'd call arachnid. One of them he's named 'Twitcher'. But which one? It's not easy to differentiate them now. 'Twitcher, is that you? Or you...?'

The one he assumes to be Twitcher indicates with wavy feelers. In response, he stimulates the wheels of the caterpillar tread beneath him, something that comes easy, feeling the hard igneous grit growl and spit in response as he powers up the slight incline. Following the spider-thing up. There's a structure standing in the hollow they're laboriously leaving. An artificial structure. So much is apparent. It's hard to categorise it further. Its contours ramble in eccentric baroques, complexifying and branching from three main stems that could be termed legs. Or struts. As though whoever, or whatever, designed it couldn't quite decide. While at its highest points the upper aerials fray, like metallic foliage, into the star-shot mauve sky.

Concentrating hard he can recall emerging from a portal set into one of those 'legs'. A smooth kind of birthing. Without effort its technological stimuli had disgorged him, and his shell, into this exterior aridity. But what came before that? He remembers nothing—beyond a name, Ahriman. Yes, the name must refer to himself. But that's a matter of little importance. He approaches the crest of the incline. His caterpillar treads shunt in close intuitive co-ordination, circling thickets of weed, gatherings of spider-things, or outcrops of ancient weathered rock in layers of geological strata. Showing eternities of time, telling a planetary tale. If only he knew how to interpret it.

Here, there are already deep tracks embedded into drifts of reddish-ochre shingle. So he's travelled here before? But he remembers nothing of previous journeys. The light is languid, throwing long listless shadows in lazy interactions. And as he hits the crest of the incline he can see the tiny red disc of the dying sun ahead of him...

Twitcher indicates impatiently with wavy feelers. Hurry. Hurry.

'I SAW THE BEST MINDS OF MY GENERATION DESTROYED BY MADNESS...'

06:21:47 am.

Shapes. Blood in spirals. Nebulae. Fractals. Orbits. Hemispheres. Ellipses. And lives trapped in circles. Repetitions. Contour lines on a map.

"So Kaukonon topped himself?" Huxley shrugs. No emphasis. A tall, bohemian, middle-aged European, his untidy hair tangled with beads of perspiration. His stick-insect body subdivided into slices of light filtered through the battered venetian blinds. "His paranoia's been getting worse for months. For all we know it was him responsible for all those decapitated rats."

"I hear tell he only came here 'cos he got the call while his bath was running," adds Vendon, slack-jawed and unshaven. "They say he said the first thing that came to mind. Quick, to terminate the conversation. Thought he was accepting an invitation to a glide-party."

"Why do you have to tell us that now?"

"I'm not telling you anything, I'm telling myself." His face glistening in planes and angles of reflected light.

There's a dutiful response of nervous laughter. Quinn watches them, eyes shifting from one to the other. He feels vaguely ill. A residue of the revulsion that hit him when he first found the body. And he keeps seeing it even now. Over and over. Confusion too. Surely he should be feeling more? More than just a need for fresh air. Away from these irritating faces. He moves through the sweltering atmosphere of the TV room, and out onto the first-floor balcony. It overlooks the outlying edge of the dilapidated town. His absence doesn't seem to have been noticed. For a long moment he stands unmoving, waiting for his gut-queasiness to settle, leaning out onto the rusting metal of the balustrade. His hands grip tight as though to draw strength from its corroding solidity. What are you supposed to feel in circumstances like this? How are you supposed to react? Don't listen. Ignore the internal narratives out of existence. Perhaps Vendon's right, and humour's the only meaningful response?

Looking to his left, directly ahead of this communally group-occupied house, a grid of cobbled streets bordered by bright colonial-era houses, a café-edged plaza with little shops selling jewellery and artwork, fruit-vendor stalls and street-musicians, and the bay ebbing away into the late-morning sky. To his right there are narrow streets of pretty two-storey houses, shuttered windows and flowers draping over wooden balconies, ornate carved doors and re-tiled pantiles breaking up the clean white walls that lean together like drunken old men. Then the gradient gets more abrupt as it shifts sharply inland. Earth. Rock. Worn away. Gradually growing more thickly wooded as it climbs steeply upwards to a Spanish-styled villa high above them.

That is the fortress of Mario Tristan Ormuzd and his family. He's the reason they're here. The left-wing émigré theorist from Europe sequestered in a villa continually patrolled by an armed retinue of personal bodyguards. He's why they're holed up beneath the building in which he works, producing political philosophies in the face of an insular reactionary world. Theirs is just one of the Ormuzd-clusters. There are other cells, small, constantly changing commune-groups of disciple-followers. To know more would be to compromise their security. But they're there. The other groups. He's why they wait—almost symbolically, thinks Quinn, at his feet.

The group now consists of Quinn, Huxley, Vendon and his wife Naomi, and Ahriman. Until the previous day, it had also included a morose and uncommunicative guy with a haywire mass of black hair. A guy called Kaukonon. But now Kaukonon is dead. Dead.

Quinn feels the trembling begin again. Beauty and brutality. So close. From below, outlined against the sky, he must look to be solid and self-assured. A firm clumsiness and grounded discipline that assembly-line years have instilled in him. If that's so, it's deceptive. Yet a sense of reality does stand out around him like so much air. A force-field against all of this. There's a book stuffed in-between the close-set rungs of the balustrade. He sees it only obliquely. A discarded paperback, dog-eared and well thumbed. At length, without real volition, he moves to pick it up. And as he straightens, he catches sight of the Ormuzd villa again. The villa that houses the wild-haired prophet of a man whose face graces the book's cover. Ideas extrapolated from Marcuse and the Frankfurt circle, set to transfigure and renew the world. Visionary narratives advocating extreme realities. If only this. If only that.

The air is already thick with noon heat. The days are always long and hot, and smell of fresh cedar. The sun seems to rise just a few miles south of here, and sets somewhere over... *there*, after making only the laziest of arcs across the sky. How can that be? We're scarcely a point on the map between nowhere and no-place, he supposes, but closer to the equator. It's somewhere barely twenty-something degrees north of here. Whores and street-vendors move in the alley beneath him from shade to shade as though swimming against tides of air, their words garbled and lost by the undertow of its sluggish currents. Gypsy children are squabbling in the dust.

Further away he watches a woman descending the street. An American mid-life tourist? Outsize wide-brim sun-hat, dark shades, loose floral top, ludicrous shorts. He watches with idle curiosity. She looks lost. Out of place. Thoughts occur and drift without the exercise of conscious flow. Too much junk-food and failed health-regimes. Too many enhancements and reductions. Too much bleach-blonde lips-reddened flesh. He runs his left hand through his lank unruly hair. Has she left a husband back in the hotel? No, more likely she's weekending 'with the girls', hunting some darkly Latin Boy-Toy. She knows what she wants. But what is *he* here for? At one time he'd never have admitted such a degree of weak indecision. This place, the bay, the house, the company, it's all taking its effect. The Glide, too. He watches his hand gripping the balustrade, blood vessels standing out, nails cracked and barbed. It's as though he's never seen it before.

At first he'd thought this a magical place. But there's no magic in Kaukonon's death. Only the shock of extinction. The random knife-edge of death that makes all action and aspirations absurd and pointless. A sad, shoddy, unpleasantly real suicide. Over the preceding weeks there had been much abstract talk of imminent deaths in corrupt, decadent and morally bankrupt Europe. Militant action. Terrorism. But seeing mutilated self-murder is different. This is tactile. No magic or romantic apocalypse, no reason. No geba, no Gewalt, no jihad, or divine violence. Just flesh wretchedly abandoned of life. He wants to cry, but there are no tears.

He opens Ormuzd's book at random, without real motivation. As though it's the I-Ching, and randomness itself will provide its own answer. 'Europe has fragmented from unity into a system of isolated fascist nation-states on the northern rim of the world, a backwater incestuously plundering its past in a blood-stained orgy of internecine regret...' And so on. As he expected, as he knows, the book is a structure of clinical reassuring logic. Reason abstracted from a messy world. He's suddenly aware of its frailty.

And simultaneously he becomes conscious of Naomi, Vendon's enigmatically silent wife, standing behind him...

'A UNIVERSE IN A GRAIN OF SAND...'

Through the arrangement of lenses and light-sensitive cells that serve as his eyes he watches the spider he's named Twitcher navigate its way determinedly through the moist shadows along the crest of the ridge. Not quite a spider. Almost a starfish at its core, but the point of each star extending into a random number of long spidery-thin legs.

And just as slowly, but just as purposefully, memory is returning to the device that thinks of itself as Ahriman. But the drip-feed of memories consists largely of remembered questions. Firstly, the triple-branched structure in the hollow is ancient. For surely its smooth moulded steel and angular alloy sections must have been interlocked and fused into their configuration millennia ago? Further, the complex must be alien in origin, for there's nothing on this bleak world capable of its construction. Not now. Probably not ever.

Twitcher waits, indicating with wavy feelers.

The tracks of his vehicle grind impatiently at the grit, as if forward-motion will stimulate forward-thinking, but it only causes the machine to lurch and slew. Almost overbalancing. That would be fatal. Or—in more appropriate machine-code, terminal. But he regains momentum, teeters over the brow, and begins descending the slope beyond. And all the while, the pale disc of the sun hangs low and unmoving just above the frigid horizon. Forming a static arrested sunrise... or sunset. So secondly, if this is Earth, it is Earth at the very end of time. There's no Moon. But maybe over billions of years it's drifted off free into its own orbit. There's no day and night either. So, the world must still be revolving, but in a gravity-locked orbit so the same side faces the sun at all times. Just like the same side of the moon always faced Earth. When there was a Moon.

Alternately, it might not be Earth at all. Just the world of some red dwarf star. There are slight rifts ahead of him, wrinkled fissures silted with fine crystalline ochre dust that has coagulated into drift-patterns of irregular waves. The limp spiders-web vegetation casts grid-lines of drab shadows across them, turning them into mythical maps of lost continents. Silence hums like a song, weighted down by time.

And all the while there's the memory of questions. And the question of memory. Enigmas that he's surely intended to interpret. And resolve. Proposition two—or is it three? Questions are concerned with language. But words have a tendency to erode, rather than construct meaning. Language is a slippery thing of nuance and intonation, a step apart from reality, above finite definition or analysis. Words are complex semantic games, randomly evolved sounds and structures, hopelessly imprecise. So instead, *he* must be the catalyst. The Key.

Systems. Numbers. Patterns. Digits. Data sequences.

It must be in *this* way that it's possible to decipher the mathematical constants that underlie it all...

As Twitcher leads, and Ahriman's caterpillar tracks direct him down towards their objective, through a moist, thickly vegetated grove in which living creatures thrive, he realises forcefully—and with sudden insight, that he is a machine. But that he has not always been a machine. Once he'd been made of flesh. Of vulnerable protoplasm. And he'd been called Ahriman. But now he is this machine of ancient metal...

'THE CRASH OF DOOM ON THE HYDROGEN JUKE-BOX...'

"Predators have to be quick."

"But—if they are to survive, so must their prey."

"Which means that, yes—predators also must become smart. They must learn stealth. They must acquire cunning."

"Yes, yes. But here—now, who are the predators? Who the prey?"

"Situations are fluid. Revolutions simply replace one ruling class with another. Every political philosopher from Hegel, Kropotkin, through Trotsky and Marcuse agree on that. No, meaningful change must be accelerated by a corresponding raising of consciousness to meet the demands of new freedoms." Huxley stabs the air vehemently to emphasise his point, like a slightly disreputable schoolmaster. Not the kind you'd want teaching your kid, if you had one. Behind him a widescreen blow-up of a blurred newspaper photograph is frozen across the wall. It fluctuates and dances with waves of static from the television. "Access to digital media synched to neuro-pharmaceutical expertise, enables us the potential to cascade global cerebral revolution—used and co-ordinated by a cadre of enlightened initiates, it upswitches us from prey to predator..."

"Glide is unprecedented in terrestrial history. A short-cut to psi-abilities, little phasings opening phantom twitchings in neural pathways a million years of future evolution may have eventually stumbled upon. But we have now. Ormuzd interprets those implications for us. It's his work that shows the synaptic retuning underlying it all, as part of the same cerebral upgrading."

"You're talking a lot, but you're not saying anything" says Quinn.

"We've been here before" says Huxley wearily. "We've done this thing, Quinn. You know as well as we know it. So why play stupid games? There has to be an informed cadre prepared to guide and shape the coming changes. Just like the Bolsheviks in Russia. They were small in number. But they were disciplined, tightly organised, and prepared. So that when the opportunity presented itself, they were ready to take advantage of it. We must be the new Bolsheviks in the new upheavals to come..."

Dusk is approaching. Paul Quinn sits beyond the circle of silver TV light with Naomi. They drink coffee, opting out of the evening's eternal political tirades. For there's no space here that is not known. No space that does not contain a memory. An experience. A conversation. A coupling. A house full of long silences and uncanny moments, empty talk and dissimulation. A house of unfinished projects where even the clocks tell lies. The walls here are black. But someone has added dribbling yellow panels, to match the black-and-saffron drapes that keep out natural light at all times. The ceiling is deep red, almost burgundy, and—to give an oriental effect, a mandala at the centre has been given Rastafarian colours, green, gold and black. A green jade Buddha is conspicuous among the exotic bric-a-brac beneath the TV, with a nest of votive candles cowed into melting question marks by occasional use. Ahriman, from the Arabian Confederation, lies on the floor in a trance-state, pumped up to the back-teeth with Chemical Glide.

"Tomorrow we'll initiate a new series of dialectics." He thinks it. But he doesn't say it. "Something more harmless, like a Unified Field Theory. Because all day Kaukonon has lain there, sprawled, bleeding, fly-crawled. Blood drip-drip-dripping. And all we do is sit around talking shit." He catches Naomi's profile in shadow. Those large haunted eyes that saw her strange childhood in Boston, New England. He can see inside her head. Or perhaps that's just the enhanced reality-kick of Glide too? Watching her grow from lawyer-stock, a family who originally fled pogroms in Eastern European cities, now grown fat on corporate law. She'd hooked up with Vendon during the Occupy and eco-green protests of the great crash. Of course, Vendon had been younger then, a romantic idealist. A revolutionary providing political form to formless gut-level rage. Shadowed black against the petrol-bomb glare, and the smoke coiling from looted hypermarts. But she'd stayed with him during what came next, betrayal, fear, and their enforced journey south. Through affection? Or habit? Naomi is a little too plump, beneath her long loose shift dresses, for the accepted definition of beauty—that is, if you accept the accepted definition of beauty. But her presence is strangely stimulating. That—in itself—is pleasurably disturbing.

He talks back to her in his head. But says nothing. "Me? I'm tech-serf from way back, started out screening Korean nano-components for assembly a hemisphere away, into—what? Phones, palm-pilots, smartglass, medbots? Then I did everything and whatever else. To survive. You know that. Or perhaps you don't. And I've lived stuff you can't even dream. All this now seems such an odd alliance..." He smiles cynically while Huxley is talking at no-one in particular, enjoying his own rhetoric, using that rasping voice for its maximum irritant effect, regurgitating ill-digested Ormuzd as they've been doing for months of lethargic waiting. Come on, Huxley, you're supposed to be smart, but *that's* not even what Ormuzd said. But then, perhaps that's why educated fools are drawn to him? Because he *is* imprecise enough for each of them to extract whatever they want from his texts?

Quinn thinks, all the time I've been here I've never spoken to a single person who was from the place I was speaking to them in. We've all come from somewhere else. This place is a sanatorium for those who don't fit anywhere else. A pause between other places, other, more real places. And whatever happened before coming here, feels as though it happened to another person. All those memories, both guilty and gilded, blurred by the fact that they're irreversibly lost. Unknown quantities.

Eventually he stands up and moves to the door. The TV is suddenly annoying, always on, always deliberately out of phase—to baffle uplinks, downfeeds and contaminated data-dumps. He jabs the remote. Making it hurt. Killing the light. An action based more on irritation than on any conscious plan of action. But satisfied now, he moves towards the landing beyond the TV. Towards the kitchen, visualising the waiting shelves of coffee and powdered milk, alongside ravioli and tagliatelli, bags of brown rice and peppers. The vivid yellow coolerator stacked with cans of lager. One shelf is stacked with labelled manila folders of notes and manuscripts, zippy-disks and digi-chips. Some postcards are tacked to the blue-tile facing of the wall. And propped up on the highest shelf is a goat's skull that Vendon had found in the dried-up river-bed near the Complex...

But before he can reach the kitchen, sitting upright on a chair, there's a decapitated rat impaled on a pen. The clear plastic tube replaces its missing head like an extended neck. And instead, its blue plastic cap forms a tapering eventual head. Which is watching the now-blank wafer-screen wall-mounted TV. Its fur is matted. Its body sunken, as though deflated. As though its fluids have been drawn off. Its intestines dissolving to nothing.

It wasn't there this morning. So it hasn't stopped. So Kaukonon wasn't responsible. So it will go on.

He goes to shift it. And stops. There's a spider stilting its careful way around the edge of the amputation. A spider on a rat popsicle. A spider like a ten-legged disc. But no, that must be shadows, or retinal TV after-image.

He turns. Naomi is standing behind him. "So you're going to leave it? Just like you leave Kaukonon."

"What else do we do?" Defensively.

"Help me."

"Why me?"

"Because you're here. And because you're... functioning."

"And the others aren't?" Yes. To ask the question is to provide the answer.

Kaukonon's room. The pungent scent of dried blood. But the bed has been stripped. Kaukonon's body now a mummy of tightly-wrapped sheets. Blood-discoloration visibly soaking through in places. And he's heavy. "I can't do this." "We must do it. The local authorities barely tolerate our presence here at best. If they get to investigate this they'll use it as a pretext to deport us. Trust me." He's a dead-weight. *Dead*-weight. Lurching step-step-step down the stairwell arrowed by their bulky triple shadows cast from a single shadeless bulb. Until Quinn is pacing, heavy-laden, out into where the paved street is rutted between huge uneven cobbles. Empty now. Empty but for a garbage-bin. A wheeled bin. She's thought this out. She's prepared it. He shrugs Kaukonon head-first. The strange shape awkwardly slumping, sticking, flags of loose sheet billowing. He shoves at it. Stabs at it, until it goes in. It. *It.* This is not a thing, it is Kaukonon.

No-one is watching. But there are ghost-voices coming through walls. Through the gathering night. The tall shuttered houses of biscuit stone that angle into each other like overcrowded teeth. A woman laughing, the way some women do. The American tourist trapped in her flesh? She's found her boy-toy? Other voices that argue in a speed-language he can't decipher. And an erotic moaning, or perhaps that's just the salt-breeze moving in the trees? And American juke-box music that filters through the cool air from a Cantina a block away. On another night, in another world, he'd be considering the merits of visiting that bar. Ruefully turning coins over in his pocket. The metal discs seem foreign and impersonal. "What now?"

"This way." She leads, they walk—him trundling the garbage -bin ahead of him, splayed legs disguised by sheeting protruding over its plastic lips obscenely, navigating it between the squat adobe buildings that are edged with weed and rubbish. Do the house-shutters resemble coffin-lids, or is that just morbid imaginings? All the while Quinn glances this way, then that, expecting at every moment to discover they're being followed. Not that you always know. There are thermal-imaging night-vision detectors. Orbital spooks capable of pinpointing individual mosquitoes. But purposefully, without the speed that might attract attention, they move from the perimeter of the town, around mud-rutted street corners that look out over the bay, where the wooden boats are beached to their gentle decay, and spiders-web fishing nets drape from ill-repaired drying frames. They move parallel to the chaotic tangle of trees that margin the landward side of the festering of buildings. Foliage searing the encroaching twilight sky, making its own night of shadows. But the path continues.

Above the trees Quinn can imagine the armed guards pacing the fortified length of the house where Ormuzd writes. Sometimes, dreams can hover. Above and beyond you. Close enough to see. Distant enough to be unreachable. Mario Tristan Ormuzd must be old now. How old? His bio-systems failing. Incontinent? Dribbles of piss darkening the groin of his trousers as he sits at his writing-desk, writing ideas that will transfigure the world. Words of power winking onscreen. But not enough power to control his own urine-flow. How old? One of the biog-files must give a birth date. Must search it out. Soon. Later. Some time.

The night is intoxicating. The ill-defined path they're walking is made up of mud and slight wells of stagnant water. The earth is moist and humid beneath him. The wheels stick in ruts and pools.

The beach. A huge moon. A glowing wash of broken diamonds shimmering deceptively. "Why does it look like this? Is

365

it the Glide-residue still percolating in my blood-stream?"

"Phosphorous. There's a high phosphorous content in the water. That's what gives it the gleam. Nothing else."

"For twenty years I worked assembly lines," he tells her, the dead Kaukonon, and the trees, as he cuffs the ground with his heel. "After all that time it really was good for me to come here and be accepted by these articulate intellectual people. And all the while, up there above me, the mighty Ormuzd is re-ordering philosophy and the universe, until that time when he decides to come down like the Messiah of the Apocalypse and make every-thing right. And all we have to do is sit and wait. It really made me feel good. At first. But none of this is real. It's just word games. Word weaving. How long can we wait? Until he wakes up one morning with an ice-pick embedded in his skull? Just lately I've begun to wonder, what if he's on Chemical Glide too and no longer gives a shit... like everyone else?"

"I heard that Glide is extra-terrestrial in origin. That they're germinating it from alien-spores extracted from a meteorite found in Antarctica. Did you hear that? I don't know for sure. But that's what I heard. In Europe they're already using subcu-taneous implants to regulate its feed across the blood-brain barrier. That way you can Glide forever..."

"I also heard it's a spin-off from ESP-enhancing research done in the old Sov-block. So who knows? Not me." 'Life is magical' someone had told him, long before the days of Chemi-cal Glide and decapitated rats, 'all you need is the perception to see it...'

"With Glide you're bleeding into other people's reality. Once you've done that you can never go back. Once you've been there you're forever changed. Altered. It's tipping the next evolutionary phase of human consciousness. The Coming Race. Or at least, that's what Ormuzd says..."

'ENERGY IS ETERNAL DELIGHT'

A sun erupts over the ridge, sending down slanting shafts of light. But no, it's not a dawn, there's never dawn here. This strange sun was just temporarily hidden behind the ridge. It's more like the reappearance of the sun after an eclipse. Except no, it isn't much like the sun either. This situation is intriguing. Those first suggestions of light give shape and scale to things. Watch the phony sunrise over the warming rocks. And he can see where they're heading. The objective that Twitcher is leading him towards. Another artificial structure.

If the planet he finds himself on really is Earth, then it must be an Earth at a point incomprehensible billions of years into the future. A kind of end-of-time Earth. A dying Earth stilled in its endless cold orbit around a dying sun. All life devolved down to crude primitive organisms with nothing ahead but slow extinction as the last wisps of atmosphere leak away into space and the entropic chill becomes terminal. Possible. Unlikely— but not inconceivable. There's something that reminds him of North Africa, only too many of the details conflict. No, it's nothing like North Africa. But this planet could just as easily be another world anywhere in the universe, or perhaps even—in some way beyond understanding, beyond the universe. Some 'Twilight Zone' parallel dimension?

"Y'know, Twitcher, I used to have teeth. I used to have hair. I used to have intestinal guts that sometimes made impolite noises. Now I don't. Now I have... this. What do you make of this, eh, Twitcher? What do you make of it?"

If it is Twitcher. He watches it. They all look alike. But there's always one here to guide him. He assumes it's the same one. Or at least, linked into the same one by some kind of shared hive-mind consciousness.

He thinks it over carefully. Considers it this way and that. His identity is in flux. A machine that thinks it's a man. Or a man who thinks he's a machine. The human mind, whether encased in flesh—or metal, measures and evaluates through senses that interpret and decipher what it perceives through comparison with known constants. Hence he's attempting to gauge the distance from the crater-bed to the hillcrest, down the incline through plants and spider's nests towards the glade and its odd inhabitants. And beyond, towards this other structure. Each distance seems relatively brief, measured by eyes that note the angle of shadow, the complexity of leaf arrangement, the strata-veins on rocks.

But how is this experience any more real than that? He has no *real* way of knowing what relationship the distances bear to those he remembers on the Earth. An Earth that, by now, is merely a dim and hazy memory. The ambiguities extend into every facet of this new world he's entered. What scale of size operates here? Are the spider-things big? Is Twitcher big? Or is he incredibly tiny? How to tell? There's no way to tell.

He'd emerged from a structure that could conceivably be native to this world, created as some kind of monitoring station by a species long since made extinct by gradual climatic deterioration. Yes, that makes sense. Perhaps it's still transmitting its findings back through time to its creators? Details about him. They're curious about him. Maybe he should signal? Ahriman turns the conjecture over in his mind. It seems neither plausible, nor improbable. Considering that he's here. Wherever here is? But there's no way of testing it. He holds onto the idea, but goes on to consider that equally, the structure might have arrived here as some kind of robotic probe from another world, gathering information that's being beamed back into space. But again, it's been here a long time. Its creators might be dead. Long dead. Or they've forgotten its diligent existence, and its endlessly pointless task.

And how does any of that help define his own role, both on this world, and within the scheme of the structure? That's equally ambiguous. Self is a tenuous thing. A figment. A construct of memories. Which the fabrication? Things cascade, flit like shadows. How to tell one from the other? How to differentiate? Yet there's an internal consistency here, something that makes a kind of warped sense. Something within the pattern of his actions that, although inexplicable, seems almost reassuring. If only he could figure out what it is.

*

'THOSE DYING GENERATIONS AT THEIR SONG...'

On the beach.

Spilling the mummified body into the sand. Unfurling it. He's naked. She's anticipated all of this. There must be nothing to connect the body with Ormuzd's cluster. Nothing. Just an anonymous cadaver washed up on an anonymous beach. He hauls Kaukonon's cold body, the limbs dangling, the heels dragging, grooving shallow sand-channels behind them. Kaukonon's white slug-penis lolling ludicrously... down deep into the surf while she meticulously collects up the sheets and returns them to the bin.

Shingle shelving sharply now. Steeply. Slithering slippily underfoot. A wave-wash of sudden force, shoulder-high. The burden of weight shifting, slurring him sideways—and down, swallowing sour salt, thrashing unsteadily in a lifeless tangle of cold limbs. Submerged, over his head, blind and breathing water. Deadness holding him down.

Who's the predator now? And who the prey? Savage scribbles of fire behind his eyes burst in phosphor constellations. A drunken Glide terror. Then a rippling numb silence of luring calm. Punctuated by flashes of memories—not all of them his. A contact-high of remembered incidents, pain, long cellular aches of longing and craving dependence. A crawling junk sickness. A need dissolved, and communicating through this fluid medium. From corpse face. To facing corpse face. An inviting welcoming suicide...

But instead, he's exploding back up into huge moon whiteness. Drooling spume and snot. Gasping greedy mouthfuls of night air.

And Kaukonon is gone. Thrashing about in a sudden panic, but his cumbrous weight is no longer there.

He drunk-lurches back until the tide-wash merely foams impotently around his ankles. The sea a shimmering field of broken diamonds. A dark shark-shape lurking some way off. Some way out. A safe non-threatening distance. Face down. A curve of shoulders. A curve of buttocks. Out of reach. But that's what they'd intended all along—wasn't it? He's gone. Disposed of. This is an end to it. An end to it all.

Quinn and Naomi walk side by side. Not touching. His clothes sea-dry already. But sweat-damp.

"You feel bad about Kaukonon?" she asks.

"Of course I feel bad. Whatever that means anyway." He concentrates on shoving the wheeled bin. Lighter now that all it contains is bloodied sheets. His discontent is difficult to articulate. But it's tied in with the suicide... and has been brought to the surface by it. And by this strange aftermath. "Briefly, for a moment, I envied Kaukonon. I was so close it scares me."

Of course he feels bad about it. It's natural to feel bad. Whatever 'natural' means too. But there are other things he can't put into words, things that lie deeper. So the question hangs in the air. If he just says 'yes' will it be enough to deter her further, more personal probing? Or will a denial open up some kind of healthy self-analysis? He's not sure he really needs such dubious solace.

"Did you like him?"

"He was OK, I suppose. But I don't think I ever really got to know him. Not properly." Perhaps he should add 'just like I don't really know any of you.'

But she curtails the process of thought by continuing. "It was the Glide that took him to suicide. He told me how he was going back down gene-counts into his Mother, then his Father. I've never been able to decide if Glide visions are actual biological phenomena—they sure seem real enough, or if they're just hallucination, beautifully distorted symbolisms, warped reconfigurations of real-life. But I do know that to the person experiencing them—they're real and three-dimensional. To Kaukonon it must have been the ultimate Oedipal trip. Can you imagine that? Wow! He probably saw no other way out but suicide."

"No, you're wrong. It's more—and less than that. We killed him. We all killed him. Every last one of us. Glide opens you up. It amplifies your sensitivities to what others are feeling. That's what it does. That's what it did to him. All the lethargy, all the pointlessness. He drowned in our collective poison."

"Is that really what you think? That's horrible." She pauses, her long black hair filtering the twilight. "So what about Ahriman? He's been permanently blocked-out on Glide over the last few months. He was strung out on various substances when he arrived here, but now he seems to do nothing else. He doesn't even involve himself in discussions any more. You just can't get through to him. In his fantasies he materialises into some kind of extra-terrestrial tracked vehicle to talk to spiders or something. He did Glide two days ago and hasn't come out of it yet. So is that real? Or is it just another amplified metaphor of our collective failure? I'm afraid for him. I'm afraid for us all."

In the tangle of trees and the wilderness of weed there's a decaying car, like precision-sculpture it had been wrecked and abandoned. Its metallic paint peeling and corroded around the shattered spidered windscreen.

"I remember when I first came into close contact with the Ormuzd clusters." Quinn braces his foot against a tyre-less wheel-hub. He looks at her. "All these strange people who debate ethics and world revolution all the time. I knew then what I wanted to attain. What I wanted to be. That's what led me to this place. You didn't know it, but you were re-writing my life. Only Chemical Glide and beheaded rats never figured in that plan."

"They call this a commune," she said. "Commune is also a verb. To commune. So let's commune..."

'ENDGAME...'

Every nerve alert. But no, he has no nerves. Only the habit of nerves remains.

There's the memory of questions. And the question of memory. Vague recall-images of being taught English at Abu Dhabi Uni. Windows glaze-full of sun-glare. Raised autoways stilting across dunes luminous green with GM-soya. Girls in hijabs. He'd naively assumed the new language to be some kind of code. And all that's necessary is to find the basic linguistic key to crack that code—after which all else would follow according to logical and rational rules. Only later coming to appreciate that no, languages aren't built that way, they spread like weeds, over centuries, through a process of inbreeding, through colloquialism, idiosyncrasies, diverse and formless influences, a multitude of regional variations and haphazard oddities.

Twitcher waits, indicating with wavy feelers. It's as though he can feel the twittering of its thought-streams, somewhere between a gasp, and a sizzle.

At first it seems he must have journeyed in a full circle, and returned to his point of origin. Back to the three-legged structure he'd emerged from. But no, this one is different. Bigger yes, but more ornate too. As though it's grown extra limbs with super-thin tubular fingers, sprouted forking branches that stand out black against the pale sky. Yet it has the same basic three legs. Its gravitational pull is inescapable. Its weary end inevitable.

If familiar dimensions can be trusted, the arachnid-things in the grove must be small. Twitcher's kind are barely four to five centimetres across. They resemble protoplasmic discs without internal skeletal or central brain structure. Starfish. Spiders. Yet their compensatory nervous systems must be incredibly complex, and evolutionarily advanced. Each creature fringed with a multitude of spider-legs, the exact number varies from one to the other, so each is unique. Each leg covered with fine hair gradiated in patterns of length and thickness. They communicate by rippling co-ordinated leg movements to produce

cricket-sounds well beneath the level of normal human perception. But he can pick them up. It forms their 'language', made
up of finely modulated nuance amid a multitude of interacting
sounds built up and evolved over millions of otherwise change-
less centuries, until its symbolic content has swamped all original meaning and structure. If the English language-code is the
product of hundreds of years, theirs has taken millions, a kind
of ancient off the biological rather than cultural timescale

By swivelling his lensed eye-stalks he can see the strut-legs
clearly. Each leg has four planes. Each plane has the outline of
a portal similar to the one he'd emerged from.

The bugs cross and re-cross the dell swarming in an eternal
dance, scuttling by indirect but obviously purposeful routes,
feeding on the condensation of dew, hoar-frost and the wispy
plant-life. They reproduce by cellular fission, so have no need
for the concept of family, or even close relationships, yet they
chatter continually on what appears to be an advanced intellectual plane. They ignore his presence. But for Twitcher... or
maybe a series of Twitchers.

He watches and records both the movements, and the conversations. From the tracked vehicle he inhabits, and the structure from which he emerges, Ahriman is now the direct heir to
millions of years of such observations made on this unchanging
community of creatures. And he's aware that the unit he inhabits has made this trek from crater-structure to the creature's
dell continually each 'day' over a period of time that has lost all
meaning in its immensity. It has recorded, it has analysed, and

it has attempted to extrapolate patterns and tabulate structures from the creature's multi-layered yatter-nattering conversations. To find the language key that will crack the code. But machines have limitations. They can go only so far, and no further. Now, it needs an organic element.

He can see the portals set into the legs of the structure. The upper receptor arrays draw energies from the pale sun. Others are tuned in to the eternal background cosmic radiation. Pinpointing the bright signals of unseen worlds around other suns. Locating and opening pathways between them. He can see rain. Framed in the closest portal, a lush window into a sweltering forest-world dominated by the immense dome of a blue-white sun. Winged lizards glide through spiky foliage on fans of spread membranes. Then, around the corner of the leg, another portal, into a glistening icescape. A sky so clear it is a seamless blue vault of glass. A column of shaggy white beasts file across a frozen ocean...

Once this world-enigma is resolved, it can move on. Other suns, other systems, other planets. But first, the enigma. So, for only the most recent of its journeys, the unit has captured this sentience that once called itself Ahriman. In some way he can't understand it reached out across space and time, touched his mind, and sought out his help. The capture was deliberate. Made possible through the 'set' of his mind, its 'dislocation in space / time' under the influence of Chemical Glide, but purposeful. The device had decided to introduce the element of sentience into its semantic research. It needs a catalyst. So he has become that catalyst. Together they have eternity, and they can wait without impatience. Then move on, to other tasks.

Ahriman now so closely identifies himself with these new objectives that he feels no sense of loss, no amputation, no sense of alienation. This is where he belongs. This is where he was always intended to be. There is no regret.

'IT ALL MUST FALL WITH A CRASHING BUT MEANINGLESS BLOW...'

"In all those old Steve Ditko Science Fiction comic strips I used to read when I was a kid each frame had moons, planets, Saturns or comets in the sky. Like cosmic decorations in the sky-corner" says Quinn quietly. "It seems odd, but just looking up through the trees now at the moon reminds me of those old comic-strip alien worlds. Makes you think, almost as if this is not just 'the Moon', but a 'moon', an alien planet. That the so-familiar shape in the sky that has become so clichéd, is a completely strange magical world in ways I've never seen before."

"What you're saying is that this is a new starting-out point, instead of an exhausted end-of-the-line" adds Naomi. "Like all of life is magical. It's just our grimy perception that gets tired and blind to it all. Now is the time to make a wish. "Ladybird, Ladybird, what is your wish? Your wish is not granted unless... it's a fish...?""

The car door protests loudly in strident metallic tones as Quinn forces it open. He cuts his finger on a windscreen-diamond of glass, and watches a bead of crimson blood swell from the cut to stand out bright and opulent against the rust-dust. It seems three-dimensionally sensual. The revealed car interior is overgrown with tall white spindle-limbed weed growing in through shatteredwindows, and damp dead pulpy leaves carpeting the floor. A cluster of dead flies grimed into the edge of the windshield-shards. Sniff deeply, and there's something dank and animal in the richly humid musk of decay that hangs in the air.

There's a snail on the worn car-seat in tree-filtered moonlight. Its perfectly moulded shell a vortex patterned by white-light play. Its gleaming body distended and erect, four delicate pronged

antennae sensing the air. A glistening slime-trial across the miraculously dry seat-cover behind it. Quinn and Naomi watch its sensual movement, its slight swaying questing head-motion, its intricately whorled shell.

"My Mother used to tell me that human beings were created to be custodians of all animal life" says Naomi softly. "I still believe that."

Quinn smiles. "Yes, my old man worked in a factory all his life. He was a hard man with no time for weakness. But he used to take early morning walks, removing snails from the footpath so they wouldn't get stomped on. I felt I understood him when I knew that. As though I'd glimpsed something special about him through that one insight."

"But that's what this is all about, don't you understand? A failure to communicate. That's all. Nothing more. Let me see your hand. Hold it up for me." He does so. She takes his hand in hers. And kisses the blood away. A smudge of it stays on her lower lips. A delicate cannibal. Looking for love, in all the wrong places.

"Touch is also a medium of communication. The first one we experience. And the last. Perhaps it's the only one we ever really have."

"No. There's more. Make a wish, Paul. Do it on Glide, and you can enhance your empathy."

A sudden glimpse of intuition. "Is that what it was like with Kaukonon?"

Her bare arms have a neat interlacing of white-line slash-scars. Meticulous mutilations, scoring symmetrically in twos so that her cuts match. She shrugs. "Sure it was."

"And it was good?" "Better than good." "For you both?" "It's a two-way thing. That's what Glide does."

And that's it. That's the way we poisoned him. Killed him. We drowned him in our abject wretchedness. Except he doesn't verbalise that. Because it belongs to him as much as it belongs to her. To each of them. Amplifying each other. Intensifying their whole sick dialogue through Glide.

They sit in the car. Watch the snail intersected by patterns of moonlight. They watch slight traces of blood well up along Quinn's finger in scarlet quivering tears. And they watch each other.

"Is it like this for everyone? Is this really all there is?"

"You don't have to stay here, you know. You can leave" says Quinn.

"But what if I leave now, and Ormuzd emerges with all the answers tomorrow, what then? How do you think I'd feel?"

For a while their bodies communicate. Almost becoming one in a sense, for as long as it takes for fumbled and unsatisfactory moments. The urgent probing of her fingers. Her skin cool and damp against his. Then she returns towards the town. Shoving the garbage bin, with the sheets for laundering. He watches her go. Above him, a Spanish villa is lost in darkness. Sometimes, dreams can hover. Above and beyond you. Close enough to see. Distant enough to be unreachable. Perhaps now, it indicates by its invisibility that he no longer belongs here, at its feet?

Instead he strikes out through the thicket for the highway that leads inland.

Without regret.

'IT'S NOT DARK YET... BUT IT'S GETTIN' THERE'

08:18:18 am

...and Ahriman is dead.

It's Naomi who first registers his stillness. Through the half-light of the room's interior, where the wall-mounted TV flickers silver soundless snow-storms of static which wash at the black walls. Her eyes grow accustomed to the gloom, tracing the shapes of sleeping figures. Huxley. Vendon. Then Ahriman—on the fourth day of his Chemical Glide trance. She can trace the configuration of his limbs, curled foetus-like across the floor. As though he's asleep. But there's no discernible movement, no sound to betray the inhalation of breath. The corpse-skin is pale, but his eyes are open, as though his vision persists. Elsewhere...

Author Biographies

ALLEN ASHLEY is a British Fantasy Award winning editor whose most recent books are "Sensorama" (Eibonvale Press, 2015) and "Dreaming Spheres: Poems of the Solar System" (PS Publishing, 2014, co-written with Sarah Doyle). Allen works as a creative writing tutor and is the founder of Clockhouse London Writers. www.allenashley.com

DAVID BIRCH is a writer from South Yorkshire who has published work in anthologies such as "10 by 5", "Jingle Hells", "Patterns in Darkness" and Big Pulp's "Lot's Crawlers" anthology. He also writes scripts. He is currently writing a crime novel.

GARY BUDGEN grew up and lives in London. He has had fiction published in many magazines and anthologies. Recent stories are in "Sensorama" from Eibonvale Press and "We Can Improve You" from Boo Books. He is a member of Clockhouse London Writers and can be found at: https://garybudgen.wordpress.com/

ADRIAN COLE: A native and resident of Devon, Adrian has had some two dozen novels and many short stories published, some also as e-books and audio books over the last 40 years. SF, fantasy and horror and his recent "Nick Nightmare Investigates" (Alchemy Press) has been shortlisted for the BFS 2014 collection of the year.

STORM CONSTANTINE is the author of over 30 books, both

fiction and non-fiction, across the fantasy, science fiction and dark fantasy genres, and has written around sixty short stories. She is also the founder of the independent publishing house, Immanion Press. She lives in the Midlands of the UK. http://www.immanion -press.com

ANDREW DARLINGTON debuted with the poem "Anthem For A Lost Cause" in "underground"-arts magazine "Sad Traffic" (1971). Over 3,000 published items follow, from Music Journalism to Erotica, from closely-researched SF-features to interviews with culture icons – a selection collected into "I Was Elvis Presley's Bastard Lovechild", 2001. Fiction too – in the NEL "Stopwatch" anthology (1975) through multiple magazine and hard/softback appearances around the world to "The Mammoth Book Of Sherlock Holmes Abroad" (2015). www.andrewdarlington.blogspot.com

PAULINE E. DUNGATE is a short story writer, reviewer and poet (as Pauline Morgan). Her work has appeared in many anthologies including some from Alchemy Press and in "Phantoms of Venice", an earlier Shadow Publishing anthology. She has served on judging panels for the Clarke, Rubery and BFS awards. She is currently looking for a home for a novel.

DENNIS ETCHISON is a three-time winner of both the British Fantasy and World Fantasy Awards. His most recent books include "A Little Black Book of Horror Tales" (Borderlands Press) and "It Only Comes Out At Night & Other Stories" (Centipede Press).
(Allen adds: Dennis is a living legend of our genre.)

EDMUND GLASBY began writing after studying Archaeology and Anthropology at the University of Oxford. His first book, "Disciple of a Dark God", was published in 2010 and to date he is the author of two mystery crime novels, five horror anthologies and one Lovecraftian thriller, "The Weird Shadow over Morecambe".

JOHN GRANT has received the Hugo (twice), the World Fantasy Award and a number of other recognitions, including the Chesley Award. His most recent books are the story collection "Tell No Lies", the nonfiction "Spooky Science" and "A Comprehensive Encyclopedia of Film Noir", and "Debunk It!", a book for young adults on critical thinking. He lives in New Jersey with his wife and too many cats.

TERRY GRIMWOOD teaches, plays harmonica, occasionally growls a little blues, acts and writes; both novels, and short fiction, which has appeared in various magazines and anthologies including "Sensorama", "Tales from the Vatican Vaults" and "Madame Morte". Terry runs both theEXAGGERATEDpress and Wordland magazine http://exaggeratedpress.weebly.com/

ANDREW HOOK'S most recent publications are the neo-noir crime novel, "Church Of Wire", and - as editor - an anthology of punk-inspired stories titled "punkPunk!". His fifth collection of short fiction, "Human Maps", will appear from Eibonvale Press in 2016. He is an editor for Salò Press, and can be found at www.andrew-hook.com.

MARK HOWARD JONES comes from a town in south Wales where it once rained fish. A former BBC journalist, he is editor of the anthology "Cthulhu Cymraeg: Lovecraftian Tales From Wales" and author of the collections "Songs From Spider Street" and "Brightest Black". He lives in Cardiff.

ALAN KNOTT - In "Dissolute Evolution" the author used his own location for the sequence where the organism ascended the cherry tree to slide onto the roof. Not only does the garden have a cherry tree but a small apple one too; rhubarb, raspberries, strawberries, spring onions and potatoes.

ROBIN LUPTON is a speculative fiction writer. She is originally from Albuquerque, New Mexico but has lived in the UK for the past 10 years. Robin is a member of Clockhouse London Writers and the British Fantasy Society. She was recently shortlisted for the 2015 Baen Fantasy Adventure Award. This is her first professionally published solo short story.

RALPH ROBERT MOORE'S fiction has been published in a wide variety of genre and literary magazines and anthologies. His books include the novels "Father Figure", "As Dead As Me", and "Ghosters", and the short story collections "Remove the Eyes" and "I Smell Blood". His website SENTENCE is at www.ralphrobertmoore.com

RICHARD MOSSES - Word shaman, lapsed scientist, technology cluster manager. Richard has had a number of short stories published in magazines and anthologies like this one, but has still to sneak past the elusive novel publishing guardians. www.khaibit.com

MARION PITMAN has written weird stuff for many years; her first short story collection, "Music in the Bone and other stories", is published by Alchemy Press in October 2015. She has a vendetta with woodworm and clothes moths, but rather likes woodlice and tsongololos, and non-venomous spiders.

DAVID RIX is an author and publisher. His published books are "What the Giants were Saying" and the collection "Feather", which was shortlisted for the Edge Hill prize. In addition, his shorter works have appeared in various anthologies, including many of the "Strange Tales" series from Tartarus Press.

DAVID TURNBULL is a member of Clockhouse London Writers. His short fiction has appeared in print and online as well as at live events such as Liar's League London. His most recent short fiction appeared in "Beware the Little White Rabbit" (Leap Books) and "We Can Improve You" (Boo Books). www.tumsh.co.uk

Also available from Shadow Publishing

Phantoms of Venice
Selected by David A. Sutton
ISBN 0-9539032-1-4

The Satyr's Head: Tales of Terror
Selected by David A. Sutton
ISBN 978-0-9539032-3-8

The Female of the Species And Other Terror Tales
By Richard Davis
ISBN 978-0-9539032-4-5

The Whispering Horror
By Eddy C. Bertin
ISBN: 978-0-9539032-7-6

The Lurkers in the Abyss and Other Tales of Terror
By David A. Riley
ISBN: 978-0-9539032-9-0

Worse Things Than Spiders and Other Stories
By Samantha Lee
ISBN: 978-0-9539032-8-3

Tales of the Grotesque: A Collection of Uneasy Tales
By L. A. Lewis (Edited by Richard Dalby)
ISBN: 978-0-9572962-0-6

Horror on the High Seas: Classic Weird Sea Tales
Selected by David A. Sutton
ISBN: 978-0-9572962-1-3

Crawling Horror
Edited by Allen Ashley
ISBN 978-0-9572962-2-0

Haunts of Horror
Edited by David A. Sutton
ISBN 978-0-9572962-3-7

Death After Death
By Edmund Glasby
ISBN 978-0-9572962-4-4

The Spirit of the Place and Other Strange Tales:
Complete Short Stories
By Elizabeth Walter
ISBN 978-0-9572962-5-1

Such Things May Be: Collected Writings
By James Wade
Edited by Edward P. Berglund
ISBN 978-0-9572962-6-8

The Black Pilgrimage & Other Explorations
Essays on Supernatural Fiction
By Rosemary Pardoe
ISBN 978-0-9572962-7-5

Shadmocks & Shivers
New Tales inspired by the stories of R. Chetwynd-Hayes
Edited by Dave Brzeski
ISBN 978-0-9572962-8-2

Bloody Britain
By Anna Taborska
ISBN 978-0-9572962-9-9

The Evil Bones: Stories from the Dark Side
By David A. Sutton
ISBN 978-1-3999-3283-5

The Black Pilgrimage 2: Further Explorations in Supernatural Fiction
By Rosemary Pardoe
ISBN 978-1-3999-4431-1

Tales of the Grotesque: Special Expended Edition
By L.A. Lewis
ISBN 978-1-3999-6355-8

www.ingramcontent.com/pod-product-compliance
Lightning Source LLC
Chambersburg PA
CBHW020508020726
47493CB00001B/240